A TOWER
—— OF ——
HALF-TRUTHS

Arcane Pursuits:
Book One

N.J. PRYNNE

*To everyone who has, for better or worse,
spent time within the ivory towers of academia*

Author's Note

PRONUNCIATION GUIDE

Geography

Dauphine · (doe-**feen**)
Dauphinian · (doe-**fen**-ee-uhn)
Fenutia · (fen-**ooh**-sha)
Maroba · (mah-**roe**-buh)
Nilandor · (**nil**-an-door)
Nilandoren · (nil-an-**door**-in)
Perrun · (**pair**-un)
Tanarim · (tah-**nar**-im)
Zakarza · (zuh-**car**-zuh)

Names

Aganast · (**ag**-ah-nast)
Alain · (ah-**lehn**)
Aventus · (ah-**vent**-us)
Corenta · (cor-**in**-tah)
Ellice · (**elle**-iss)
Enodus · (ee-**no**-duss)

Itri · (**ee**-tree)
Kazamin · (**kaz**-uh-min)
Lythandus · (lie-**than**-duss)
Nezima · (nez-**ee**-mah)
Noxanthyan · (nox-**anth**-yun)
Rel'Sclayne · (**rel**-suh-lane)
Selemin · (**sell**-uh-min)
Seringoth · (**sir**-in-goth)
Tesseraunt · (**tess**-er-awnt) *Except in Dauphinian;
the final 't' is silent.*
Volsegar · (**vole**-suh-gar)
Yuriva · (yuh-**ree**-vuh)

Magic

Aumbremancy · (**ahm**-bruh-man-see)
Etherean · (uh-**thee**-ree-uhn)
Faisancy · (**fay**-zawn-see)
Gardemancy · (**gar**-duh-man-see)
Mysticism · (**miss**-tuh-siz-um)
Soudremancy · (**soo**-druh-man-see)

Miscellaneous

Enferné · (ahn-fair-**nay**)
Fervidor · (**fur**-vid-or)
Kutauss · (**coot**-ouse)
Nivose · (**nee**-vohs)
Pluviose · (**ploo**-vee-ohs)
Potin · (**poe**-tuhn)
Yvernal · (ee-**vur**-null)

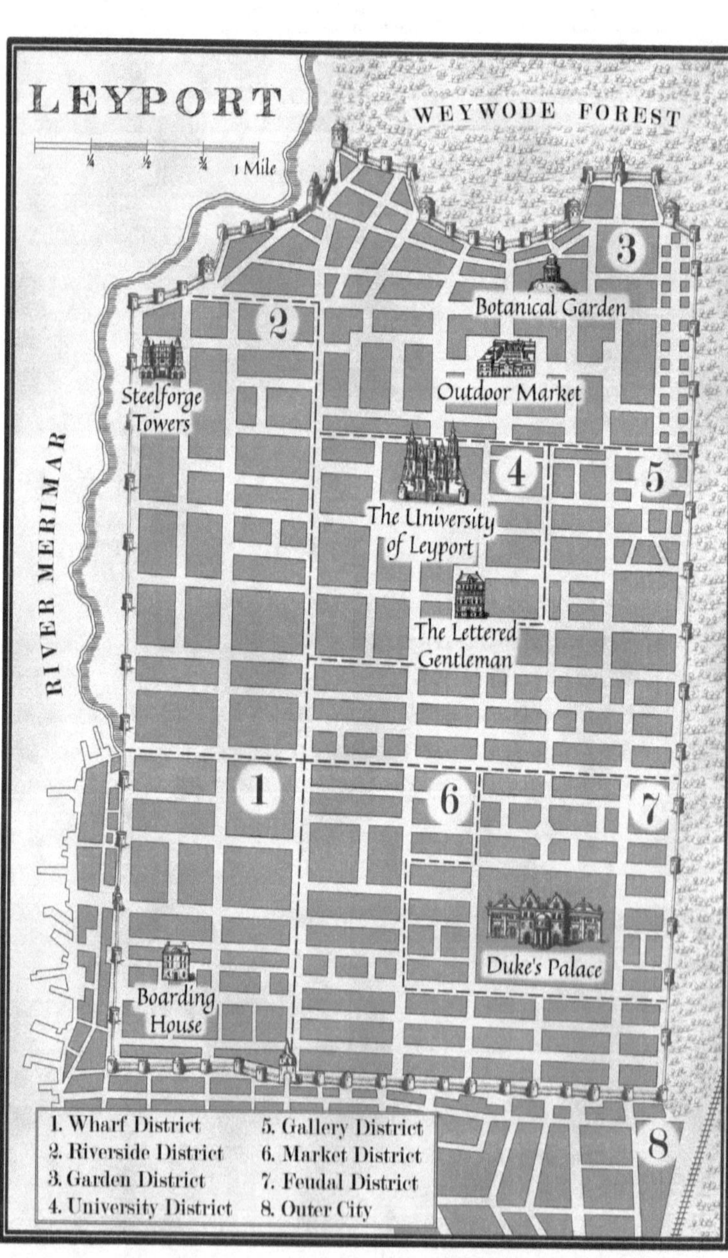

LEYPORT
¼ ½ ¾ 1 Mile
WEYWODE FOREST
RIVER MERIMAR
2
3
Botanical Garden
Steelforge Towers
Outdoor Market
4
5
The University of Leyport
The Lettered Gentleman
1
6
7
Duke's Palace
Boarding House
8
1. Wharf District
2. Riverside District
3. Garden District
4. University District
5. Gallery District
6. Market District
7. Feudal District
8. Outer City

Part One

The Thief

ONE

Of all the outrageous wastes of money Mavery had encountered while robbing manors, a four-foot-tall painting of hellhounds topped the list. The artist had depicted the beasts' scarlet eyes, umber fur, and barbed tails with such chilling accuracy, it took her a moment to recover from shock and notice the blue aura peeking out from behind the canvas.

To hang this painting directly across from his four-poster bed, Baron Roven had to be fearless, eccentric, or—the more likely answer—a little of both. If this were Mavery's bedroom, she would never get a good night's rest, despite that luxurious bed. And that was to make no mention of the *real* hellhounds prowling about the manor's lower levels.

"The safe is behind that painting," she said. "Seems to be guarded with your run-of-the-mill protective ward."

Her partner, Neldren, crossed the master bedroom in three strides and lowered the painting to the floor, revealing the safe embedded within the wall. Mavery began to follow him, but her green eyes flicked to the two pairs of red ones, and she froze again.

"Er, Nel, could you do me a favor and turn that around?"

He obliged with a chuckle. Mavery knew she was being ridiculous; it was only a painting. Still, she couldn't deny how her shoulders relaxed once those demonic eyes were no longer staring back.

"Remind me again why you agreed to this job, knowing we'd be dealing with demonspawn?"

"*We* are not dealing with demonspawn," she said. "Fennick and Itri are. And the pay was too good to pass up, as you reminded me at least a dozen times."

She tucked a strand of golden brown hair behind her ear as she stepped forward to examine what, to Neldren's eyes, would appear an ordinary safe. Only Mavery could actually see the magic emanating off it. Tendrils of blue light were loosely entwined like a sweater made with thick yarn. Mavery didn't need to break the ward completely to reach the metal beyond it.

As she spread her fingers, the tendrils pulled apart, creating a gap large enough for a hand to slip through. With a turn of her wrist, the tendrils froze in place. It was so effortless, it was almost insulting.

According to this job's buyer, the baron wasn't a mage, nor did he employ any. The magic must have been contracted out to a freelancing wardsmith. Mavery had occasionally dipped her toes in that line of work. Making a steady income had been difficult when her wards lasted weeks at a time, even without anchoring spells. To guarantee repeat business, she could have instead created second-rate wards like the one guarding this safe.

But no, there was more satisfaction—and money—in ward-*breaking*. Especially when it came to breaking the wards of mages who took little pride in their craft.

She reached through the gap and tugged the safe's handle. It didn't budge.

"It's locked," she said, looking over her shoulder. With his slate-gray skin, Neldren blended into the darkness, but Mavery glimpsed his leather boots dangling off the footboard. In the seconds it had taken her to manipulate the ward, he'd made himself comfortable on the baron's bed.

"Paranoid bastard," he snorted. "Magic wasn't enough for him?"

"He was right to not put much faith in it. A child could break this ward, given enough time."

She pushed her hands apart, stretching the gap until the ward created a thin border around the safe's door, completely exposing it. She could very well crack the combination, too. But since the payout for this job was being split five ways, she wasn't about to do more work than was necessary.

"All yours," she said.

Neldren slung himself off the bed, landed on the carpet with a soft thud.

"It better not explode in my face when I open it."

"I'm not Sensing any blasting wards. If you need me, I'll be in the library."

She turned to leave, but he took her by the wrist.

"Are you sure? Cracking this safe won't take long, and it'll be some time before we need to regroup with the others." He placed a finger beneath her chin, tilted her head upward. "I figured, seeing as we have this bed and a couple of minutes to spare—"

"Come on, be serious." She laughed, batting his hand away.

"Oh, but I am, Mave. *Very* serious."

Even in the dim glow of their lanterns, the desire on his face couldn't be more clear. But she still suspected he was only joking; he would never take such a risk. The only part she fully believed was that he'd only need "a couple of minutes." Such had been the case the last time they shared a bed.

"Maybe later."

"As you've said every night this week," he grumbled, then shooed her away with a wave of his hand. "Fine, go enjoy your *books.*"

He turned his attention to the safe, body stiff and shoulders hunched. She didn't need to see his face to know he was scowling, and she knew that arguing with him would be pointless.

Mavery headed down the darkened corridor and entered the library, where moonlight poured through the floor-to-ceiling windows. She touched the lantern on her hip, severing the connection between her arcana and the stone that fueled the light.

In most manors, the private library was little more than a status symbol. Roven's was no exception. His shelves were coated in a thick layer of dust; even his servants didn't give this room much attention. A neglected library presented a perfect opportunity.

Mavery searched the bookshelves for anything that stood out. She had a personal code when it came to pilfering books. She never took anything that was signed, gilded, or looked expensive enough to draw attention. Books with cracked spines and dog-eared pages were also off-limits, as they were more likely to be missed. Her prime targets were somewhere in the middle: mass-produced, but with enough literary or scholarly merit to be worthy of her collection. And if the book was small enough to slip into her pocket, all the better.

Finding a target among Roven's collection was more challenging than she'd expected. The top three rows were filled with exquisite leatherbound encyclopedias. She would bet her cut for this job that the baron had never read a single entry. Below those books was a shelf filled with other reference materials: legal codes, dictionaries, almanacs...

She wasn't expecting a non-mage to own any tomes on spellcasting or arcane history, but she was hoping for at least *something* with a little panache. Roven didn't seem to own so much as a book of poetry.

At last, a book on the bottom shelf caught her eye. A less discerning observer would have missed it entirely. Tucked between two large tomes on animal taxonomy was a thin clothbound book with yellowing pages: *The Modern Gentleman's Field Guide to Mushroom Foraging*. It had been published fifty years ago, but its spine was pristine.

Flipping through it, she found dozens of detailed drawings of mushrooms. She wasn't sure why this book was specifically for "the modern gentleman," but she would have plenty of time later to discover that. She tucked the book in her pack as footsteps thundered up the main staircase. Her pulse quickened. Arcana hummed beneath her skin, waiting for her to unleash it on the approaching threat.

She was reaching for her dagger when a familiar mop of black hair passed the doorway. The youngest member of the crew, Itri, skidded to a halt. He doubled back and leaned against the doorframe, panting. Sweat glistened on his dark skin.

"Mave!" he gasped. "Oh, gods, we have to leave—*now!*"

"What? Why?"

"Hellhound! Coming this way!"

"You and Fennick couldn't handle a pair of hounds?"

"Not a pair. There's eight of 'em." Itri shook his head. "No, nine. Fen missed the others when he was scouting the place."

"How the hells does someone miss *seven* hellhounds?"

"Roven's a breeder. Got a whole operation down in the kitchens and everything. A half-dozen pups and a bitch. Gods, was she pissed when she spotted us."

She glanced over Itri's shoulder and realized the boy was alone. "Where's Fennick?"

"He distracted the bitch, told me to run for it and come find you. We only brought enough sleep tonic for two hounds, so—"

As if on cue, an otherworldly screech ripped through the manor. Mavery flinched, blood chilling and skin prickling.

Once she reclaimed her senses, she dashed out of the library with Itri on her heels. In the corridor, they narrowly avoided crashing into Neldren. From the look on his face—which was livid in every sense of the word—he'd overheard everything. He rounded on the boy, who flinched.

"Our mark is a fucking hellhound breeder? That's a detail I should've known about!"

"Even the buyer didn't know," Itri squeaked. "Fen swore that Roven only had the two guard dogs."

"And *I* swear to *Fen*, when we—"

The hound shrieked again. Louder, closer. Without another word, Neldren sprinted down the corridor.

"Wait!" Itri called. "What about Fen?"

"The bastard got himself into this mess, he can get himself out of it. Come on!"

Mavery and Itri exchanged glances, then ran after Neldren.

They retraced their steps from the break-in, scrambling down the corridor and up a narrow spiral staircase that led to the servants' quarters. Three young women lay on cots, exactly where Neldren and Mavery had left them. Thanks to the sleep tonic Mavery had brewed earlier that day, they would continue sleeping soundly through the night.

One by one, Mavery and her accomplices tossed their packs through the window, then hoisted themselves out onto the roof. Mavery closed the window behind them. They tiptoed across the shingles, crouching as low as possible, lest a patrolling guard look in their direction. The hellhound's cries had to have drawn someone's attention. As Mavery climbed down the trellis, she tried to not think about that—or how high off the ground she currently was. Every movement made the wood rattle, and she had only the light of the first moon to illuminate the footholds. The climb down was somehow infinitely worse than the climb up.

The trellis held her weight, and her feet met solid ground once more. There was no time to pause and catch her breath, however. She followed Neldren and Itri across the back garden. As they wove around spindly bushes and barren patches of soil, they encountered no guards, no hounds, no Fennick.

They reached the stone fence, where the final member of their crew, Ellice, peeked through the hole she'd made earlier. Even in near-darkness, her red hair was vibrant as a lighthouse beacon. She threw a hand signal: the way forward was clear.

Itri climbed through the hole first. As Mavery and Neldren stood and waited, a hulking figure stumbled across the garden. With its broad shoulders and plodding gait, Mavery knew at once it was Fennick.

"You there! Stop!" cried a distant voice, gruff and unfamiliar.

A second figure chased after Fennick. This one was much smaller and carried a rifle. It stopped and aimed said rifle at Fennick.

"Fuck me," Neldren groaned. He trudged toward Fennick and the guard. The breeze carried a hint of ash as Neldren raised his arms. Tendrils of darkness coiled around his limbs. He swung his arms forward and loosed those tendrils upon the guard, who began to yelp as his entire body became engulfed in shadow, but his voice cut out at once.

Mavery grimaced. She knew what the man was feeling. Or, more precisely, what he *wasn't* feeling. Being caught unaware with no sense of light, no sense of anything, there was nothing left but to give into that all-consuming void. And that's exactly what the guard did. When Neldren pulled the shadows away, the man lay unconscious on the ground, his limbs splayed at unnatural angles. It wasn't far off from how Mavery had looked after her first attempt at a shrouding spell.

Neldren clenched his fists as Fennick shuffled closer, favoring his right leg while grasping his left side.

"Thanks, Nel. I—"

"You idiot!" Neldren barked. Fennick came to a halt. "All that racket you made, you're lucky it was only one guard. And you better not've killed that hound. Anything happens to those beasts, we forfeit the payment."

"I know, but the buyer only mentioned the guard dogs," Fennick said through gritted teeth. "Said nothin' about the others."

"The others that *you* should've noticed!" Neldren shook his head. "If I didn't know any better, I'd say you bungled this job on purpose."

"C'mon, Nel. Don't..." Fennick squeezed his eyes shut as he took a shallow, rattling breath. "Don't be ridiculous. 'Sides, I didn't kill the hound. Just choked it out."

"For your sake, you'd better hope—"

Footsteps and voices echoed from around the corner of the manor. It was difficult to discern what they were saying, or how far away they were. Not taking any chances, Neldren turned on his heel and jogged toward the fence.

"Move!" he hissed. "Before the rest of them catch up."

His lithe figure slipped through the hole, joining Itri and Ellice on the other side. Before Mavery could follow, the sight of Fennick up close gave her pause. Dark blood saturated his shirt, oozed between his fingers. His tan face had turned pallid. His sandy hair, saturated with both blood and sweat, was plastered across his forehead.

"I'm fine," he muttered; he'd no doubt heard Mavery's gasp. "Just a graze, is all."

Before she could argue with him, Neldren ordered the two of them to hurry up. Mavery tossed her pack through the hole, then pulled herself through. The hole was only three feet off the ground and just as wide, but Fennick couldn't manage it. He winced as he tried to lift his leg, then lowered it with a shake of his head.

"Stand back," Ellice said, pushing up her coat sleeves.

She crouched and placed her palms flat against the wall, just below the hole. The smell of saltwater filled Mavery's lungs—a hint of summer cutting through the sharp, wintry air. Cracks appeared in the stone wall. Though Ellice was a mender, destruction magic came just as naturally to her. A chunk of wall broke free, and Neldren pushed it out of the way.

Fennick ducked as he walked sideways through the enlarged hole. His hand briefly slipped away from his abdomen, revealing a gash roughly the size and shape of a hellhound's maw. Blood gushed, spattering the dirt at his feet. Mavery shuddered and had to glance away. She usually had an iron stomach when it came to this sort of thing, but Fennick's wound was enough to test her limits.

Neldren and Itri replaced the slab, then groaned as they hoisted another into the original hole. As Ellice seamlessly mended the fence, Fennick swayed on his feet. Mavery rushed to his side.

"Here, lean on me," she said.

He slung an arm around her shoulder, and her knees buckled beneath his weight.

"All right," Neldren said. "Let's move."

He and Ellice fed a little of their magic into their lanterns and held them aloft, casting globes of warm light on the forest floor. Mavery did the same to the lantern on her hip, though it only illuminated her feet.

Neldren took the lead, his black ponytail whipping behind him as he hurdled snow-dusted roots and felled trees. They were only a mile from the closest village, where they would regroup with their contact and collect their payment. The trek to Roven's estate had taken all of twenty minutes, but Fennick's injury now made that pace impossible. Neldren, Ellice, and Itri trudged forward, stopping every so often to let Mavery and Fennick catch up. Mavery's bad knee sent stabbing pains up her leg, but she clenched her teeth and focused on pushing ahead. Letting Fennick use her as a crutch was enough to keep him moving, albeit slowly. But before long, even that wasn't enough. He stopped, untangled himself from her grasp, and leaned against an oak tree.

Neldren turned to Mavery. "Can't you heal him?"

"Even if I could, patching up a wound this severe would probably kill me."

"I told you, I'm fine," Fennick gasped. "Just leave me here for a minute. I'll catch up."

His skin was whiter than the patch of snow at his feet, his eyes were ringed with darkness. He wasn't remotely in the realm of "fine."

"Nonsense," Mavery said. "You'll get torn apart by wolves out here, if you don't bleed out first."

"Leave him," Neldren said.

She blinked, mouth agape. "You can't be serious."

"Just look at him, Mave. He's beyond saving."

"If we could get him to a healer—"

"And then what? We'll strut up to the nearest temple and hope they don't ask too many questions? For starters: How did he get mauled by a hellhound at half-past midnight?"

"We're not leaving him," Mavery said. "He's—"

"The reason we almost got caught, or did you already forget?" Neldren scowled. "He didn't want this job in the first place. He fought me on it every step of the way, told me anything involving the Rovens wasn't worth any amount of money."

"So, this is how you deal with those who disagree with you? You just leave them to die?"

Mavery gestured to Fennick, who was breathing heavily, mouth hanging open. A moan and a trickle of blood were the only things that escaped it. Neldren's eyes narrowed as he looked to Fennick, then to Mavery.

"You're right," he said in a low voice. "We shouldn't leave him to die."

Mavery began to breathe a sigh of relief, until an eerily unfamiliar look crossed Neldren's expression. His hand inched toward his blade.

"Wait!" she cried.

A metallic tang hit her tongue as she pushed her palms outward, creating a translucent blue barrier between the two men. The scent of ash filled the air again as Neldren vanished, then reappeared on the other side of her protective ward a heartbeat later. With neither a word nor hesitation, he unsheathed his knife and swiped it across Fennick's throat.

Fennick reached for the wound, but his fingers could find no purchase amid the gushing blood. His gaze flicked to Mavery, and she swore she could see the slightest glimmer of fear behind his eyes. He then turned to Neldren. Nostrils flaring, he flashed the crew's leader a cold, hard glare. As the final embers of his life extinguished, Fennick's body slid down the tree trunk and into the brambles.

A deafening silence fell across the forest.

Mavery looked to Ellice and Itri, who silently stared at Fennick's corpse. She hoped their lack of reaction was due to disbelief, not indifference.

"Neldren!" Mavery yelled. "Why would you—"

"No point in delaying the inevitable," he said flatly. He cleaned his blade on Fennick's shirt, then wiped a spatter of blood from his own face.

"But—"

"Quiet down before you wake the whole province." He sheathed his blade and continued onward. "No time for a funeral. Let's go get paid."

Two

While Mavery gazed into the depths of her tankard, the rest of the crew was in high spirits, celebrating their payout. Odd, how a bit of money could make them forget all about what had transpired not even an hour ago.

Then again, none of them were strangers to death. That was especially true for Mavery. She'd been a member of everything from well-oiled mercenary organizations, to fly-by-night crews like this current group. Over her nearly twenty-year career, she'd lost more colleagues than she could count. She'd lost count well before she'd learned to stop counting altogether.

This most recent death stung, but it wasn't as if Mavery and Fennick had been particularly close; they'd only known each other for a month. But that had been long enough to learn how he'd once been a nobleman's bodyguard, until his heavy drinking and gambling left him with no job—only debts and divorce papers. He'd traded his once comfortable life for one that was far less savory, where he soon fell in with Neldren.

Fennick's story was one Mavery had heard dozens of times. Though the details differed, they all led to the same place. Very few people chose this life. More often than not, it was the only viable path after they'd burned every bridge.

Despite his shortcomings, Fennick had deserved a better death.

Would Mavery face a similar fate? Had she been the one bleeding out in the woods, she couldn't say for certain whether Neldren would have acted any differently. And now he sat beside her, drinking and laughing with Ellice, as though he hadn't killed his own crewmate. Even Itri was now three tankards deep and plunking out a tune on the taproom's poorly tuned piano.

Mavery, taking a page from their book, tried to focus on the wad of potins in her pack. This had been her biggest payout in over a year, and her first job in weeks. Now that practically everyone in Osperland was carrying a pistol in their back pocket, there was little need for mercenaries' protection these days. After months of attempting to strike out on her own as a mage for hire, only to come up short, Mavery had had no choice but to fall back in with Neldren.

Though his accomplices changed faster than the seasons, Neldren had always been consistent when it came to finding work—and getting paid decently for it. Now that the payout had been split four ways instead of five, Mavery had over five hundred potins to her name. It wasn't a life-changing sum, but for the first time in ages, she didn't need to pinch every copper until the next job came along. She could begin thinking in broader terms.

She sipped from her tankard and winced at the sour, watery ale. It was no surprise that this low-end establishment would serve low-end drinks. This place appeared to be made of driftwood and held together with dust. The handful of other patrons were what you'd expect to see in a backwater village's public house at nearly two in the morning: passed out in their cups, or well on their way to it.

The only thing that stood out was the painting behind the bar. It was a crude rendition of a wizard with a long white beard and blue robes, raising his staff against an eldritch horde of black wings, red eyes, and countless fangs. A plaque hung beneath the painting:

SERINGOTH'S REST—EST. 1012
NAMED IN HONOR OF THE WIZARD SERINGOTH
THE FIRST, WHO CLEANSED BURNSLEE VILLAGE
OF DEMONS IN 534

Mavery held back a scoff. Perhaps wizards had been more heroic five centuries ago, but she doubted it. Saving villages was the type of work your average wizard would contract out; they would never risk damaging their precious spellcasting fingers. They preferred keeping to their towers, crafting spells and writing books. Stashed away in Mavery's pack were pages from some of those books—all that remained of her far-too-brief wizarding education.

Now *that* was something she hadn't thought about in some time.

She wasn't foolish enough to entertain the idea of completing her studies, much less becoming a wizard. She'd dropped out of university nearly twenty years ago, which meant she would have to start over anew, and she was too old for that. Though mages often lived for a century or more, she assumed these past two decades had shortened her lifespan by just as many years—likely more. But with the payout from this job, maybe she could scratch the itch, take a class or two...

"Mave? Are you still with us?"

She blinked as she came to her senses, starting with Neldren's voice, followed by a slight pressure against her upper back, a taste of blood, a sharp pain along her thumb. Another blink, and she realized Neldren had draped his arm around her while she'd been gnawing on a hangnail.

"Where'd you drift off to?"

She wiped her bloody thumb on the hem of her shirt, then shrugged off his arm without making it too obvious she wanted to put some space between them. She still couldn't reconcile the man next to her with the man from earlier that night, with the man she'd known off-and-on for eighteen years. Neldren was many things—a smooth-talker, a thief, a charlatan—but he'd never been a *killer*. He'd promised her that from the night they first met.

"Nowhere," she muttered, but Neldren's cocked eyebrow was proof that he didn't believe her. "I'm just a little tired, is all. I think I'll call it an early night."

"Oh, but we're just getting started!" Itri said, slurring his words. At some point during Mavery's musings, he'd abandoned the piano and returned to the table. Now, only snoring filled the taproom, and the innkeeper looked all the happier for it.

"Go easy on her," Ellice said. "The thrill of a good score lasts a lot longer for you than it does for us older folks."

It took all of Mavery's resolve not to roll her eyes. *Older folks.* Ellice was twenty-four—only five years older than Itri. Her red hair didn't have a streak of gray, her fair skin not a single blemish. Mavery doubted the girl started her mornings with her joints protesting as she rolled out of her bunk. What did *she* know about being old?

Mavery would be thirty-seven in a few days. Maybe she already was. The days tended to blend together when you spent your life hopping from one town to the next, sleeping in a different inn every night. Regardless, she had well over a decade on both of them. And for someone in this line of work, she was practically near retirement age—though the typical "retirement plan" was death.

"I know what's going on here," Neldren said. He leaned in, and Mavery fought the urge to lean away from him. "You're still upset about Fen. Look, I did what I had to do, and at least he didn't suffer."

She scoffed. It hadn't appeared that way to her.

"He was slowing us down," Neldren continued. "But if we'd left him alive, like he wanted, what do you think would've happened once Roven's guards found him? At best, they would've tortured the bastard to death. Worst, he would've ratted us out and led them straight to us. You can't deny I made the pragmatic choice."

A man was dead, and Neldren wanted to discuss *pragmatism.* Mavery was in no mood to argue with him. She pushed back her chair and stood up.

"Good night," she said. "Enjoy the rest of your celebrations."

She lay on her bunk, gazing at the ceiling. The inn's thin walls did little to drown out the crew's lively chatter from downstairs. Without her around, their spirits had lifted again. In the far corner of the room, a stranger snored loudly. Mavery lowered herself over the edge of her bunk and dropped to the floor.

She hadn't changed out of her travel clothes, so packing up her belongings took very little time. As she laced up her boots, a shadow crossed over her. She looked up to see Neldren leaning against the doorframe, arms crossed, his figure limned by the light from the hallway.

Even in shadow, she could still make out the features that had made her nineteen-year-old self fall for him so hard and fast. As a native of Nilandor, he had slate-colored skin, tar-black hair, and subtly pointed ears. He stood over a head taller than Mavery, who was already a taller-than-average woman. Nilandorens aged slowly, thanks to their elven ancestry. Though Neldren was in his mid-forties, Mavery looked more his age than he did: her golden brown hair was streaked with gray, her beige skin was weatherworn, her green eyes were framed with fine lines.

Their scars seemed to be all they had in common anymore. Mavery bore a slash spanning the bridge of her slightly crooked nose, along with dozens of marks elsewhere on her body. Neldren sported gashes across his bottom lip and left eyebrow. His goatee hid a jagged lesion on his chin, a souvenir from his own run-in with demonspawn years ago. No amount of magical blood could prevent scars. Not when you lived the kind of life they did.

She had loved him once, and for this past month, she had thought she could learn to love him again. But tonight's events had quelled those already tenuous feelings.

"Where are you going?" he demanded.

"I can't sleep. I thought I'd step outside and clear my—"

"Don't bullshit me, Mave. You're leaving."

"And? As you've said countless times, you're not running a guild, we can leave whenever we like."

"So, after barely a month, you've decided you've had enough?" His furrowed brow darkened his gaze. "What is it this time?"

She sighed. "What happened with Fennick—"

"I told you, he was a dead man either—"

"Let me finish. *Please.*" She forced her trembling hands into white-knuckled fists. And then she forced herself to ask the question that had lingered deep within her mind, the one she'd been too afraid to ask downstairs. "That wasn't the first time you killed someone, was it?"

Neldren remained silent.

"Answer me, Nel."

He hung his head. "No, it wasn't."

Mavery released a held breath. She'd already known the answer, though that didn't make the truth any less painful. She shouldered her pack and began to move forward. Neldren stepped in front of the doorway, blocking it with his body.

"Look," he said, holding out his palms, "I only killed when it was absolutely necessary."

Mavery laughed coldly. "And that's the difference between you and me. I would *never* think it was necessary." She lowered her eyes. "So would the Neldren I knew a year ago."

"A lot has changed since then. You would know, had you bothered to stick around for any of it."

That was a low blow, even for him. But instead of enraging her, his words only made her all the more exhausted.

"I can't do this anymore," she said.

"Do what?"

"All of *this*." She gestured vaguely at the dim room. "Roaming from village to village, never knowing what tomorrow will bring, never having a place to call my own. Yes, we had a good score tonight, but that money won't last forever. And then what? I'm not getting any younger, and so—"

"You think *you're* getting old? What does that make me?"

She scoffed. "Oh, please. You'll live another century at least."

"Not in this line of work."

"See? You've just proved my point! If there's little hope for you, then there's even less for me. And everything that happened tonight proves I'm not cut out for this life anymore."

"Then what'll you do instead?"

She shrugged. "Maybe I could return to my studies, or—"

"Gods, not this again." He shook his head, laughing incredulously. "You think living in dusty libraries, surrounded by ink-stained blowhards, is going to make you happy? Even Ellice couldn't hack it, and she's..."

Mavery crossed her arms as she waited for him to finish that thought. Like Mavery, Ellice had once attended wizarding university. Unlike Mavery, the brat had squandered the opportunity by failing out during her first term. Ellice's family had banished her for it, but that didn't erase all the years she'd lived in privilege, attending the finest boarding schools, wanting for nothing.

"She's *what*, Nel? Cultured? Well-bred?"

"All I'm saying is, don't throw away everything just to go chasing old dreams. We've become a good team again."

"Good for *you*, you mean. In all the years we've run together, never once have you asked me what jobs *I* would like to take."

"Then let me ask you now, Mave. What do you want to do?"

She hesitated. All that came to mind was the bundle of textbook pages stashed in her pack. Beyond that, her ideas were all abstract.

"I... I don't—"

"And now you've just proved *my* point. You never know what you want, which is why those decisions always fall on me." He pinched the bridge of his nose. "Fine, go fuck off with the wizards, be my guest. But we'll see how long that lasts before you change your mind again."

"I don't need your permission to leave."

"Then leave!"

"Yes, *leave*, so I can get some godsdamned sleep!" snapped a voice from the darkness.

"This is none of your business," Neldren snapped back.

"You made it my business the moment you decided to have your lovers' spat next to my bunk!"

As Neldren and the old man bickered, Mavery seized the opportunity. She shouldered past Neldren, who didn't move from the doorway but also didn't prevent her from leaving. No doubt their heated argument had traveled downstairs. She took the back exit to avoid receiving Ellice and Itri's questions, too—assuming they would even care. From what Mavery had seen tonight, Neldren was molding his newest protégés in his own image.

It was still a few hours until sunrise, so Burnslee was dark and quiet. Only the light of the second moon and the glow from the windows of Seringoth's Rest illuminated the village; it lacked even a single lamppost.

Mavery turned onto the main road and followed it out of the village. She had no goal in mind, other than to put as much distance between herself and Neldren as possible. Flurries danced in the bitter breeze, and snowmelt soaked through her worn boots. But her coat remained unbuttoned. The residual anger from her argument had left her arcana flaring in her veins; that alone was enough to warm her.

After walking for a few minutes, she came to where the building-lined roads gave way to open fields. The River Merimar was just over the horizon. From there, she could hitch a ride on a boat and make her way...somewhere. So long as she wouldn't have to cross paths with Neldren again, her destination didn't matter.

A few paces later, the ash-tinged scent of shadow magic made her stop in her tracks, but she did not turn around.

"Of course you followed me," she sighed. "Thought you could change my mind?"

The scent faded as Neldren dismissed his shadows.

"No." His voice lacked even a hint of emotion. "I realized you left with something that belongs to me—to the crew."

She turned to him with a hard stare. He could control the shadows as though they were an extension of himself, but she had a more varied arsenal of magic at her disposal.

"You're talking about my cut from the job."

"It stopped being *your* cut the second you decided to leave."

"Oh, piss off."

As she turned away, he reached a hand inside his coat and whipped it out again with a flash of silver. She threw up her left hand, summoning a ward, while her right hand reached for her dagger. She sensed in quick succession a metallic taste, a small explosion, a white-hot pain deep in her gut. She looked down to see a dark red spot blooming on her shirt. She gripped her stomach, and her fingers became slick with blood.

Neldren had stabbed her.

No. She'd summoned her ward before he'd struck; a mere blade couldn't pass through her magic that easily. This pain was deeper, more agonizing, than a stab wound.

Neldren had *shot* her.

Her eyesight blurred. She blinked, and the pistol in his hand came into focus. She could almost forgive him for stabbing her, but shooting her was an even greater betrayal. In her delirium, the only thing she could focus on was the weapon that had made their line of work all but obsolete.

"You...have...a gun?"

Speaking those four short words pushed her pain over the edge. Her legs gave out. Her bad knee screamed in agony as she fell forward, landing on her stomach, but the pain from her gut promptly drowned it out. As she began to fade out of consciousness, she heard Neldren rummage through her pack.

"Bastard."

She wasn't certain if she managed to speak the word, or only think it. One thing *was* for certain: if she needed a sign that she was due for a career change, she doubted she'd ever get one clearer than this.

THREE

S he awoke to the scent of blood and bile mixed with something she couldn't quite place. Pine, or was it juniper berries? At first, she thought she was in her bunk at the inn, but the room was too bright, the air too clean, the blanket covering her too thick. She was not lying on a rickety bunk, but a single bed with an iron frame. To her left, someone coughed, and the noise echoed through the spacious, high-ceilinged room. She looked to the source of the coughing, but a wood-paneled divider blocked her view.

She was in an infirmary, that much was clear. But why was she here? How had she gotten here? More importantly: how long had she been here?

Mavery winced as she sat up; though her body was stiff, she felt no pain. She wore a thin white gown. On a chair near the bed, she recognized her clothes—clean and folded and resting atop her pack. Her coat was draped over the back of the chair, her boots sat beneath it.

And then she remembered everything: the coldness of Neldren's voice, the thunder of the gunshot. Tears stung her eyes as her breath caught in her tightening throat.

She'd trusted him, and he'd shot her in the street like she was nothing more to him than a stray dog. Her fingertips prickled with white-hot arcana that begged to be let loose.

Focus, she thought. *Stay in control.*

She clenched her fists, blinked away the tears. Then, as she'd learned years ago, she forced those troublesome emotions to the deepest depths of her mind. Her arcana subsided.

To ensure it stayed that way, she needed a distraction, and assessing the physical damage seemed as good as any. She pushed aside her blanket and hitched up her gown. To the left of her navel was the scar from the first time she'd ever been stabbed. Below her ribcage was the scar from the second time. But there was no sign of a bullet wound.

A healer stepped around the room divider. No doubt Mavery's stirring had drawn her attention. She was a short blonde woman in a gray and white smock. Embroidered across the front was a pair of clasped hands, dripping with blood.

"Careful, now," she said, though there was little trace of concern in her tone. "You had surgery three days ago. You need to rest."

"Where am I?" Mavery rasped.

The healer sighed, then delivered in a flat voice, "You are in the infirmary at the Temple of Lavestra, in Burnslee. I am Acolyte Emma, and I have been assigned as your healer this afternoon."

Mavery couldn't recall how many times she'd ended up in infirmaries like this one. And, like all those times before, she must have appeared a penniless drifter. The temples were duty-bound to treat anyone in need of healing, regardless of their ability to tithe, but that didn't mean every acolyte was going to be thrilled when a charity case was placed under their care.

"You were found outside our door three nights ago, unconscious after suffering a gunshot wound," Emma said, reading from Mavery's chart. "You were taken into surgery, and you've been in and out of consciousness ever since. Now, lie back down."

"How did I get here?"

Emma shrugged. "Don't know. I don't work the night shift."

She appeared at least a decade older than Mavery, but it was always difficult to tell with healers. Healing magic—Soudremancy, the scholars called it—was one of the more demanding Schools of Magic. Healing required giving up part of your life force. A small cut required only a tiny sliver, but a life-threatening wound could prove fatal to the healer. That was why Mavery couldn't have saved Fennick, even if she'd known the proper spells. Career healers were constantly giving up their life force, and so they aged more rapidly than other mages. Healers tended to be quite literally the self-sacrificing types. That was especially true for the ones who served Lavestra the Benevolent; to them, shortening their lives for the sake of extending others was the ultimate way of serving the Goddess of Afflictions. Mavery couldn't wrap her head around any of it—the altruism, the religious devotion—but she was nonetheless grateful to have found her way here. Somehow.

Had she regained consciousness long enough to drag herself to the temple? No, more than likely, some kindhearted stranger had seen her bleeding out and had stopped to help her. Neldren had wasted no time breaking into her pack. He would have vanished the second he claimed her share of the payout.

Her breath hitched.

The payout...

"Can you hand me my pack?"

Emma begrudgingly obliged, handing Mavery a patched-up rucksack that was far lighter than she remembered. Dread tightened in her chest as she unfastened the front flap.

"You want something to eat?" Emma asked.

"Sure, fine," Mavery muttered. While the healer stepped away, she took inventory of her few possessions: her comb, the book she'd stolen from the manor, her Compendium, her lockpicking tools...

"Damn it!"

Just as she'd suspected, her cut of the payout was gone, as well as her lantern and dagger. She only hoped Neldren hadn't gotten too greedy and stolen *all* of her money.

With Emma away, Mavery swung her legs over the side of the bed. After three days of lying prone, her unsteady legs nearly collapsed beneath her. Using the wall for support, she inched closer to the chair. She picked up her left boot and prised away the insole to find a wad of notes, along with a few coins, she'd stashed away ages ago. She then checked the hidden pockets she'd sewn into her clothing: one inside the right cup of her brassière, and two along each inner thigh of her trousers. Since her clothes had been laundered, the notes clung together but were otherwise untouched. She peeled them apart and totaled up what now comprised her life savings: forty-seven potins and twelve coppers.

She would leave a few potins in the tithing box before she left this place. Even the entirety of her money was a pittance compared to the value of being brought back from certain death. But she needed to leave *something* behind. She hated being thought of as a charity case—even if she was one. She returned her money to its hiding spots and padded back to bed.

Emma returned, carrying a tray with a bowl of hot broth, a hunk of brown bread, a glass of milk, and a newspaper. Mavery placed the newspaper aside and devoured the food. She nearly choked on a mouthful of bread, and Emma scolded her to slow down.

"How long do I need to stay here?" Mavery asked when Emma reached for the empty tray.

"That's for the Head Healer to decide. She will need to examine you before she discharges you."

"Is there anything stopping me from leaving right now?"

Emma frowned. "No, but I would advise against it. You'll just find yourself right back in this bed."

She was right. The two paces between the bed and the chair had been enough to wear Mavery out. She felt a familiar twinge of pain from her knee. Well, since she was already here...

"My right knee has been bothering me for some time. It's not related to the gunshot, but could you take a look?"

"Lie down," Emma sighed.

She removed the tray, then pulled back the blanket and touched Mavery's knee. A clean, herbal scent filled the air. Emma's magic gently, but not painfully, probed the joint and tendons. A moment later, she removed her hands and shook her head.

"You've got a lot of scar tissue. Much like that mark on your nose, it's a very old wound, and even magic has its limits. Best I can do is prescribe you a poultice to ease any pain you're feeling."

"No, thanks." Mavery was disappointed but unsurprised. In

the years since she'd injured that knee—she could no longer remember what, exactly, had caused it—she'd tried an entire apothecary's stock of poultices, ointments, and serums. All to no avail.

Before Mavery could make any additional requests, Emma snatched up the tray and left.

Mavery reached in her pack and pulled out the book she'd stolen from the baron's library: *The Modern Gentleman's Field Guide to Mushroom Foraging*. She quickly learned why "the modern gentleman" was its target audience. The majority of the guide was devoted to mushrooms with aphrodisiac properties. She came across a detailed diagram of the most phallic-looking fungus she'd ever seen—one purported to "increase virility tenfold." This book wasn't a good fit for her Compendium, but it gave her a good laugh.

Unfortunately, her laughter caused a sharp pain in the pit of her stomach, in the very spot where Neldren's bullet had lodged itself. Once again, Emma was right: she still needed to rest. At least that gave her some time to plan her next move.

She put the mushroom book aside and turned to the newspaper, *The Burnslee Herald*. The current date was the second of Germinal. She'd turned thirty-seven two days ago, while she'd been unconscious. That realization deepened the ache in her stomach. Upon seeing the front page headline, her pain flared even more.

PROVINCIAL POLICE INVESTIGATING
BREAK-IN AT ROVEN MANOR: HOUSE
FALLSTAD STILL TO BLAME

If the job had garnered that much attention, she didn't want to linger in this village longer than necessary. It wouldn't be long before someone made a connection between the robbery at the manor and the stranger in the infirmary only a mile away. But her options were even more limited than they'd been the other night. Even if she lived as frugally as possible, her savings wouldn't last her a fortnight.

If she was serious about making a career change—one that

involved more honest work—the "help wanted" section was the best place to start. She flipped to the back of the newspaper and was greeted, front and center, by an enormous ad in elegant, bold lettering. A filigree border framed it on all sides:

WANTED: ABLE-BODIED MEN & WOMEN
Wincoff & Sons Rail Co. seeks laborers for Tanarim's
first cross-country railroad. A RARE OPPORTUNI-
TY to become part of history! Daily wages & meals.
SIGNING BONUSES for all menders. Write to Wincoff
& Sons, 155 West High Street, Durnatel.

"Rare opportunity" or not, the thought of hard labor made her knee ache all over again. If only she were ten years younger, it would be somewhat tempting. She shifted slightly, which aggravated a twinge in her lower back. On second thought, maybe if she were *fifteen* years younger...

She continued reading.

GRAVEDIGGER NEEDED
Talk to Sexton Jerrod at Burnslee Cemetery.
NO vagrants. NO criminals.

Mavery rolled her eyes. Yes, she was both a vagrant and a criminal, and one who had *indirectly* stolen valuables from the dead. But she'd always drawn the line at looting corpses. She had standards.

Her eyes glazed over the long list of calls for menial, unskilled labor. Most were offering a pittance, and nearly all of them made it clear they had no use for a not-so-hale, not-so-youthful woman with a dubious work history.

She was about to give up hope altogether when an ad near the bottom of the page caught her eye. Whoever had placed this one hadn't requested a larger space. The verbose copy had been squeezed into a two-inch square. Mavery had to squint to read it.

Esteemed Wizard & Professor
Seeks Assistant
Duties include, but are not limited to, facilitating arcane research & experiments. Ideal candidate must be a mage Gifted in the School of Gardemancy. Other desirable qualities include: exceptional organizational skills, university-level literacy, excellent penmanship, a cheerful disposition, & a willingness to tolerate obstinacy. Pay is negotiable, based on qualifications. Inquire at Steelforge Towers,
Riverside District, City of Leyport.

Mavery reached the end of the ad with a raised eyebrow and a heaping measure of skepticism. She read it again to make sure she hadn't imagined it. From what little she knew of wizards, they typically plucked their assistants from the pools of recent university graduates. To see one advertise such a position in the newspaper was unusual, to say the least. And the village of Burnslee was about fifty miles from the city of Leyport, so he was searching far and wide.

She assumed "he" because the vast majority of wizards were male. She also assumed he had to be desperate, and perhaps a tad insane. This ad was practically a public invitation to visit his tower. No, *towers*. Whoever he was, he must have been distinguished enough to own more than one, which further intrigued her. She couldn't recall seeing any wizard towers the last time she was in the city—apart from the ones that comprised the University of Leyport—but a lot could change in nearly twenty years.

She chewed on a nail as she read the ad for a fourth time.

Enchanted talismans, magical staves, rare potion ingredients... A wizard's tower was a treasure trove. She had a good idea of how much those treasures fetched on the black market, courtesy of her brief tenure with the Brass Dragons, the kingdom's largest criminal network. A single artifact could make up for what Neldren had stolen from her. An entire display case of artifacts could have her living comfortably for years.

Wizards collected magical artifacts like the nobility collected unread books. Of course, they tended to contract out artifact *fetching* to people like Mavery. She'd done it a handful of times, but she'd rarely interacted with the wizards directly. They preferred to conduct that sort of thing through their assistants—the bookish types who had no business delving into old ruins.

But that didn't mean being a wizard's assistant was a *safe* job. Mavery recalled Draconus the Vile, the Necromancer who'd died over five centuries ago but still held the record for the most assistants to die under his employ: thirty-three. And those were only the recorded deaths.

Whether this wizard in Leyport was as ruthless as Draconus was none of Mavery's concern; she had no intention of sticking around long enough to find out. She would travel to Leyport, convince this wizard to hire her, and then clean his tower of valuables at the first opportunity.

Convincing him that she was the right woman for the job wouldn't be too much of a challenge. He just so happened to be looking for a Gardemancer, which she knew was the fancy, academic word for warding magic.

She also knew that her ability to detect magic was something of a rarity. The average mage could not see the color of a ward, taste a spell being cast, or differentiate the pungent odor of shadow magic from the calming aroma of healing magic. What she lacked in formal education, her abilities would make up for in spades. The wizard would never even know she'd failed to finish university, so long as she kept the details vague enough.

And even if the wizard saw through her ruse and didn't give her the job, she would at least use the interview to case out his tower. The only challenge would be getting to Leyport before any other applicants.

She ripped out the newspaper ad and tucked it in the front pocket of her pack. Though she wouldn't yet be leaving the criminal life, it was within reach. All she needed was one final score.

FOUR

A train whistle sounded, and with a clamor of whinnying, the wagon lurched to a halt. Mavery dodged crates and barrels as they tumbled forward in the wagon bed, colliding into one another. Thanks to her protective wards, the abrupt stop hadn't damaged any merchandise. She couldn't say the same for her Compendium of Knowledge, however. It had slipped from her hands, and then had been promptly crushed beneath a crate of cabbages.

"Sorry about that, Jayne!" the merchant called from the driver's seat. He'd told her his name was Herold; she'd given him a fake one in return. "The train spooked the horses."

Mavery groaned as she grabbed one corner of her Compendium. She was about to pull it free when Herold snapped the reins and the wagon moved forward again. The cabbage crate slid backward—and took a section of her Compendium along with it. Mavery emitted a colorful string of expletives as she gathered the torn pages.

Whether out of fear of the unknown, or fear of bruising his ego, Neldren had always been content relying on shadow magic alone. But dropping out of university had never quelled Mavery's thirst for knowledge. Once she'd squeezed as much as she could from Neldren, she'd begun pilfering books while performing jobs.

Thus, her Compendium of Knowledge had been born: hundreds of loose pages, bound together with needle and thread.

A life of constant travel meant she could only carry so many books at a time. When she finished one, she would cut out the most interesting sections and add them to her Compendium. Sections would come and go as she grew bored with the material or had committed it to heart. Arcane knowledge was the one exception. Things like Gardemancy textbooks were difficult to find outside of university campuses and wizards' libraries, and so anything on magic had a permanent place in her collection.

She'd been poring over those pages on her journey to Leyport, in case the wizard wanted to test her skills. At least the rogue cabbages hadn't destroyed anything useful. The only casualty had been a tedious but thorough chapter on the history of the First Reforms. Unless the wizard was also a historian, she doubted he would quiz her on that.

She lowered herself onto the sacks of grain she'd arranged into a chair. After being discharged from the infirmary yesterday, she'd tracked down a merchant who was heading to Durnatel, the capital city. In exchange for some protective wards, he'd promised to drop her off in Leyport. They had to be close by now. She pulled a section of canvas aside and peered through the gap.

To say Osperland's largest port city had changed over the years was an understatement. Much of it had spilled outside the original city walls, and the southern outskirts were now a hive of working-class activity. Shipyards, fisheries, and factories stretched on for miles. Beyond that, the landscape was dotted with villages robust enough to be cities in their own right.

The University of Leyport's five white towers loomed over the heart of the city. The University was the largest wizarding school in the country, and it boasted one of the largest libraries on the continent—over a hundred thousand books. But the wizards kept that vast hoard of knowledge behind their warded gates. It was off-limits to someone like Mavery, who had to make do with her portable, illegally acquired library.

They were still a few miles out, and so she decided to get some rest before the next leg of her journey began. She turned away from the view, closed her eyes, and tried her best to ignore the rattling wagon wheels and distant train whistles.

The wagon stopped outside the city's southern gate. She climbed out the back and winced as her feet collided with cobblestone. Though her arcana allowed her to heal much faster than someone without magical blood, an overnight trip in a cramped wagon had hampered her recovery. And being in Leyport didn't help her feel any more refreshed. Her stomach lurched at the stench of rotting fish and burning coal. Her ears rang at the endless din of noise. Even her arcana felt more subdued than usual, as if it, too, wanted to escape all this chaos.

She remembered now why she avoided cities whenever possible. But it was too late to turn back.

"How well do you know your way around Leyport?" she asked Herold.

"Well enough. I stop here at least once a season."

"You wouldn't happen to know where I can find Steelforge Towers?"

"Steelforge Towers?" He scratched his whiskered chin. "Doesn't ring a... Oh! You must mean the old armory."

Mavery had only vague memories of an armory along the riverfront. Given her profession, she tended to avoid areas swarming with armed guards.

"Yes, that's the place," Herold mused. "They decommissioned the armory fifteen years ago, give or take, when they opened the munitions factory. Completely gutted it and turned it into some hoity-toity apartments."

Mavery frowned. An apartment building sounded a far cry from a wizard's tower, but she wouldn't know until she confirmed it for herself.

"It's on the north end of the city. Just follow the river for about three miles. You can't miss it."

In theory, Herold's directions had sounded simple. In practice, she was in no condition to walk nearly three miles.

When she reached her destination, she'd worn another hole in her right boot, she was drenched in sweat, and she couldn't find a muscle that *didn't* ache. She almost wished she'd hired a city carriage. But until she knew her plan was feasible, she didn't have a single copper to spare.

Steelforge Towers was, indeed, the old armory. The enormous red-bricked building resembled a castle. It even had battlements running along its roof, turrets on its northern and southern ends. The entrance—glass double-doors accented with mullions—was definitely not part of the original building.

Nor was the lobby, with its gleaming, black-and-white tiled floor. The room was flanked by staircases with marble steps and curved wrought-iron balustrades. A chandelier hung from the ceiling; dozens of tiny lights glowed with warm auras. Sitting at the desk in the center of the room was an elderly man bearing an umber complexion and a tailored suit.

Perched on his shoulder was a kutauss. This variety of demon-spawn resembled a ferret, apart from its red eyes and coal-black fur. To Mavery's relief—though probably not to the creature's—it had been declawed. Even a tiny scratch from those poisonous claws would stifle a mage's arcana. Mavery had learned that the hard way during a job when she'd transported a cage full of kutausses.

The old man gave her a long, scrutinizing look, as if evaluating her appearance: worn boots, ragged trousers, bloodstained blouse, hair ending in a shaggy cut just below her jawline. The kutauss seemed to eye her with an equal amount of suspicion.

"Good day, er, *madam*," he said with a forced smile.

Mavery approached the desk and leaned her elbows on the counter. The kutauss hissed. The man recoiled, but his smile didn't budge.

"A fine day to you, too," she said. "I'm looking for a wizard who lives here."

"*You* are looking for Aventus?" Eyes widening, his smile finally faltered. "I'm sorry, he doesn't accept visitors."

The old man flinched again as she reached in her pocket, then relaxed when she only retrieved the newspaper clipping. He donned a pair of spectacles, but he still needed to hold the paper up to his nose to read it.

"Well, it appears I stand corrected." He handed back the clipping. "You would be the first to call on him in ages. It's been weeks since I last spoke to him."

No one else had jumped at the opportunity like she had; that was reassuring.

"Are you sure he's around?"

"He paid his rent on the first, but he once again failed to pick up his mail. Seeing as you're heading upstairs, would you mind bringing that to him?"

"Er...all right."

The man clicked his tongue, and the kutauss hopped onto the desk. He took his cane and hobbled into an antechamber to the right of the lobby. While he shuffled papers and emitted a few grunts of exertion, Mavery remained by the desk, trying to avoid eye contact with the kutauss, which was staring at her, unblinking, with its head tilted to one side. Though it was somewhat cute, its red eyes were unsettling enough to make her shudder. She could almost understand keeping demonspawn around for protection; she couldn't fathom keeping one as a *familiar*.

When the old man returned, she balked at the size of the box in his trembling arms. She took it before his strength failed him. She'd expected only a handful of mail, but this box was roughly the size of an apple crate, and it was filled to the brim with unopened letters and rolled-up issues of *The Leyport Gazette*.

The man returned to his chair with a groan, and the kutauss returned to his shoulder.

"I tossed the oldest newspapers," he said, "and I had half a mind to toss the entire lot. I've tried leaving it at his door, but that's easier said than done."

"What do you mean?"

"You'll see soon enough. Sixth floor, apartment six-oh-five. I recommend taking the lift."

She followed his outstretched hand to the lobby's back wall. The lift's cabin was barely large enough for two people. She had to place the box at her feet and use both hands to crank the lifting mechanism. Her arms ached and her forehead gained a new layer of sweat as she slowly ascended to the sixth floor, but she supposed it was preferable to the stairs.

When she stepped off the lift, her thoughts became peppered with doubts.

Turn around and tell that old man you're not his errand girl.

You don't really want to be here.

It's not too late to change your mind.

Mavery blinked, and her mind quieted once more. The first thought had seemed to be her own, but where had the others come from? She shifted the box to one arm, then closed the gate behind her. The rattling reverberated down the long wood-paneled corridor. It contained no windows, but was lit by a handful of sconces—all infused with magic, judging by their halo-like auras.

As she proceeded down the corridor, a new wave of doubts washed over her. These were shorter but more tempestuous than before.

You have no business here.

Turn around.

Leave.

Mavery stopped. She closed her eyes and breathed deeply.

And there it was: the taste of copper. The air was filled with warding magic strong enough to manipulate her thoughts. With a shudder, she wondered if there was some Mysticism involved. She couldn't make herself immune to magic this powerful, but simply being aware of it dampened its effects.

As she pressed forward, she focused all her thoughts on the act of putting one foot in front of the next. The intruding thoughts persisted, but now they were suggestions rather than commands.

She did not need to see the number on the door to know she had the right place. The door at the end of the hall was radiant with magic. The thoughts now screamed at her, begged her to turn around. She ignored them and instead focused on the warding magic itself: a half-dozen spells, each represented by a tendril of colorful light, and woven together like an intricate tapestry—a masterpiece crafted from arcana. Rarely could she recall seeing magic so breathtakingly beautiful, so *flawless*.

This was a test, she deduced. The wizard must have planned for his applicants to prove their worth by getting through the front door.

She lowered the box and leaned as close as the magic would allow. Even the most complex ward could be manipulated; it was just a matter of finding a weak point. With her nose inches away, she could identify the individual spells by color. Blue for protective wards; violet for soundproofing; gold for alarms; sage green she couldn't identify, but assumed it represented the thought manipulation spell. Luckily, she Sensed no red-hued blasting wards, so at least this wizard didn't intend to maim anyone.

"Aha!"

She spotted the weak point at last: a single thread whose aura was duller than the others. This spell had nearly run its course. She raised her hand and pinched the thread between her thumb and forefinger. Of course, she couldn't *physically* touch it, but it responded to her magic as though she had. With the precision of a surgeon, she pulled it loose and created a hole no larger than a pinhead. Using the same technique she'd used on Baron Roven's safe, she tried coaxing the tiny hole to widen. It refused to budge. She held firm and focused her arcana.

"Come on, you," she muttered.

Like an invisible game of tug-of-war, she pulled, and the ward pulled back. The hole widened to the size of a coin, then the size of an apple. But no matter how hard she fought, she couldn't freeze the hole in place, much less break the ward. She would have to act quickly.

In one swift movement, she slipped her hand through the hole, gave the door two quick raps—the soundproofing ward muffled them—and pulled her hand back. With a *snap*, the hole shrunk to a pinprick again. Heart thrumming against her ribcage, she sighed with relief. Early in her career, she'd managed to ensnare herself in a ward—an unpleasant experience she never wanted to repeat. Moreover, she didn't want to look like a novice to the wizard she planned to impress.

The magic didn't take kindly to her efforts. The intruding thoughts now pounded inside her skull, too loud to ignore.

YOU'RE NOT WANTED.

BEGONE, TRESPASSER.

LEAVE, OR ELSE.

She would not leave, not when she'd come this far.

A moment passed, and then the door opened an inch. A face, partially hidden in shadow, peered at her through the gap. The violet tendrils vanished; the stranger had dismissed the soundproofing ward.

"Who are you?" The voice was masculine, though soft and somewhat strained.

"Hello, I'm Mave Reynard."

She'd put enough distance between herself and Burnslee; it felt safe to resume using her real given name. The surname, however, was fake. It was the go-to alias for thieves who wished to remain anonymous, but she doubted a wizard would know that.

"Did Declan send you?" the voice asked.

"Who's Declan?"

"Volsegar?"

She shook her head; she didn't recognize either name.

"Never mind. Why are you here?"

"I'm inquiring about the position."

"What position?"

"The wizard's assistantship."

The door opened wider. The remaining wards dissipated, taking the intruding thoughts along with them. Mavery's ears rang from the sudden silence.

She stood eye to eye with a disheveled-looking man in a tartan dressing gown. His dark brown hair hung limply past his shoulders. It was paired with a thick beard that obscured the lower half of his face, including his mouth. Though his age was difficult to place, his croaky voice wasn't due to advanced age. He had few wrinkles, no noticeably gray hairs.

Even the youngest of Mavery's professors had been middle-aged, and she couldn't recall ever meeting a wizard younger than that. Earning that rank took years—sometimes decades—of training, and that was *after* completing six years of university.

The man standing before her was definitely too young to be a wizard. And she doubted someone in this state of undress was a wizard's assistant. Perhaps he was a relative, or even a lover. Whoever he was, she assumed he was suffering from some illness. His complexion was deathly pale, his eyes sunken.

He cleared his throat.

"I believe there's been a misunderstanding." His voice grew slightly more robust. "I'm not looking for an assistant."

Mavery raised her brows. She'd been expecting an elderly man with a beard. Well, he met *two* of those criteria.

"I saw an ad in the newspaper—"

"What ad?"

She produced the clipping, and he snatched it from her hand. He read beneath his breath, pausing on occasion to add his disjointed commentary.

" 'Esteemed'?... Oh, for the love of... 'Obstinacy'!?... Mother." He read it a second time, then snapped, "Was this in *The Gazette*?"

"No, *The Burnslee Herald*."

"And when did you see this?"

"Two days ago."

As he raked his fingers through his hair and muttered something she couldn't discern, disappointment sank in. Mavery should have recognized an opportunity that sounded too good to be true.

"Sorry for bothering you," she said, taking a step back from the door. "I'll be—"

"Would you like a cup of tea?"

She paused mid-step. "What?"

He cleared his throat again. "I imagine coming here—and so quickly—took a great deal of effort. Though I cannot deliver on what this ad promised, it would be discourteous of me to turn you away without at least offering you a cup of tea. Your timing was most auspicious, as I was about to put on a kettle when you knocked."

She blinked as she tried to reconcile the posh, upper-class accent with the disaster of a man standing before her. This entire situation was becoming more mystifying by the minute, but she wasn't about to pass up the invitation he'd just offered.

"Sure, why not? Er, I mean—"

Mavery had always found her own voice too raspy and unrefined, her provincial accent too persistent despite her attempts to suppress it. She'd built up a wide vocabulary over the years, but no amount of reading could prevent her from sounding like a yokel putting on airs whenever she spoke a word containing more than two syllables. She cleared her throat, hoping she could suppress her inner yokel long enough to trick this wizard into thinking she was worthy of his time.

"Thank you," she said, bowing her head for good measure. "A cup of tea sounds *lovely*."

He opened the door the rest of the way and gestured for her to enter. She picked up the box of mail and crossed the threshold.

She was bombarded with the musty scent of leather, paper, and ink. She could hardly call this a sitting room, as there was no place to actually *sit*. There were books everywhere she looked—a collection that rivaled even the wealthiest noble's library. The bookcases lining the right-hand wall were filled to capacity; their shelves bent under the weight of the hefty tomes. Books that hadn't fit on the shelves had been scattered over every surface, from the tea table in the center of the room, to the fireplace mantel on the left-hand wall. But most of them had been dumped on the floor. Mavery took another step and nearly tripped over a stack.

Her stomach lurched when she saw a fire crackling in the hearth but Sensed no fireproofing wards. This wizard was either insane or had a death wish.

"Oh, this is your mail," she said, showing him the box. "The old man at the front desk asked me to bring it to you."

He shook his head. "I should have known Bertie would find a way to get that to me eventually. You can put it...oh, wherever."

She placed the box and her pack beside the desk in the corner closest to the door. This, too, was piled high with papers and books, but she was glad to keep at least *some* potential kindling away from the open flames.

"May I take your coat?" the wizard asked.

She pulled it tightly around herself and hoped he hadn't noticed the bloodstain on her shirt.

"Er, I'm still a bit cold from the outside." The sweat pooling on her forehead betrayed her lie. "I'll keep it on."

The wizard—Aventus, the man downstairs had called him—pushed aside a stack of books on the sofa and motioned for her to sit. He then navigated a path that snaked around the piles of books, leading to what Mavery assumed was the kitchen.

She wasted no time scoping out the room. The walls were decorated with a few maps and paintings—all cheap reproductions, at first glance. There was a rather alarming number of empty wine bottles scattered about. A dust-coated one lay on the tea table. Directly below it, a purple stain marred what had once been a vibrant Maroban rug.

Aside from the book collection, Mavery could identify nothing of value here. If Aventus owned any rare artifacts, they were hidden beneath the mess. It would take some digging—maybe literally—to uncover them.

Clinking porcelain announced Aventus's return from the kitchen. Mavery vaulted over a stack of books and sat on the sofa, as though she hadn't just been snooping around. He balanced a tray atop the books on the tea table, then lowered himself into a well-worn armchair—the only surface that was completely free of clutter. While his living space was chaotic, his approach to tea-making was the opposite. He spooned loose leaves into the pot and then filled it with steaming water, spilling not a single drop.

"As I said before... Sorry, what did you say your name was?"

"Mave Reynard."

He blinked at her as though he'd misheard, but then nodded. "Mave, apologies for the misunderstanding. That newspaper ad was placed by mistake—one that I will rectify immediately after you leave."

"Who placed it, then?"

Aventus stiffened. "Someone who, I'm certain, was looking out for my best interests. But that someone failed to realize that I prefer an...*independent* approach to research these days."

He strained the tea into a pair of teacups. The teapot had a hairline crack down its side, the cups were chipped in several places. This set wasn't a valuable heirloom, handed down through the generations. Another sign that his *real* valuables—Mavery was still optimistic they existed—wouldn't be left out in the open.

"Cream or sugar?"

She shrugged. "However you take it is fine. I'm not picky."

In Osperland, even the lowest of low-end taverns served tea, but it wasn't the kind worth sitting down and savoring. More often than not, it looked and tasted like dishwater. She couldn't remember the last time she'd had a cup of something even *half*-decent. Whatever Aventus was preparing, it was bound to be luxurious, despite the state of his tea set.

He added a single sugar cube and a generous splash of cream. He stirred the liquid until it turned the color of old parchment, then passed her the cup upon its matching saucer. She took a sip with as much poise as she could muster, not wanting to look too obviously out of her element. The tea smelled strongly of bergamot and was warm, earthy, comforting.

"Does it need more sugar?"

"Oh, no," she sighed. "This is perfect."

She drank heartily as he prepared his own cup.

"Since you took the initiative in coming here," he said, "I will at least do you the courtesy of passing along your information to my colleagues at the University." He glanced at Mavery's pack. "I assume you brought some application materials with you."

"Such as?"

"Letters of recommendation, university transcripts, any spell tomes you contributed to..."

She should have known a *wizard* would prefer written evidence. She sipped her tea, buying herself a moment to craft a response.

"Oh, I left Burnslee in such a hurry, I'm afraid I didn't have time to gather all my, er, papers. How about I deliver everything to you verbally now, then I'll mail them to you the first chance I get? What do you want to know?"

"Your education, for starters."

"I attended Atterdell College."

Beneath his mess of hair, his eyebrows raised.

"What?"

"Nothing," he said, shaking his head. "Only... Well, Atterdell's reputation in the wizarding community is, shall we say, short of prestigious." If he noticed her frown, he made no mention of it. "Anyway, which Schools did you study?"

"Gardemancy, of course."

"*Gar*-duh-man-see."

Didn't I just say that?

She forced a smile. "I'm also studied in alchemy, shadow magic—I mean, Ambermancy—and Souder—"

"*Ahm*-bruh-man-see and *Soo*-druh-man-see." He articulated slowly, as if he were speaking to a child.

Her smile fell. "Right, well, some of those terms have gotten a little rusty. I've been out of the academic circles for a while."

"Personally, I don't mind if you use colloquialisms, but some of my colleagues are sticklers for using the proper terminology. Before you meet with them, you'll want to brush up on that—as well as your Dauphinian, by the sound of it."

Over a thousand years ago, the First Reforms had established Dauphinian as Tanarim's language of law, commerce, and magic. Even the names of the months and days of the week originated from Dauphinian. It was the closest thing the continent had to a common tongue, though Mavery had never been capable of wrapping her own tongue around it.

"Do you know *any* foreign languages?" Aventus asked.

"I can speak Fenutian well enough."

He uttered a small sound that Mavery could only interpret as disapproval.

"What is it now?" she demanded.

"To paraphrase one of my colleagues, anyone can speak Fenutian. All that's required is stuffing a sock in one's mouth and speaking Osperlandish at half-speed."

While he lowered his gaze to his teacup, she gave him a hard glare. She'd also picked up some Nilandoren from Neldren, though none of it was suitable for polite conversation. The way *this* conversation was heading, it wouldn't be long before she introduced the wizard to some of her favorite phrases.

"What of your field experience? Have you ever assisted any other wizards?"

"Look, we could talk about my qualifications until nightfall." *And you'd likely disparage each one.* "But shouldn't the fact that I'm sitting here be enough evidence of my skills? I managed to break through your wards, and that was some of the most intricate magic I've ever *Sensed.*"

"Fair enough. Even the University's best Gardemancers couldn't—" He stared at her over his half-raised teacup. "Wait. When you say 'Sensed,' you don't mean—?"

"I can see magic. Taste and smell it, too."

"Y-you're a Senser?" he asked. When she nodded, his eyes widened. He placed his cup on the table, then raised a finger. "Wait there just one moment."

He stumbled over the blockade of books between his armchair and his desk, then riffled through the stacks of papers. Mavery watched him with a satisfied smirk. She'd had a card hidden up her sleeve—one that even a pompous ass like Aventus couldn't disregard. He returned to his chair, opened a notebook, readied a fountain pen.

"I hope you don't mind if I take some notes."

"Not at all," she said cloyingly.

"When did you first develop arcane hypersensitivity? 'Sensing,' if you prefer."

She relaxed into the sofa. "Since I first showed signs of magic, I suppose. When I was a child, I described it as seeing colors and shapes. For the longest time, everyone in my family thought that was normal. I was the first mage in my family in at least four, maybe five, generations."

"Were there any Sensers in your family before then?"

"No idea. Neither side of my family kept many records. Any that did exist are long gone."

"Still, that's consistent with the current body of research." He tapped his pen against his cheek, leaving behind a black smudge that he didn't seem to notice. "When a magical bloodline skips several generations, the next mage's arcana tends to be exceptionally strong. Most often, that takes the form of uncontrolled bursts of magic during the developmental years. 'Magic surges,' if you will."

"Oh, I had plenty of those, too. Still do, on the very rare occasion. But, as I said, everyone around me thought random outbursts were normal. We had no one in living memory to compare me to, and we didn't leave the family farm very often. Once I started school and met other mages, I learned that few people experience magic like I do."

"That's putting it lightly. There have been only a dozen or so Sensers in the past century."

"In Osperland?"

"Across the entire continent."

Mavery gaped at him. She'd always known her abilities were rare, but no one had ever told her they were *that* rare.

"The last Senser in Osperland," Aventus said, "was Deventhal the Fifth, and he died about thirty years ago. He was a reclusive one, even by wizard standards. He rarely left his tower, never hired a single assistant. So, to have a Senser show up at my door, you can see why I'm eager to ask questions."

"Then ask away."

"What do you Sense, exactly? Colors, scents, *anything*. The more specific, the better."

Mavery began by explaining how she'd identified the different wards on his door by color, before delving into other Schools of Magic. She spoke for nearly half an hour. Aventus feverishly took notes, only stopping once his fountain pen ran dry. At that point, he paused the interview to return to his desk and search for his inkwell. As his search progressed, paper-shuffling and drawer-slamming grew increasingly more frantic.

"I swear I left the blasted thing here," he grumbled. "Can't find another pen, either."

"May I make a suggestion?" Mavery asked. Here was an opportunity if she ever saw one, but she couldn't sound *too* eager. He gave up on his cluttered desk and turned to her.

"Yes?"

"I know you said you weren't looking for an assistant, but from what I can tell, you could use a little help around here."

Aventus slowly gazed around the room, as if noticing its disordered state for the first time. Slouching his shoulders, he groaned.

"Loath as I am to admit it, you're right. The 'independent approach' to research hasn't been very fruitful—unless my goal was developing a book-hoarding habit." He laughed flatly. "If that were the case, I would say I've been a resounding success."

"Believe it or not, I can relate to that." Mavery gave him a small smile. "May I ask why you don't have an assistant? Not to be crass, but is it a matter of money?"

"No, not at all. My reasons are...personal."

He picked his way across the piles of books and slumped into his armchair. As he scratched his bearded chin with his blackened fingers, Mavery could almost see the thoughts buzzing inside his head. A moment passed before he spoke again.

"If your goal is to become a wizard, I should warn you: I'm one of the last people you'd want to work for. I've barely the capacity to conduct my own research these days, much less be any sort of mentor for yours."

"Oh, that's no problem at all. I'm not looking to become a wizard. I was thinking I could tidy up your books, and you can ask me anything about my Sensing abilities."

"A tempting offer, though one I can't help but notice weighs heavily in *my* favor. What would *you* gain from this arrangement?"

"Remember how I said I've been out of academic circles for a while? Well, I'm looking for a way to dip my toes back in. Seeing as I'm a natural Gardemancer—"

"Innate," he corrected.

"An *innate* Gardemancer," she said through another forced smile, "this seemed like a good fit. And, of course, I wouldn't work for free."

"Nor would I expect you to. I paid my last assistants eighty potins per week, if that sounds reasonable."

"Very reasonable." She hadn't a clue if it actually was, but for that amount of money, she could overlook the wizard's lack of social graces.

"Well, then, I'm open to giving this arrangement a trial run.

Let's give it a week. I'll even pay your wages in advance. Take some time to get settled in Leyport, then return here on Onisday at, let's say, nine in the morning."

He stood up, and Mavery followed him to the desk. From one of the drawers, Aventus retrieved a billfold and counted out eight ten-potin notes. She pocketed them without hesitation. She had expected a cheque, which would leave a paper trail in the event she didn't fulfill her end of the bargain. By paying her upfront in cash, he either trusted her completely, or he didn't care about losing his money. Assuming he had something worth stealing, he was shaping up to be the perfect mark.

"I'll see you in a few days," he said, opening the door.

"Until then." She gave him a nod and, by virtue of the eighty potins in her pocket, a smile that was almost genuine.

FIVE

H e pressed his forehead to the closed door. He was exhausted in a way he could scarcely remember feeling. His mind reeled, his hand ached from that bout of frenzied writing. His throat was raw from speaking the most he'd spoken to another person in...gods, he couldn't even remember how long.

His conversation with Mave had been far from a perfect example of human communication. But it had gone better than he would have anticipated, had he anticipated *anything* of interest happening today—a visitor, least of all.

Upon hearing the knock at his door, he'd wondered whether he would find one of the Elder Wizards of the High Council, if not the Archmage himself, standing on the other side of it. Instead, he'd found a woman with striking green eyes and an air of quiet determination about her. At first, he'd assumed he'd been on the receiving end of another of Declan's pranks; his colleague *would* be the type to use an attractive woman to lure a reclusive wizard from his cave. But Mave was just an ordinary mage.

No, "ordinary" was doing her a disservice. She'd managed to bypass his wards long enough to knock. No one, not even anyone from the University, had managed that over these past months.

Without the wards in place, the air was eerily still. There was no familiar, steady rhythm of magic—a sensation so subtle, it was detectable only by spending years learning to attune oneself to it. Or, by nature of being a Senser, like the woman who had just exited his apartment.

The woman he had just *hired*.

He considered throwing open the door, running down the corridor, stopping her before she reached the lift. He'd apologize profusely for his momentary lapse in judgment, but he had no business taking on a new assistant. Though she claimed to have no intention of becoming a wizard, he was certain he would find some other way to fail her, just as he'd failed all the others before her.

He wasn't ready for this. Definitely not now, and potentially never again.

But it was likely too late to catch up with her now.

He turned away from the door and returned to his armchair. With shaking hands, he seized his teacup and drained it. The liquid had gone cold, but it calmed his nerves enough to allow him to think practically about what had just transpired.

Mave Reynard—if that was actually her family name—was more than a talented Gardemancer. She was a *Senser*. He couldn't pass up an opportunity that had so serendipitously arrived at his doorstep. She would return on Onisday, and today was...

For the life of him, he couldn't remember. Before she returned, he would need to reacquaint himself with a calendar.

He picked up his notebook and skimmed the notes he'd recorded during their interview. The end result of his hastiness was dreadful penmanship accented with inkblots, but he couldn't blame himself for being excited. This was the first spark of inspiration he'd had in ages. Not since—

Gods, no. Of all the things to dwell on, don't dwell on that.

He instead forced himself to refocus on his notes. When he reached the final unfinished sentence, he let loose a sigh of...satisfaction? Relief?

Mave's testimony aligned with everything he already knew about arcane hypersensitivity—a subject that had long fascinated him, if only because the body of literature on it was so sparse. Most scholars approached Mave's condition with a heaping dose of skepticism, as they tended to do with anything that didn't fit neatly into one of the eight Schools of Magic. But where others saw anomalies, he saw possibilities.

Already, ideas were beginning to form. They would either lead to the break his career needed—or the final nail in its coffin. Regarding the latter, he doubted it was possible to tarnish his reputation in the wizarding community any further.

And so, with nothing left to lose, he would give this new assistant a chance, see where his ideas led. He would have started his research right then and there, had he any clue where he'd left his books on Sensing. He looked around the room and sighed again. This time, it was out of frustration with himself. He'd grown so used to living in these conditions, he'd forgotten how dire he'd allowed them to become.

Months ago, he'd attempted to tidy up the place. But no matter how hard he tried, it seemed the piles always continued to multiply, the dust always continued to thicken. At some point, he'd decided it was easier to simply live with the mess than to attempt to mitigate it. Even if Mave stayed in his employ for only a week, she was bound to make more progress than he'd done in nearly a year.

But he had a more pressing matter to attend to: he had to put an end to those blasted newspaper ads. He ripped a blank page from his notebook, then found his spare pen at last. It had been with him all this time, lodged between the cushions of his armchair. He spared a single laugh at his own foolishness, then set to work.

He was halfway through writing his letter when he realized he'd never given Mave his name.

Six

Over the next few days, Mavery reacquainted herself with Leyport. By Onisday morning, she'd rented a room in the cheapest boarding house she could find, identified the bakery with the least expensive bread, and patronized the taverns with the least watered-down ale. Though her first week's wages would allow her to live a bit more comfortably, it was still too early to indulge in frivolous things.

She arrived at Steelforge Towers promptly at nine. She waved to Bertie at the front desk, tossed a chunk of baguette to the kutauss—whose name she learned was Klaus—and ascended to the sixth floor. This time, she wasn't inundated with thoughts to leave, though the rest of Aventus's magic was still in place. She repeated the trick she'd pulled the other day.

Several minutes passed before he finally answered the door. His dressing gown was open, revealing a sleeping shift that hung below his knees. His hair was even more tousled than before, as though he'd come straight from bed.

"You're early," he yawned.

"I'm on time, actually. For a moment there, I thought you'd forgotten all about me."

"No, I overslept, is all." He glanced at his stockinged feet. "Come in while I put on something more presentable."

She returned to the sofa as he walked around it and into the bedroom. He stumbled into a stack of books, toppling them over, and muttered something under his breath. His incoherent ramblings continued until he closed the door behind him.

Clearly, he was not a morning person. Nine o'clock was late for Mavery, who had awoken at dawn as usual. She chewed her baguette while she picked at a loose thread in her new blouse. Well, it was new to *her*, not the woman who'd left it in the boarding house's washroom. It was several sizes too large, and its oatmeal color made her look like a walking corpse. At least it was better than the shirt with the bullet hole and bloodstains. With the advance on her wages, she could have bought some nicer clothes, but that seemed like another frivolous indulgence.

When Aventus reappeared, she recalled from the newspaper ad that he was a professor. Now, in his tweed trousers and matching vest, he finally looked the part. Though his clothing was made of quality fabrics, not a single article fit him properly. His trouser legs were baggy, his sleeves were rolled up past his elbows, his vest hung loosely despite being completely buttoned. But he was still the better dressed between the two of them.

"Well," he said, "shall we begin?"

She polished off her baguette as she followed him to the bookshelves. The books here had been arranged by subject—to an extent—while the ones on the floor had been lumped together at random.

"I've accumulated a rather large collection of overdue books from several universities' libraries," he said. "Your first order of business is to track them down."

"Sounds simple enough."

"Simple, though I doubt it will be *easy*. I've long neglected my cataloging system, so those books could be anywhere. You'll have to pick through every book in this apartment, I'm afraid."

To further prove his point, he showed her how the books had also overtaken his bedroom. Stacks of them had been shoved into corners, atop the dresser, beneath the bed. Aside from the mess, the room was cozy—and private. Since they were on the top floor, with nothing but the River Merimar in sight, only a sheer curtain hung in the window. The iron-framed bed was excessively large for a single sleeper, and it was covered in a heap of plush blankets and pillows. Mavery now understood why Aventus had overslept.

Back in the sitting room, she spotted a door that she assumed led to a second bedroom. He noticed her gaze linger on it. He took her by the shoulders.

"That's the storage room, nothing of importance in there," he said, steering her away. "Here, let me show you the kitchen."

It was equipped with modern luxuries: the sink had running water, the stove was powered by Elemental magic, and the larder glowed with a blue aura that Mavery suspected was a food preservation ward. Though Aventus had called it a kitchen, the room looked more like a laboratory. Alchemy equipment lay strewn about on every surface, and a few bundles of herbs hung from the rafters.

"Though it's not my primary focus," he said, "I've always enjoyed dabbling in alchemy."

"Seems a little dangerous, considering all that paper in the next room."

"Oh, I always place a fireproofing ward before engaging in my experiments. You've nothing to worry about."

"Uh-huh..."

"Speaking of wards, I should augment the one guarding the front door. That way, you'll no longer need to break in, so to speak."

They returned to the sitting room, where the spectrum of auras pulsated in front of the door. He opened a desk drawer and extracted a smooth black stone about the size of a goose egg. This, too, glowed with an aura. Mavery peered closer and spotted ley lines—silver threads that connected the stone to the warded door.

"This is the anchor for my Personage-Based Augmentations."

"Ah, of course." She nodded, pretending that he hadn't just spoken complete gibberish.

"Your hair, if you will."

"*Excuse me?*"

"Well, it doesn't *need* to be hair. A fingernail clipping, a drop of blood, a severed digit... but hair is far less morbid."

"True, you don't strike me as the type to dabble in Necromancy, especially considering it's illegal and all."

"Only for ordinary mages. Wizards are allowed certain privileges." Aventus furrowed his brow. "Surely you learned that at Atterdell?"

"Probably, but it's been almost twenty years since I last stepped foot in a classroom."

"Hmm." It was impossible to tell whether he believed her. He gave his head a slight shake. "Now, a hair, if you please. I'll let you do the honors."

With a brief twinge of pain, she plucked one of her gray hairs—she was more eager to part with those—and passed it to him. He draped it across the stone and recited a few words of Etherean.

Etherean was born of the Ether, the energy that produced magic, and so it was the language of spellcraft. Its cadence commanded reverence, while its lyricism inspired awe. Simple spells sounded like stanzas from a song, while the most complex spells were akin to epic poems. Mavery had only studied the language long enough to recognize it; she'd never accomplished even the most basic incantations on her own. Mispronouncing a single word could result in a failed spell at best, an explosive disaster at worst. After one too many close calls, she'd given up on teaching herself this aspect of magic.

Aventus, however, spoke Etherean as though it were his mother tongue. His words produced a slight chill in the air, and Mavery shivered in spite of herself. The stone glowed in response. But she knew these were all side effects of her Sensing abilities. Anyone else would notice nothing out of the ordinary—apart from a man speaking strange words to a rock.

"There," he said. "You'll now be able to pass through the wards, though you'll still need me to unlock the door."

"Oh, that's all right. Next time you don't answer, I'll just pick the lock."

He laughed, but when he realized she was serious, his face blanched—which was saying something, given his already pale complexion. Divulging that piece of information may not have been her wisest move, but the look on his face had been worth the risk a thousand times over. Mavery turned away, failing to suppress a smirk as she surveyed the bookshelves.

"I've been meaning to ask," Aventus said. "What, exactly, does your work history entail? We never got around to discussing that."

She trailed a finger along a shelf, leaving a streak in the dust as she considered how much more to divulge. She rubbed her fingers together, and dust particles dissipated into the air. A crumb of truth wouldn't hurt. Just enough to test his reaction.

"Oh, a bit of this and that. After I left school, I worked as a wardbreaker for a time. That's where I picked up lockpicking, among other things."

"Really? I'd always assumed that sort of work was for the un-learned types."

" 'Unlearned types'?" she said stiffly.

"Yes, considering how wardbreaking requires no formal ed—"

"I understood your meaning."

Unlearned types. Oh, she was going to *enjoy* robbing this man when the time came.

"Well, it's unexpected, to say the least," he said. "I don't need to see your transcripts to know you are an educated person. For you to partake in a venture like *wardbreaking*..." He spat out the word as though it were the most vile profanity.

She spun around, and he recoiled at the pointed look she gave him. He was still standing in the same spot, still holding that stone. Briefly, she fantasized about chucking it in his smug face. She re-membered now why she'd stopped working for wizards. They were an insufferable lot, and this man was proving to be no exception.

Keep it together. Breathe...

After a few heartbeats' worth of uncomfortable silence, her anger tempered. She only needed to tolerate his company for as long as it took to thoroughly case his apartment. At least he didn't seem the type to put a knife to her throat or a bullet in her gut. As far as positives went, those were too significant to ignore.

"How about we move past you belittling my former line of work, and on to work that you deem more acceptable?"

He blinked. "Er, yes. Why don't I make some tea first?"

This time around, he prepared something that smelled less like tea and more like flowers. Aventus explained how a long steep in lukewarm water was necessary to extract every bit of flavor from the delicate herbs. After fifteen minutes, he passed Mavery a cup of what looked like watery ale. She took a sip and almost gagged; it tasted like perfume. Aventus enjoyed his liquefied flowers from his armchair, while Mavery sat on the sofa and only pretended to drink.

Though she hated to admit it, he was right. She *was* an "unlearned type," at least to some extent. Despite her best efforts to study magic on her own, the spells in her arsenal were practical but simple. They required neither magical stones nor ancient words. What Aventus did was an *art*—one that she desired to learn.

"I was wondering," she said, breaking the lull of the ticking clock and clinking porcelain, "if you could teach me some Etherean?"

Aventus sputtered on his tea. "Gods above, did they teach you *nothing* at Atterdell?"

She'd barely covered the alphabet by the time she was forced to abandon her studies. But she wasn't about to tell him that; he'd kick her out of the apartment before the tea turned cold.

"I learned it once, but it's yet another thing that's gone rusty over the years."

"What about Venetum's First Principle?" he asked. She gave him a blank look, and he threw her an incredulous one in return. "Venetum's First Principle: 'Etherean must be practiced daily, for fluency can slip away with surprising ease.'"

He'd rattled it off with the fervor of an acolyte reciting scripture.

"Well, excuse *me*," she huffed. "Not all of us have the luxury of time for daily language practice. Besides, I've survived just fine without incantations."

She should have kept her mouth shut. From the way he blinked at her, mouth agape, he was readying another tirade. She braced herself.

"No incantations! All this time, you've been using only rituals, like a schoolchild? That's like...like being a painter, but limiting your palette to a single color."

She shrugged. "You'll end up with a painting all the same."

"Yes, but what a *boring* painting that would be!"

For the second time that morning, Mavery considered throwing something in his face. This time, it was her teacup. She settled on throwing him a scathing look instead.

"You're doing it again," she said.

"Doing what?"

"Belittling me." She clenched her cup. By some miracle, it didn't shatter. "I'm going to assume you're the same as every other wizard I've ever known: you rarely cast spells outside the comfort and safety of your tower. Or apartment, in this case."

Aventus's beard sagged. But, as he issued no rebuttal, Mavery forged ahead.

"I've actually used my magic out in the world, and I'd argue I've been pretty godsdamned good at it. I might not know Ven-whoever's Principles, but I know it's best to avoid unnecessary risks—especially when you have a history of surges. I'd rather stick to my 'boring' magic than blow myself up because I used the wrong word."

As her frustration subsided, regret settled in. She hoped her little outburst hadn't been a mistake. Most wizards had such fragile egos, they couldn't handle even the smallest bit of criticism. He was liable to fire her on the spot. He sipped his tea, avoiding her eye. Though the clock on the mantel continued to tick away the seconds, time seemed to stand still.

"Point taken," he said at last. She nearly dropped her teacup in surprise. "But let me raise a counterpoint: if you're so confident in your skills as they are, why ask me about learning Etherean?"

"Curiosity, mostly." She ran her thumb along the rim of her cup as she chose her next words carefully. "And, as long as I'm here, I thought I'd seize the opportunity to learn from someone who's very clearly a master of his craft."

When in doubt, a bit of flattery never hurt. Aventus scratched his chin as he grew lost in thought. She pretended to drink her tea as they sat in uncomfortable silence. Again. This was happening far too often for her liking.

"We could both benefit from this," he said at last. "You see, I've been on sabbatical for the better part of a year. Before I return to teaching, I ought to revisit my lecture notes, conduct a trial class or two for good measure. Those can serve as your lessons." He raised a finger, paired with a warning look. "But that will happen *after* you've found the last of the library books."

"Sure, that's fair." Sticking around that long was not part of her plan, but at least he'd given her an offer and not a rejection.

"Though, be warned: once you get a taste for advanced spell-casting, you'll find those basic spells lacking. You may very well end up taking back everything you just told me."

"I'll be the judge of—"

A high-pitched chime sounded from the door. Its tone was bright and pure, as though the Ether itself had been plucked like a harp. This alarm was more pleasant than the ones Mavery had encountered in manors, bank vaults, and other places she'd intended to rob.

"That would be my resonating ward," Aventus said, then spoke something in Etherean. Another chill swept through the room, and the chiming stopped. "It means we have a visitor."

"Is that what you heard when I was outside your door?"

"No, *this* ward was augmented for one specific person." He groaned. "Well, this is about to be a painful, yet necessary, conversation."

"Why? Who's your visitor?"

"You'll see—or hear, rather—soon enough. Go to the kitchen and keep quiet. I'd rather she not see you, and I doubt she'll snoop around in there."

Mavery placed her teacup next to his before retreating to the next room and closing the kitchen door. Curiosity getting the better of her, she leaned against it so that she could eavesdrop. She heard Aventus take a few deep breaths before opening the front door.

"I see you received my letter," he said.

"Oh, I received your letter, all right," replied a woman's voice. She spoke with guttural 'r's, nasally vowels, and an air of superiority. A textbook Dauphinian accent. "After weeks without a word from you, worrying myself sick, not knowing if you were even *alive*, you send a letter. A *letter*! To your own mother!"

"What would you have preferred?" Aventus asked.

His mother scoffed. "I would have *preferred* you speak to me in person. Or, is a trip to the Garden District too much of a burden?"

"No, but I—"

His sentence was cut off with a rustling of fabric, followed by a surprised yelp. Mavery could only assume his mother had forced him into a hug.

"Oh, Aventus, you poor thing! How did you get so thin? Are you remembering to eat?"

"Yes, I know how to feed myself."

"Your hair—and that *beard!*" She gasped, then tutted in Dauphinian. "Oh, you used to be so handsome. Now look at you."

"On the contrary, I saw in the newspaper that the Duke of Leyland himself plans to sport a similar look this Season." He took a few steps and closed the door. "While we're on the subject of newspapers, what were you thinking, placing that ad on my behalf? Using the 'help wanted' section as though I were looking for a common laborer... If someone from the University had seen—"

"I never mentioned your name, and I did not place it in *The Gazette.*"

"There were enough identifying details, someone who knew me would have pieced it together."

"You are too—oh, what is the word?—paranoid."

"All right, let's assume none of my colleagues saw the ad. Even so, you had no right—"

"I had no *choice.* The High Council tired of you ignoring their letters. I received *this* almost two weeks ago."

The room fell silent. Mavery had to press her ear to the crack between the door and its frame to hear what followed: paper being crumpled into a ball, then thrown against something with force.

"You understand now, yes?" Aventus's mother asked. "I was

only trying to help."

"I don't need your help."

"You and your stubbornness! It is why your assistants resigned, why you have turned away every—"

"Can we not talk about this now?"

"Why not? What are you doing that is more important?"

"I was—"

"Is there someone here?"

"Er...no?" he said. "Why would you think that?"

"You are hiding something."

"What are you talking about?"

His mother did not answer. Instead, heeled shoes clacked across the floorboards.

"Where are you going?"

A door opened. The one to the bedroom, Mavery assumed. Aventus and his mother argued back and forth in Dauphinian, until the door slammed shut and he reverted to Osperlandish.

"You'll find nothing *in the kitchen*, Mother!"

Mavery sighed. Though she appreciated the warning, she would have preferred a more subtle one.

She backed against the wall and made a hugging motion to call the shadows to her. As she wrapped them around herself like a blanket, her arms trembled, and the scent of ash prickled her lungs. She held her breath, lest she cough and defeat the purpose of shrouding herself.

Spellcasting was a bit like speaking a foreign language, even when there was no Etherean involved. Warding magic was like Mavery's mother tongue. Despite not knowing any incantations, nor the inner workings of its mechanics, the magic still felt intuitive. Shadow magic was like a language she dabbled in only occasionally. She could stumble through it and achieve something that, though it lacked nuance, still had the desired effect. But even the simplest spells took a great deal of focus, and no one would ever mistake her for a "native speaker."

The kitchen door opened, and Mavery's gut reaction was that this woman could not possibly be the wizard's mother. Aventus had her pallid complexion and dark eyes, but their similarities ended there. The woman was shorter than Mavery, even in heels, but her raised chin and perfect posture gave the illusion of someone much taller. She wore a high-necked dress the same shade as the amethysts dangling from her ears, and her silver hair was pulled into an elegant bun.

Aventus appeared behind her. His grimace relaxed as he looked in Mavery's direction. He must have noticed a flicker in her faltering shroud, or glimpsed her own grimace as her arms grew weaker by the second. He gave her a subtle nod, then took his mother by the arm and attempted to steer her back to the sitting room.

"See? There's nothing here. Do you believe me now, or shall we start tearing up the floorboards?"

Refusing to budge, she narrowed her eyes. "I still think you are hiding something. Or some*one*."

"Nonsense. Why don't you take a seat on the sofa, and I'll fix you a cup of your favorite jasmine tea."

"Ah, that was it! I saw *two* teacups on the table. There *is* someone here!"

"No, I... That was from—"

"Aventus, tell me the truth. Now."

Mavery swore under her breath; the shadows had finally slipped from her grasp. Aventus's mother flinched as Mavery appeared out of thin air. Once she'd recovered from the surprise, she shot them both a smug look, which promptly morphed into disgust as she took in Mavery's appearance.

"Oh, Aventus." She clicked her tongue. "I knew you needed company, but a streetwalker?"

Mavery scowled. She no longer doubted that these two were related. Evidently, condescension ran in the family.

"Mother," he groaned, "I can assure you she's *not* a streetwalker."

"Then who is she, and why is she here?"

He shot Mavery a pleading look. She returned it with one that conveyed that he was on his own here; he wasn't paying her to manage *this* sort of mess. Especially when seeing him so flustered was more than a little satisfying.

"Well?" his mother pressed.

Aventus sighed. "This is Mave...my new assistant. Before you ask, *yes*, she answered one of your ads. Mave, meet my mother, Priscilla Tesseraunt."

Priscilla grinned more smugly than before. "So, my plan worked!"

"No, not necessarily. We only agreed to a temporary—"

She ignored him as she turned to Mavery. "Hello, dear. It is a pleasure to make your acquaintance."

Priscilla extended her gloved right hand. Mavery shook it, though a curtsy felt more appropriate. The woman was dressed for a visit to the duke's palace, not her son's disorderly apartment.

"As a supposed expert on the subject, the *pleasure* is all mine," Mavery said, her voice dripping with sarcasm. Aventus glared at her from behind Priscilla's back.

"Well, now you know," he said. "Are you happy?"

"I am happy that you *do* remember how to accept help."

His beard sagged. "I'm thirty-four, Mother. I'm quite capable of helping myself."

Mavery's brows raised slightly. He was even younger than she'd expected.

"I know this." Priscilla patted his arm. "But that does not mean you can do *everything* on your own. Well, I shall leave you both to your work."

The three of them returned to the sitting room. At the front door, Priscilla said something in Dauphinian that, judging by her stern tone and Aventus's glowering, wasn't particularly affectionate.

"And Mave, if you ever wish to wear something more ladylike than *that*..." Priscilla's lip curled in disgust as she gave Mavery's outfit another long, critical look. She opened her handbag and extracted a lavender-colored calling card. "Call upon my boutique sometime. Tesseraunt's, in the Garden District. I am certain my son will pay you well enough to afford something more befitting of a wizard's assistant."

"*Goodbye*, Mother," Aventus grumbled as he opened the door. She left with a dainty wave of her hand, and he shut the door with a drawn-out sigh.

"Well, she was charming," Mavery said.

He laughed dryly. "Not the word I would choose. And please, pay no mind to her nonsense about your attire. I wouldn't dare ask you to hunt down books in one of her evening gowns."

Mavery had nothing against dresses, or feminine clothes in general. She defaulted to wearing trousers for the same reason she kept her hair short: it had always been the more practical option. She looked down at the threadbare pair she was wearing and could no longer deny she was in need of new clothes—and not ones she swiped from her neighbors. Mercifully, Leyport had no short-age of clothiers. She would find a way to "accidentally" misplace Priscilla's calling card.

"So, I take it you're Dauphinian."

Aventus nodded. "I was born in Dauphine, though Mother and I moved here when I was only a few months old."

"Never would have guessed. 'Aventus' doesn't strike me as a Dauphinian name."

"Oh, no, that's just my honorific."

"Your *what*?"

"When you earn the rank of wizard, the High Council bestows upon you an honorific. A 'wizard name,' if you will. It's always three syllables—for reasons I doubt anyone remembers—and many wizard names have been recycled throughout the years. I'm Aventus the *Third*, actually."

"Why 'Aventus'? Did you choose it?"

He shook his head. "No, that was the High Council's doing. Aventus the First invented the resonating ward, and Aventus the Second is hailed as the greatest Gardemancer of the ninth century. I suppose they deemed me worthy of filling those rather enormous shoes."

With a half-hearted laugh, he folded his arms across his chest and lowered his eyes.

"Are you required to use your wizard name?"

"Only professionally, though most wizards use their honorific as though it were their real name. *My* real name is Alain." He shrugged. "Not that it matters. I'm sure you noticed how even my own mother prefers my wizard name over the one she gave me."

"What about you?"

He looked up at her. "Me?"

"Yes, which name do you prefer?"

"Alain," he said without hesitation.

"Good choice. Rolls off the tongue a bit easier."

Aventus—*Alain*—nodded in agreement. "It's odd... People have always assumed which name to use, one way or the other, without my input. You're the first I can recall who's ever *asked*."

"I know what you mean. My name is Mavery, but everyone has always called me Mave, ever since I was a child."

"And which name do *you* prefer?"

The nickname was so persistent, even she had defaulted to it. But she'd always seen herself as Mavery. Speaking it aloud just now had felt familiar, *right*.

"Mavery," she decided.

"Likewise, a good choice. Mavery suits you much better than Mave."

Her face suddenly warmed.

"Well, then," he said, "if you agree to call me Alain from now on, I will call you Mavery."

"Deal."

His scraggly beard twitched, suggesting a hint of a smile that she couldn't help but return. This new agreement between them seemed to have lifted a heavy burden. He now stood a little taller, his shoulders were a bit more relaxed. Enough so, Mavery doubted he would berate her for admitting to a bit more of her ignorance. She decided to test that theory.

"All this time, I thought Archmage Seringoth was Seringoth the First's great-grandson or something."

He shook his head. "No relation whatsoever. Very few wizards have children, in fact. Many will argue it's to prevent nepotism, but the real reason is that most of us prefer research over child-rearing. Or, to put it more bluntly, we prefer the company of books...over...people..."

He fell silent as his thoughts seemed to transport him elsewhere. Mavery lingered awkwardly, wondering whether she should leave the room and give him a moment to himself. Just as she was about to step away, he met her eye and spoke again.

"I'm sorry."

"For...?"

"For belittling you earlier, for my lack of decency in general. I never intended to insult you, but I still managed to accomplish that at least twice in a single morning. To be completely honest, my opportunities for socializing had been rather...limited before you came along. I'm woefully out of practice when it comes to conversing with others—not that I was ever much good at it to begin with." He sighed, shook his head. "Gods, I'm only proving my point, aren't I? What I'm trying to say is, going forward, I promise to be less of a..."

"Pompous ass?"

He laughed. "Precisely."

She would believe it when she saw it. Still, his apology seemed sincere enough.

"All right," she said. "And, er, thanks."

He nodded, then turned to his hoard of books. Thanks to Priscilla's surprise visit, they hadn't so much as touched a single tome.

"If you'd like to call it a day," he said, "I completely understand. You can come back tomorrow and—"

"No, I'm ready to work. Where should I start?"

Only an hour ago, she would have accepted any excuse to avoid tolerating Aventus's company for gods knew how much longer. It was too soon to know for certain, but Alain seemed significantly more tolerable.

And, with his guard lowered, robbing him would be significantly easier.

SEVEN

B y the end of her first week as a wizard's assistant, Mavery had made two crucial discoveries.

First, her *real* task was proving more difficult than tracking down hundreds of library books. With Alain constantly around, her casing had been confined to book pages. While searching the libraries of the wealthy, Mavery would often come across bond certificates and currency used as bookmarks. Somehow, the affluent couldn't resist flaunting their wealth in subtle ways, even in the privacy of their own libraries.

Alain tended to use whatever flat debris had been closest at hand: scraps of paper, playing cards, silk ribbons, the occasional tea envelope that left a hint of herbs and spices on the pages. Mavery had been removing these as she came across them and adding them to a pile that now resembled a magpie's nest. An eccentric, but completely worthless, collection.

Her second discovery was that wizards' books were incredibly *boring*. Alain had told her she could borrow anything from his personal collection that piqued her interest. But she was more likely to find a sack of jewels than an entertaining book. Most of them were so full of complicated diagrams and scholarly babble, she couldn't read more than a paragraph or two before her eyes glazed over.

The books Alain himself had penned weren't much better. Mavery had come across one of his recent texts, *On Etherean Metaphysics*. It had more to do with the philosophy of magic than the mechanics of it, but she had only tolerated a single page of jargon-filled sentences before setting it aside.

Presently, she was leafing through *The Historical Uses of Gardemancy Spells on Merchant Marine Vessels*. She landed on a chapter devoted to barnacle-repelling wards. With a scoff, she turned to the book's front matter and made some notes for the new cataloging system she was in the early stages of developing.

"What is it?" Alain asked from his armchair. Her sounds of boredom had been louder than she'd realized.

"Just wondering why you wizards insist on stripping all the magic from, well, *magic*." She held up the book she'd just cataloged.

"I think a colleague gifted me that one," he said.

"Seems less of a gift and more of a punishment."

He chuckled. "Such things usually are."

Her lower back twinged in protest as she rose from the floor. Gods, what she wouldn't give for proper seating. But the room was too cluttered to move any of the furniture, not even Alain's spindly desk chair.

"I have another stack for Chitterton College," she said. "When did you say their courier was coming?"

"Next Trisday, if memory serves."

"We should move these to the storage room, get them out of the way until then."

She lifted the stack, then inched her way across the room. Alain closed his book and sprung from his armchair.

"Oh, no, it's already filled to bursting," he said quickly. "Let me fetch one of my transmutated bags. Stay right there."

He unlocked the door with one of the keys he wore around his neck. Sparing a glance over his shoulder, he opened the door just wide enough to squeeze through the gap, but not an inch more. From the little Mavery could see, the room hardly looked "filled to bursting." There was no avalanche of forgotten belongings, no floor-to-ceiling stacks of crates, nothing keeping him from opening the door all the way—other than his desire to prevent her from looking in. Whatever valuables Alain owned, they had to be in that room.

He returned with what appeared to be an ordinary satchel, until he showed her the iridescent void that filled the inside. He offloaded the books from her arms, but no matter how many he placed in the satchel, the canvas didn't stretch, and it didn't become weighed down in the slightest.

"It's a rather basic spell," he said, apparently noticing her raised brows. "Well, 'basic' for the Transmutation School, at any rate."

"I definitely skipped those lessons."

"Transmutation spells have the highest risk of fatal accidents, and so they are only taught to sixth-year students. Judging by your reaction, I assume you didn't make it that far in your studies."

She'd only made it six *weeks* into her education—a far cry from the six years required for prospective wizards, or even the four years required for everyone else. Instead of admitting to that, she only shook her head.

"If you can make a bag larger on the inside," she said, "couldn't you turn that small room into limitless storage space?"

He laughed. "You really *have* gotten rusty if you've forgotten Elymor's Law of Proportions."

"Let's pretend that I have."

"Well, in essence, the larger the spell's area of effect, the larger the anchor required to power the spell. This satchel requires only a tiny anchor." He tapped one of the silver buckles on the shoulder strap; it glowed with a silver aura, and a ley line tethered it to the enlarged pocket. "To transmutate my storage room, I would need an anchor, oh, at least twice as large as this satchel. But an Ether-sensitive boulder wouldn't just be absurdly expensive; it would completely clash with my décor!"

Mavery pulled a face as she gave his mess a sidelong glance.

And then she realized that he was *joking*. Alain's face reddened. As he turned away and placed the satchel beside his desk, she felt the slightest pang of guilt. He was trying to make good on his promise to be more cordial, even if his sense of humor left a lot to be desired. She scanned the room for something to help her steer the conversation away from awkward silence. The book on his chair seemed the most promising.

"So, er, what were you reading just now?" she asked.

"I've been going through my old research journals, seeing if there's anything worth revisiting." He retrieved the book from his armchair. A wistful look passed over his face as he stroked the cover. "This one contains my notes from the project I'd been working on just before my sabbatical." He sighed. "It's a project best left shelved, but you can take a look."

She startled at being given permission to read his private journal, then realized that a *research* journal would likely be as riveting as everything else in this room. Still, not wanting to be rude, she took it. She skimmed through the earliest entries, pausing on occasion to admire his elegant handwriting. And then she noticed a name any mage for hire would recognize.

"I see you, too, were drawn to the Innominate Temple."

Alain's eyes lit up. "You know of it?"

Mavery laughed. "The old ruin that's baffled scholars for centuries? Of course I know of it."

Of all the ruins wizards paid others to investigate on their behalf, the Innominate Temple was, by and large, the most popular request. Mavery and Neldren had once accepted that job together, though her memories of it were so muddled, she couldn't even remember the route they'd taken. She had only a vague idea of where the temple was located: in northeastern Osperland, somewhere within the forests of Dyerland Province.

Since then, Neldren had tried his luck several more times. Once, he'd managed to get within a few yards of the temple, but the warding magic had prevented him from getting any closer. To this day, no one had yet discovered the temple's purpose, much less found their way inside.

"I've never seen it in person," she said. "I came close once, about twelve years ago, but the magic overwhelmed my Senses so badly, I had to turn back."

"Oh, I see." Alain's shoulders slumped, his excitement evaporating. "It's probably for the best you didn't get any closer. The area around the temple is inundated with traps. Very *lethal* traps."

"Have you ever been there?"

"No, only my..." He frowned, lowered his eyes. "No, I haven't."

She couldn't blame him for being so forlorn. Whoever found their way inside the Innominate Temple—whether a glory-seeking scholar or a fortune-seeking adventurer—would be renowned across the continent. And, of course, they would lay claim to whatever treasures were inside that ruin.

"So, what's your theory?" she asked. "Are you among those who think it was for some long-forgotten pre-Pantheonic god?"

"Hardly," he scoffed. "I have reason to believe the 'temple' had nothing to do with worship. Here, take a look at this."

Rather than asking her to hand back the journal, he stepped over a pile of books and bridged the space between them. He stood over her shoulder, then reached across her as he turned the pages. He stopped at an entry that was dated a few weeks shy of one year ago.

Dredisday, 12 Pluviose, 1040

Despite my initial skepticism, Lorcan's decision to spend the past month combing through old tax records may not have proven a waste of time after all. He uncovered a letter from 533, addressed to the Wizard Aganast, from Dyerland's Solicitor General. Aganast had fallen delinquent on his taxes for a property of some sort. The writing was too faded to parse. This seems promising, but will require further investigation.

"Who's Lorcan?" she asked.

"One of my former assistants. What's more important is *this* name." His finger prodded the center of the page.

" 'The Wizard Aganast'? Can't say it rings a bell."

"I'm not surprised. He's been all but scrubbed from the history books." Alain shook his head. "Oh, I remember spending *days* researching him, only to find a half-dozen references in just as many books. I must have torn apart the University's library. That didn't win me any favors with the arcanists, I can assure you."

Mavery imagined him picking through shelves upon shelves of tomes, as she'd been doing this past week. But instead of neatly sorting the books, he would chuck them aside as he worked himself into a frenzy, leaving nothing but chaos in his wake. She stifled a laugh at the thought.

"One of my colleagues teaches a class on the history of the Second Reforms," he said. "The mere *mention* of Aganast's name prompted a meeting with the High Council. In the end, the Council decided that Aganast could be named—but only in an objective, historical context." He scoffed. "As if such a thing were even possible..."

"So, who *was* this Aganast, exactly? What did he do?"

"He founded the Order of Asphodel, a short-lived but notorious society of Necromancers, and he was one of the most outspoken critics of the Great Demonic Cleansing."

The Second Reforms of the early sixth century had, among other things, outlawed most practices of Necromancy and instigated the Great Demonic Cleansing. Demonspawn, the offspring of demons and wild animals, contained no demonic magic and therefore had been allowed to persist. But there hadn't been a full-blooded demon on the continent of Tanarim in over five centuries.

"Oh, I'll bet the churches *loved* him for that."

Alain nodded. "So much so, they ordered his execution. Though they managed to follow through on it for the other members of the Order, Aganast himself disappeared, never to be seen again. It's likely he, like many others who'd gained the churches' ire, fled on a ship to Nilandor."

"And you think he was behind the Innominate Temple?"

"At the very least, I found evidence that connects it to the Order of Asphodel. Let's see here..."

He now lingered closely enough for Mavery to feel the warmth of his body, his quickened breaths against her ear. As he turned the pages, his fingertips briefly brushed hers. But she was too intrigued by his research—and by this sudden change in his demeanor—to move away.

They'd spent most of the past week in silence, keeping to opposite sides of the room. From nine in the morning to four in the afternoon, Mavery sorted through books while Alain read them, only pausing for midday meals, when they exchanged a few words over sandwiches and tea. Their conversations usually centered around Mavery's Sensing abilities. If the mood struck, they would delve into more risqué topics, such as the weather or the newspaper headlines. This was the most they'd spoken to each other since Mavery's first day of work.

Alain turned to the final entry, then froze. Before Mavery could even finish reading the date, he snatched the journal from her hands and snapped it shut. As she turned around, he clutched it to his chest.

"Gods, I completely lost track of the time! It's nearly four-thirty. You should have left ages ago."

Mavery's eyes narrowed. "What was in that journal entry?"

"Nothing you need to see." He shifted on the spot, avoiding her eyes. "I...I think I must have mistaken my research journal for my personal one."

If he knew how often she dealt in half-truths, he would be a bit more careful with his own. The storage room was no longer the only thing piquing her curiosity.

"Then can you at least tell me about the evidence you found?"

"I don't remember the specifics. Even if I did, it makes no difference. I doubt it would be enough to crack that mystery. No, as I said, this is a project best left shelved."

Before she could say any more, he sidestepped a pile of books. He placed the journal inside a desk drawer, then took another key from around his neck. With a click of the lock, he put the matter to rest.

"And now, I suppose we've come to the end of our 'trial run,' " he said.

"Last time I checked, there were seven days in a week. We still have one day left."

"True, but seeing as the University doesn't hold classes on

Finisdays, I would always give my assistants the day off. Though I'm on sabbatical, I'd still like to offer that to you."

"You want to keep this going?"

He nodded. "It would be a shame to part ways now, just when we're beginning to make progress. So, why don't we turn this into a more permanent arrangement?"

He didn't trust her enough to forgo his keys and secrets, but he *did* trust her enough to keep her around. That was a promising start. To uncover his secrets, Mavery would need to play the long con, and patience was the only "key" she would need.

She smiled. "I was hoping you would say that."

She left Steelforge Towers with another eighty potins in her pocket—another advance on her wages. If she kept this up, it wouldn't be long before she earned back the money Neldren had stolen from her. And she was certain she *could* keep it up. Sorting through a seemingly endless pile of books made for tedious work, but a job that didn't require risking death or imprisonment made for a welcome change of pace. Maybe she could—

What are you thinking!?

Even if she decided to abandon her scheme and become a legitimate assistant, it would only be a matter of time before Alain discovered her lack of credentials, her sordid past, her reasons for coming here in the first place. Sooner or later, he would discover the truth. She doubted he would keep her around after learning how much he'd been deceived.

Their arrangement would never be permanent. Thinking otherwise would only lead to disappointment.

EIGHT

At the beginning of her third week on the job, Mavery received a sign—quite literally—that her patience was beginning to pay off. She arrived on Onisday morning to a note attached to the door.

> Out running errands this morning. Should return around thirteen o'clock, midday at the latest. Door is unlocked. Please begin work without me.
>
> -A

Finally, she could give Alain's apartment a thorough casing. He had likely taken his keys with him, but she'd glimpsed the storage room's lock enough times to know it would be no challenge for her lockpicking tools.

Upon stepping inside the apartment, the metallic scent cutting through the musty books was stronger than usual. She looked to her left. Alain had placed a protective ward over the storage room door. But that did little to dampen her spirits; now, she had no doubt he was hiding something in there.

She stepped closer. The ward was simple—a bit *too* simple. He wanted to keep her out, but he knew that magic would do little to deter her. She leaned forward until the tip of her nose almost brushed against the tendrils of light. Entwined with the shimmering blue aura was a silver ley line, barely thicker than a hair. She focused her gaze and traced where it led, which was easier said than done; it was like trying to detect a spiderweb in a snowstorm. If she so much as blinked, she lost sight of it.

Her eyes watered from strain as she followed the ley line's trail clockwise around the room. First, it snaked around the bedroom door, then under the windows along the western wall, then stopped at the kitchen door, where it ran diagonally across the floor to Alain's desk, only three feet from where she'd started. It led her to a drawer that contained only two items: the iron coin it was anchored to, and a folded piece of paper.

> Mavery,
> If you are reading this, congratulations! Senser or not, your observational skills are truly unparalleled. Now, kindly stay out of the storage room. The augmentation will inform me if you attempt to tamper with the ward.
>
> Sincerely,
> Alain

Mavery laughed. "You win this one, cheeky bastard."
She returned the note to the drawer, then surveyed her surroundings. Though she hadn't yet earned Alain's trust, at least she'd succeeded in tidying up his living space. It was far from clean, but she could finally see the floorboards. There was now enough room to sit on one of the kitchen chairs while she worked, and her back was all the more thankful for it. But if Alain had any treasures among his books, she'd yet to uncover them.

Of course, the books were potentially worth a small fortune, but finding a buyer would be no small task. With the exception of rare tomes and first editions, the wealthy preferred to stock their libraries with brand-new books. She wouldn't know which of Alain's books held any real value until she had cataloged them—the job he was actually paying her for. The irony was not lost on her.

The bathroom was filled with modern plumbing—a claw-footed tub with a dedicated tap for hot water, a pedestal sink with the same, and a flushing toilet—but ripping out copper pipes was far from the subtle approach she preferred. The alchemy equipment in the kitchen could fetch a fair price, but as she was working alone, she needed something easy enough to move by herself.

So, she had a go at the bedroom. She rifled through Alain's belongings, taking care to not leave anything out of place, though she doubted he would notice. In the wardrobe, she found only a few wizard robes, a winter coat, an old suit. Atop his dresser, she found no jewelry, no pocket watches, no family heirlooms.

The more she searched, the more of an enigma this man became. As a wizard *and* a professor, he had to be well-off, but he seemed to spend his wealth exclusively on old books and exotic teas.

She returned to the sitting room and plopped herself on Alain's desk chair. It wasn't even ten o'clock yet; she still had a few hours before he returned home. She could search for secret compartments, loose floorboards, safes behind paintings. But she assumed a wizard would prefer magic over mundane methods. She would have Sensed *something* by now.

Her only option was to continue biding her time until he trusted her enough to show her the storage room, or she found some way in there without him noticing. At least she was getting paid for her work, and she'd started spending some of her earnings on herself. Over these past weeks, she had treated herself to new clothes, bottles of half-decent wine, and even a few novels that *weren't* stolen. But she couldn't continue wasting her money on these luxuries, as small as they were. At this moment, she didn't even have two hundred potins to her name.

The work itself was another luxury. Alain was the least demanding employer she could ever recall, and the tedium of the work was strangely comforting. So, too, was the constant presence of old books paired with the warding magic that separated this apartment from the outside world.

It was a shame none of it would last.

Seeing as she still had plenty of time before Alain returned home, she decided to do some snooping of another nature. She hadn't forgotten about his Innominate Temple research—and the journal he'd hidden from her. To her surprise, the desk drawer was unlocked. Even more surprising, instead of finding the research journal inside it, she found a stack of letters addressed to Alain. Though he'd hidden his valuables from her, he'd neglected to hide his mail. She started with the letter on top, though it took her three full passes to decipher the dreadfully sloppy handwriting.

> Alain,
> The most curious thing happened when I attempted to call on you yesterday. If I didn't know any better, I'd say I succumbed to a Diversion Ward. But I know you wouldn't use my own spell against me!
>
> Seeing as you are obviously <u>not</u> accepting visitors at this time, perhaps you will accept a letter. I do miss seeing you around the common room. Department meetings are not as entertaining without you there. (Not that they ever were in the first place!)
>
> Please write back soon. I would <u>thoroughly</u> enjoy catching up over a pint...or six!
>
> All the best,
> Declan

Now she knew who to thank for the intrusive thoughts that day she'd first arrived at Steelforge Towers. She moved on to the next letter. The handwriting was shaky—from a feeble old hand, perhaps—but it was leagues more legible than Declan's.

Dear Aventus,
I regret to inform you that once Chancellor Drusilla learned you were not returning for the spring term, she threatened to report you to the High Council. I offered to issue the report myself. I believe I presented your case far more charitably than the Chancellor would have done. You should expect a letter from the Archmage within a week's time.

Sincerely,
Kazamin

And beneath this letter was a heavily wrinkled one—an impressive feat, given the thickness of the stationery. It had been penned in sapphire ink; at the top of the page, THE HIGH COUNCIL OF WIZARDS was embossed in matching foil.

To the Wizard Aventus III:
After multiple failed attempts to contact you at your home address, the High Council of Wizards (hereinafter, "the High Council") has resorted to contacting your next of kin.

It has come to the High Council's attention that, for two consecutive terms, you have failed to submit a written request for personal leave. Your actions are in violation of *The Covenants of Wizarding Decorum (134th Edition)*. In addition, it has been nearly two years since you last produced research before the High Council.

Your supervisor has granted you leave, with pay, for the Spring 1041 term. The High Council requests that you use this time to demonstrate your commitment to scholarship.

You are hereby ordered to present to the High Council an original Gardemancy spell on Siddisday, the 6th of Verdure, 1041. Failure to do so will result in immediate revocation of all academic ranks and titles.

The High Council once again offers its sincerest condolences for the passing of your assistant, but you would do well to remember that you are still obligated to fulfill your scholarly duties.

Kindest regards,
Archmage Seringoth II
The High Council of Wizards
Montesse, Dauphine

P.S.: It has also come to the High Council's attention that you have accumulated 627 library books from five wizarding universities. The arcanists have requested the prompt return of any books that are not directly related to your research. For your convenience, an exhaustive list of these titles is enclosed.

This had to be the letter Kazamin had warned Alain about, and the one that had prompted Priscilla to place her newspaper ads. Alain's presentation was just under six weeks away—forty days, to be precise—which explained why he'd been revisiting his old research. Yet, he'd not mentioned any of this to Mavery.

There was one more letter on the desk. Even if Mavery hadn't been fully committed to her snooping, she would have still read this one, as it mentioned a very familiar name: her own.

Dear Aventus III,
The former student you inquired about was Mavery Culwich. She began her studies in the Autumn 1021 term and withdrew six weeks later, citing personal

reasons. As she failed to complete even a single term, enclosing a copy of her transcript would be superfluous. However, it contained one note of interest: Miss Culwich claimed to have arcane hypersensitivity, but her condition was never verified.

Sincerely,
Garnevar III
Keeper of Academic Records
Atterdell College of the Arcane

The letter was dated over a week ago. Alain had known for a few days that Mavery hadn't been fully truthful about her education, but he'd made no mention of this, either.

Was he waiting to catch her in another half-truth, or waiting for her to come clean?

In either case, she wouldn't say a word about it—or anything in these letters. He knew one of her secrets, but she now knew *several* of his.

NINE

"I'm afraid I must be off," Kazamin said. "I look forward to continuing this conversation next week."

"As do I, sir," Alain replied with a shallow nod.

Upon the tablecloth, Alain's supervisor laid a ten-potin note to cover both the bill and a generous tip—despite Alain's insistence that *he* would pay for lunch—before pushing back his chair. Once the short elderly man exited the restaurant, Alain finally let fall the smile he'd managed to maintain for the past hour. He hoped that his expression had appeared less painful than it had felt.

He reached up to massage his aching jaw, then startled at the prickle of blunt hair beneath his fingertips. This change would take some getting used to—a thought he'd had countless times over these past weeks.

Without Kazamin to focus on, Alain was now starkly aware of how crowded the restaurant had become. Lunch service was booming, and there was hardly an empty table in the dining room. A swell of piano chords sounded from the far corner, interlacing with the tinkling silverware and polite conversations.

Alain knew, logically, that the dozens of patrons were too focused on their own meals to pay him any mind. Yet, he couldn't help but feel exposed, as if everyone in this room knew that this was the most people Alain had been around in nearly a year.

On impulse, he began chewing on a nail. And then another impulse kicked in: the phantom sting of a rolled-up newspaper, courtesy of his mother, striking his knuckles.

He lowered his hand from his mouth and picked up his fork, though he'd long lost his appetite. As he pushed bits of cold, half-eaten cottage pie around his plate, he considered what he'd just agreed to. Taking on an assistant had been one thing. Delving back into research, another.

But returning to the University next week?

Returning to teaching *next term*?

He should have explained to Kazamin how his sabbatical had given him a newfound perspective, and that he wasn't ready to return now—or ever again.

But he'd run into his supervisor outside the barber's this morning, completely by happenstance. He'd been too blindsided to decline Kazamin's invitation to lunch, and when Kazamin had asked whether he would return to the University, "yes" had been the only word in Alain's vocabulary.

Perhaps Kazamin was right: once he returned to his old routine, he would feel like himself again. Perhaps being alone with his thoughts over these past months had—

"May I get you anything else, sir?"

Alain flinched. Amid all his pondering, he hadn't noticed the waiter approach his table.

"Er, yes, I'll take some wine," Alain said. He fully expected the waiter to balk at his request, but the man only nodded.

"Of course. Shall I bring you the wine list?"

"No need. A glass of your house red will do." As the waiter began to walk away, Alain raised a finger. "Actually, make that a carafe."

He'd held back around Kazamin, who undoubtedly would have protested at drinking before midday. The dean was as devoted to decorum as he was to his faith. The Covenants might well be holy scripture.

The waiter returned with a filled carafe and an empty glass. Alain didn't bother giving the wine any fanfare. He prepared a generous pour, then gulped from his glass like a parched man at a wellspring. The wine was cheap: thin-bodied, slightly sour, and it burned all the way from mouth to stomach. It did nothing to dampen the noise of the surrounding crowd, nor did it distract Alain from thinking about what awaited him next week.

At least he could count on Kazamin to not ask too many questions about his new assistant. The dean didn't care where his subordinates' assistants came from, so long as they didn't make a mess of the common room.

Alain could understand why Mavery hadn't come forward about being a university dropout. He knew that his colleagues—with the exception of Declan, perhaps—would have dismissed her the moment they learned about her lack of a formal education. That was assuming she would have gotten past the initial interview. Had she arrived at any of *their* doorsteps instead of his, she would have been better off stumbling blindly into a den of starving wolves.

What he couldn't understand was what "personal reasons" had forced her to leave university in the first place. She was attentive, organized, clever. Her only fault was a curiosity that bordered on nosiness. Every day, she found some way to postulate a question about the contents of the storage room. Every day, he brushed her off.

But he had to admire her persistence. In fact, he'd left her a small "gift" that she was sure to discover by the time he returned home. More than likely, she'd already found it.

He knew there was no need for scheming. The obvious thing to do would be to ask her why she left university. But if he asked her about her private matters, she would likely do the same to him, and he knew what her first question would be. Given the choice between providing the answer and returning to teaching, he couldn't say which was more daunting.

Perhaps one day she would come forward of her own volition.

Perhaps one day he would be ready to do the same.

For now, Mavery would remain a puzzle he'd made little progress toward solving. When he found no solutions at the bottom of his wineglass, he poured himself another.

Ten

Mavery gasped when the front door opened. For the first time in weeks, a jolt of panic ran up her spine. Once she realized the intrusion was only Alain, returning from his errands, she chided herself for sitting with her back to the door—a habit the Brass Dragons had drilled out of her years ago. She could only assume she'd become so accustomed to playing the role of a wizard's assistant, her old instincts were starting to slip.

Alain entered the room and shrugged off his coat.

"Back from running errands?" Mavery asked, mustering a cheerful tone.

"Errands? Oh, right. Fine. They were fine." He tossed his coat in the direction of his desk chair. It missed by at least a foot, but Alain didn't seem to notice. "I'm going to put the kettle on."

He lumbered across the room and into the kitchen while Mavery continued working. She straightened a stack of library books and pushed them aside. She was reaching for the next stack when she heard a crash, followed by a yelp.

"Everything all right in there?" she called.

When Alain failed to reply, she hoisted herself from her chair and headed toward the kitchen. She opened the door to find him on hands and knees, gathering the pieces of a shattered teacup.

"Here, let me help you," she said.

With a circular gesture, she performed a basic mending spell. The shards of porcelain scattered across the floor and clustered together, reforming a teacup on Alain's palm, though the cracks rendered it useless. Only an innate mender could flawlessly repair a broken object, but at least Alain no longer needed to continue searching for the pieces by hand. He tossed the cup in the garbage bin.

"Thanks," he said. "I don't know why I didn't think to do that in the first place."

Something pattered against the stone tiles. Mavery looked down to find blood dripping from Alain's right hand.

"You're bleeding," she said. "I also know some healing spells. I can—"

"No, no, you've done plenty already." He raised his hand, examined it. "Besides, it's only a small cut. It should heal in no time."

He turned and grabbed a tea towel to stanch the bleeding. Even with his back to her, she sensed something was different about him—apart from his odd behavior—but she couldn't place it.

Then he turned around again.

His dark hair was cropped to shoulder length and slicked back with a bit of pomade. His beard, though still full, was neatly trimmed. With that distracting tangle of hair no longer in the way, she recognized for the first time his high cheekbones, prominent yet slender nose, slightly bowed upper lip, full lower lip...

Alain's face flushed, and he averted his gaze. Mavery's blood ran cold upon realizing she'd been staring at him. He had a handsome face, objectively speaking, but she wasn't about to lose her mind over it. If she'd done that with every attractive mark, her thieving career would have been a decidedly short one.

"I know it's a bit different than you're used to seeing," he said, gesturing at his shortened beard. "Er, what do you think?"

She raised her eyebrows. He wanted her opinion on *this* sort of thing?

"It suits you," she said, and it was more than a half-truth. "You're far too young for the 'grizzled old hermit' look."

He laughed, but the sound of it rang hollow.

The tea kettle whistled. He removed it from the stove, then carried it toward the teapot on the dining table. The towel wrapped around his hand was now saturated with blood, making his grip clumsy. Scalding water sloshed out the kettle's spout and onto the floor, and he barely dodged getting burned. Mavery wrenched the kettle from his hand.

"You don't..." He paused, placed his uninjured hand over his mouth to stifle what was halfway between a belch and a hiccup. "You don't have to do that."

"If you want to risk maiming yourself further, be my guest."

With a sigh and a shake of his head, Alain slumped into the closest chair. Mavery took over the tea preparations. She likely poured the hot water too forcefully over the delicate leaves, but it was better than having him bleed over everything.

Once the tea was steeping, she sat across from him, took his hand, and removed the bloody rag. The cut was more severe than she'd realized: a two-inch gash along his index finger. And she was now close enough to catch a whiff of wine. That explained his sudden bout of clumsiness.

"Let me take care of this," she said.

He shrugged. "If you must..."

Whether he was versed in healing magic didn't matter in this case; he couldn't heal himself. He could likely recall the academic term for this phenomenon—Some-Dead-Wizard's Law of Transference, or something along those lines—but she knew from practical experience that healing was always an external transfer of magic. You could give a bit of yours to heal another person, and vice versa, but trying to heal yourself would result in the magic canceling itself out.

With one hand, she held his, keeping it still. She closed her eyes and took a deep breath to focus her arcana, which she directed toward her other hand. Her fingertips trailed along the length of his cut, leaving behind a thin white line that would fade in a few hours. Had Mavery been an innate Soudremancer, she would have left no trace of the injury. And she likely would have felt nothing from this simple spell—not even the touch of lightheadedness it had inflicted upon her.

She wasn't sure why she'd offered to mend Alain's cup, heal his wound. She needed to earn his trust, but she didn't have to go to these lengths for it. Helping him simply felt like the right thing to do, she supposed.

She was still holding his hand; he must have not realized the spell was complete. His hand was relaxed, his fingers were curled slightly around hers. He had the soft skin and lack of calluses of someone who had never done a day's worth of physical labor. His fingertips were ink-stained, which was equally unsurprising. But she *was* surprised to find that his nails were as ragged as her own. A fellow nail-biter, though a more discreet one. During these past weeks, she'd never once caught him in the act.

She was staring again, though at least now it was only at his hand. And at least now she could use her healing spell as an excuse. She looked up to find him watching her, gaze soft and lips slightly parted. Upon meeting each other's eyes, he flinched and glanced away at the same time she looked down and dropped his hand.

"Well...I'm no healer," she said, "but I think you'll live to see another day."

She slowly peered up at him as he raised his hand and assessed her work. Judging by his slight nod, she'd done well enough. He used the clean end of the tea towel to wipe away the remaining blood.

"You never trained as one?"

"Me?" she laughed. "Gods, no, I barely attended temple for the sermons. I learned a few healing spells during my...er, my studies."

"Really? If memory serves, Soudremancy isn't taught at the universities."

She swore internally as she remembered, all too late, one of the stipulations of the First Reforms. For over a thousand years, since the establishment of the High Council and the first wizarding universities, only the churches had been permitted to teach the healing arts.

"I didn't mean taking classes," she said. "I came across a textbook and taught myself the basics."

"You happened to 'come across' a Soudremancy textbook?"

One of the first times she'd landed herself in an infirmary, she'd swiped a primer from the trainee who'd been assigned to her. Excerpts from that book had remained in her Compendium for so long, the pages were tattered, the ink faded. But it was too valuable to discard; even those basic, near-illegible spells had helped her allies more times than she could count. And now, she'd just helped the man sitting across from her, though she doubted "ally" would be the appropriate word in his case.

She shrugged. "Is that so hard to believe?"

Alain threw her a skeptical look, but he said nothing as he poured himself a cup of tea. A hint of a smile tugged at the corner of his mouth.

He offered Mavery a cup as well. It was the color of fresh butter and, though it smelled like licorice, had an intensely bitter taste. Somehow, he managed to drink it without even a pinch of sugar.

"Regardless of where you learned Soudremancy," he said, "I appreciate it all the same. Can you Sense that School as well?"

She nodded. "The aura is light teal, and there's always an herbal scent, though it's different every time. Just now, it smelled like rosemary, but sometimes it's juniper, mint, something like that."

He took a small notebook from his pocket and jotted down what she'd said. He had gotten into the habit of carrying it around at all times to record Mavery's comments on the spot. And she had gotten into the habit of delivering those comments, though Alain hadn't yet told her the purpose for all his note-taking.

He slipped the notebook back in his pocket. She took another sip of tea and winced.

"You're not partial to taxwort, I take it," he said.

"Is *that* what this is? I've only ever used it to scrub the rust off iron."

"The root, yes, but the leaf is far gentler. Helps with digestion." He lifted his cup to his mouth. "Among other, er, *ailments...*"

Drunkenness, she assumed. She cracked a smile that she swiftly hid behind her teacup.

"Don't feel obligated to drink it," he said. "I'll have to find a better way to thank you for cleaning up my messes."

"You can start with gold and jewels." He laughed, and she played it off with a shrug. "What can I say? I'm a simple woman."

"You, 'simple'?" He leaned forward, rested his chin on his freshly healed hand. "No, I highly doubt that."

If he wasn't half-drunk, she would have assumed he was searching for a crack in her composure, a rift from which he could prise free her lies. He was studying her so intently, warmth began to creep up her neck. She choked down a mouthful of taxwort tea, simply for the sake of distraction.

"Anyway," she said, bitterness lingering on her tongue, "don't get used to the complimentary spells. I only offered because you seemed like you had a lot on your mind. I mean, something must be amiss when a wizard forgets to use magic."

He leaned back. "You're right, I do have a lot on my mind. After I left the barber, I ran into my supervisor." Sipping his tea, his gaze drifted to a far corner of the room. "We had lunch, and he asked me to meet him on campus next week to discuss how my research is progressing. Much as I wanted to decline, I'm in no position to."

"How long has it been since you last visited campus?" It seemed an innocent enough question; she couldn't reveal that she knew more than she was supposed to.

"Nearly a year. You'll come with me, I hope?"

"Should I?"

"Didn't you tell me you wanted to return to the academic world? I can't think of a better way than by visiting the University."

Mavery chewed her lip. Continuing her ruse for another week thrilled her almost as much as the prospect of meeting Alain's colleagues. The last thing she needed was for more wizards—more witnesses—to know her name, her face. But this could also be an opportunity. She hadn't found any valuables in his apartment, but there were bound to be plenty at the University.

"I won't pressure you," he said, "but do keep in mind that our current arrangement is a tad unconventional. Once I return from my sabbatical, we'll be expected to work on campus."

"I thought assistants typically worked out of wizards'...er, towers."

"Not when those wizards are also professors. Besides, the work you're doing now, while helpful, is glorified housekeeping. There's

plenty more you can do at the University: grade exams, help facilitate my lectures, perhaps even deliver them yourself when my
other duties pull me elsewhere..."

He still thought she was qualified for all that? He could have
been bluffing, but no, his tone was completely earnest. Not only
did she find that a bit flattering—she wasn't above admitting
it—here he was, making plans for months from now, unaware that
she would be gone in a matter of days. Weeks, at most. It was almost
enough to make her feel guilty.

Almost.

As he continued to speak, she realized that Alain could have
ordered her to accompany him. It would have been well within his
right as her employer. Instead, he was offering her a choice.

Mavery could sort his books, mend his drinkware, heal his
injuries every day for weeks on end. But if she wanted to earn his
trust, *this* was how she would do it.

"All right," she said. "I'll go with you."

ELEVEN

T he University of Leyport was located in the center of the city, a little over a mile from Steelforge Towers. Not even a minute into the carriage ride, Mavery realized they could walk faster than the city traffic. Carriages weaved through the lamp-lined streets in every direction, like a chaotic dance that somehow made sense to the drivers.

As part of winter's swan song, snow had blanketed the city overnight. Mavery poked her head out the window, but the view was little more than a drab, endless pattern of gray stone and red brick. Some of the buildings were so tall, she couldn't see the topmost windows, even with her neck craned. Smoke bellowed from chimneys, casting a gray haze over what would have otherwise been a clear blue sky. The roads had become a slurry of mud and half-melted snow. Before she could take in any finer details, she was assaulted with the stench of horse shit and leaned away from the window with a groan.

Gods, did she *loathe* cities.

The carriage was slow, but at least it was relatively warm and clean. Across from her, Alain's knees bounced as he picked at a loose thread on the cuff of his robe. Wizards and assistants were required to wear robes while on campus. Alain's reflected the University's colors: deep plum with silver embroidery. Mavery's was solid black, one of Alain's robes from his assistantship days. It smelled of mothballs, the fur lining was overly warm and itchy, and it had too few pockets for her liking. She already missed her own coat.

A wrought-iron fence, twenty feet high and imbued with the blue auras of protective wards, cut off the campus from the rest of the city. After exiting the carriage, Alain lingered on the sidewalk for a moment. He gazed at the University's main entrance with a look Mavery couldn't quite place, though she assumed returning here after his long absence had left him with a mixed bag of emotions. Alain took a deep breath, then passed through the open gate.

The University consisted of five towers that would have looked more at home atop an ornate cathedral, not arranged around this largely vacant quad. Their marble exteriors gleamed in the late-morning sun. With the recent snowfall, the campus was almost too bright to look at. Mavery shielded her eyes as she followed Alain down the stone path.

"That's the dormitory," he said, pointing to the first tower on their left. "Going clockwise, you have the library, the Great Hall, then the towers that house the classrooms and faculty offices."

The Great Hall was the largest of the buildings, with a domed roof and enormous stained-glass windows. The other four towers were, more or less, identical, with much smaller windows and staggering spires.

"How can you tell them apart?" Mavery asked.

"There are plaques above the doors, but that doesn't prevent the occasional mix-up. The first few weeks of the autumn term, it's almost a daily occurrence to see a first-year come bursting through the doors, thinking they've found the classroom they're late getting to, only to find themselves in the library—or worse, interrupting a faculty meeting." He chuckled. "I was that student a time...or ten. Never had a great sense of direction."

"You were a student here?"

He nodded. "I've lived in Leyport my entire life. Well, apart from my six years at Barcombe Academy, but that's only ten miles east of here, so it doesn't quite count."

Barcombe Academy was an elite preparatory school for mages.

Mavery recognized the name because it was the same school her former associate, Ellice, had attended. Not that she wanted to reminisce about anyone in Neldren's crew—Neldren himself, least of all. But this was proof that Alain had come from wealth. Now, if only she could find where he was hiding it...

"We have some time to spare before my meeting," he said. "Let's stop by the Great Hall. There's something I'm very eager to show you."

Despite being the main building on campus, the Great Hall was devoid of life. It was between mealtimes, so the refectory contained only empty tables and benches. As Alain led her down the main corridor, Mavery Sensed violet-hued auras that prevented sound from both entering and exiting the offices. Only their footsteps echoed off the marble floors and wood-paneled walls.

They came to a lift at the end of the corridor. Unlike the one in Alain's apartment building, this one was powered by magic. Inside the cabin was a metal panel that glowed with an aura Mavery had never seen before. It was crimson and, unlike the steady pulsation of warding magic, it buzzed with energy. Alain spotted her studying the panel and pulled out his notebook. She described what she saw, and the cabin filled with the sound of his scratching pen.

"This is a product of the Faisancy School," he said. "Mending, destruction, and fabrications such as this one. Place your hand on the 'ascend' panel and focus a little of your arcana into it."

She followed his instructions but still startled when the door shut and the lift began to rise of its own accord. She stumbled backward and collided with Alain. With her arcana no longer powering the lift, it lurched to a halt. She stumbled again, and this time Alain gripped her by the arm, steadying her.

"I had a similar reaction the first time I used one of these." He laughed. "It packs a punch, doesn't it?"

For once, Mavery had no reply at the ready; all she could think of was her own foolishness. She slipped out of his grasp and replaced her hand on the control panel. Her face burned as they rode the lift in silence to the top floor.

Here, they entered a cavernous circular room. The only window was a round skylight in the center of the domed roof. But it was so high up, hardly any sunlight reached the floor below.

A wooden desk spanned the room from wall to wall. Atop it were a pair of arcana-infused lamps that cast the immediate area in clinical blue-white light. An assistant—judging by his black robes and youthful features—was seated at the desk, reading. As Alain and Mavery approached, he held out his hand.

"Your pass," he said without taking his eyes off his book.

"Oh, we're not using any portals today," Alain said. Mavery's eyes widened. Surely she'd misunderstood him. "I'm giving my new assistant a tour, so we are only *passing* through, if you will."

He chuckled. The assistant put down his book at last and threw Alain a hard, unamused stare. Alain's laughter faltered, and he cleared his throat.

"Er, we'd simply like to see the room, if that's all right."

The attendant sighed. "Fine, but only for a few minutes. Keep to the center of the room and don't touch anything."

With a raise of his hand, a section of the desk swung forward. Mavery couldn't detect any hinges, nor could she Sense another fabrication spell; whatever magic powered the desk was buried deep within the wood.

Mavery followed Alain into some sort of gallery. The walls were lined with frames large enough to drive a stagecoach through. There were fifteen in total, and each one housed an identical painting...or were they mirrors? The magic in this room was unlike any Mavery had ever Sensed before. Her mind reeled as she tried to attune herself to it, but she couldn't grasp anything distinct. It was like trying to describe the innate taste and smell of the wind. All she could Sense was raw arcana.

"This is the portal room," Alain said.

She hadn't misheard him after all. The portals were made of a gaseous, silvery substance that flickered in and out of existence. One moment, she could see the portals shimmering in their frames. The next, only the stone wall behind them.

"Each one connects to a similar chamber at the other fourteen wizarding universities across Tanarim, as well as the High Council's tower in Montesse. That's the capital of—"

"Dauphine," Mavery said curtly. "Yes, I know my geography."

"Of course." Alain cleared his throat. "Er, anyway, these frames are more than simply decorative. They're made of silver—permanent anchors for the portal magic."

She spotted the frame engraved with ATTERDELL COLLEGE OF THE ARCANE. It was hard to believe that the place she hadn't seen in twenty years was now only a few steps away. And if that wasn't enough to marvel at, the frame alone had to be worth thousands of potins. Never had she seen so much wealth contained in a single room—and there were *fifteen* rooms just like this one.

"I thought portal magic was a myth. Or, at least, it was only theoretical."

"Portals are so highly regulated, seeing one outside of a room like this might well be like seeing a mythical creature."

"How long have these rooms been around?"

"A little over a decade, so not long after you would have graduated. The High Council created them to facilitate scholarship, though students aren't allowed to use them unless accompanied by a professor. Even full-fledged wizards aren't allowed to come and go as they please. Each room is guarded twenty-eight hours per day. You can only imagine how people would abuse them."

Mavery nodded. She could think of a few reasons why someone would want to hop across the continent in an instant. The attendant had mentioned something about a pass. One of those should be easy enough to steal...or forge...

But she was getting ahead of herself.

"On that note," Alain said, casting a glance at the front desk, "let's go before we overstay our welcome."

Mavery had hoped to glimpse the library and its hundred thousand tomes, but as they were running short on time, their final stop was the tower that housed the Gardemancy Department. Much of the life on campus had congregated inside the classrooms on the tower's lowest floor.

Warding magic emanated from the rooms as professors demonstrated spells. The taste of magic around here was more than a metallic tang; it coated Mavery's tongue like a bitter medicine.

They passed by the open door of a lecture hall, where a Nilandoren woman stood at the front of the room. There was hardly an empty seat to be found.

"Wonderful," Alain muttered. "Let's go before she notices me."

He hurried down the corridor, but Mavery didn't follow. A female wizard—a female *professor*—was such a rare sight, she was compelled to stay and watch.

The professor spoke Etherean, and Mavery Sensed the somewhat pleasant chill she felt whenever Alain voiced a spell. The professor instructed her students to repeat the incantation.

Dozens of voices called upon the Ether in unison, turning that gentle breeze into a dead-of-winter blizzard. The onslaught of arcana squeezed the air from Mavery's lungs, chilled her down to her core, froze everything from her muscles to her thoughts. And then her body, desperate for warmth, fought to regain control. Her limbs trembled, her teeth chattered within her aching skull.

The Ether dissipated once the incantation was complete, but its chill lingered. Once Mavery regained control of her limbs, she clung to the nearby wall and dragged herself down the corridor. She inched her way toward the lift, one agonizing step at a time. Alain was too preoccupied watching the floor indicator to notice that his assistant was no longer at his side.

The lift door slid open with a chime that might as well have been a gunshot. Mavery clenched at her temples, unable to shake the sensation of her head being squeezed in a vise. She desperately needed respite, if only for a minute.

"Wait," she groaned.

Alain stopped and turned, then gasped. "What happened to you?"

"Magic...too much. My head...cold..."

"Your Senses, of course." As he stepped toward her, the lift closed and ascended without him. "I should have known. Why didn't you mention something sooner?"

Mavery replied with a grunt, which was all she could manage.

"No matter, take as much time as you need."

She wanted to tell him to not risk being late on her behalf, but even the thought of voicing those words made her head reel again. She leaned against the wall, sank to the floor. Squeezing her eyes shut, she focused on taking slow, steady breaths.

She'd last experienced this during her failed excursion to the Innominate Temple. Its warding magic, even from a mile away, had brought on a similar headache, paired with a wave of nausea. She could only recall flashes of what had followed, but they all involved vomiting—in the forest, outside a public bathhouse, inside her and Neldren's rented room.

Her illness had lingered long after convincing Neldren to abandon their search for the temple. Though, as these vague memories resurfaced, she realized that her slow recovery might have had less to do with the temple's ancient magic, and more to do with her partner's sour mood. He'd sulked for days afterward, as their trip had been all for nothing.

A rustle of fabric and a pressure against her left shoulder returned her to the present. She was certain she would open her eyes and find Alain observing her, recording every painstaking detail of her episode. Instead, he sat beside her, no notebook in sight, with his hand on her shoulder. It was the lightest touch, which was fine by her. She doubted she could handle anything beyond that.

She pulled her robe more tightly around herself, but it did little to alleviate the chill. She closed her eyes again and continued to breathe, grateful that she could use Alain's hand as an anchor. She leaned into his touch, focused on the weight of his fingers and the warmth emanating from them.

After a few breaths, her headache subsided to a dull throbbing. A few more, and speaking finally felt possible again. She blinked her eyes open, then winced as she readjusted to the late-morning sun pouring through the windows opposite her. She turned her head and was greeted with a warm smile.

"How are you feeling?" Alain's voice was unusually gentle, like a healer adopting his best bedside manner.

"Better, thanks."

He nodded and pulled his hand away. A small part of her wished he'd left it there just a moment longer.

"That Senser you once told me about," she said, "what was his name?"

"Deventhal?"

"That's the one." She hugged her knees to her chest. "I think he had the right idea. Given the choice between being around this much magic all the time and becoming a recluse, I probably would've done the same."

"I, too, can empathize with him more than ever. Perhaps it's because I've been away for so long, but I find the magic here a tad stronger than I remember. And I'm only able to attune myself to the Ether after many years of studying it. I hadn't considered what this would be like for someone who can do that innately."

She hadn't considered it, either. After all, she'd managed a few weeks at Atterdell just fine. Now that she gave it some thought, that place was like a one-room schoolhouse compared to the University of Leyport, and none of her first-term classes had included speaking Etherean.

"Wait," she said. "You can also see magic?"

"Not in the same way you do. Warding magic looks like a ripple in the air, like gazing at a hot stone on a summer's day. As for how it *feels*..." Alain closed his eyes, then breathed deeply. "The air is thick with energy. There's a constant push and pull, like waves breaking against a shore. One moment, it's a light prickle against the skin. The next, it's a vibration deep within the marrow. That's how arcana, the Ether, always feels—brimming with contradictions. It's subtle and forceful, beautiful and horrible, comforting and unsettling all at once." He opened his eyes and turned slowly, meeting her gaze. "Is that how you would describe it?"

He'd spoken with a fervor she had only heard others use when discussing the largest scores, the rarest treasures. For him, maybe magic was exactly like that.

She realized she was staring at him—with mouth agape, no less. She pressed her lips together as she pieced together an answer.

"Er, maybe not in those exact words, but yes. Something like that." She cleared her throat. "Anyway, I think I'm ready to push on."

"Are you sure?"

She nodded. He stood up, slung his satchel over his shoulder, then peered down at her with suspicion—or was it nothing more than concern? As a thief, she was used to the former. The latter was unfamiliar, a touch uncomfortable.

She took his hand and, feeling foolish for the second time that morning, averted her gaze as he helped her to her feet.

The lift door opened to a spacious room with a stone fireplace at its center. Assistants, all wearing black robes, sat at tables piled high with books and scrolls. None of them opted for the plush armchairs by the fire. The room was lined with doors that Mavery assumed led to the professors' private offices. Some of them were protected with warding magic, but most seemed to make do with mundane locks. Magical barriers likely served little purpose in a place filled with expert wardbreakers.

The only thing attached to Alain's office door was a bin filled with unopened mail. Inside, the room was all of eight feet long and half as wide. His desk was covered with loose papers—research notes, newspapers, marked-up essays. Everything was dated nearly a year ago and coated in dust.

Bookshelves lined the walls. Much like in Alain's apartment, these were crammed with leatherbound books. The tiny window was packed with snow. Alain touched the lamp on his desk, and golden light filled the room. Mavery spotted no artifacts out in the open, and the odds of this office containing hidden compartments seemed unlikely.

The chair that she assumed was typically reserved for student visitors was piled high with books. So, she lingered in the doorway as she rubbed her arms, attempting to warm herself.

"Why don't you go sit by the fire?" Alain said.

"All right. At least I'm not Sensing too much magic around here. I think I've had enough of that for one day."

She picked the armchair closest to the fireplace. The moment she sat down, one of the other assistants approached her. She was a petite woman, likely in her mid-twenties, and wore thick-framed spectacles.

"Excuse me, I couldn't help but overhear." She spoke in a voice that, given her small stature, was surprisingly deep and brusque. "Did you mean Sensing, as in arcane hypersensitivity?"

Mavery nodded. And then a half-dozen assistants swarmed around her, like a pack of starving dogs rounding on a scrap of meat. Each of them wielded pens and notebooks that seemed to have materialized out of nowhere; Mavery wouldn't have been surprised if they actually had. The assistants began speaking all at once.

"Are you *really* a Senser?"

"Can you Sense anything right now?"

"Is that scar related to your Sensing in any way?"

"Honestly," sneered a male assistant who hadn't joined the others, "you're causing this much fuss over *Sensing*?"

Alain emerged from his office and, with a swish of his robe, swooped in between Mavery and the others. He spread his arms wide, as if simply shielding her from view would quell their interest.

"That's enough," Alain said. "If you wish to learn about her abilities, leave a request in my mailbox."

"Just one question?" the bespectacled assistant asked.

"*No.*"

The horde of scholars shot him looks of disappointment—one mumbled something about "bloody wizards"—but then retreated to their tables and returned to their work. Alain shook his head as he lowered himself into the armchair across from Mavery.

"I could have handled them myself," she said.

"Don't let their meek, bookish looks fool you. An individual scholar is no threat, but together, they're fiercer than a dragon."

"Well, in *that* case, thank you for saving me from the big scary dragon, Sir Knight."

She shifted her chair closer to the fire. Up close, she noticed how the flames oscillated in a pattern, there was no crackling of wood—in fact, there were no logs at all—and the heat was too tempered. This was an Elemental fire, one that had been conjured only to *look* comforting. That was for the best, considering how the common room was brimming with kindling. One errant ember would likely set the entire tower ablaze.

"That's not helping much, is it?" Alain asked.

She shook her head. "Not at all."

There was one positive: Elemental magic didn't affect her Senses. She'd always assumed because this was already the "flashiest" School of Magic; its effects were obvious to everyone, mage or not.

Alain stood up. "Well, time to get this over with." He spoke as if he were readying himself for a walk to the gallows. Suppressing a shiver, Mavery hoisted herself out of the chair. "Oh, er, no need to come with me if you're still feeling poorly. We're only going to discuss some of my research ideas. It'll be quite tedious."

"Sounds better than sitting by a fake fire with those weirdos over there." One of them turned and glared at her. "Besides, you look like you could use a little moral support."

Alain nervously scratched his beard. "All right. But remember: I warned you."

TWELVE

The dean's office was fit for a king. The room contained the vast collection of books Mavery had come to expect, and—more importantly—cabinets brimming with magical artifacts. They glowed with faint auras that she was so eager to investigate, she all but forgot about her Sensing-induced headache. Before she could do more than glimpse those artifacts, Alain steered her toward the pair of leather chairs in front of the desk. Her curiosity would have to wait.

Even if Mavery hadn't spotted his diploma from the University of Maroba, Kazamin's sepia complexion and short stature would have made his ethnicity obvious. Like most Marobans, Kazamin was tiny, not even five feet tall, yet broad-shouldered. His large ears stuck straight out and made his bald head appear wider than it actually was. While seated, only his head and shoulders were visible from across the expansive desk. He was elderly, even by wizard standards. His face was a web of deep wrinkles, he sported a fully gray beard, and his liver-spotted hands trembled as he spoke.

"First order of business," he said. He pushed a tall stack of papers across his desk. "Here are some spells and book chapters in need of peer review. This should help you become reacclimated with research. On that note, you mentioned last week you were already exploring some research topics."

Alain tucked the papers into his magically expanded satchel. He glanced at Mavery, then nodded. "Yes, sir. Well, to begin, my new assistant, Mavery Cul—er, *Reynard*—has arcane hypersensitivity."

Mavery examined her nails as she pretended to ignore his slip-up.

"Has a Mystic confirmed this?" Kazamin asked.

"No, but I don't believe it's necessary. Based on my observations over the past month, I have no reason to believe she's lying."

Mavery looked up. "Why would I lie about that?"

From the way Alain's face fell and Kazamin startled at the sound of her voice, Mavery realized her mistake. Evidently, assistants were expected to remain silent during these meetings.

"Arcane hypersensitivity is an incredibly rare condition," Kazamin explained. "So rare, in fact, there is little scholarship on this topic. Many people have claimed to have this condition to garner influence in a niche field. So, I am certain you can understand why, when an unverified Senser walks into my office—furthermore, one who is not a wizard but a *female assistant*—I would be more than a bit skeptical."

She opened her mouth, but Alain's eyes flashed her a warning to stay quiet. She decided to seethe in silence while Kazamin returned his attention to Alain.

"I will trust your judgment, Aventus. If what you are saying is true, she is no doubt the first Senser since Deventhal, Marya preserve his soul." He briefly touched his palm to his forehead. "However did you find her?"

"*She* found *me,* if you can believe it." Alain's voice quavered with a nervous laugh.

Kazamin leaned forward, resting his elbows and steepled fingers on his desk. He peered at Mavery as though he didn't know what to make of her.

"Hmm," he said at last, then turned to Alain again. "I remember the High Council requested that you present a new spell. Are you planning to use her Sensing to guide your spellcraft?"

"In a manner of speaking, yes."

"Go on."

Yes, do go on, Mavery thought as dread gnawed at her stomach.

"One of my ideas is to develop a spell that imitates her abilities. She is an innate Gardemancer, and therefore she Senses Gardemancy spells more vividly than the other Schools of Magic." Alain took out his notebook, flipped to a page in the middle, and pushed it across the desk. The dean read as he listened, brow furrowing all the while. "Over the past month, I've taken extensive notes on the specific colors, vibrancies, even smells and tastes that she Senses. The ability to differentiate between the various types of wards, just as she does, would be a tremendous boon for our field."

Kazamin offered another noncommittal "hmm" as he pushed the notebook back across the desk. "If I were you, I would seek out a Mystic to confirm that your assistant is, in fact, a Senser. I'm sure you're aware that many of our colleagues still treat Sensing as something of a pseudoscience, and would be unlikely to simply take her word for it—or even yours."

"But if my spell is successful, I can prove that it's *not* pseudoscience."

Kazamin shrugged. "At any rate, I *do* think your spell has potential. If I recall correctly, such a spell has been attempted before. Let me see here..."

He swiveled in his chair to the bookshelf behind him, then perused it for a moment before picking out a hefty tome. From what Mavery could glean from across the desk, it was some sort of encyclopedia filled with wizard names. Kazamin muttered to himself as he turned to the index, then ran a knobbly finger down the page. While he was distracted, Mavery glared at Alain.

"A Sensing spell?" she hissed. "You could have warned me."

"I *did* try to warn you," he whispered back. He glanced at Kazamin, whose focus was solely on the book.

"You could have been more specific!"

"Can we talk about this later?"

"Depends. When were you planning to tell me?"

"I didn't know if—"

"Ah, here we are!" Kazamin said, and the two of them snapped to attention in unison. "Enodus the Second of Fenutia attempted a similar spell over two hundred years ago. He died before he could complete it—may Marya keep him—but his unfinished tome resides in the University of North Fenutia's archives. That would be a good place to start. I will request they loan it to us."

"Thank you, sir," Alain said. "I appreciate it."

As Kazamin closed the book, a chime pealed from outside. It was a louder version of the resonating ward that had announced Priscilla's visit.

"Is it really thirteen o'clock already?" Kazamin asked, glancing at his pocket watch. "I have a class next period. I must go prepare the room."

"I apologize again for forcing you to cover my teaching duties for me."

"Oh, it's no bother at all, Aventus. I hadn't taught a class in almost thirty years. It's been a refreshing change." He chuckled. "That being said, you will hear no complaints from me when you return this autumn!"

As he rose from his chair with a groan, Alain stood automatically. Alain was not a tall man, but he was gigantic compared to Kazamin. Dwarven ancestry and old age had so compacted the dean's body, the top of his head barely reached Alain's chest. While the two wizards exchanged their farewells, Mavery took the opportunity to examine the nearest curio cabinet.

Her pulse quickened. This one alone contained dozens of pendants, rings, daggers, and the like. Their blue protective wards were anchored to the precious gems and metals they were crafted from. Though Alain didn't seem to own any artifacts, he'd just given her access to a wizard with a treasure trove. And if she was wrong about Alain, maybe she could pilfer something from *both* of them...

"Mavery," Alain called, "are you coming?"

With a pang of longing, she turned away from the cabinet. At the door, she shook Kazamin's unnervingly cold and bony hand; she worried it would shatter if she gripped it too firmly.

"Welcome to the University of Leyport, Marion," he said.

"Mavery," she replied stiffly. Normally, she would abhor the idea of robbing the elderly. But robbing *this* old codger wouldn't weigh on her conscience one bit.

He closed his office door and hobbled through the empty

common room toward the lift. Mavery would figure out how to get her hands on Kazamin's curios some other time. First, she had another matter to address. She folded her arms—partially for dramatic effect, partially to warm herself—and rounded on Alain. He raised his hands.

"Look, keeping you in the dark was never my intent—"

"Oh, I think it was *exactly* your intention."

"The Sensing spell was only an idea—one of several, in fact. I didn't know Kazamin would latch onto the first one I suggested."

Mavery snorted. "Please, you saw how those assistants treated me like I was some sort of specimen the second they found out I was a Senser. And what did Kazamin mean about having a Mystic confirm my abilities? Because if you think I'm going to let one of *them* poke around in my head—"

"Mysticism is perfectly safe when practiced by professionals."

"Sure, when they're not torturing confessions out of people."

"*Torture?*" Alain scoffed. "That's a rather narrow view of an entire School of Magic. While I agree that *some* of the uses of Mysticism are a bit morally questionable, that's not true for all of them. In this case, the Mystic would simply ask you a few questions and detect whether you were lying. It's a five-minute interview, quick and painless."

"And you've experienced this yourself?"

"Well, no, but—"

She closed her eyes and pinched the bridge of her nose.

"—it doesn't matter," Alain continued. "I'm not calling upon any Mystics because I don't need to, no matter what Kazamin says. You've given me no reason to doubt your abilities, especially after what I've witnessed today."

Mavery studied his expression: earnest, with a hint of that odd look he'd given her before. Though she had no reason to doubt him, nothing about this sat right with her.

She sighed. "Look, I was fine with all your note-taking when I thought it was for a book, maybe for your own amusement. But a *spell*? I don't know if I'm comfortable with that."

"Why not? Think of how it could benefit the study of magic!"

"My Sensing *has* been a benefit, but it's also been a burden.

I'm still freezing after that episode downstairs. Having a reaction like that isn't something I'd wish on anyone—even if they can just turn it off with a spell. I can't do that. I'll *never* be able to do that."

To her own surprise, this was bothering her more than she'd anticipated. But why? She would be gone long before he finished the damned spell. And there was no guarantee he *would* finish it, especially if he needed her assistance.

Because, once again, she had landed herself in a situation where someone was assuming his authority over her, not even bothering to ask for her input, and she was supposed to accept it.

"I didn't think—" Alain started.

"No, you didn't." She averted her gaze and muttered, "That's the problem with you wizards. You never—"

"Alain!"

They both turned toward a boisterous baritone voice. Upon seeing its source, Alain's shoulders sank.

"Oh, gods, not now," he groaned.

Bounding toward them was a hulking middle-aged man. Everything about his body seemed to be out of proportion with itself, from his barrel chest contrasted with his slender legs, to his bulbous nose paired with his beady eyes. His plum-and-silver robe strained against his protruding stomach. The man had a bushy red mustache that was leagues thicker than the hair atop his head. His cheeks had the ruddiness of someone who had just come in from the cold, or from downing a pint.

Despite his imposing build, the man had a jovial spirit—a little *too* jovial. His thick arms seized Alain around the middle, drawing him into a full-bodied hug. Alain stiffened and, once he was free again, gave the man a forced smile.

"Aha, so the rumors are true!" Though he now stood in front of them, the man's voice was no less booming. "The elusive Alain Tesseraunt has returned at last. Why didn't you tell me you were coming to campus today?"

"I—"

"Ah, and who is this lovely lady?"

"This is Mavery, my new assistant. Mavery, meet Volsegar the Fourth."

"Bah! No need to be so bloody formal. My Gardemancy students call me Professor Ward, my friends call me Declan. As far as I'm concerned, we're all friends here."

He extended a hand that dwarfed Mavery's. She cracked a grin as they shook hands.

"Your surname is actually Ward?"

He beamed. "Since the day I was born! That my magic and my name happened to be a perfect fit, well, I call it fate—and the good kind, too. Once knew a lad named Burncock. You don't want to know what fate had in store for *him!*"

Declan guffawed while slapping his knee. Alain sighed and rolled his eyes with the agony of someone who had heard that joke a hundred times too many. Mavery, however, gave Declan a genuine chuckle. She then laughed even harder at Alain's scowl.

"Finally!" Declan reached forward and clapped Alain on the shoulder. "You found an assistant with a sense of humor."

"Yes, Volsegar, because *humor* ought to be a scholar's most important attribute."

This comment came from the professor who had just entered the room. Mavery recognized her as the same professor whose class had overwhelmed her Senses. While the professor's blue-gray complexion suggested she was Nilandoren, her height—she was a few inches shorter than Mavery—suggested otherwise. The wrinkles around her mouth, but not her dark yet piercing eyes, suggested she was someone who frowned more than she smiled. Her wiry salt-and-pepper hair framed her hawkish face like a frazzled halo. The professor stopped in front of Mavery.

Trailing behind her was a much younger woman whose black robes marked her as the professor's assistant. She was the same height as the professor, with black curls and a heart-shaped face covered in freckles. Of all the scholars Mavery had met today, this woman was, by and large, the most attractive of the lot.

"So," the professor said, "not only does Aventus remain among the living, he's managed to hire a new assistant."

Her eyes flicked up to Mavery's face, then down to her feet. From her hard stare and even harder frown, she was not impressed with what she saw. But Mavery didn't take offense; she gathered this woman was exceptionally hard to please.

"You're a bit old to be an assistant," she said bluntly.

Well, Mavery would take offense to *that*. She placed her hands on her hips and returned the older woman's hard stare.

"I'm in the middle of something of a career change."

Declan chuckled. "Come now, Nez, go easy on the new—"

The woman veered on him. Though Declan was over a foot taller than her, he recoiled at her steely glare.

"Don't you dare use that familiar tone with me, Volsegar. It's *Nezima*. Understood?"

Declan mumbled an apology.

"As for you, Aventus," she said, pivoting on the spot, "I hope the reason for your visit is to pick up some of the slack that your colleagues, myself included, have had to assume in your absence. I'll have you know, I'm teaching four classes this term—*four*! I haven't had that kind of workload in a decade."

Alain winced. "I'm sorry for putting you in that position, Nezima."

She huffed.

"I am, truly. But I'm afraid my reasons for being here today are solely for research."

"You're conducting research again?" Nezima's eyes widened briefly before narrowing again. "How nice for you. I've little time for it myself these days. Case in point: my next class starts in five minutes. As much as I would love to stay and engage in idle chatter, I must be off."

She turned to Mavery. Perhaps it was a trick of the light, but Mavery swore she saw Nezima's expression soften slightly. There was a look behind her eye that was unreadable. Mavery glanced at Nezima's assistant, who was staring at the floor as if she were trying to ignore this entire conversation.

"Best of luck with your...career change," Nezima said to Mavery. "You'll need it."

Nezima approached the door to her right. It opened at the flick of her hand, and she pointed for her assistant to go inside. The younger woman rushed in the office, where she exchanged the stack of papers she'd been holding for a thicker one. Meanwhile,

Nezima left the common room without another word.

The assistant closed Nezima's door behind her with one hand, careful to not spill the papers pinned under her other arm. Before she trailed after Nezima, however, she stopped and looked at Alain.

"Er...hello, Aventus."

"Hello, Wren," he said flatly.

"You look well."

"As do you."

Wren looked from Alain to Mavery, then shifted her arms to keep her stack of papers from slipping. "Well...I'd best not keep Nezima waiting."

As Wren left the common room, Mavery pondered the odd exchange. Yet another mystery. Whether she could benefit from this one remained to be seen.

"Well!" Declan said, clasping his hands together. "Now that we've each gotten a pep talk, I suppose now's as good a time as any to get some work done!"

He crossed the room to his office, which now had a queue of students waiting outside.

The interruptions had forced Mavery and Alain to place a pin in their argument. She wasn't eager to revisit it. Judging by his silence, Alain shared that sentiment. He gave her a sidelong glance.

"Shall we get out of here?"

"Gods, yes," she sighed. "Thought you'd never ask."

They arrived at a café around the block from campus. On the walk over, Alain had told her how this had been his favorite spot from his university days, until his sabbatical. Its owner was Dauphinian, and it was one of the few places in Leyport where you could find authentic Dauphinian pastries. But what really set it apart from the other cafés were its alchemical teas.

"Alchemical teas?" Mavery asked as they approached the front door. The café was a quaint cottage nestled between towering brick buildings. "You mean potions?"

"In a sense. Think of it as tea, but with a touch of magic."

"I think what I need right now is *less* magic."

"Just trust me," he said, opening the door.

Her doubts persisted as he led her to a small round table beside the fireplace. He pulled out her chair and offered to take her robe, but she declined. While she attempted to warm herself by the fire, Alain went to the counter and ordered for both of them. That was fine by her, as she couldn't begin to make sense of the menu. Half of it was in Dauphinian, and the offerings were so vast, Alain's tea collection seemed primitive by comparison. A few minutes later, a server returned with a plate of buttery scones, an assortment of jams, and a pair of cups large enough to be soup bowls.

At first glance, Mavery's cup seemed to be filled with ordinary black tea. But the iridescent sheen on its surface indicated it had been enhanced with...something. She held back her hair as she leaned forward and sniffed. It smelled like cinnamon.

Alain's tea was a scarlet liquid that smelled like grass but looked disturbingly like blood. Instead of drinking from his own cup, he was watching Mavery with anticipation.

"This better not make me sprout feathers or burst into song."

He laughed. "No, but now I'm hoping it does."

She was so desperate for relief, she decided to not argue with him further. She lifted the cup with both hands, brought it to her lips, and took a careful sip. Warmth flooded her body the second the liquid reached her stomach. All at once, it was like soaking in a hot bath, bundling up in a thick blanket, and napping in a sunny meadow. Alain's smile broadened as she relaxed in her chair.

"Finally, I feel *warm*," she sighed, then took a large gulp. After that, she shrugged off her robe.

"I suspected all you needed was the right mix of alchemical ingredients."

He raised his cup, then paused as a distant look crossed his face. It was one she'd grown familiar with over these past weeks. So, she wasn't the least bit shocked when he lowered the cup, took out his notebook, and began writing.

"What does your tea do?" she asked. It was a futile attempt to reel him back in. Once he started recording his thoughts, he was unlikely to stop until every last one had been committed to paper.

"Try it for yourself if you'd like," he said without looking up. He nudged his cup toward her with his right hand while his left continued to scrawl feverishly.

She had to close her eyes as she drank because, gods, the liquid really *did* look like blood. But it tasted just as it smelled: like grass. And then a sense of calm trickled over her from head to toe. It was not the typical sensation from a normal cup of tea. It was as if her thoughts had become muted, pushed into the background. They were still present, but if she tried to focus on any details, they became fuzzy, detached. What instead became more pronounced—more important—were her breathing, her heartbeat, the liquid slipping down her throat, the warmth of the cup against her hands. For a moment, she had no concerns, no worries.

All too soon, the sensation passed and her thoughts returned to normal.

"I think you need this more than I do." She nudged Alain's cup back toward him. But he continued to write as if he'd forgotten she was there.

She studied his pen gliding across the page. In one swift movement, she leaned forward and snatched it from his hand. At last, he paused and looked up. He blinked at her, seeming more surprised than irritated.

"What were you writing about?" she asked, twirling the pen between her fingers.

"It's nothing."

He reached for the pen, and she returned it without a fight. Getting him to stop had been her only goal. Instead of resuming his writing, he pocketed the pen and tipped his notebook away from her as he closed it. Not that there was any need to hide anything. During his note-taking frenzies, his perfect script regressed to a scribble that she doubted even he could decipher.

"For 'nothing,' that sure was a lot of *something*."

"Just another research idea I had."

"Oh."

Mavery took a long drink of her tea, thankful that the cup was large enough to hide the sour look on her face. His research was the last thing she wanted to talk about right now.

"I'm sorry for what happened in Kazamin's office earlier."

With a sigh, she lowered her cup. Of course, *he* wanted to talk about it.

"I'm sorry for not being transparent with you," he continued. "Since you are my research subject—not to mention, the highest authority on Sensing that I know—I should have asked your opinion on the matter before diving in head-first. But, once again, I got ahead of myself and I..."

"Was an ass."

He nodded. "Yes."

"Well, at least you admit it. *Again*. But I'm not just your research subject, Alain. I'm your assistant." She leaned forward, resting her elbows on the table. "I'll help you with this Sensing spell however I can, but you need to be honest with me. You need to keep me informed about *everything* you're researching."

She looked him in the eye, wondering if he would understand her true meaning behind those last three words. Would he admit that he'd looked into her past? Would he admit that he knew she was lying, bending the truth, omitting key details, whatever he wanted to call it? Or, would they both continue to keep their secrets?

"I will," he said, holding her gaze, "in due time."

Finally, he drank his tea.

THIRTEEN

When Mavery arrived at his apartment the following morning, Alain was abuzz with something that she suspected had kept him up all night. He was still wearing his faculty robe, his eyes were ringed with dark circles.

She'd barely taken off her coat when he steered her to the sofa. She lowered herself beside a pile of books that hadn't been there the previous day: alchemical recipes, herbalism field guides, medical texts on arcane maladies. He paced back and forth as he spoke. Watching him was like following a frenzied game of shuttlecock.

"Kazamin has given me so much to think about," he said. "Peer review, for starters. The book chapters, I can read on my own time, but as for the spellcraft...well, that will be more complicated. I think it's time we talk about my protocol."

"Protocol?"

"In case of my accidental death."

"What?"

He stumbled, then yelped as his shin collided with the tea table. "You told me you worked for wizards before," he said as he rubbed his leg. "Did they never mention such a thing?"

Were these theatrics a ruse to catch her in a lie? She opted for a bit of truth, but not enough to give herself away.

"That work was always temporary. The *wizards'* accidental

deaths were never a concern."

He planted himself beside her with so much force, the sofa shifted back a few inches. He grasped her shoulders and looked her squarely in the eye. She laughed nervously at his bloodshot, unblinking stare.

"I'm about to tell you something of grave importance," he said.

"Pun not intended?"

He narrowed his eyes. "Mavery, I'm being serious."

The phrase "deadly serious" danced on the tip of her tongue, but she thought better of it.

"Sorry." She flattened her smile. "What is it?"

"Have you ever wondered how wizards manage to be so long-lived? How even those without elven ancestry can live as long as the Nilandorens?"

"I'd always assumed it had something to do with magical blood."

"You're halfway there. If it were merely a matter of arcana, *all* mages would live a century and a half or more. Archmage Seringoth is among the oldest wizards in the world—a hundred and forty-three, if memory serves—but he should have died *decades* ago, dozens of times over. Remember when I once told you wizards are given certain privileges?"

She nodded.

"Well, chief among those is that we can be resurrected."

"What!?"

Her jaw dropped. She had heard rumors of resurrections, but had always assumed they, like most things pertaining to wizards, were nothing more than that.

"Spellcraft, alchemy, what-have-you...these all come with risks. And when those risks prove lethal, assistants are duty-bound to follow their wizard's resurrection protocol."

"Why the hells didn't you tell me this upfront?"

"Because this knowledge is not meant to be shared with the general populace. But now, I will be testing some potentially volatile spells. The chances of a fatal accident are not *incredibly* likely, but they are more than zero. If that happens, I will need you to resurrect me."

Her eyes widened. "And how am I supposed to do that? I know a little healing magic, but—"

"Don't worry, you won't need to cast any spells. There is a loose floorboard beneath my bed. Beneath *that*, you will find a box containing everything you need. It is imperative, though, that you follow the protocol as soon as possible. The longer you wait, the less likely I will be able to return. And, of course, there are other stipulations, but..." He shook his head. "We need not get into those now. My protocol will explain everything, if and when the time comes."

" 'If *and when*'?"

He winced. "Er...one should always prepare for the worst."

She glanced over her shoulder at the bedroom door. Whatever this "protocol" entailed, it had to be valuable, if it was capable of bringing someone back from the dead. She should have trusted her instincts and checked for loose floorboards when she'd had free rein of the apartment.

"Why not show me now, give it a trial run?" she asked.

"I'd rather not, but I can assure you it's all very straightforward. If you're capable of learning Soudremancy on your own, this will be child's play. Just follow my instructions and you will be fine. *I* will be fine." He absently scratched his chest. "Don't forget: I was once an assistant in your exact position. I myself have been through the protocol several times. I wouldn't task you with this if I didn't think you could handle it."

She should have been thrilled that he trusted her with this secret protocol, that her plan was working. Yet, she was left with a sense of foreboding. Was the procedure so horrifying, he thought she would back out once she knew what it required?

"All right," she said. "But tell me you're not going to test any dangerous spells *right now*. You don't look like you're in any state to do that."

He ran his fingers through his thoroughly mussed hair. "I won't, and I know. I didn't get much sleep last night."

Mavery narrowed her eyes.

"None at all." Alain shrugged. "Can't let something as mundane as *sleep* get in the way of a research breakthrough."

"What breakthrough?"

"I can't tell you yet." When she opened her mouth, readying a rebuttal, he added quickly, "This isn't related to the Sensing spell. Not *directly*, at least. But you can assist me with something else in the meantime."

He pulled his notebook from his pocket, tore out a page, and handed it to her. At first, she struggled to decipher his scribblings, but she soon recognized them as a list of alchemical herbs, minerals, and solvents. Nothing looked out of the ordinary, until she came to the final item on the list: powdered kutauss claws.

Kutausses were often bred in captivity, declawed, and sold as exotic pets. Mavery suspected the one presiding over the lobby downstairs was a victim of that very practice. Their claws were ground into a powder that was popular among poisoners, while the kutausses themselves were popular pets among the wealthy. Neither could be sourced from an ordinary shopkeeper; the demonspawn trade was exclusive to the black market.

What business did Alain have with such an ingredient? A single teaspoon was enough to sap the arcana from a dozen mages, and he wanted *two ounces* of it. Was his alchemy hobby more nefarious than he let on?

"Some of these ingredients are a tad...exotic," Mavery said.

"Oh, I'm well aware, but the apothecary I use is nothing short of a miracle worker. I've yet to request an ingredient Enid can't source."

Mavery had an uneasy feeling about this, but she had no choice but to play along.

"I suppose you want me to go shopping for you," she said.

"Yes, but I'll come with you this first time, get you and Enid properly introduced. Besides, I could use some fresh air."

"I think you could use some *sleep*."

Maybe she could convince him to lie down on the sofa before heading out, which would buy her a little time to check under the bed. Maybe even the storage room, if she could manage it.

"My eagerness to start this project means I couldn't sleep right now even if I tried. Don't worry about me, I'll get some rest later. If we leave now, we should arrive as soon as the shop opens." He stood up. Mavery cleared her throat, eyeing his wrinkled robe. He looked down. "Er, but perhaps I should change first."

The Cracked Pestle was a little hole-in-the-wall tucked down an unassuming side street in the Market District. The walls were lined from floor to ceiling with bottles of every size and color. Bundles of dried herbs hung from the rafters, giving the air a medicinal scent. To get to the front counter, they had to weave around stacks of barrels filled with minerals waiting to be scooped and weighed, or solvents and serums waiting to be tapped and bottled.

One corner of the shop was devoted to broken alchemy equipment—a heap of cracked glass and tarnished metal that had been pushed aside and forgotten. It was little wonder. Everything in this place exuded chaos, much like Alain's apartment had weeks ago.

Behind the counter was a woman with russet skin and long graying dreadlocks. She stood over the hearth, stirring something in a small cauldron. She wore a red-orange dress with ragged hemlines and flared sleeves. It seemed a risky outfit for working over an open flame. No wonder Alain liked this woman; perhaps they'd bonded over their shared disregard for fire safety.

Alain rang the bell at the counter.

"Be with you in a minute!" the woman called over her shoulder. She gave her concoction another stir, then donned a pair of thick gloves. With a grunt, she heaved the cauldron off the fire and onto the flagstones.

"Working on a tincture, Enid?"

"No, this is just breakfast for Peaches." She paused. "Hold on a tick, I know that voice." She whipped around so quickly, the hem of her dress fanned the flames. "Mr. Tesseraunt! Well, I'll be godsdamned. It's been a hound's age!"

She tossed off her gloves as she rushed around the counter, then pulled Alain into a hug that was no less enthusiastic than the one Declan had given him yesterday. But Alain didn't seem to mind this one. He returned it with a friendly pat on the shoulder.

"I can't tell you how good it is to see my favorite customer again," Enid said as she released Alain.

He blushed. "Oh, you only say that because of my order from three years ago."

"One thousand, four hundred, seventy-six potins—and twenty-eight coppers. A record sale that has yet to be beaten. Until then, you'll be my favorite!"

She turned to Mavery and gave her an appraising look that settled somewhere in the vicinity of Mavery's waist. Enid leaned closer—and so did the generous swell of her bosom. Heat trickled up Mavery's neck. She forced her gaze upward, where she caught a glint of something dangling from Enid's ear: a brass pendant depicting a dragon.

That explained how Alain's apothecary was able to source *anything*. Did he know his money was helping fund private armies, smuggling operations, backroom deals, and gods knew what else the Brass Dragons had their fingers in these days?

For a Dragon, Enid played fast and loose with security. She had no rookie guild members on guard duty. There wasn't even a single ward cast over the storefront. Mavery subtly glanced around the shop, searching for anyone who might be lurking in the corners, shrouding themselves in shadow, but she could Sense nothing. She caught the faintest hint of ash, but that was likely from the open fire—or any number of ingredients lying around. From what she could tell, the three of them were alone.

"Who's your friend?" Enid asked. Though she addressed Alain, her gaze remained fixed on Mavery.

"This is Mavery, my new assistant."

"Well, well! If she was *my* assistant, I doubt I'd ever get any work done." Enid threw Mavery a wink. "Does this Mavery have a family name?"

"Reynard," Mavery said with a knowing smirk.

"Exactly my type, too," Enid sighed, then returned her attention to the man who was about to continue lining her pockets. "Well, I suppose you're here for more than playing catch-up. My ledger will be all the happier for it. What can I do you for?"

Alain handed her the list. She mouthed the words and quirked an eyebrow as she read over it.

"You're in luck!" she said. "I just so happen to have everything in stock. I had another buyer for that powder you're looking for, but he didn't pay up. Only a single ounce, though."

"Anything you have, I'll take it."

"All right, then. Hold tight."

She flitted about the shop, humming to herself as she gathered jars from the shelves and brought them to the counter. She carefully weighed out ingredients and poured them into smaller jars and pouches. She stood on a stool to gather some bundles of herbs, then bound them in twine. Finally, she headed toward the pile of broken equipment and vanished behind it. There was the creak of what was likely a trapdoor opening and closing.

Mavery turned to Alain, arms crossed and lips pursed.

"What is it?" he asked.

"Your apothecary really *can* source anything."

"Just as I told you. And?"

"And you don't find that suspicious? Convenient, even?"

He peered at her with a slight tilt to his head. "Whatever you're insinuating, I genuinely haven't a clue."

Mavery sighed. "Did you know she's a—"

The trapdoor opened again.

"We'll talk about it later," she muttered as Enid reappeared, holding a black pouch that could only contain the powdered kutauss claws.

At the counter, Enid totaled up everything in her ledger; it came out to nearly five hundred potins. Alain counted out notes with the nonchalance of someone who regularly spent six weeks' worth of his assistant's wages in one fell swoop. Meanwhile, Mavery pondered what other illicit merchandise was stored in the room below. Though she knew better than to steal from a Dragon, the Cracked Pestle's lack of security would make it so simple. Why wasn't there at least a guard keeping watch?

"Gods above! In all this excitement, I completely forgot," Enid said. She looked up and bellowed, *"Peaches!"*

The ceiling rattled as thunder erupted above their heads. It rolled across the upper floor and down the staircase along the back wall. Mavery recoiled, nearly knocking over a barrel of serum, when a hellhound appeared at the bottom of the stairs.

The hound was a sleek black and umber blur as it sprinted to the cauldron. Then, with a din of panting and squelching that made Mavery's stomach lurch, it gobbled up its breakfast within seconds. Thick strands of drool oozed from the beast's maw. It raised its head, and its glowing red eyes met her stare.

"Oh, gods damn it," she muttered.

The hellhound galloped around the counter and skidded to a halt, nearly colliding into her. With a gasp, she squeezed her eyes shut and clenched her fists.

"Not a dog lover, I take it," Enid said with a touch of amusement in her voice.

Dogs were fine, but this creature was no dog. Its sniffing sounded more like a rutting boar than anything dog-like. And that was to make no mention of its *fangs*... Only weeks ago, Mavery had seen what they could do to human flesh. Instead of telling Enid that, all she could manage was a disgusted groan as the hellhound's snout prodded her in a rather inappropriate place.

"Peaches is harmless, so long as you don't try to nick anything."

Though Mavery had serious doubts about that, the hellhound backed off after determining she posed no threat to Enid—or Enid's wares. She opened her eyes with a sigh of relief, only to discover that it had moved on to Alain...who was *petting* the gods-damned thing.

"You remember me, don't you, Peaches?" Alain said. The hound's barbed tail whipped about as its slobbery tongue lolled. "Of course you do, because you're such a good boy!"

"Good thing you're my only customers at the moment," Enid said. She rolled her eyes, though she did so with a faint smile. "Can't have word getting out that my guard dog's got a soft side. Peaches, *come!*"

The hellhound snapped to attention, then trotted over and sat on its haunches while Enid packed up Alain's order. She escorted Alain and Mavery to the door, each of them carrying a large satchel over one shoulder.

"Don't be a stranger," Enid said with the cheerfulness of

someone who was now a tad wealthier than she'd been earlier that morning. "That goes for you, too, Reynard. Kindred spirits are always welcome here."

She winked at Mavery again before closing the door.

"What did she mean by that?" Alain asked.

Mavery didn't answer him. Her eyes scanned the shop's exterior until she spotted an etching below the left windowsill: an X, followed by an O with a vertically stacked B and D in its center. As she'd suspected, the Cracked Pestle was a Dragon-operated establishment.

Not wanting to loiter here any longer, she readjusted her satchel and hurried down the street.

"Wait!" Alain called.

Bottles clinked as he jogged to catch up. Once the Cracked Pestle was out of sight, Mavery stopped and leaned against the wall of another shop.

"If only we'd remembered to bring one of your enchanted bags."

"Transmutated," Alain panted. "Can't...enchant...inanimate objects. Common misconception. Now, will you please explain what has gotten into you?"

She looked up and down the street. Though there was hardly another person around, she still asked in a low voice, "Did you know your apothecary is a Brass Dragon?"

Alain blinked at her, mouth agape. "Enid, a Brass...? What? How did you—?"

"She was wearing their emblem."

"You're certain about that?"

Mavery nodded. "I'd recognize it anywhere. Not to mention, you'll only find kutauss claws on the black market."

Alain collapsed against the wall, looking more exhausted than ever. "I suppose it was always odd how she's never accepted bank cheques—not to mention the hellhound—but gods, I never would have guessed. And I've been patronizing her shop for years!" He narrowed his eyes at Mavery. "How do *you* know so much about this sort of thing?"

She winced. By even mentioning the Dragons, she'd already

revealed too much. Being a university dropout was one thing. Being a former—albeit low-ranking—member of Osperland's largest and most notorious criminal organization was a far worse transgression.

Alain wouldn't be able to trust her. She needed him to continue trusting her until she could fully case Kazamin's office. Not to mention, she still needed to investigate his storage room and the box beneath his bed. But saying nothing was just as likely to raise his suspicions.

"I had some run-ins with the Dragons in my younger, dumber days."

"Did those overlap with your wardbreaking days?"

"Something like that."

"I suppose that's all you're going to say on the matter."

She shrugged. "There's not much else *to* say."

Alain observed her for a moment. She once again adjusted her satchel, which felt as though it had tripled in weight, as she avoided meeting his eye.

"All right, then. Let's track down a carriage," he said. "And quickly. These bottles are heavier than they looked."

FOURTEEN

Mavery removed the final bottle from her satchel and handed it to Alain. He stored it inside the larder that now contained more alchemy ingredients than actual food. The kitchen itself, now more than ever, looked like a laboratory. The dining table was covered in bundles of dried persilweed, fallowroot, and feygrass, all waiting to be ground up and brewed.

"How are you going to eat with all this in the way?" she asked. "Or, more importantly, make tea?"

"I'll manage," he said with a drawn-out yawn.

She placed her hands on her hips. "That does it. As your assistant, I demand you get some sleep."

He laughed. "That's not how this works."

"Then I *insist* you get some sleep."

Her words weren't motivated solely by her desire to snoop around his apartment again. She was genuinely concerned about him. The trip back had drained every last bit of his stamina. He swayed on the spot, barely keeping his eyes open.

"As I told you before, I won't be able to sleep until I start this project."

"Fine."

She plucked a sprig of fallowroot and dropped its violet-hued petals into a mortar. She handed it to him, then the pestle.

"Grind that," she said.

With a shrug, he humored her. But he gave the pestle only two rotations around the bowl before she snatched the tools from his hands and set them back on the table.

"There, you have officially started." She pointed out the door. "Now, go take a nap."

With heavy-lidded eyes, he opened his mouth and raised a finger. Before he could say a word, she grasped his shoulders, steered him out of the kitchen, and closed the door behind them.

"Gods help me, Alain, I will put a blasting ward on this door if I need to."

"*Detonation* is the proper terminology."

She scoffed. "I thought you didn't care about being 'proper.'"

"Regardless... One day soon, you will think back on this moment and wish you hadn't delayed me." He held up his hands. "But, if you insist, so be it."

He stumbled to the sofa, lay down, and closed his eyes. Mavery knew better than to jump straight to work. She waited a moment, then waved a hand in front of his face and prodded his shoulder. He was out cold.

First, she considered the storage room. He always kept it locked but unwarded while he was at home. She wasn't about to reach for the key around his neck, so she would need to pick the lock. But that risked making too much noise. If he woke up, she would be directly in his line of sight. The bedroom, which was behind him and always unlocked, was the safer option.

She removed her boots, then tiptoed around the sofa and to the bedroom door. She winced as the hinges creaked, and she wished she knew the Etherean words to create a soundproofing ward. She glanced at the sofa; the noise hadn't disturbed him.

Once inside the bedroom, she wasted no time. She closed the door, then dropped to her hands and knees beside the bed, and pressed the floorboards one by one. The loose one was directly in the center, and she had to lie flat on her stomach to reach it. Carefully, silently, she prised the board free and placed it aside, uncovering a thin metal box. She reached a little further—

The sofa creaked.

"Damn it!" she whispered. Pulse racing, she replaced the floorboard, followed by the rug, then rose to her feet. She froze, waiting for another sound to follow.

A few heartbeats later, Alain's footsteps approached.

There was no use wasting her arcana on a shrouding spell when he'd detected her so easily the first time. So, she did the only thing she could think of: she would get caught on purpose. She grabbed a pillow and a blanket from the bed, then turned and pulled the door open. She feigned surprise as she almost collided with Alain face-to-face.

"Oh! Awake already? I didn't hear you get up."

"What are you doing in here?"

"You didn't look very comfortable, so I wanted to bring you these."

She raised her arms, showing him the pillow and blanket. His gaze softened as he gave her a weak smile.

"Thank you, Mavery. That was very thoughtful of you."

With a pang of guilt, she smiled. A small part of her wished her gesture had been genuine.

"And you're right," he said, taking the linens. "The sofa isn't particularly comfortable. I'm afraid I won't be much company, but you can continue working if you wish."

"I'll stay a little while longer, just in case you need anything."

She left the bedroom, then swore under her breath as she leaned against the closed door. She didn't know when she'd get another chance to check under the bed, but at least now he would be out of the sitting room for the foreseeable future. At last, she could try her luck with the storage room.

She rummaged through her pack and retrieved her lockpicking tools. She hadn't used them in ages, and her skills had gotten rusty. Bypassing the tumblers took her several attempts. Her quick pulse, shaky hands, and need to glance at the bedroom door every few seconds, all slowed her down. Finally, there was a soft click as the latch released. She returned her tools to her pack, then slowly opened the door.

The storage room had no windows, and the light from the sitting room only did so much to illuminate it. She took the lamp from Alain's desk, infused it with arcana, and carried it inside. When she'd glimpsed this room once before, she hadn't seen the ladder in the center, bolted to the floor and ceiling. She raised the lamp, revealing a hatch overhead.

She set the lamp at the base of the ladder, then climbed until the hatch was within reach. With one hand grasping a rung, she pulled the door downward. The hinges creaked, echoing through the room and sending her heart into her throat. She waited for any stirring from the other side of the wall. When she heard nothing, she opened the hatch the rest of the way, then winced as light flooded in from above.

She pulled herself into a round room with a high ceiling and tall, thin windows. The walls were made of the same red brick as the building's exterior. This had to be the northern turret, and Alain had turned it into an art studio. An easel held an oil painting in its earliest stage: blue streaks across a white canvas. Propped against the curved wall were more paintings: pastoral landscapes, floral arrangements, bowls of fruit. The paint was dry on all of them; they'd been completed some time ago.

So, Alain had another hobby aside from potion-brewing and book-hoarding. Mavery wasn't sure why he'd gone through so much trouble to hide it from her. To her inexpert eye, he had some talent, though the subjects he'd chosen to paint weren't exactly inspiring.

She descended the ladder. She left the hatch open but still needed the lantern to investigate the crates in the far corners of the room. Most of them contained art supplies, linens, summer clothes, nothing of real value. The rest contained items that only held sentimental value: stuffed animals, textbooks, and Barcombe Academy uniforms. Curiously, she found his University of Leyport diploma—he'd graduated with the highest honors—tucked behind a stack of crates. She also found a wizard's staff, but without any Ether-sensitive gems, it was little more than an ornate walking stick.

Then, a paint-spattered tarp caught her eye. She pulled it away to reveal a half-dozen portraits. They all depicted the same subject: a young man with light skin, auburn hair, and mismatched eyes—one brown, one blue.

The first was a close-up with muddled features, the proportions slightly off-kilter. Next was another close-up, but this one had more detail, as if it had been painted from a reference. The man's nose was long and regal, his chin pronounced, his features symmetrical. All except for his eyes, which only heightened his beauty.

The next two paintings depicted the man sitting stiffly on a stool, then relaxing in an armchair that was identical to Alain's. The final painting was incomplete; the charcoal sketch was still visible beneath sheer blocks of color. From the man's pose—relaxing on a bed—and the abundance of flesh tones, Mavery assumed this was the beginning of a nude portrait.

"I should have known I would find you in here."

Mavery flinched. She'd let herself get too absorbed in the paintings. And, once again, she'd left her back to the door.

Slowly, she turned around. Alain stood in the doorway, arms crossed. His face was obscured in shadow, but she could only assume his expression was one of anger. She thought back to Neldren confronting her at the inn.

"Alain, I—"

The silhouette of his raised hand compelled her to be silent. Cold prickled the back of her neck as he spoke a brief incantation. She flinched again, thinking he was about to use his arcana on her, but he only conjured a small orb. A flick of his wrist sent it toward her, casting the storage room in white light. Now that she could see Alain's face, she found no trace of anger. But he was nonetheless disappointed and profoundly *tired*.

"Whatever excuse you're about to give, don't bother," he said in a voice so calm, she almost wished he'd lashed out instead. "I was planning to show you my studio—and my paintings—eventually, when I was ready."

"Your paintings are fine. Some of them are quite good, actually. They're nothing to be ashamed of."

An emotion she couldn't identify passed over his face. His shoulders slackened.

"Er...thank you," he said, then shook his head. "But the *quality* of the paintings was not my concern. Some of them are a bit personal. I'm certain you can guess which ones I'm referring to, and no, I'm not going to tell you who he is."

"I'm sorry. I shouldn't have—"

"Yes, I'm glad we agree on that," he said sharply. Mavery braced herself for the inevitable. "I think it would be best if you leave. Let's both get some rest and revisit this tomorrow."

"Tomorrow?" She blinked at him. "You're...not firing me?"

"Not now, at least. But if you continue to pry, I may change my mind."

She nodded, then avoided making eye contact as she ducked out of the room, grabbed her pack and her boots—she didn't bother putting them back on—and left the apartment. Halfway down the corridor, she stopped and leaned against the wall. At last, she felt like she could breathe again. She took a deep gulp of air, and the tension slowly released from her body.

Alain hadn't fired her. He'd given her another chance.

But now what? Now that she knew what was in the storage room, her only options were to pursue Kazamin's artifacts or whatever was beneath Alain's bed. As for the former, she didn't know when Alain would make his next trip to campus—or whether he would want her to accompany him. As for the latter, she doubted he would leave her alone in the apartment again. She wasn't sure which dampened her spirits more: her plan falling apart, or the disappointed look he'd given her.

She laughed incredulously as she realized the answer.

FIFTEEN

After Mavery scampered out of the apartment and slammed the door behind her, Alain released a heavy sigh. The weight of everything that had happened over these past minutes came crashing down all at once, and his body sagged against the door-frame.

He had known this day would come, though he'd hoped he could have delayed it for a while longer. It had been days since Mavery had last commented on the storage room. But he'd noticed the way her gaze would flick toward the door when she thought he wasn't paying attention. The way her brow would furrow as she no doubt pondered what lay beyond it. He couldn't fault her for sating her curiosity after he'd created such an aura of mystery about this room. If anything, he should have been more upfront, perhaps shown it to her from the first day of their partnership.

After all, she'd complimented his paintings. She hadn't disparaged him as some of his colleagues once had.

And why would she? She wasn't like them. She wasn't like anyone he'd ever known in the wizarding community.

Alain secured the trapdoor and retrieved the desk lamp without sparing a look at the paintings. The glimpse he'd gotten moments ago had been more than enough. He could go another year—or a lifetime—before he glimpsed them again. He closed the door, though he didn't bother locking it. Now that this secret was out, he no longer saw a need for it.

Back in the bedroom, he lay down and closed his eyes, but sleep would not come. His mind kept returning to what Mavery had revealed to him outside Enid's shop. All along, his apothecary had been a Brass Dragon. And Mavery had once had "run-ins" with them.

Perhaps she'd been a member of law enforcement, tasked with infiltrating the guild and cracking down on black market operations.

That would have been a viable theory, had he not recalled Enid's parting words. She'd called Mavery a "kindred spirit."

He already knew Mavery had once been a wardbreaker. What if her other pursuits had been more nefarious?

With a low groan, Alain opened his eyes. Sleep was a fickle enough mistress on an ordinary day, and today's events had been anything but ordinary. As he did whenever sleep failed him, he threw himself away from his bed and into work.

In the kitchen, the small mountain of herbs remained on the table. Mavery had ordered him to begin grinding the fallowroot petals, and so he continued what he'd started. Having something to do with his hands brought him immediate relief, though the sound of stone scraping against stone quickly faded to his stentorian thoughts.

What did he know about his assistant?

First: She bore callused fingers and a smattering of old scars. Whatever life she'd lived before coming to Leyport, it had been far from a pampered one.

Second: Despite having no formal education, she'd somehow managed to acquire a patchwork knowledge of several Schools of Magic—including Soudremancy.

Third: That knowledge included not-so-savory subjects. He doubted black market ingredients and criminal organizations were the extent of it.

Alain couldn't necessarily assume the worst. He himself had first come across kutauss claws in a tome he'd picked up at an antique dealer's, not realizing at the time that the High Council had banned the book nearly a century ago. Per the Covenants, he was duty-bound to turn in banned books to an arcanist, but this one had proven so useful, he'd selfishly kept it. Besides, he saw little harm in doing so. He would never use a forbidden book for his *real* research.

He wiped his violet-stained fingers on his trousers, then made a quick detour to the sitting room to fetch that very book. Thanks to Mavery's efforts in culling his collection, he'd had little trouble finding it last night, and he'd taken copious notes for his current project. Book in hand, he returned to the kitchen to put those notes into action.

He turned to the page on kutauss claws. In their current state, they were incredibly poisonous. But the alchemist who had penned this tome—simply, "the Maker"—had discovered that bringing the claws to a supergressive state reduced their arcana-sapping properties. That seemed the most promising place to start.

Alain placed the book aside, then performed a fireproofing ward. As it did whenever he performed the most rudimentary of spells, his mind wandered. This time, he was transported to a moment from a little over a week ago, in this very room, when Mavery had healed his injured finger. She'd never trained at any temple, so where else would she have learned Soudremancy?

Perhaps she'd been a medic in the military. That would explain not only her healing skills, but her shorter-than-fashionable hair, her toughened hands, her blunt manner of speaking.

No, he couldn't imagine her wearing a uniform while someone barked orders at her, much less taking those orders without question. The thought alone made him laugh.

He retrieved his torch—and reminded himself to focus. Though his fireproofing ward would stop a fire from spreading beyond the kitchen, it wouldn't prevent him from catching *himself* on fire.

He began with a tiny amount of powdered claws, barely enough to fill a thimble half-way. He deposited them in the bowl of a calcinator and, with an infusion of arcana, ignited his torch. He guided the flame in a circular motion, carefully heating the powder from above until it blackened, then continued until it turned white as fresh snow—purification. Had this been any other alchemical recipe, he would have stopped here. But he continued until the ashy substance began to glow from the inside out, much like a brick of charcoal. Ordinarily, reaching the point of supergression would render an ingredient useless, but the Maker had yet to lead him astray.

With this step complete, he now needed to render the powdered claws into a liquid state. For this, he didn't bother referencing the Maker's recipe. Many alchemical recipes used water as a solvent, but Alain knew from experience that most types of claws required a solvent with a touch more potency. He doubted kutauss claws, even in their powdered form, would be an exception.

For this, he would use alkahest: an odorless liquid that could be easily confused with water. But if one were to drink an entire glass of it, their melting insides would quickly inform them of their mistake. There was little alkahest *couldn't* dissolve.

He wondered if Mavery knew that. She could heal, yes, but were poisons also part of her repertoire? As Alain grabbed a bottle of alkahest from the larder, his breath hitched.

What if she's an assassin?

Perhaps one of his colleagues had hired her to bring his guard down and turn his year-long sabbatical into a permanent leave of absence.

He shook his head, then poured the alkahest into a metal bowl. No, he was letting his imagination get the better of him. If Mavery were a hired killer, he'd given her ample opportunities to follow through on the killing part.

As he tipped the powdered claws into the bowl of alkahest, he considered how this afternoon was a prime example. She would have knifed him in his sleep, not broken into his—

The alkahest and powder combined with an angry hiss. Instead of bubbling and then dissolving, the mixture erupted into a plume of white vapor aimed directly at Alain's face.

Too distracted to react in time, he inhaled a lungful of it. The taste and scent—a bit like rotten eggs—made his stomach churn, and his eyes burned as he bolted for the window. He threw it open, but the burst of fresh air only heightened the tempest in his stomach. He then lunged at the sink, where he spat a mouthful of white phlegm into the basin.

Alkahest is a bit too potent, he thought as he gulped down handfuls of water. He shouldn't have trusted his instincts. If he believed in the afterlife, he could imagine the Maker, whoever they'd been, chiding him from the Beyond.

Once his coughing subsided, he wiped his mouth with the back of his hand before taking a deep breath. He'd only used a small amount of kutauss claws, so he hadn't wasted too much of an expensive ingredient. His mishap hadn't proved lethal—just very unpleasant.

Furthermore, it had given him a bit of clarity. Mavery being an assassin was absurd, but what if he wasn't too far off the mark? There were many ways to end a wizard's career prematurely. Death, while the most common, was but one of them.

What if a colleague *had* hired her—not to kill him, but to get the dirt on him? What if Mavery had expected to find that dirt in the storage room?

It wasn't lost on Alain that he and Kazamin had a close relationship, and that the dean had a history of giving him special treatment. Alain couldn't recall the last time someone in his department had been granted a year-long sabbatical, much less after failing to follow the proper protocol for it. Alain wouldn't put it past someone like Nezima to resent him for that. But hiring someone to sabotage him? Would she go to those lengths for petty revenge?

Yes, Nezima most definitely would. If she was scheming something, he only hoped Mavery had nothing to do with it. No, he was *certain* she had nothing to do with it. Either Nezima and Mavery were exceptional actresses, or that moment in the common room yesterday had truly been their first meeting. He recalled how Mavery had returned Nezima's glare with an even steelier one, how she'd taken Nezima's critique without so much as a flinch...

Alain realized he was smiling.

He couldn't deny that, just as he couldn't deny that he enjoyed Mavery's company—and that he was beginning to let it color his judgment. Had Wren or Lorcan broken into his storage room, he would have dismissed them without a second thought. Not only had he told Mavery to come back tomorrow, his initial reaction had been to blame *himself* for his assistant's transgression.

Wanting to keep her around was only natural. After all, she comprised the entirety of his social circle most days. But he knew there was more to it than that. If all he desired was human inter-action, he could call upon Declan at any time. Or, gods forbid, his mother.

Declan expected him to endure bustling taverns, cheap ale, and off-color jokes. His mother expected him to accept a deluge of criticism and be grateful for the kernel of affection buried within it. His colleagues' expectations weren't much better. As the Wizard Aventus the Third, he was to carry himself with decorum, to be the stoic academic who never showed a hint of weakness.

It was all so *exhausting*.

He'd always found books much easier than people. They never expected anything from you, never demanded that you alter the essence of your being, never hurt you in the way another person could. And so, for the better part of a year, he'd believed that he could forgo people and get by with only his library for company.

But books made for terrible conversation partners. Even the Ether, for all its wonders, had its limitations. It wasn't until Mavery came along that Alain realized how lonely of an existence he'd created for himself.

With her, there were no expectations. No matter how many times he stuck the proverbial foot in mouth, she never demanded that he change himself into someone she found more favorable. It was refreshing to simply *be* in someone else's company for once. Of course, there was a chance she only tolerated his company because she was working for Nezima, or another of Alain's disgruntled colleagues. If there was any truth to his suspicions, then so be it. He would do anything to secure another day in Mavery's company, even if it came back to haunt him.

And so, he measured out another sample of kutauss claws. The sun now hung low in the sky, and a long night of experimenting awaited him.

Sixteen

A cloud of black smoke and an acrid stench greeted Mavery at the door. She pulled the neckline of her blouse over her nose.

"Sorry about that," Alain coughed, wafting the smoke away from his face. "My latest experiment went a bit awry."

His face and the front of his clothes—the same ones he'd worn yesterday—were covered in soot. Colorful splotches of plant material had joined the ink stains on his fingers. Tangled locks hung over eyes that were more deeply ringed with fatigue than Mavery remembered.

"Come in while I clean myself up."

He kept the door open to air out the smoke. With the violet soundproofing ward spanning the threshold, anything they said inside the apartment would remain private. Dread clenched Mavery's chest, but she tried her best to ignore the discomfort.

As Alain stepped toward the bathroom, she grasped him by the sleeve. He turned to her with bemused, slightly unfocused eyes. Either the alchemical fumes had gotten to him, or he was more exhausted than he was letting on.

"Alain, I wanted to apologize again for yesterday," she said. "I shouldn't have broken into your—"

"Apology accepted."

Her eyes widened. "Are you sure? I had a whole speech prepared and everything."

"Yes, I'm sure," he said with a smile.

Instead of returning it, she frowned. "So, all is forgiven?"

"You seem surprised."

During the hours they'd been apart, she had expected his dis-appointment to have evolved into anger, then resentment.

"A bit," she said quietly as she released his arm. "In my experience, people aren't so easily forgiving."

"Then I suppose I'm not like most people you know."

"No, I suppose you're not."

The room had grown uncomfortably warm. It was little wonder, given the crackling fire on the other side of the room. Mavery's eyes stung, though she was certain the lingering smoke was the reason for it.

Alain shrugged. "Honestly, I should have been more upfront. Had I told you an art studio was the only thing of interest beyond that door, I could have assuaged some of your curiosity."

She gave him a small smile. "I'm not sure that would have helped. It's not every day I get to see an artist's private studio."

" 'Artist'?" he said with a scoff and a wave of his hand. "Oh, I wouldn't go *that* far. It's nothing more than a hobby—and not even a recent one. It's been ages since I last picked up a paintbrush."

"Where did you learn? Did they teach you that at Barcombe?"

"Gods, no," he laughed. "Barcombe only taught me a bit of figure drawing to help with field research. Cameras are not only expensive and unwieldy, arcane interferences cause photographs to come out wrong, so we must record things the old-fashioned way. But beyond that, the wizarding community views the arts as a colossal waste of time. No, when I was first curious about painting, I found a book on the basics and taught myself."

Though learning this left Mavery a bit dispirited, she laughed.

"What's so funny?" he asked.

"Of course you learned how to paint from a *book*."

Alain looked around the room. Though they had returned most of the library books, hundreds upon hundreds of his own remained. Mavery had just barely started implementing her new cataloging system, so many of those books were pushed against the walls in unorganized stacks. At least they no longer posed a tripping hazard.

"I see your point," he said. "Speaking of books, I still haven't started peer reviewing any of the ones Kazamin gave me."

Mavery stifled a groan. It seemed nothing would take this man's mind off work.

"Are you sure you don't need a break first?" she asked. "Did you get any sleep after I left yesterday?"

"Er...a bit, off and on. But I promise this project will be well worth the sacrifice."

"Worth running yourself ragged, you mean."

"I won't have to for much longer. Just a few more days, and I'll have this thing cracked."

He reached for her shoulder, then glanced at his stained fingers and, seeming to think better of it, dropped his hand.

With each passing day, Alain's face became a little more gaunt, his beard a little more unkempt, the dark circles around his eyes a little more pronounced. But he assured Mavery that she had nothing to worry about, that his mysterious project—which he only worked on when she wasn't around—was inching ever closer to completion. And so, she pushed her concerns aside and focused on her own project.

On a bitterly cold Siddisday morning, Mavery arrived to find the door wide open. Alain was in the kitchen, balancing on a chair and securing a sapphire blue bundle of feygrass to one of the rafters.

"You went shopping without me?" Mavery demanded.

Alain yelped, clinging to the rafter with one hand. Once he'd stabilized himself, he grumbled, "I would have appreciated a warning knock—or a simple 'good morning,' for that matter."

Mavery gave the doorframe a quick rap. "Good morning. I thought you said supply runs would be my job from now on."

"I did, but in this instance, I only needed feygrass."

"Still, I could've stopped by Enid's shop on my way over, saved you the trouble."

"Oh, I didn't go to the Cracked Pestle. Now that I know of Enid's Brass Dragon ties, I can't in good conscience associate with a criminal, much less patronize her shop, can I?"

Mavery's stomach lurched. She was thankful he was too preoccupied with tying a knot to notice her mouth hanging open.

He sighed. "Compared to Enid's prices, the other apothecaries charge a small fortune. I suppose crime *does* pay. Pity." He gave the knot a final tug, then hopped down from the chair. "Are you feeling all right? You're looking a little peaky."

"I'm fine." She glanced away. "Just a bit chilled from the walk over, is all."

"Good thing I restocked on feygrass. If you need me to brew you a cup, just say the word. But, for now, out with you! The project's not quite finished, but you've seen quite enough." Alain shooed her into the sitting room, then closed the kitchen door behind them. "On a similar note, yesterday you said that *you* had something to show *me*."

Mavery's stomach performed another leap. She'd completely forgotten about her plan to show him the catalog. She retrieved the book from her chair, and her knuckles paled as she gripped its leather cover. Like Alain's project, this one was nowhere near ready; she had hundreds of books left to catalog, and her system would likely need some revising.

But a glint in Alain's eyes, like that of a child anticipating an Yvernal gift, compelled her to hand over the book. When he turned to the key on the first page, she rushed to his side, then lingered over his shoulder as she quickly explained the shorthand she'd devised: a string of letters, numbers, and symbols representing each book's author, publication date, subject matter, and location on Alain's shelves.

"I wanted this to be more than a simple list of every book you own," she said quickly. "With a single line of writing, you'll know what each book is about, and where to find it."

"May I?"

Mavery nodded. She chewed a hangnail while she watched him

test her system. He turned to a random page, picked a book from the list, then located it on the shelf. The process took him not even half a minute.

"This is your own invention?"

She nodded slowly.

He grinned. "This is *brilliant*!"

She released a held breath before returning his smile.

"Finding a single book used to take me the better part of an hour, assuming I didn't grow so frustrated, I gave up altogether. Where did you come up with this idea?"

"Previous employment. Let's just leave it at that."

Her shorthand had been adapted from the Brass Dragons' code for marking buildings—the same one she'd used to confirm the Crackled Pestle's affiliation with the guild. A handful of letters and symbols could denote a wealth of information: whose protection the building was under, the type of loot inside, the locations of weak points to exploit during break-ins. Of course, she couldn't tell Alain any of that.

"In any case, this is excellent work." He handed back the catalog. "It's a bit different than what the University's library uses, but every arcanist devises their own system."

"Oh, please." She rolled her eyes. "If I'm an arcanist, then you're a master painter."

Arcanists were a step above librarians. Apart from cataloging books and spells, they would occasionally pen translations or delve into ruins to recover ancient tomes. Most importantly, they controlled what knowledge was housed within their libraries—and who was granted access to them.

"Fair enough," Alain said. "Had you ever considered becoming one?"

Mavery nodded. "It was why I enrolled at Atterdell in the first place."

Becoming an arcanist was more straightforward than becoming a wizard—it required only four years of university, then sitting a certification exam—but it was by no means easier. Some wizards hired arcanists to manage their private libraries, but becoming a university's arcanist was far more prestigious. Not to mention, far more lucrative. While the University of Leyport's library boasted three arcanists, that was the exception to the rule; most wizarding schools had only one. Such positions were so rare, becoming a wizard had once been Mavery's *backup* plan, as ridiculous as that seemed in hindsight.

"You attended *Atterdell* for arcanist studies? No wonder you—"

He blanched as the two of them locked eyes. The unspoken truth hung heavily in the air between them. It had been nearly three weeks since Mavery had come across the letter from Atterdell. And yet, Alain still hadn't mentioned it.

Since then, she'd felt as though she were balancing on the edge of a blade, and every revelation about her past nudged her a bit further from the center. He'd kept her around despite her lack of credentials, her vague ties to the Brass Dragons, her invasion of his private room. She wanted to know *why*, even if it meant revealing that she'd violated his privacy—again. Even if it delivered the final push that tipped her over the edge.

"Go on," she said, clutching the catalog to her chest. "Say it."

"Er...say what?"

She sighed. "I'm a dropout. There's no use hiding it; you've known for weeks now. I found your letters. Not just the one from Atterdell, but the one from the High—"

"Good."

She blinked at him. "Wait, what?"

"It never occurred to you that I *wanted* you to find those letters?"

It *had* struck her as odd that he'd left them in an unlocked drawer after he'd so carefully hidden everything else. Her breath hitched as she realized he'd intentionally led the ley line to his desk, to make the letters easier to spot.

"Why?" she asked.

Alain lowered his head. "I wanted to tell you that you were working for a wizard who had tarnished his reputation so tremendously, he was on the verge of losing his rank. But when I couldn't find the words, I decided to let those letters speak for me. You'd already proven the inquisitive sort. I knew if I left you to your own devices, you would discover them."

"But that doesn't explain the Atterdell letter. Why have you kept me around, knowing full well I don't have an education?"

"Because you're a Senser, of course! I would be a fool to turn you away. And, Senser or not, you've already proven your worth." He pointed at the catalog, then smiled wryly. "Besides, that letter only confirmed what I'd already suspected from your first day of work: that you had, at most, a first-year education. Believe me, no university graduate *ever* forgets Venetum's First Principle.

"Furthermore, I doubted your family name was actually Reynard. It seems you're unfamiliar with the Dauphinian folktale, *Reynard the Three-Tailed Trickster*, else you would've chosen a less obvious alias."

"If you knew all along, why didn't you say anything?"

"I assumed you would eventually come forward on your own." Alain shrugged. "And, well, here we are."

Mavery gazed at her feet. "Here we are."

For a moment, she'd feared that this would be the end of everything: steady wages for work that she'd grown proud of, afternoon teas that had become far more enjoyable, and—above all else—

Alain cleared his throat, jostling her from her thoughts.

"Well, to return to what we were saying: you may not be an arcanist *officially*, but I'll consider you one in my book, if you'll pardon the play on words."

Without thinking, she nudged him in the ribs.

"Ouch!" he cried, then paired it with a chuckle.

"Careful. Make one too many puns, and this arcanist will start tossing your books out the window—or into the fireplace."

"Yes, you're definitely an arcanist." He sighed, rolled his eyes in mock exasperation. "You've held the title for not even a minute, and already you're drunk with power."

They shared a laugh, though for Mavery the moment of levity was short-lived. Alain didn't care that she wasn't a university graduate. He didn't even seem to care that she'd lied about it. But one detail about her past still remained a secret, and if it ever came to light, she doubted he would be so forgiving.

I can't in good conscience associate with a criminal.

If he thought that of Enid, someone he'd known for years, he'd certainly think that of someone he'd known for only a month. And wasn't Mavery's relationship with him equally transactional in nature? She was nothing more than a commodity to him. He only kept her around because she was a Senser with a knack for organizing books.

She should have left the day she discovered those letters and learned that Alain had begun looking into her past. Deep down, she knew this man had nothing worth stealing; the only thing keeping her here was a foolish belief that she could make this arrangement last in the long term. The longer she stayed, the greater the odds he would learn what kind of person she truly was. She needed to cut her losses and leave before he made that decision for her.

Seventeen

Mavery spent her day off plotting her next move. She'd first considered taking her savings and running off in the middle of the night. But no, she'd done enough of that for one lifetime. Alain had been decent to her in the short time they'd known each other; she at least owed him a proper goodbye.

Ultimately, she decided to announce her resignation first thing on Onisday morning. She would keep the details vague: she'd been presented with another job opportunity that was conveniently far away from Leyport. She would wish him luck with his current endeavors, then bid him farewell with a shaky promise to keep in touch. Then, she would seek out another mark or, gods forbid, another crew.

It was far from an ideal plan, but what choice did she have?

Alain opened the door before she barely had the chance to knock. She wondered whether he'd augmented a resonating ward for her, or if he'd been standing by the door with his ear pressed to it.

"At last, you're here!" he said, though she was precisely on time—same as every morning. He grasped her by the shoulders and steered her toward the sofa, moving so quickly he nearly caused her to trip over her own feet. "Come in, take a seat. I have something to show you."

"I need to talk to you about something," she said, but he was already halfway to the kitchen. "Alain, did you hear me?"

"Yes, we'll speak in a moment. But first..."

He slipped through the doorway, and the clinking of alchemy equipment soon followed. Mavery dropped her pack at her feet, then dropped herself onto the sofa. No doubt, he'd finally completed his experiment. She would humor him, let him indulge in his excitement for a moment before she snuffed it out.

He returned carrying a single teacup. He placed it before her on the table, then bounced on his heels as he waited. Simply watching him made her exhausted.

She raised the cup and peered at the liquid. It was black as tar and nearly as viscous, with a medicinal smell that made her nose scrunch.

"Remember the café we visited almost a fortnight ago?" Alain asked. "Think of this as my own take on alchemical tea."

Whatever he called it made it no less unsettling. Mavery thought back to the assortment of ingredients he'd bought from Enid. Based on how his supplies had dwindled, every ingredient had gone into making this potion, including...

"Don't tell me you put the powdered claws in *this*."

"Only a very small amount." She balked, and he dismissively waved a hand. "As the old saying goes, the difference between medicine and poison is all in the dosage. I've tested it myself multiple times and found that it's perfectly safe. As for its effectiveness, well, only *you* can determine that."

"And what, exactly, is this supposed to do?"

Alain sighed. "A healthy dose of skepticism is a virtuous trait for a scholar, Mavery, but you *can* have too much of a good thing."

She gave him a hard stare. "I'm not drinking this until you tell me what it does."

"But that would spoil the surprise."

"*Alain...*"

"All right!" He threw up his hands. "I'll give you a hint: I'm hoping this alleviates some...*symptoms*...that are specific to you."

"I hope, for your sake, you're referring to my Senses." She raised an eyebrow, then stifled a laugh as his face turned red.

"I...I've already said too much," he sputtered. "You're just going to have to trust me."

Mavery's instincts told her to never trust a suspicious drink—especially if said drink contained poisonous ingredients, and doubly so if said drink was a potion crafted by someone who only *dabbled* in alchemy. On the liquid's dark surface, her reflection stared back at her, then rippled as she exhaled.

"All right. How much of this do I have to drink?"

"This dosage is based on a rough estimate of your weight—"

She narrowed her eyes at him.

He cleared his throat. "Er, all of it. Best do it quickly."

She closed her eyes and threw it back like a shot of liquor. It had an astringent, slightly bitter taste, paired with the bergamot tea she liked. It was a bit gritty and didn't taste *good*, but she was able to keep it down.

She placed the empty teacup on the table and waited. A moment passed without feeling anything, not even a hint of protest from her stomach. She opened her eyes again to find Alain watching her intently.

"Well, do you feel anything?"

"No."

"Try looking at the door."

She peered over his shoulder, then gasped.

The warding magic had vanished.

She rose from the sofa and approached the door. The wards were still present, but she was likely seeing them as Alain did: a rippling effect instead of vibrant auras. There was no longer the hum of arcana, nor the metallic taste she'd grown to ignore whenever she was this close to the door. She turned to Alain, who hadn't taken his eyes off her. A smile tugged at the corner of his mouth.

"I take it the potion is working as intended." His tone was much calmer than she'd expected. She could only assume it was taking every crumb of his willpower to not boast right now.

She nodded. "I can't Sense a thing. This is... I don't know what to say."

"Before we get too carried away, let's test how it works on incantations."

He spoke a few syllables of Etherean. An orb of light appeared above his palm—the same one he'd conjured after catching her in the storage room. She felt no rush of Ether, no change in temperature.

"Nothing," she breathed. "How did you...?"

Alain made a fist and snuffed out the orb. He stepped forward, close enough for her to see how the brightness in his eyes outshone the darkness encircling them.

"Walking you through the entire process would take all morning. Key to it was determining the exact amount of kutauss claws to negate the side effects of your Senses, without negating any of your arcana. I used myself as a test subject. But because my ability to detect magic is a poor substitute for yours, there was much trial and error involved. Many late nights sampling far more potions than one ought to."

That explained the dark circles, the gauntness of his cheeks, the complexion that was more deathly pale than usual. It was no wonder he'd kept her in the dark. Had she known he was going to spend the past ten nights poisoning himself and forgoing sleep solely for her benefit, she would have put her foot down.

"Don't get me wrong," she said, "I appreciate it, but why go through all that trouble?"

"We'll soon be taking more frequent trips to the University. Eventually, we'll return there full time." He smiled. "We'll never get any work done if you're having endless headaches and chills."

She nodded as her heart sank. Of course he'd done all of this for practical reasons; a useful tool needed to be kept in prime working condition. It was ridiculous to hope, if only for a second, there had been more to it than that.

His smile faded. Softly, he said, "When your Senses overwhelmed you so much, you could hardly breathe..." He lowered his eyes as he raked his fingers through his hair. "I can't tell you how many times I've thought back to that. And later that day, when you drank that tea, I knew I could find some way to help you. Not to remove your Senses altogether, but to give you more than a single moment of relief."

He took another step forward and, just as he'd done in the corridor outside Nezima's classroom, he touched her shoulder. She glanced at his hand, then upward, until her eyes met his. His gaze was so soft, so focused, a different instinct urged her to look away. But she held it, even as her pulse raced and the air around her became sweltering.

"I once said I would find a way to thank you for cleaning up my messes. I hope this potion is adequate."

"It's…"

Her breath caught in her lungs. Her mouth suddenly turned dry.

"Er…excuse me," she muttered.

She rushed into the bathroom and closed the door. As she leaned against it, tears stung her eyes, but trying to blink them back was no use; they broke free in hot, wet rivulets. She lunged for the sink, turned the tap, hoped the running water would drown her out as she leaned against the basin and sobbed.

Gods, when had she last allowed herself a good long cry?

Paired with relief was a cascade of every emotion she'd tamped down and tucked away for over a month. Altogether, they were too strong to suppress. Individually, they were too fleeting to grasp.

And it was all because she couldn't recall anyone in recent memory doing something so kind for her, because she'd done nothing in recent memory that made her worthy of such kindness. She especially didn't deserve kindness from the man she intended to, if not rob, then use as a means of robbing someone else. And at the heart of this whirlwind was Neldren, that godsdamned *bastard*, for betraying her, for being the reason she was in this mess in the first place.

With the next sob came a surge of arcana. Like a rushing flood against a cracked dam, unbridled magic broke through her body and ricocheted off the bathroom mirror. She yelped, stumbled backward, collided with the linen cabinet. The bolt of magic dissipated midair but left behind a spiderweb of cracked glass.

Right. That's *why a good long cry is a bad idea.*

Now that the surge had passed, she turned off the tap and examined her face in the broken mirror. Her eyes and nose were red and swollen, her cheeks damp. And she was certain Alain had heard the commotion, even over the running tap. She couldn't hide in here forever. She dried her face with the hand towel and opened the door.

In unison, she and Alain flinched, gasped. He had been waiting outside, leaning against the doorframe.

"Are you all right? The tea didn't make you ill?"

"I'm fine." Her voice was thick, her throat raspy.

"Oh, that's a relief," he sighed. "I was considering whether to change the—"

She threw her arms around his shoulders. His body stiffened as he emitted a chuckle that sounded equal parts surprised and nervous.

"It's more than adequate," she whispered.

He relaxed against her.

"I'm glad," he whispered back.

His arms wrapped around the small of her back. And then her breath hitched as what she'd intended to be a brief, appreciative hug escalated to a far more intimate embrace. He pulled her closer, leaving no space between them.

A bit to her own surprise, she rested her chin against his shoulder. He clung to her even more tightly, as though afraid of what would happen when he let go. She didn't want to find out, either. So, they remained that way for a moment longer, his body warming hers, her breaths slowing to match his.

When he pulled back, his hands shifted to her waist, just above her hips. Hers skimmed down his arms and came to rest at his elbows. There was a mistiness to his eyes, and she wondered if he'd suppressed a sob of his own.

"Are *you* all right?" she asked.

"Me?" He cleared his throat. "Never better."

It was the least convincing lie she'd ever heard.

"I'm just relieved that my little experiment was successful."

She scoffed. " 'Little experiment'? Don't be so godsdamned modest. And you didn't need to do all that just for me."

"I know I didn't need to." He smiled at her. "But I *wanted* to."

There was no fire in the hearth, but the room had turned oppressively hot again. Then, with a grimace, she remembered what had happened in the bathroom.

"Well, as a token of my gratitude, I broke your mirror."

He laughed. "Not on purpose, I hope?"

"No, of course not! I had a magic surge just now—my first in over a year, actually."

"Do you think the potion had something to do with it?"

"Er, not directly. My surges have always been more of an...emotional reaction."

She looked down and realized their hands were still on each other. She cleared her throat and shifted her eyes, drawing his attention to how his fingers still pressed into her hips, though not uncomfortably. From the way his eyes widened and his face flushed, he'd also forgotten how they were standing. They both dropped their hands, backed away, exchanged a nervous laugh. But the awkwardness carried an undercurrent of regret for breaking their connection so soon.

"So, er, how long will this potion last?" Mavery asked.

"A dose of that quantity should last four hours, give or take," Alain said. "That will give us ample time for the second phase of this test run, if you're interested."

"What did you have in mind?"

"We'll take another trip to the University, see how the potion works against larger, more concentrated sources of magic. Plus, Kazamin sent word the other day that the incomplete Sensing spell he'd told us about is now available. There's but one problem: the tome is so old and delicate, it cannot leave the library. So, if we want to study it thoroughly, what I'd hoped would be a quick trip to campus may take a few hours."

"If you found out days ago, why haven't you gone already?"

The High Council presentation was now less than three weeks away. She had expected him to jump at the first opportunity to continue the research that would secure his wizard rank.

"Well, I *did* promise to involve you with every step of this spell. I had to make sure the potion was ready, so you could join me without any ill effects."

She smiled. If he continued on like this, she would feel obligated to embrace him again...though she supposed there were worse things she could do.

"By the way, what did you want to talk about?"

Mavery blinked at him. "Oh, er... Honestly, I don't remember." She shrugged. It wasn't a complete lie; she'd almost forgotten about her plan to resign and leave Leyport. "Must've not been all that important."

In hindsight, perhaps she'd been too hasty. Her life had been little more than an endless string of temporary arrangements, all born out of convenience and built on half-truths. Wasn't this just the latest one? Why not stay a little longer and enjoy it while it lasted?

Eighteen

When they arrived at Kazamin's office, the old wizard was hunched over a tome that took up the full width of his desk, examining it with a magnifying glass. Alain knocked on the doorframe, and Kazamin peered up at them with a comically enlarged eye.

"Ah, Aventus! Come in, come in," he said. With a grunt and a creaking of joints, he closed the massive book. "It's good to see you again! But, er, remind me why you are here. Did we have an appointment?"

"I'm here to see Enodus's spell tome. Your letter said to report to you first."

"Oh, of course! Bear with me for one moment while I write your pass for the portal room."

From a desk drawer, he pulled out a leaf of vellum and a quill—archaic, even for a man his age—and began to write. While he was distracted, Mavery took the opportunity to inch toward the closest curio cabinet.

"It's not in our library?" Alain asked.

"No, the tome is too delicate to leave the University of North Fenutia's library. Did I not mention that in my letter?"

"You said I could view it 'at the library.' Now that I think on it, you didn't specify which one."

"My apologies. My mind has been a bit addled as of late."

That was excellent news to Mavery. Even better, the curio cabinet's lock appeared more decorative than protective. She wouldn't even need her tools; a hairpin or a letter opener would do.

"Here you are," Kazamin said. "One pass for the University of North Fenutia's portal. When you arrive, ask to speak to Dolokir. He will be expecting you."

"Thank you, sir, but I see this pass has only my name on it. What about my assistant?"

"Oh, no, she cannot go with you."

That tore Mavery's attention away from the cabinet. She stepped forward.

"What do you mean I can't go?"

Alain winced. Kazamin balked at her, much like he had during their first meeting when she'd spoken out of turn.

"The tome is in the special collections, which are only accessible to wizards," Kazamin said tersely. "Since you are *not* a wizard, you are not allowed entry."

"But the whole point of his research is to make a Sensing spell. Shouldn't the fact that I'm a Senser count for something?"

"I'm sorry, Margery—"

"*Mavery!*"

"—but these are direct orders from North Fenutia's arcanist. Even if I had any say in the matter, your lack of decorum would make me loath to write you any passes, I can assure you of that!"

She opened her mouth. Before she could continue her tirade, Alain grasped her arm.

"Don't," he whispered, then dragged her toward the door. Over his shoulder, he called to Kazamin, "Thank you, sir. I appreciate the efforts you took to arrange this."

"Think nothing of it," Kazamin said, cheerful once again. "I hope your research proves fruitful. Oh, and Aventus?"

Alain stopped and turned to the dean.

"You would be wise to review the Covenants with your new assistant."

Mavery continued fuming in silence as Alain led her into his office and closed the door behind them. The room was so small, they were practically standing on top of each other. The tiny window provided little natural light, but it was enough to half-illuminate Alain's frown as he rubbed his temples.

"I understand your frustrations, Mavery, but please watch your tone around my supervisor."

"I will once that old codger bothers to remember my name," she muttered.

"What was that?"

"Nothing." She sighed. "I'll try to be on my best behavior from now on. And what did he say on the way out? Something about some Covenants?"

"*The Covenants of Wizarding Decorum*. Essentially, it's a long list of professional standards all wizards are expected to follow. I have a copy around here...somewhere." He glanced at the mountain of dust-coated papers on his desk, then shrugged. "Well, what matters most is that we treat our fellow scholars with respect."

She rolled her eyes. "That 'respect' goes in one direction, I take it. Does that arcanist think my non-wizard fingers will taint their precious books?"

"Trust me, I like this as much as you do, but if that's how the arcanist wishes to run their library, then that's how it must be."

Mavery scoffed, though she should have known better than to expect anything else from the gatekeepers of arcane knowledge. Alain placed his hand on her shoulder. Her mood turned slightly less sour.

"I'll be sure to take copious notes," he said. "If need be, I will stay there all afternoon, until I've made a perfect copy of the spell tome."

"And what am *I* supposed to do all afternoon?"

"Go about campus, attend a class or two. Assistants do it all the time. No one will bat an eye, so long as you're wearing that." He nodded to her black robe.

She *was* eager to learn more about magic. Almost as eager as she was to break into Kazamin's office and stuff her pockets with curios. She didn't even care if they were worthless; she was motivated purely by spite. Maybe she would have time for classes *and* some petty thievery.

"All right," she said, "but how am I supposed to know when you're back?"

Alain walked around the desk and began rummaging through the drawers.

"There's one," he muttered. "Now, where is the other...?"

While he was preoccupied, she swiped a letter opener from atop his desk, then slipped it in her pocket. Just in case.

"Ah, here we are."

Alain held out his palm, revealing a pair of stones that were roughly the size of hen's eggs. They were identical, from their deep scarlet backing, to their bands of rose-tinted quartz.

"Bloodstones," she said.

"I assume if you recognize them, you're also familiar with how they work."

She nodded as she took one of the bloodstones. It was cool to the touch. Stones cut from the same vein, like this pair, were perfect mirrors of each other. She channeled a small amount of arcana into it, and the bloodstone warmed her skin as the quartz glowed. Alain's stone glowed simultaneously. Together, they bathed his office in pink-hued light. When she cut off her magic, the stones dulled, and the room darkened again.

"I'll send you a signal once I've returned to campus. Let's meet at the fountain," he said. Mavery slipped the stone in her pocket. As she grasped the doorknob, Alain added in a low voice, "I know it'll only be for a few hours, but...I'll miss having your company."

From the opposite side of the desk, he was too obscured in shadow for her to see his face, but she could feel his gaze on her. A tightness in her throat made it impossible to speak; even if she could, she wasn't sure what she would say. All she could manage was a brief nod before opening the door.

As she rode the lift back to the ground floor, her thoughts cycled between losing her temper at Kazamin, crying in the bathroom, bringing about a magic surge, *embracing* Alain...

Stop letting your emotions get the better of you.

Yet, was that really such a bad thing?

Being a career criminal meant being constantly on her guard; a single slip-up stood between pulling off a successful scheme and getting caught, thrown in prison, or worse. Compared to that life, being a wizard's assistant was akin to living in the lap of luxury. She could afford to let her guard down, even if that meant risking the occasional magic surge. And she couldn't think of anyone better equipped to handle those than a wizard.

If she wanted to make an honest living and become a legitimate wizard's assistant, she needed to be honest about *everything*. Coming clean about her past would be the first step.

Or, it could very well be the last.

"Gods damn it," she groaned as the lift opened. The student who'd been waiting outside the door gawked at Mavery as she trudged past.

The potion was still working. The corridor appeared as it had on the way up to the common room: completely devoid of magic. She passed by a classroom where a score of students practiced incantations, and she didn't Sense a thing. She continued past a few more rooms as she tried to gather her thoughts.

"—members of the Order of Asphodel—"

Mavery stopped. Where did she know that name? She carded through her memories, then recalled when Alain had shared his theories about the Innominate Temple. Or, at least, he'd *begun* to share his theories.

If her life as a wizard's assistant was on borrowed time, she wouldn't squander an opportunity to use one of its perks. She doubled back and approached the lecture hall.

The room had seating for at least fifty, but there were only eight students scattered between the two front rows. Mavery slipped into a chair in the back row. The professor glanced at her and, exactly as Alain had implied, continued on as if nothing had happened.

Around their neck, the professor wore a pendant depicting an hourglass. It marked them as a follower of Chroniclus, the Deity of Time and Records. Chroniclers, believing themselves to be observers of the world rather than participants, eschewed many societal norms: marriage, bearing children, owning property. And, like the deity they followed, they eschewed the concept of gender.

The professor was tall and willowy, with a light olive complexion. Their wrinkles suggested they were middle-aged, though their waist-length brown hair didn't have a single streak of gray.

"The Order was tried together, all twelve of them, on the eighth of Fervidor, 533," the professor said. "Does anyone remember from the reading what made this trial so significant?" Half the students raised their hands. The professor pointed at a blonde girl in the front row. "Yes, Ms. Harrow?"

"It was the shortest one in history."

"Exactly! From the opening statement to the final verdict, the trial took only two hours. It was presided over by Guiscard Pomeroy. That name should ring a bell or two, yes?"

Only Harrow and one other student nodded. Mavery vaguely recognized the name, though Dauphinian history had no shortage of Pomeroys. The professor sighed, then wrote the name on the blackboard.

"Do pay attention, as this *will* be on the final exam." At that, the students bowed their heads and readied their pens. "Guiscard Pomeroy was born in 466 to one of Dauphine's five Great Houses, he was the first Chancellor of the College of Mystics, and he was one of Tanarim's leading experts on Mysticism at the time of the Great Demonic Cleansing.

"Despite Pomeroy's lack of a legal background, the Church of the Dyad and the High Council of Wizards appointed him to preside over all Cleansing-related proceedings. There were no juries, no evidence presented during his trials. Pomeroy's rulings were based solely on his memory-reading spells."

That was a detail Mavery's history lessons had failed to mention. Now that she knew Mysticism had been involved, she would take those rulings with an ocean's worth of salt.

"He found all twelve members of the Order of Asphodel guilty of illegal uses of Necromancy, possession of demons, and conspiring to hide their founder's whereabouts. Can you guess what the punishment was for those crimes?" The professor raised their hands like an orchestra conductor. "Say it with me..."

"*Hanged by the neck until dead*," the class chanted in unison.

The professor chuckled. "Of course, you have no problem remembering the Church of the Dyad's execution method of choice. Yes, the members of the Order of Asphodel were hanged—all except for their founder, Aganast, who went missing a few weeks before the trial.

"When we next meet, we will cover another of Pomeroy's landmark cases, in which he ruled that demon*spawn* were to be treated as a separate species from demons."

A chime sounded, signaling the end of class. The students rose from their desks.

"Remember," the professor said, raising their voice over the scuffle, "your term papers are due at the beginning of class on Dredisday. Five pages—not four, not six, *five*."

As the students trickled out the back of the room, Mavery made her way to the front, where the professor was stuffing papers in their satchel. They glanced up as she approached.

"Hello, I'm Mavery—"

"Aventus's new assistant, and our resident Senser." They smiled. "Word travels fast around our department. I'm Selemin."

The two of them shook hands.

"So, you're a Chronicler?" Mavery pointed at Selemin's hourglass pendant.

"That, I am!" They smiled even wider. "Not many recognize it, so color me surprised—and a little impressed."

"I once met some Chroniclers in my travels." She recalled waking up with the worst hangover of her life—and one of those Chroniclers in her bed. "Though we didn't engage in many, er, *scholarly* discussions."

"Oh, you've met *those* Chroniclers." Selemin chuckled as Mavery furrowed her brow. "We fall into two camps. First, you have people like me, who practice our faith as professional historians. And then you have my..." They shook their head with a drawn-out sigh. "My *siblings in Chroniclus*, who use our faith as an excuse to gallivant about the continent and commit all sorts of debauchery. All in the name of 'recording events for posterity,' of course."

"If you're a historian, why are you in the Gardemancy Department and not the History Department?"

"Because it no longer exists." Mavery gawked at them, and they nodded gravely. "See, when the dean retired six years ago, the department was dismantled and I was thrown in with the Gardemancers. I'm an innate Soudremancer—not that I practice it much these days—so the higher-ups didn't know where else to put me." They shrugged. "At least it was better than getting sacked, like the rest of my colleagues."

"You're the University's *only* history professor?"

Selemin nodded. "When I first started teaching, Arcane History was part of the core curriculum, but now it's only an elective—and not a popular one, as I'm sure you noticed. These days, anything that's not directly related to fabrication research has to fight for the scraps." They cleared their throat. "Anyway, that's a topic I'd much rather get into after a couple of strong pints."

The arts had been one thing. To find out wizards also had little love for *arcane* history... But Mavery had a more pressing concern on her mind.

"Do you know anything about the Innominate Temple?" she asked.

"Only rumors and speculation, which is to say, not much at all." They tilted their head to one side. "Why do you ask?"

"Alain has a theory—"

"Who?"

"Er, Aventus."

They smirked. "Seems all that time he's spent with Declan has finally rubbed off on him, if he's also dropped his wizard name. All right, I'll bite. What's his theory?"

"He thinks the temple is connected to Ag—"

"Come now, Selemin, you've had your turn with this room. That is, unless you're planning to deliver my next lecture for me."

Mavery and Selemin turned to the door. Nezima had entered the classroom, flanked by three young women—including the black-haired woman Mavery had seen before, the one who knew Alain somehow. Once again, she'd been burdened with a large stack of papers. The other two assistants were empty-handed.

"Sorry, Nez," Selemin said. "I was having a chat with—"

"None other than the talk of the department," Nezima said. She stopped at the front of the room. Her assistants stood a few paces back, hovering like a trio of black-robed phantoms.

Selemin tilted their head, this time in the other direction. " 'Talk of the department'?"

"You missed the show, unfortunately. Mavery gave our dean quite the verbal thrashing."

Mavery scoffed. "It was hardly a—"

"Really!" Selemin's eyes widened. "What did she say?"

"I only caught a few words, but it was the first I'd heard him raise his voice in *ages.*"

Selemin cackled. "Oh, what I would've given to see the look on that miser's face!" They turned to Mavery. "I owe you a pint sometime. Maybe then we can get back to discussing that theory."

"What theory?" Nezima asked.

"Oh," Mavery said, "just one Al—*Aventus,* has about the In-nominate Temple."

Behind Nezima, papers scattered to the floor. The black-haired assistant yelped, then dropped to her knees.

"Gods above, girl," Nezima sighed. "Look at the mess you've made!"

As the assistant scrambled to gather up the papers—neither Nezima nor the other two assistants made any effort to help her—students began to fill the classroom. Selemin took this as their cue to leave.

"Nice meeting you, Mavery," they said. "And I'm serious about that pint."

"Likewise, and thanks."

"I must begin my preparations," Nezima said. "I do hope you'll stay and watch, Mavery. Perhaps you can relay to Aventus some advice on how to manage his classroom more effectively." Her lips curled into a wicked smile.

The professor snatched the papers from her assistant, who shot Mavery a glance as she received Nezima's hushed bout of criticism. Mavery, meanwhile, returned to her seat by the door.

Though Nezima had said *she* needed to prepare, her three

assistants did the majority of the work. They walked the perimeter of the room, reciting incantations that Mavery assumed were for protective wards. Though the spells were complex, she saw not a single aura and felt not even a hint of cold. Once their spellcasting was complete, the assistants sat in the back row, in the seats farthest from the door.

Nezima began her lecture immediately after the second chime, not wasting a second. She paced about the front of the room, delivering her lecture with the same intensity Mavery had once seen her use with Alain and Declan.

From what Mavery could gather, this was an upper-level course on advanced spellcraft. Some of the jargon Nezima spouted was familiar—the bits and pieces Mavery had absorbed from cataloging Alain's books. But it was still too technical for her to grasp, as were the spells Nezima demonstrated. At least Nezima's authoritative tone discouraged any nodding off.

"Taking into account Velimar's Principle of Arcana Conservancy, it follows that—"

In the front row, a pair of students exchanged whispers. Nezima stopped mid-sentence and turned to them with an icy glare. She continued to stare at them, completely silent, until the whispering subsided. The room grew so quiet, Mavery could hear nothing but her own heartbeat. Inside her pocket, her bloodstone warmed. She'd left Alain's office not even two hours ago. How could he be back this soon?

"Is there something you wish to share with the class, Mr. Pitchard?" Nezima said.

"N-no, ma'am."

"How about you, Ms. Apton?"

"Nothing, ma'am."

"Are you certain?" Nezima crossed her arms. "For you to interrupt my lecture, it must be of *world-shattering* importance."

While Nezima harangued her students on the importance of classroom decorum, Mavery slipped out of the lecture hall. She took a few steps down the corridor, then stopped and turned toward the lift.

She couldn't keep Alain waiting too long. And if she wanted

to make an honest living, going back upstairs was the last thing she ought to do.

But some habits were difficult to break.

Taking off at a slight jog, she headed for the lift.

Her heart skipped a beat upon finding the common room empty and every door closed—including the one to Kazamin's office. The potion had worn off, and so she could see that Kazamin hadn't warded his door. She hurried across the room, the plush carpet dampening her footfalls.

Kazamin's door was locked, and her soft knock received no response. She removed Alain's letter opener from her pocket, then jammed it into the slit between the door and its frame. It wasn't the most sophisticated break-in method—she wasn't skilled enough at Faisancy to manipulate a mundane lock—but it was the best she could do with the tools at her disposal. She shimmied the blade against the latch.

Behind her, another door opened. She stifled a curse as she tucked the letter opener inside her left sleeve.

"Old Kaz is out to lunch." The voice was familiar, as was the chuckle that followed. "This time, only literally."

Mavery clasped her hands behind her back as she turned to Declan. "Oh, this is *Kazamin's* door?" She glanced at it, then shook her head. "Well, no wonder my key wasn't working! These doors all look the same to me."

"That they do, hence the name plates."

He pointed to Kazamin's name, embedded in the wood at Mavery's eye level. She looked at it with faint surprise, as though she were seeing it for the first time.

"Gods, it's been a long day," she sighed. "I could use a drink."

"It's not even midday yet!" Declan's eyes widened, but then he gave a hearty laugh. "That's a feeling I know a little too well. I reckon you were looking for Alain's office."

Declan made a beckoning gesture, and she had no choice but

to follow him across the common room.

"What did he send you up here for?" he asked.

"Oh, just a book."

"Which one?"

Mavery was thankful Declan was leading the way and couldn't see her scowl. "Er...his copy of *The Covenants of Wizarding Decorum.*" It was the first thing that came to mind.

Declan shook his head. "Knowing the state of his office, you'll be in there all night trying to find the damn thing." He stopped outside Alain's door and turned to her. "Why don't you borrow my copy? About time someone put it to good use."

She smiled, hardly believing her luck. "That's so kind of you."

As Declan disappeared inside his office, she slipped the letter opener beneath Alain's door. Getting rid of it was her best option; she doubted she would have another chance at Kazamin's office. Declan returned and handed her the book. It was much smaller than she'd expected—barely larger than a field guide. As she slipped the book into her pocket, she decided to indulge another of her curiosities.

"Can I ask you something? It's about Alain."

Declan raised his brows. "Er...sure."

"I was wondering why he went on sabbatical."

"He hasn't told you himself?"

"He doesn't want to talk about it. I was thinking, considering you're good friends, he would have told *you.*"

Declan's bushy mustache twitched as he passed his fingers through his thinning red hair. He was stalling, but Mavery pegged him as the type who wouldn't dare turn down a woman in need. She gave him her best pleading look: knitted brow, wringing hands, a slight pout.

"All right," he groaned, "but, by Tanar's beard, don't tell him I told you any of this."

"Of course." She gently touched his arm. "Your secret is safe with me."

"A year ago—almost to the day, come to think—he sent his three assistants on a research trip. Only two of them came back." He sighed. "In our line of work, death's simply part of the job, but the poor lad was in a right state over it. Missed Conor's funeral because he'd drunk himself into a stupor. He canceled half his classes, then stopped showing up to work altogether—during final exams, no less.

"Kazamin put him on personal leave, and I had to step in and help Alain's last two assistants cover exams. Then Lorcan resigned, and it was just down to Wren. And then *she* resigned a few months later and started working for Nezima."

That explained Wren and Alain's frigid exchange from the other week. If only Mavery could separate Wren from Nezima for a few minutes and hear her side of the story...

It was then she realized Declan was staring at her pocket. She looked down to see pink light emanating through the black fabric.

"That's Alain," she said. "I shouldn't keep him waiting. Thank you again for the book—and for the chat."

"Any time," Declan said with a nod. As Mavery hurried across the common room, he called after her, "And tell that wizard of yours to answer my letters once in a while!"

Nineteen

Alain shivered. The linen version of his faculty robe did little to protect him from the chill. Though the ground was warm enough for the jonquils to unfurl their yellow blooms, the air was too frigid to linger outside without a proper coat. Save for a handful of students who were not only forgoing coats, but *lounging* on the quad as though it were the peak of Fervidor. Alain shook his head, doubting that he'd ever been that foolhardy.

He blew hot air on his shaking hands, then stuffed them inside his pockets. He fed the bloodstone a second burst of arcana.

What's taking her so long?

Perhaps she'd taken his advice and was currently engaged in a lecture. Or, perhaps she'd stopped by the University's library and was lost within the pages of a book.

Or, perhaps she was informing Nezima of her progress. After all, compared to the first visit, Mavery had seemed far more eager to visit campus today...

Stop it.

That was one of his many half-baked conspiracy theories, nothing more. He needed to believe that she was here of her own accord, that she was truly working for him, that the embrace they'd shared had been as genuine as her reaction to the potion.

As he thought back on that moment, a fluttering sensation

rippled through his chest. It had been so long since he'd last held anyone in that way—since *he'd* last been held in that way. He'd certainly not received any warmth from his mother; hugging her was akin to wrapping one's arms around a statue. Even when he was a child, her displays of affection had been, at best, perfunctory.

His stomach twisted into a knot. Had he returned Mavery's friendly gesture with too much enthusiasm? What if he'd come off too strongly, and she was now avoiding him?

To his left, the doors of the faculty tower opened. At the sight of Mavery passing through the arched entrance, his stomach stirred again, but this time the sensation was lighter, more pleasant. In the midday sun, her hair was the color of wheat at harvest. She tucked a lock of it behind her ear as she approached him at a jog.

"Sorry," she said, a bit short of breath, her cheeks flushed. "I got tied up chatting with Declan."

He'd been fretting over nothing. Declan wouldn't ever conspire against him. Well, not regarding anything *career-ending,* at least. Alain could have laughed—or perhaps even cried—with relief, but he forced himself to retain his composure.

"How was the library?" Mavery asked. "Did you learn anything from the spell tome?"

"Did I!" He pulled his notebook from his satchel. "My appointment was limited to only an hour—something else Kazamin failed to mention. Thankfully, the tome itself was so short, that was just enough time to make a complete transcription."

He'd brought a fresh notebook for this occasion but had only filled a quarter of it. Most of his writing was devoted to the incantation—Etherean runes that he knew Mavery couldn't yet decipher. She skimmed past those and instead focused on the pages that were in Fenutian. The longer she read, the more her brow relaxed and the corner of her lips quirked into a smile. Alain recalled that she'd once mentioned something about knowing Fenutian...and then he winced at the asinine comment he'd made. He would have to find some way to apologize for that.

When she reached the final page, she closed the book and looked up. Her eyes glinted with a spark of inspiration that made them even more vibrant than usual. They were a spring green that, like a budding flower, had the hint of something even more brilliant beneath the surface, waiting to burst with life. Were he to capture that color in paint, he would need to add a touch of ochre, or perhaps...

She smiled at him with that slightly crooked smile, and his head swam as though he'd drunk an entire glass of wine in a single swallow. Gods, she was stunning. She was—

Oh, no.

No, no, no.

This line of thinking could only end in disaster.

Mavery was his assistant. Perhaps he could even call her his friend. But she wouldn't—she *couldn't*—ever be anything more than that.

He cleared his throat, hoping he'd retained enough of his wits to avoid gawking at her like some lecher.

"Er...well?" he asked. "What does it say?"

"I'll need to sit with this for some time, but from a quick skim, it seems to be some sort of treatise on Sensing. I saw the words 'I' and 'my' quite a lot, so he must have based much of this on his own experiences. That alone makes his tome worth its weight in silver."

"Could you translate it?"

"His writing style is a bit antiquated, so it would take some time—and a dictionary. But yes, I think I can manage that." She handed back the notebook. "What about the incantation? Do you think you can complete it?"

He nodded. "With heaps of modifications based on recent advancements in Etherean Studies. At least our late Fenutian friend has given us a head start." He tucked the notebook back in his satchel. "Speaking of Etherean Studies, I'd say it's about time for those lessons I promised you."

Mavery pursed her lips, and Alain desperately searched for another place to focus his gaze. Her chin was still too close, staring at her nose seemed a bit rude, returning to her eyes was completely out of the question. He settled on her left earlobe.

"Didn't you say that would happen *after* I found all the library books?" she asked. "Last time I checked, there were still some left."

He shrugged. "Close enough. If you're to assist me with this spell, you need to at least know the basics. Besides, when I made that stipulation, I was dreading the idea of teaching again." He gave her a coy smile. "But I don't dread the idea of teaching *you.*"

The words slipped out automatically. Before he could fully consider what he'd just said, a pair of arms grasped him around the middle.

The quad dissipated.

He was in the back room of a dimly lit pub. He could almost taste the sour ale coating the back of his throat, smell the cigar smoke permeating the air. A different pair of arms—leaner, yet stronger—now clung around his abdomen, pulling him into an embrace that had lost all semblance of comfort. Despite the warm breath against his neck, he'd never felt so cold.

What are you doing?

Didn't you say you wanted me?

Not here, of all places! You know we have to follow the—

Shh. Not another word about those bloody Covenants.

The arms tightened their hold on him.

Ensnared him.

His lungs burned.

Air. He needed air.

"Alain?"

He gasped. The dark, smoke-filled room faded, and he now found himself back on the quad, hunched over the fountain. His knuckles, bone-white, gripped the stone basin. Another set of fingers rested against his forearm. He turned, meeting a pair of green eyes beneath a deeply furrowed brow.

"Alain, are you all right?" Mavery asked.

He blinked slowly as he tried to recall what had happened over the past few...hours? Minutes? No, it must have been only seconds.

Mavery pulled her hand away as he stood up straight, adjusted his robe.

"Yes, I'm fine." He cleared his throat. "Er...do you recall what I said earlier about decorum?" Mavery nodded slowly. "Well, the University frowns upon displays of affection while in public. Can't have professors showing any favoritism."

She opened her mouth, hesitated. "That makes sense." She

tucked another lock behind her ear. "I suppose I got a bit too excited about those Etherean lessons. Sorry."

His stomach sank. "You did nothing wrong. I should have told you about the Covenants long before now. I'd give you my copy, if only I remembered where—"

Mavery smiled as she pulled that exact book from her pocket.

Alain's jaw slackened. "How—?"

"Declan let me borrow his copy." She shrugged. "It's a long story."

Knowing Declan, the man had sought any excuse to offload that book.

"Are you sure everything's all right?" Mavery asked.

Alain waved a hand. "Oh, you know me. Just lost in thought, especially now that I have this spell tome to pore over."

Her frown indicated that she didn't believe a word of it. But how could he even begin to explain what was actually on his mind?

I just relived a moment from what was not only the worst night of my life, but a precursor to my greatest failure.

No one, especially not his assistant, deserved to be burdened with that knowledge; it was his alone to bear. He shouldered his satchel and turned away from the fountain.

"Let's call it a day and get some rest," he said. "Tomorrow, our *real* work begins."

TWENTY

"Please tell me you did something other than study that spell tome all night."

"That depends. Does eating count?"

"*That* depends. Was it something other than tea and bread?"

Alain hesitated. "I think this is a conversation best cut short."

Shaking her head, Mavery crossed the threshold and dropped her pack in its usual spot by the desk. Gods help her, she would find some way to force this man to take a night off. There was still an abundance of alchemical supplies in the next room, including dried nightshade hanging from one of the rafters. A single petal, ground into powder and mixed into his tea, would put him to sleep for a few hours...

No, she wasn't yet that desperate.

"I know what you're thinking," he said. "I failed to take my own advice and get some rest. But you won't believe the progress I've made!"

His notes blanketed the tea table. To her, they were gibberish. One page was completely covered in inkblots; either Alain had spilled an entire well upon it, or his pen had ruptured under the strain of his frenzied writing.

He paced around the tea table as he explained what had kept him up all night. Mavery nodded as she tried to follow along.

"...And so, Enodus's incantation will reveal the auras of warding magic, but only in the color of the Ether, which is not actually a color, as the Ether is an interaction of wavelengths and energy. That would be akin to saying light itself is a color, when it's really a spectrum of—"

"Alain, focus!"

"Right." He cleared his throat. "First, we will need to complete Enodus's spell, which will serve as the primary incantation. Then..."

From his mouth flowed a deluge of names and theorems. Each was more obscure than the last, but he rattled them off as easily as recalling his own name. When he finally paused to take a breath, Mavery seized the opportunity and placed a hand on his shoulder.

"You lost me about halfway through all that, but I gather you have a plan for finishing the spell."

"In essence, yes. But first things first: are you ready for an Etherean lesson?"

"Do you need to ask?" Remembering the decorum Nezima had demanded yesterday in the lecture hall, she threw Alain a smirk. "Though I hope you're not expecting me to address you as 'sir' the entire time."

He returned her smile. "Only if you want me to address you as 'Ms. Culwich'...or, is it '*Mrs.* Culwich'?"

She raised her eyebrows. "You think I look like the marrying type? I should be flattered."

He laughed, and it was then Mavery realized she was still grasping his shoulder. Though he made no mention of it, she snatched her hand back anyway. Her heart thrummed annoyingly against her ribcage as she took a seat on the sofa. Meanwhile, Alain retrieved something from his desk.

He seemed in much better spirits today. Since parting ways yesterday, she'd replayed their exchange by the fountain countless times. She'd been so thrilled by the idea of Etherean lessons, she'd impulsively thrown her arms around him. And he, just as impulsively, had pushed her away and collapsed against the fountain. She'd worried about him flinging into the water the remains of his breakfast, if not himself. Before regaining his senses, he'd muttered something she'd had to lean in closely to discern.

Not here...not here...not here...

Last night, she'd read *The Covenants of Wizarding Decorum* from cover to cover. While she'd found nothing that forbade a simple embrace between colleagues, she'd come across a covenant that was along those same lines:

> Faculty holding the title of Professor are prohibited from engaging in romantic relationships—including, but not limited to, courtships and marriage—with any Wizard's Assistant.

Had he feared that the handful of students and professors on the quad would mistake them for something beyond colleagues, beyond even friends? Either way, she wasn't stung by his rejection; it was clear he hadn't been himself in that moment. And it was clear that whatever had forced that sudden change ran more deeply than he was willing to admit.

He turned away from his desk, and nothing in his expression indicated that he was also thinking of yesterday afternoon. He had a battered notebook tucked under his arm, and he placed an equally worn book on the tea table. Upon reading its title, Mavery's worries vanished—along with her enthusiasm.

"*The Etherean Alphabet Primer.*" She frowned. "I thought you were going to teach me something."

"I am. This is how I begin every first-year Etherean course."

"By practicing letters?"

"*Runes.*"

Her eyes narrowed. "Do you use that tone with all your students?"

"What tone?"

"The same one you used when we first met, when you corrected my pronunciation, dismissed all of my credentials—well, all except for my being a Senser."

He stared at her blankly, mouth agape, as if he couldn't find the words. Then, a flush of scarlet crept up his neck.

"Oh, that," he said, gazing downward. "I wasn't thinking at the time. Well, I *was* thinking, but about the reaction you would receive from one of my colleagues, should I have passed you along to, gods forbid, someone like Nezima."

Mavery replied with a slight nod. She could only imagine how Nezima would react to a prospective assistant showing up without so much as a transcript.

"At least, that's the way I saw it," Alain continued. "But as for just now, I honestly hadn't a clue. And if that's how I came across to my *students*, well..." For a moment, he trailed off with that blank look on his face again. "Well, that explains quite a lot."

Mavery sighed. "Look, if there's one thing I remember from my studies, it's practicing these runes for hours on end, until my hand turned numb and I was bored senseless."

"I understand it's tedious, but memorizing the alphabet is the first step toward learning Etherean. That's been the pedagogical standard for decades."

"But, despite all that writing and memorizing, I can't remember a single rune. Isn't that proof that the 'standard' is, if not useless, then at least flawed?"

His eyes widened, and he placed his hand to his chest as though she'd just stabbed him in the heart.

"What if you started by teaching me a very basic incantation?" she asked.

"But even the 'basics' can be dangerous without sufficient training."

"Then why not place some wards? I saw Nezima's assistants do that before her class yesterday."

He flinched, nearly dropping his notebook. "You...you attended one of *her* classes? Er, what did you think?"

"It all went over my head—but don't change the subject." She wagged a finger at him. "What I'm suggesting is, maybe if your students saw a little success with Etherean early on, that would keep them motivated through the more tedious lessons." She glanced at the primer. "At the very least, it might help those lessons stick."

Alain looked at the notebook he was holding. For a long moment, he didn't say anything. He broke the silence with a deep sigh.

"Though I hesitate to abandon my tried-and-true lesson plans," he said, "I suppose it's worth a shot."

He placed his notebook on the tea table, then walked to the closest corner of the room and recited an incantation. Mavery shivered as the nearby walls glowed with the violet aura of a sound-proofing ward. She'd expected a protective ward, but she supposed this spell was designed to keep the Ether itself from listening in, so to speak. Alain moved to the opposite side of the room and repeated the incantation. This time, the chill of Ether was weaker than before.

As he continued his preparations, Mavery examined his note-book. The spine was cracked, the pages' outer edges were curled and yellowed, some of the writing was smeared with tea stains. The oldest entries were from the Autumn 1033 term—almost eight years ago.

"These are your lecture notes?" she asked, though she had no doubt the handwriting—and the tea stains—were his.

"Yes, I've used that same notebook since my first year of teach-ing."

"As an assistant?"

"No, as a professor."

She furrowed her brow as she mentally rechecked her math. After he placed the final ward, he stood in front of her and held out his hand. She passed back the lecture notes.

"Then you became a professor at—"

"Twenty-six." He averted his eyes as he paged through the book. "Technically speaking, I was only *appointed* at twenty-six. I began teaching on my twenty-seventh birthday."

"But to become a professor, you have to be a wizard first."

He closed the book with a sigh. "Yes, I earned my rank a few months prior to my appointment."

She gawked at him. She'd known he was young for a wizard, but she never would have guessed that he'd held his rank for *eight years*.

As if he'd read her mind, he threw her an exasperated look. "Let's just say I was assistant to a wizard with impossibly high expectations and little tolerance for failure, which gave me ample motivation to extricate myself from that relationship.

"I graduated from the University at twenty-three, worked under Seringoth for two and a half years, earned my rank at twenty-six, and—thanks to an auspiciously timed opening at the University of Leyport—became a professor that same year." He raised his hands with an air of finality. "There, that ought to cover it."

"You were *Archmage Seringoth's* assistant?"

He winced. "Er, yes, though he was only an Elder Wizard at the time."

" '*Only* an Elder Wizard,' he says." Mavery scoffed, shaking her head. "If you worked for the most famous wizard on Perrun, how had I never heard of you?"

"Nothing kills a young wizard's notoriety faster than a quiet life in academia." He shrugged. "Now, if I'm not mistaken, *Etherean* is the subject of today's lesson. Shall we begin?"

She nodded, and he lowered himself beside her on the sofa, immediately to her right. He was so close, his thigh nudged hers when he leaned forward to push aside his ink-smeared notes. When he leaned back again, their shoulders were barely an inch apart. Whatever reservations he'd had yesterday out in public, they were no issue here in private.

She caught the scent of bergamot tea in his hair, on his breath. He had a black smudge on his left cheek, and she had an overwhelming desire to reach up and wipe it away. But she remained still, her hands clasped together in her lap.

"Rather than beginning with the alphabet, let's begin with a number," he said. "Twenty-eight. What does that bring to mind?"

She nearly sighed with relief for being given something more productive to focus on.

"Time, for starters," she said. "There are twenty-eight hours in a day, twenty-eight days in a month, two hundred and eighty days in a year. Oh, and I remember that Etherean has twenty-eight letters—sorry, *runes*."

He nodded. "The number twenty-eight has mathematical harmony, as it is the sum of all its divisors. But it also has Etherean harmony. You'll find many incantations that use exactly twenty-eight runes—each one representing a single syllable—though divisors and multiples of twenty-eight are more common. The one I'm about to teach you requires only seven syllables."

As Alain leaned forward again to lay out a blank sheet of paper, Mavery tried to ignore the slight pressure of his knee against hers. He wrote a line containing seven runes. Below that, he spelled them out phonetically.

"*Etero rah mira shah.*" His finger trailed along as he enunciated slowly. This incantation sounded familiar.

"*Etero rah mira shah,*" she repeated. The wards mitigated the full effects of the Ether; instead of a wintry gust throwing open a door, a draft slithered in through the keyhole.

"Remember to *roll* every 'r.' That's very crucial."

She repeated the incantation three more times before Alain nodded.

"I think you're ready to recite it without the warding magic," he said.

"Are you sure? Maybe I need one more go of it."

"Don't worry." He placed his hand over hers. "You'll be perfectly safe."

She turned her head and met his gaze. As usual, his eyes were a bit sunken and ringed with fatigue. But there was warmth within those pools of deepest brown: a glint of amber she'd never noticed before now, a softness she'd once impulsively turned away from, a reassurance that he wouldn't let her come to harm.

"All right," she said.

He unfurled her fingers and lifted her hand, palm facing up. He then raised his other hand overhead and, with a turn of his wrist, the violet-hued wards vanished.

"Remember," he said, "the Ether is very sensitive. You can whisper the words, or bellow them like an opera singer, if you so desire." From his soft laugh, she suspected he'd done the latter at least once. "The volume makes no difference, so long as your pronunciation is spot on."

She nodded, took a deep breath, then directed her next words to her palm. Her voice quavered as she spoke.

"*Etero rah mira shah.*"

Instead of feeling it against her skin, the flow of Ether was internal. In quick succession, it chilled her from the marrow, filled her lungs with ice, then streamed out with her breath. It left her tongue slightly numb, as if she'd eaten a mouthful of snow from a mountaintop.

She gasped when a small orb of white light appeared above her palm. It was bright enough to make her eyes sting, but it was too beautiful to look away from.

"You've just conjured a bit of the Ether itself," Alain said. "And on your first attempt, no less!"

She tore her gaze away from the orb and back to him. His smile was nearly as brilliant as the light hovering above her palm.

His fingertips remained against the back of her hand, to help her keep the orb at eye level. While she'd been focused on the spell, his free arm had draped along her upper back in a sort of half-embrace, as though he'd sensed that the rest of her also needed support.

"It will remain tethered to you until your arcana is completely expended. It's yours to do with as you wish. You can sever that connection by making a fist, or you can send the light elsewhere in the room."

"How do I do that?"

"Just move your hand upward and focus on where you want the orb to go."

He lowered his hand, but his arm remained against her shoulders. She focused on a point near the ceiling and flicked her wrist. The orb floated upward, coming to rest where she'd intended.

"If you were to go into the other room, it would follow you in there," Alain said. "To call it back, just focus your attention on it."

By simply imagining the orb returning to her palm, it responded as if it and her thoughts were one. She formed a fist, then blinked as her eyes adjusted to the suddenly dim light.

"Can you teach me something else?"

He scratched his chin. "Since you mastered that so quickly, we could try something a bit more advanced."

His hand left her shoulder so that he could retrieve his notebook. She leaned into him slightly—to better see his notes, of course. He stopped on a page in the latter half of the book.

"How about a brief overview on the basics of spellcraft?" When she nodded for him to continue, he cleared his throat. " 'Spellcasting includes at least one, and up to four, components. Almost every spell requires a ritual component: touch, hand gestures, even simply focusing on a spell. But ritual-only spells are the most basic form of spellcasting, and are therefore the weakest.' "

She scoffed.

"Hmm, I see what you mean. I really ought to revisit these lessons more often." He grabbed his pen, crossed out the last sentence, and made a correction. " 'Ritual-only spells are *limited,* but are still a completely valid form of spellcasting.' How does that sound?"

"Much better," she said.

" 'The more components a spell includes, the more complex it becomes. We just covered incantations. Next, we have anchors. Stones are the most common because they're the easiest to acquire. Metals, while the more expensive option, will power a spell indefinitely. But anything that resonates with the Ether could serve as an anchor.' "

"I've always wondered, does an anchor *have* to be some sort of object? Could you use another person?"

"Inorganic materials are ideal, as they don't need to replenish their arcana. But yes, you could use another mage—or several—for short-term spells. Once a mage's arcana is depleted, so too will the spell end. And, of course, you'd need someone willing to serve as one."

"Why 'willing'? Is it painful?"

"No, but it's incredibly draining, and it means having all the negative effects of burning through your arcana, but for someone else's benefit." He turned to the next page and continued to read. " 'Finally, we have augmentations. They are the most complicated component by far, especially if you are using a material that is not Ether-sensitive.' Do you remember how I once used your hair to augment my protective ward?"

She nodded as she thought back to that day five weeks ago. No time at all, in the grand scheme of things, yet so much had transpired since then. On that first morning of her assistantship, she never would have imagined sitting this close to Alain, much less not minding it.

"Well," he continued, "I could have used that strand of hair to allow any woman entry to my apartment, or to allow anyone with light brown hair—"

"Actually, I think I gave you a *gray* hair."

"I never would have noticed." He smiled. "So, you can see just how complex augmentations can become. For now, how about you try a simple incantation combined with an Ether-sensitive material?"

He stood up and retrieved something else from his desk. Mavery was acutely aware of how cold and empty the spot to her right had become.

Alain returned to the sofa a bit more sluggishly than before, and when he sat down, he looked dangerously close to nodding off. After setting up the wards and delivering the lesson, both his arcana and his energy had to be nearly spent.

He handed Mavery an iron coin. On another piece of paper, he wrote another line of runes—fourteen in total—and the pronunciations below it. He turned his wrist counter-clockwise, reinstating the violet auras around the room.

"This incantation will turn the iron into a basic compass," he said. "It will glow with Ethereal light when you point it north. It's a touch more difficult than conjuring an orb, but it's nothing you can't handle."

It quickly proved to be more than she could handle. Her tongue tripped over the strange phonics. She would successfully remember to roll one 'r,' then forget to roll the next one. After a quarter hour, she only managed to speak the entire incantation once without having to restart from the beginning. Reciting it without the wards was completely out of the question.

"It takes practice," Alain said. "I'd say this is a good stopping point for today. I should return to working on the Sensing spell."

At the rate he was going, he would work himself to death before he could present the spell to the High Council. But she knew pressing the matter would be a waste of breath.

"Do you want your coin back?" she asked.

She held it in her open palm. Instead of taking it, Alain curled her fingers around it and laid his hand over her closed fist.

"Why don't you keep it? Consider it a gift."

"What for?"

"Er...when is your birthday?"

"The twenty-eighth of Nivose."

"Then consider it a belated birthday present."

He glanced at their joined hands, then promptly pulled his away. With a tinge of red coloring his face, he rose from the sofa. It seemed he finally remembered what they'd discussed yesterday about decorum.

As he busied himself with his research notes, she examined the coin. It was a century-old potin, minted long before paper currency became the standard. An antique like this would fetch maybe a hundred potins from the right pawnbroker—a paltry "score" for over a month of work, not counting her wages.

Though the coin wasn't worth much, it was another sign that her persistence had paid off. Alain trusted her enough to give her something of his.

She should have been ecstatic.

She stared at the back of her hand, where his own had been moments earlier. The warmth and gentleness of his touch were soon drowned out by the guilt that came with planning schemes, sneaking around, telling half-truths, breaking into private rooms...

"I can't do this anymore."

"Do what?" Alain asked, looking up from his notes.

If she told him the truth, he would want nothing to do with her. That coin would be all she had to remember him by—assuming he didn't demand she give it back.

"Er...my Senses are acting up again," she said. "I don't think I can work without more of that potion."

"Of course. I made a large enough batch to last the week. I'll go fetch you another cup."

While Alain puttered around in the kitchen, Mavery chided herself for her cowardice. As much as she wanted to put an end to her lying and scheming, she wasn't yet ready to let go of all of this...to let go of her employer, her friend. When he returned with a cup of the off-putting liquid, she choked it down as a small penance.

They then both resumed their work. Mavery returned to her usual cataloging and sorting. Alain paced around the room while taking notes and muttering incoherently. She pieced together that he was making adjustments to Enodus's unfinished incantation, much like a poet trying to find the perfect turn of phrase. After a few minutes of this, he stopped in front of her.

"I'm not distracting you, I hope."

"Is this what you do when I'm not around?" she asked. "Talk to yourself while walking holes through your floorboards?"

He laughed. "Only when I'm pondering new ideas. But I'll try to keep my monologuing more *internal* going forward."

As promised, he resumed his pacing, but the only noise came from his footsteps. Though Mavery wouldn't typically use the word "charming" to describe this sort of behavior, she couldn't think of anything more suitable. Alain *was* charming...in his uniquely odd way.

Once afternoon tea had come and gone, he took his work to his desk, where he began reciting the incantation aloud. Whereas Mavery had struggled to string together only fourteen syllables, he managed to recite what must have been pages' worth of runes before stuttering, shaking his head, and marking a correction in his notes. She hadn't realized she'd been watching him until he gave her a sidelong glance and beckoned her over.

She leaned against his desk as she watched him work. These past few hours of minimal talking, keeping to their own tasks, had reminded her of the earliest days of her assistantship—something she was loath to return to. There was something comforting about being by his side again.

Though the potion had long worn off and the soundproofing ward was still in place, listening to him speak Etherean gave her chills nonetheless. There was no denying he was on the brink of collapse. Performing a single spell outside of the wards' protection would likely drain him entirely. Only then would he have no choice but to get the rest he so desperately needed.

Suddenly, a new plan formed. As Alain paused to make another correction, Mavery put it into motion.

"If you want to become a wizard, you need to invent your own spell, yes?"

"That's the usual way," he rasped, then cleared his throat. He put down his pen and turned to her. "But you could invent a potion, retrieve a lost relic, translate an ancient text. Any contribution to arcane scholarship will do, so long as the High Council deems it significant enough."

"What did you do?"

"I took the traditional route and invented a spell."

She smiled. "Could you demonstrate it for me?"

He mussed his hair with a grimace. "Even on an ordinary day, that spell leaves me absolutely knackered." At that, Mavery stifled a laugh. "But I suppose it would be a fitting way to cap off your first Etherean lesson. It won't be easy, especially as I've never performed that spell with another person."

"Well, now I'm even *more* intrigued."

He gazed around the room. "This is not the proper place for it, though. To get the full effect, we'll need to go outside. Ideally, somewhere that's bustling with activity."

"You're not going to elaborate, are you?"

"And spoil the surprise?" He gave her a tired but nonetheless enthused grin. "No, you know me too well."

TWENTY-ONE

I t didn't take Alain long to find a suitable spot. The street immediately outside Steelforge Towers wasn't exactly "bustling" in the middle of the afternoon, but there was a steady flow of pedestrians and horse-drawn carriages. After a wave of traffic lulled, Alain walked into the middle of the street and stopped.

"What are you doing?" Mavery called from the curb.

He waved for her to follow him. She glanced up and down the street to ensure the way was still clear, then came to his side.

"You must be out of your godsdamned—"

He grasped her by the shoulders, spun her until her back was flush against his chest.

"Don't move," he said.

"What are you—"

"Keep looking forward. Focus on that lamppost."

She hadn't known what to expect from this spell demonstration, but playing in the street like a pair of schoolchildren hadn't been her first guess. Feeling ridiculous, she laughed but decided to humor him.

"Are you ready?"

"Sure," she said with a nod.

"All right. Stay perfectly still."

A chill cut through the air as Alain spoke Etherean. Like the incantation she'd heard him practicing upstairs, this one was a long string of syllables spoken in a steady meter. Etherean had always sounded a bit like poetry to her untrained ear, but never had that comparison been more appropriate.

She relaxed against him, letting the vibration of his voice resonate through her. Though she wanted to close her eyes and lose herself in those strange yet beautiful words, she continued focusing on the lamppost.

When he finished the incantation, the final syllables were barely above a whisper. Calling upon the Ether for so long had left him breathless, as if he'd been running for miles. Mavery knew he hadn't moved, but she somehow could no longer feel the pressure of his hands on her shoulders, his chest against her back. Even her own body seemed lighter.

She tore her gaze from the lamppost long enough to see that they were no longer alone. Traffic passed by them, but no one paid any mind to the two people standing in the middle of the street. She looked back to the post. A carriage, led by a pair of horses, had just rounded the corner.

It was heading straight toward them.

"Er, Alain, we need to move." Her voice was delayed, distant, like an echo in a deep cave.

"Just wait." His voice contained that same echo-like quality. He was too calm for someone who was about to be run over.

The carriage moved closer. How were the horses not startled? How could the driver not notice them?

"Trust me," Alain said when the horses were only three feet away. Then two, then...

Mavery winced, but then the horses completely passed through her, followed by the carriage, as though they'd only been in her imagination. She'd felt nothing, not even the cobblestones beneath her feet. She'd heard nothing—no hooves, no wheels, no wind. Though she could see the world moving around her, it had grown completely silent.

She looked down and gasped. Her body had become translucent, and it glowed with the same pure light of the orb she'd conjured earlier. She began to turn around.

"Don't move," Alain said softly. "Too much movement will break the spell."

"Are we invisible?"

"Think of it as a bit like Aumbremancy, but calling upon the Ether itself instead of the shadows. Instead of obscuring us, it's turned us incorporeal." He paused. "But yes, to the casual observer, we're invisible. A trick of the light, in a sense."

To Mavery, shadow magic had always been stifling, like trying to breathe in smoke. But this... She had expected this amount of magic to overwhelm her Senses. Being shrouded in Ether—or, perhaps *veiled* was the better word—being one with arcana itself, its hum and chill were more soothing than oppressive. She had never experienced anything like this when shrouded in shadow, not even when Neldren had been in control.

She banished that name to the deepest corner of her mind. Because this was nothing like the shadows, nothing like *him*.

Alain continued to breathe slowly, steadily. Though his explanation had been more concise than usual, it had still drained most of his stamina.

"Remember what I said earlier about using another mage as an anchor?" he whispered.

"Of course," she whispered back. "What do I need to do?"

"Just stay right here."

There was nothing she would rather do.

She stood motionless enough to feel his presence. Not in the form of physical touch, but in the pull of his arcana against hers. Her own trickled through her veins, gathering along the surfaces where his incorporeal body met her own, creating pools of calm, yet electric, warmth.

Her pulse slowed to match the cadence of his as they shared the same magic, the same breath. Each inhale brought about a small controlled surge of heat. Each exhale left her body a bit lighter than before.

The world continued on around them, occasionally *through* them, but they were merely observers. The only sound was their shared breath, the only sensation was the gentle tug of arcana as her magic replenished his.

They were fully clothed, doing nothing more than standing together in broad daylight. And yet, Mavery had never felt a closeness quite like this.

Alain emitted a quavering exhale, and the Ethereal veil dissipated. As their bodies returned to their physical forms, she once again felt the weight of his body pressed to her back. His chin rested on her shoulder, his right cheek touched her left. At some point during the spell, he'd wrapped his arms around her waist. Even now, he continued to hold her. She suspected being an anchor didn't require this much touching, but she didn't mind at all. In fact, she didn't mind standing like this a little longer. Her eyes fluttered shut—

"Oi! Get outta the feckin' road!"

—and snapped open again. Barely three feet to her right was a man on a horse-drawn cart. He glared and rudely thumbed his nose as he passed by.

"Alain." She'd been jolted from her reverie, but his body was dead weight, as if he were in a drunken stupor. Her knees began to buckle.

"Hmph?"

"The spell wore off. We need to move."

He nodded, but he stumbled only two paces on his own before Mavery took his arm and slung it across her shoulders. Being his anchor had completely drained her arcana. Fatigue settled beyond her deepest muscles. She doubted she could conjure even the simplest protective ward. But she still had enough physical strength to drag Alain out of the street, then prop him against the exterior of his apartment building.

She'd grown used to seeing him exhausted, but this was something else entirely. Without the brick wall at his back, she suspected he would be a useless puddle on the ground.

"So, what did you think?" he asked, peering at her through half-closed eyes.

"Amazing," she sighed. "I've never experienced anything like that. I see now why they made you a wizard."

"Of course, only *now* do you see it."

"You know what I mean." Cracking a smile, she suppressed the urge to roll her eyes at him. "Now, let's get you inside."

Walking side by side, his arm over her shoulders once more, they reentered Steelforge Towers. Bertie had stepped out of the lobby, but Klaus was perched atop the front desk. The kutauss watched Mavery ungracefully drag Alain toward the lift. Its beady scarlet eyes shot her what she could only interpret as a judgmental glare. If the creature could speak, she assumed it would give her a snide comment as well.

"Oh, don't look at me like that," she muttered.

Inside the lift, she had to release Alain to turn the crank, but the small space made it impossible for him to fall over. He slouched against the wall, watched her with a dazed but intent look that made her heart race. It seemed that spell had turned them both delirious.

"Why can't this building have a lift like the ones at the University?" she asked, if only for a distraction. They'd passed the third floor, and her arm muscles were on fire. What she wouldn't give for a bit of magic to speed up the process.

"Only-for-wizards." Alain's speech had devolved to something halfway between mumbling and yawning. Had his mouth not been six inches from her ear, she would have failed to differentiate one slurred word from the next.

"But *you're* a wizard. You could've installed one yourself."

"Fabrications...not-in-my-wheelhouse."

Mavery brought the lift to a halt. She tried to ignore the dull ache in her arms as she resumed half-carrying Alain down the sixth-floor corridor. She supposed it was fortunate he was barely taller than her, and he was much lighter than he appeared, or else her knees and lower back would have already given in.

Once inside his apartment, Alain lurched toward the desk, but Mavery tightened her grip on his arm and pulled him in the opposite direction.

"No more work today," she said. "That's not where we're going."

"And where *are* we going?"

"You'll see."

She guided him around the sofa and into the bedroom. Only

once they crossed the threshold did she release him. He took a single step before he stopped, glanced at the bed, and turned to her with his eyebrows raised.

"That little demonstration left you 'absolutely knackered,' " she explained. "Exactly as you said, and exactly as I wanted you."

He leered at her—or, at least, that was what she assumed he was attempting to do. He was so spent, the faintest trace of a half-smile was all he could manage.

"Mavery, my dear, there are much easier ways to take me to bed."

She laughed, though her face burned as she considered to what extent his delirium was to blame for *that* specific choice of words.

"Oh, I've no doubt," she said, and the burn became a blaze. "Now, get some sleep."

"But it's only—"

"I don't care. You're not leaving this room."

She blocked the doorway with her body and pointed at the bed. With a dramatic sigh, he dropped onto the edge and slumped over to take off his shoes, but even his fingers were too fatigued to untie the laces. Mavery couldn't help but laugh.

"I'll handle those," she said. "You just worry about lying down."

She moved to the footboard, where she unlaced one shoe and dropped it to the floor. By the time she'd removed the other shoe, his eyes were closed. If he wasn't already asleep, he would be soon. Her work complete, she headed for the door.

"Wait," he said. "Stay for a moment."

She paused, hand gripping the doorframe. She needed to wish him goodbye before she took this any further. But the earnestness of his request reminded her of another long-forgotten need.

So, against her better judgment, she unlaced her boots and approached the bed. The iron frame creaked as he inched over and turned onto his side. It creaked again as she lay down and faced him.

She knew they'd been physically closer while veiled in Ether, but she hadn't been able to see his face then. Now, she could take in more details she'd never noticed before: a smattering of freckles down the length of his nose, traces of silver hair against his temples. Once again, she spotted that ink smudge on his cheek, persistent as the stains on his fingertips.

She glanced down at his hand inching toward her. He raised it slowly, brushed a lock of hair from her eyes, tucked it behind her ear. It was the most gentle of gestures, his movements no longer clumsy, and her eyes closed for a moment. When she opened them again, she met his gaze: soft, yet focused, despite his heavy-lidded eyes.

"Remember how I told you I'd never tried that spell with another person?"

She nodded, and he tucked back another lock of hair. The lightness of his touch warmed her, clouded her thoughts.

"That was the truth. I'd never done that before, but I'm glad I did. And I'm glad it was with you." He gave her another weak smile. "Even though you tricked me."

"Sorry," she said softly, "but I wanted you to get some rest for once."

She couldn't change him. It would be foolish to think so, considering they'd known each other for only a few weeks. She couldn't force him to stop sacrificing his wellbeing for his research, for the High Council, for *her*. But maybe she could guide him toward a different path.

"I worry about you," she said.

His hand cupped her cheek, his thumb brushed the hollow of her cheekbone. His caress was so tender, so sincere, that her throat clenched. It grew sore as she smothered a surge that contained no arcana—only raw emotions that she dared not name. He continued, unaware of how each pass of his fingers against her skin roused the storm inside her. She closed her eyes tightly, and only opened them when he answered her confession with one of his own.

"I worry I don't deserve you."

"What do you mean?" she asked.

But her question went unanswered. His eyes closed, his breathing slowed, his fingers trailed down her cheek as his hand fell, coming to rest between them. At long last, he was asleep.

She wondered how much of this exchange he would remember

come morning. One thing was for certain: this would be the most restful sleep he'd had in ages. To reverse some of the damage he'd done to himself over these past weeks, he would need more than a single night. But this would be a start.

Lying on this soft and spacious bed, she became aware of her own exhaustion. The familiar, dull aches in her body reintroduced themselves. Her arcana would continue to lie dormant, not even the faintest ember, until rest replenished it.

She would close her eyes for a brief nap, enough to restore her strength for the walk back to the boarding house. As sleep took hold, her thoughts drifted to the loose floorboard directly beneath her, and the box she'd once been so determined to uncover.

It had been the furthest thing from her mind.

TWENTY-TWO

A distant crash roused her from the depths of sleep.

It took her a few seconds to remember where she was: not on her tiny cot at the boarding house, but on Alain's double bed. Stars dotted the night sky, thick clouds obscured the moonlight. As her eyes adjusted to the darkness, she felt around but found only an empty bed beside her.

"Alain?" she called.

Silence.

"Etero rah mira shah."

However long she'd slept, it had been enough to recover her arcana. She shivered, then winced as an orb of light appeared above her palm. Her excitement from remembering the incantation vanished when she confirmed that she was alone.

She tossed aside a thick blanket that she couldn't recall covering herself with, then slung herself off the bed. The orb of Ether followed her into the main room. She flicked her wrist and sent it to the ceiling, where it cast the space in white light.

"Alain, are you in here? What happened?"

The clock on the mantel said it was a quarter to midnight. She'd been asleep much longer than she'd anticipated, though it wasn't surprising; she couldn't remember the last time her arcana had been drained so completely.

Aside from the clock ticking away, the apartment was eerily quiet at this time of night. The air itself was more stale and stagnant than usual. She looked to the front door, and her stomach lurched. Most of the wards had vanished. All that remained was the blue aura of the protective ward—the one that was anchored to the stone inside a desk drawer. She looked down and found Alain motionless across the tea table.

"Shit!"

She rushed to his side, dropped to her knees with a twinge of pain. She grabbed his shoulder, but he didn't respond. His body was warm but unnaturally still, lacking even the most minute movement.

"Oh, no-no-no, don't you fucking *dare*..."

When she pulled him from the table, he landed on the floor like a felled tree. She rolled him onto his back. His skin was even more pallid than usual, his lips were tinted blue, his widened eyes lacked any semblance of warmth. No breath, no heartbeat, but no sign of what had killed him. The only thing out of the ordinary was a thin book that had been pinned beneath his body. Its crumpled pages were covered in Etherean runes. Though Mavery couldn't make heads or tails of the text, she knew this had to be one of the spells Kazamin had given Alain to peer review.

Why he'd decided to resume this sort of work in the middle of the night, effectively by himself, gods only knew. All *she* knew was that something had gone horribly wrong.

Mavery hoisted herself off the floor, then hurried back to the bedroom with her orb of light trailing behind her. As she'd done nearly two weeks ago, she removed the rug, then the loose floorboard. This time, she snatched the long, thin box.

She laid out the box's contents: a syringe with a needle so thick and severe looking, it made her skin prickle; a thumb-sized vial filled with silver liquid; three pairs of surgical tweezers in various sizes; a folded paper with READ THIS FIRST writtent upon it; and a bundle of potins.

Her own heart nearly stopped upon realizing how thick that bundle was. But she put it aside and unfolded the paper. The protocol instructions were written in Alain's most elegant script.

In case of fatal accident:
1. Remove any clothing covering the heart area. If necessary, use tweezers to remove foreign objects that may pose a lethal threat upon revival.
2. Fill syringe with one vial of resurrection serum.
3. Aim syringe directly over heart.

Below that step was a sketch of a torso; an X indicated the exact spot to insert the needle. He'd said his instructions would be straightforward, though Mavery wished he'd informed her of the details. Still, she'd seen worse than this not long ago. Fennick's slashed throat flashed in her mind's eye as she forced herself to continue reading.

4. Pierce chest with a firm, downward movement.
5. Slowly inject serum. (For best results, count to 30.)
6. Remove syringe and wait. Revival may take several minutes.

Serum must be administered no more than ONE HOUR after death. If serum is unsuccessful, deliver body and enclosed funds to a Resurrectionist within THREE HOURS. They will make house calls for an additional fee. (Addresses are listed below. Use the password "camellia.")

In the event that three hours pass without a successful revival, please notify next of kin: Priscilla Tesser-aunt in the Garden District.

She'd heard him fall only moments ago. There was still time to administer the serum. But then her attention drifted back to the money, and her curiosity got the better of her. She counted out the notes.

Two thousand potins.

She was holding the equivalent of the payout from the Burnslee job—the *full* payout, and she wouldn't have to split it with anyone. She then picked up the vial of resurrection serum and held it to her eye. It was metallic and viscous—a bit like quicksilver with an iridescent sheen. How much would this fetch on the black market? A serum that was only accessible to wizards had to be worth another thousand, if not more.

Here it was, the score she'd been looking for all along. For the past ten hours, she'd been quite literally sleeping on it. She laughed as tears muddled her vision.

Had she gotten her hands on this weeks ago, she would have taken it and slipped out of the city without a second thought. Now, she would still use it, but not in the way her past self ever would have expected.

With the resurrection kit tucked under her arm, she returned to the sitting room. She pushed back the tea table with a grunt—it was much heavier than it appeared—and cleared enough space to sit by Alain's side. As she fumbled with his shirt buttons, she recalled the last words he'd spoken to her.

"You were wrong," she whispered, though she knew he couldn't hear a thing. "*I'm* the one who doesn't deserve *you.*"

Once she revived him, she would have to tell him the truth—and there was a not-so-small chance she would never again be on the receiving end of his warm smile, or his even warmer embrace. Once he turned her away, she would never again hear his impassioned ramblings or words of encouragement. Never again would they engage in deep discussions or playful arguments. But she couldn't keep her ruse going forever; he deserved better than that.

When she unfastened the final button and parted the fabric, she gasped. A thin scar ran down the length of his torso, from sternum to navel. Beneath a wisp of dark hair, there was another scar—no larger than the head of a nail—in the exact spot where she needed to insert the needle. But she could ponder all that later—*after* she revived him.

She filled the syringe, taking care to avoid pricking herself with the needle, then held it directly above his heart. She took a deep breath as her vision focused on the tiny round scar. Everything else faded to darkness.

In one swift movement, she plunged the needle into his chest, then depressed the plunger as she counted to thirty. In a sense, this was nothing more than a healing spell. And as with any healing spell, all she needed to do was focus and breathe. When the syringe was empty, she pulled it out and tossed it onto the tea table. A spot of blood bubbled from where the needle had been.

She'd saved him...or had she? Her heart lodged in her throat as she recalled the instructions—and the caveats. What if the serum didn't work? What if she'd misjudged the time, and more than an hour had passed? Could she find a Resurrectionist this late at night?

As the seconds stretched on like hours, she chewed on a hangnail until her skin turned bloody and raw, and her eyes stung with more tears. But never once did she leave his side. When she placed her hand upon his chest, his heart remained still as stone.

Come on. Come back to me...

Even more seconds passed, even more tears filled her eyes.

Then, the lightest pulse stirred beneath her fingertips.

Alain's eyes widened. He inhaled sharply, followed by a fit of ragged coughing that made his entire body quaver. He bolted upright, and Mavery was relieved she'd had the foresight to move the tea table.

"Careful," she said. Standing up was likely out of the question, so she helped him turn around, lean his back against the sofa.

He continued to cough, but with each one, more color returned to his cheeks. She noted to herself that she would never again think of his complexion as "deathly pale." Compared to the real thing, he was *radiant.* She rubbed small circles against his shoulder as his coughing fit subsided. He then turned to her.

"Mavery," he gasped. Coming from his voice, her name was like the most beautiful music she'd ever heard. "Thank—"

She lunged forward and threw her arms around him, nearly knocking him to the floor again. Simply feeling his breath and pulse strummed up a well of emotion and arcana. The former sprung free in a shuddering sob, while the latter coursed through her veins like a gathering storm.

She pulled away at once, not wanting to risk her magic surging beyond her control. She recalled what she'd done to his bathroom mirror, and she had no intention of seeing what would happen if Alain was on the receiving end of that. Besides, it probably wasn't a good idea to squeeze someone whose lungs had started working again only a moment ago.

"Sorry about that." She dried her eyes with the back of her hand. Yet another emotional impulse had gotten the better of her. "I just...for a minute there...I thought..."

"No need to apologize. Now that you've gone through the procedure, I'm sure you understand why I was reluctant to tell you more."

"I wish you had. You're lucky I don't have a debilitating fear of needles."

"Further proof that I picked the right person for the job."

He smiled weakly, and she averted her eyes as shame washed over her.

"So, er, what happened?" she asked.

"I awoke feeling so well-rested, I thought I'd get an early start on peer review. That way, we could focus on more important matters: the Sensing spell and your Etherean lessons." He looked at the orb of Ether floating overhead. "Speaking of, I see you remembered the incantation. Excellent work!"

Any other time, she would have welcomed his praise. Instead, she frowned at him.

"You told me it was too dangerous to peer review spells by yourself."

"But I wasn't by myself. You were here...technically speaking."

"*Technically speaking*, I was asleep!"

"And when did you wake up?"

"When I heard you collapse."

"See? Everything worked out. No harm done."

" 'No harm done'?" She blinked at him. "Alain, you fucking *died*!"

He winced. "I'll admit, that was a poor choice of words."

She fought an overwhelming urge to throw herself at him again—and shake him. Her frustration must have been written plainly on her face. Alain placed his hand on her shoulder.

"It was a stupid mistake," he said. "I was reviewing a simple voice-based augmentation developed by an, at most, entry-level wizard. Somehow, I managed to botch the incantation, which caused me to suffocate." He sighed and shook his head. "I used a *guttural* 'r' when I should have *rolled* the 'r.' Must have been my mother's influence popping up at the most inconvenient of times."

He chuckled, but even that seemed to be too strenuous. With a pained expression, he gingerly touched his chest. His shirt remained unbuttoned, and a bruise had begun to darken the spot where his breastbone had collided with the tea table. Mavery caught another glimpse of his long scar and thought of a coroner slicing open a cadaver.

"You're being awfully casual about this," she said. He looked down, biting his lip, and that was enough to confirm her suspicions. "How many times has this happened?"

When he didn't answer, she took him by the jaw, gently turned his face until he looked at her again.

"How many times have you been resurrected?" she asked, enunciating each word.

"Er...only once before."

Not even the most gullible idiot would fall for that. She narrowed her eyes and tightened her grip.

"Twice?"

"Alain, tell me the truth."

He closed his eyes and sighed deeply. "Twelve. Counting tonight, I've now been resurrected twelve times."

For a brief moment, all she could do was gawk at him. Then, she scowled as she released his jaw and gave his arm a swift punch.

"Ouch!"

"Twelve? *Twelve*!?" Her frown deepened at the sheepish look he gave her. "You ass! Keeping your protocol a secret was one thing, but you could have at least told me you'd been through this before!"

"In all fairness, I *did* say I'd been through it before."

"I'd assumed you meant as the one doing the resurrecting, not the one being resurrected—and definitely not *eleven fucking times* before tonight!"

As she formed a fist again, arcana ignited her blood. But seeing him wince tempered her rage, and she settled on continuing to glower at him. He must have noticed her gaze linger on his scar again; he began buttoning up his shirt.

"My record pales in comparison to those of the Elder Wizards," he said. "Collectively, the High Council has died hundreds of deaths. Seringoth alone has died over fifty times, and one of his resurrections was performed by yours truly."

If cheering her up had been his intention, he'd failed miserably. Her stomach clenched just thinking of how many times Alain had been stabbed with that needle—or had undergone whatever gruesome procedure a Resurrectionist performed. His scars were permanent reminders of his many close calls, though knowing they had that in common gave her little comfort at this precise moment.

"Seringoth may have died fifty times, but he's ancient," she said. "You're only thirty-four. A dozen resurrections at your age can't be... That can't be *normal*, can it?"

"If it helps you feel any better, it had been over two years since my last. I might have been imprudent tonight, but this is nothing compared to how I used to be. I once had four resurrections in a single year."

She frowned. "I can't say *any* of that helps me feel better."

"Well, regardless of how many times I've been through it, thank you for bringing me back."

He placed his hand on her shoulder again as he gave her a look she recognized all too well. She'd often been on the receiving end of it after several pints of ale, a particularly thrilling score, or a closer-than-expected brush with death. If recent events didn't count as the latter, she didn't know what would. A small part of her wouldn't have minded that look—and everything that would follow it—had guilt not been clawing at her insides.

"Don't thank me," she said. "There's something I need to tell you—something I should have told you ages ago."

For a moment, she struggled to find the words. She could

only stare at her lap. Alain's hand released her shoulder, skimmed down her arm. His fingertips brushed the back of her hand, then hesitated. Her eyes met the soft gaze that, as he'd lain lifelessly on the floor, she'd longed to see again. But now it made her stomach twist into knots, her throat tighten.

"If this is about your lack of education," he said softly, "you have nothing to be ashamed of. As I already told you, I don't care about any of that. What you did just now only confirms that you're worthy of being my assistant."

"It's not about that. And no, I'm *not* worthy." Her hands clenched into fists. No matter what happened next, he deserved the truth. "When I arrived at your door nearly six weeks ago, my aim wasn't to become your assistant, but to rob you."

She continued to gaze downward; she couldn't bring herself to look him in the eye.

"R-rob me?" He laughed weakly. "You're joking...er, aren't you?"

She shook her head. "Over the years, I've been a little of every-thing: wardbreaker, mage for hire, con artist. I even worked for the Brass Dragons for a time. Before I came to Leyport, I was running with an independent thieving crew. Let's just say we parted ways on less-than-favorable terms, and I needed an easy score.

"That's when I came across your ad—your mother's, I mean—and thought a wizard mad enough to put his address in the newspaper would be the perfect mark. My plan was to impress you with my Sensing abilities and earn your trust. When the time was right, I would rob you of your valuables and skip town." She shrugged. "But, for what little it's worth, I changed my mind."

"So, you came here of your own accord?" Alain asked.

She nodded.

"Nezima didn't hire you?"

"Nezima?" She looked up, blinked at him. "What does she have to do with—"

Mavery startled as Alain began to *laugh*. It wasn't a soft chuck-le like before; he threw his head back as tears beaded in the corners of his eyes. All she could do was stare incredulously as his laughter gave way to another bout of wheezing.

"Alain, what—"

He gasped for breath as he clutched his chest. "Gods, that's a relief! Well, not the fact that you came here to *rob* me, but I was worried you were working for a disgruntled colleague. I even thought they'd hired an assassin to do me in—and that's but one of the harebrained ideas I'd concocted."

She laughed nervously, unsure if he was only saying this to ease the tension. As Alain recovered his breath, the clock continued to tick. She couldn't help but think of it as the death knell for their partnership, for whatever else existed between them.

Alain shook his head. "I knew I was right when I told my mother those newspaper ads were a terrible idea. But I was worried about my academic reputation when I should have been worried about would-be thieves. This building could have been infested with them, but I only ever attracted the one. I suppose I should consider myself lucky."

He nudged her shoulder. His smile faltered when she failed to react.

"So, what made you change your mind?" he asked.

"I..." She looked at him. "I decided you were worth more to me than any potential score."

All this time, she'd expected him to raise his voice, to demand she leave and never return. A tiny part of her wondered if he would turn to his arsenal of spells; even the most unassuming types could be provoked into rage. The last thing she'd expected was for him to lean forward and embrace her. Her eyes widened, her entire body clenched. Surely this had to be some sort of trick.

"I just confessed to being a career criminal! I was even a Brass Dragon once."

He pulled back, hands still grasping her shoulders. "But you're not one presently?"

"No, I severed those ties years ago."

"Then I fail to see the problem."

"But you said you couldn't associate with a criminal."

He furrowed his brow, then realization crossed his face. "Oh, you're referring to what I said about Enid. Well, that's different. She's just my...and you're..." He sighed. "You might have lied about why you came here, but what of everything since? Everything you've done as my assistant, as my friend, was that also a—"

"No. All of it was real." She held his gaze, searching for a sign that he believed her. "And I want to continue being both, if you'll still have me after all this."

"Then how about we forget about the past and start anew?" He removed his right hand from her shoulder and held it in front of her. "Hello, I'm Alain Tesseraunt."

She choked out a laugh as she blinked away tears. "Hello, Alain. I'm Mavery Culwich."

They shook hands.

"A pleasure to meet you, Mavery. Would you do me the honor of being my assistant?"

She smiled. "Yes, I would."

"Wonderful. As your wizard, I promise to not be reckless with my spellcraft."

"And as your assistant, I promise to not rob you."

"Then I say we have a deal."

When he embraced her this time, she allowed herself to relax into him, to let her head nestle against the crook of his neck, to let him stroke her hair as the last of her tears fell upon his shoulder.

Her confession hadn't dispelled her guilt entirely. But it was enough for her to savor being held like this. It was enough for her to believe that, when the sun rose in a few hours' time, a new day would break, and the two of them would continue on as before. Only now, there would be fewer secrets between them.

Part Two

The Scholar

Twenty-Three

Mavery slammed the dictionary shut and threw down her pen.

"Experiencing the joys of research, are we?" Alain asked from across the room. They had traded places for the day: while she worked at his desk, translating Enodus's treatise on Sensing from Fenutian to Osperlandish, he was stretched out on the sofa with a stack of books at his side.

"Oh, hush." She rolled her eyes, though her back was turned to him. "There's a word I don't recognize. Here's the full sentence: 'According to one local folklorist, Sensing is a form of K-T-O-N-I-C magic.' Do you recognize that 'k'-word?"

"It's not Fenutian?"

"Doesn't look like it, and it's not in the dictionary."

"Let me see."

Alain closed his book, then crossed the room. He cast a shadow over Mavery as he leaned over her shoulder, one hand on the back of her chair while the other reached for her translation.

Four days had passed since his accident. Since then, his eyes had become less sunken from getting more consistent sleep. His face was a bit fuller from eating more substantial meals. He'd even managed to keep his beard neatly trimmed and his hair combed.

Now, as he reviewed her work, Mavery breathed in a heady

aroma of ink, bergamot, and a hint of orange blossom that she suspected came from the new soap she'd spotted in the bathroom. It was difficult to focus on anything else.

" 'Kay-tonic'?" Alain shook his head. "No, 'kuh-tone-ick' seems the more likely pronunciation."

"Do you know what it means?"

"Not a clue. I've never seen it before."

"Then how do you know how it's pronounced?"

"I..." He looked to her, then returned her smirk with a chuckle. "Point taken. I'll admit, this word could simply be an error on my part. Given the limited time I had with the spell tome, transcribing the Etherean was my priority; I was less cautious with the Fenutian."

"Maybe the word *is* Fenutian, but it's too archaic for this dictionary," Mavery said.

"Possibly. The University's library should have one from Enodus's time."

She nodded. "When can we go?"

"Whenever you want. The arcanists here are more lenient than the ones in North Fenutia. Just wear your assistant's robe, and they'll grant you access to anything in the library—even the special collections."

"Wait." She pivoted in the chair. "You mean I could have gone to campus by myself all this time? Why didn't you tell me?"

"You never asked," Alain said with a shrug. "Maybe you ought to reread the Covenants."

Mavery scoffed. "Trust me, they didn't mention a thing about assistants and libraries. Sounds like *you're* the one who needs to reread the Covenants."

He opened his mouth, but his rebuttal died on his lips as he looked up, blinking. "Gods, when did it get so late?"

According to the clock, it was almost seven. Outside, a pink-orange sunset bled across the cloudy sky. The sun had already sunk below the horizon.

"This is the third time this week you've stayed long past your shift," Alain said. "If I didn't know any better, I'd say you were developing a habit."

She could argue it was to keep a closer eye on Alain after his accident, but that wouldn't be the full truth. This apartment was leagues more comfortable than her room at the boarding house. Not to mention, the company here was leagues more enjoyable.

She bowed her head as she tidied up her papers, heat gathering in her cheeks. She stashed her translation in a drawer, then rose from the chair. Alain had returned to the sofa, where he now skimmed a book about famous Sensers throughout history. It was a relatively short volume, and one of only a handful in his library that even mentioned Sensing.

Lying on the sofa, he appeared more comfortable than he was letting on. Mavery had noticed how often he would rub his chest; in fact, he was doing it now. The bruise from his injury—a fractured sternum, courtesy of his collision with the tea table—peeked above his collar. Over the past four days, the livid blotch had paled to a sickly yellow. He'd been adamant about letting it heal without spells or potions. He wanted to live with the pain for a bit, as a reminder of his recent mistake.

That was but one of the areas where his stubbornness persisted. In the hours following his resurrection, he'd returned to his research as though literally *dying* didn't entitle him to a day off. And now he appeared to be settling down for another long, tireless night. Tomorrow was Finisday—Mavery's usual day off—and without her around, he was likely to work straight through Onisday without pause.

"There's a pub two blocks from here," she said. "I was planning to go there for dinner. Why don't you join me?"

Not bothering to glance up from his book, he shook his head. "I know the one you're talking about. The wine is overpriced, and I find the clientèle too crass for my taste."

She crossed her arms. "I'll have you know, I've become somewhat of a regular there."

"I fail to see how that refutes my point," he said flatly, though he neglected to hide his smile.

She snorted. "Do you plan to stop and eat *at all* this evening?"

"Of course." He licked his finger, turned a page. "Sometime...eventually."

She strode forward, plucked the book from his hands, and tossed it on the tea table. Alain gawked at the unceremoniously discarded tome, then frowned at her.

"Mavery, I appreciate your concern, but the presentation is—"

"Two weeks away, as if I could forget. You deserve *one* night off between now and then."

They locked eyes—a silent challenge to see who would relent first. This time, Mavery proved victorious when Alain lowered his gaze with a sigh of defeat.

"All right," he said, "but no pubs."

"Then what do you suggest?"

He scratched his chin as he gave it some thought. "Have you ever been to the Night Market in the Garden District?"

Mavery shook her head. Though she'd heard of it, anything in the Garden District had always been too rich for her blood.

"It's held every Siddisday evening. I haven't been in well over a year, but I remember there was no shortage of food merchants."

"Fine by me." Mavery grasped his arm and hoisted him from the sofa before he could change his mind. "Whatever gets you out of this room for a few hours."

The Garden District was Leyport's most affluent area, with manors butting against the eastern city walls. As its name implied, the district was home to the famous botanical garden, with its exotic plants and glass-domed roof.

Central to the district was a plaza that boasted the equally famous outdoor market. Though the days had grown warmer, the night air remained frigid. The entire plaza was enveloped in a shimmering blue dome that turned the air so warm and comfortable, Alain loosened his scarf, and both he and Mavery unbuttoned their coats.

Many of the market-goers were dressed in their finest, likely passing through on their way to the nearby theaters and opera house. But plenty had stopped to queue in front of the stalls, where merchants peddled luxuries from all across the continent. Scattered around the plaza were musicians, jugglers, and magic-wielders, each drawing their own small crowds. Mavery couldn't recall the last time she'd seen this many people in a single area. She and Alain were but two in a crowd of hundreds, perhaps upwards of a thousand. This fact seemed to have put Alain on edge; he stiffened beside her.

"Are you all right?" she asked.

"Evidently, the Night Market is more popular than it used to be. Not to mention, I'm remembering how most of my colleagues live in this part of the city."

Mavery doubted any of them would recognize him in this vast crowd, especially without his faculty robe. Dressed in a black peacoat, he looked not like a professor or a wizard, but a completely ordinary man. It was a look she could get used to seeing.

"You'll be fine." She took him by the arm. "Come on, I'm starving."

Following the scent of spiced meat wafting through the magically warmed air, they weaved through the crowd together. They passed by stalls overflowing with floral arrangements, rare alchemical ingredients, jarred spices in every color of the rainbow. Each lot of merchandise was more ridiculously priced than the last. A jeweler showcased necklaces that he claimed were enhanced with magic that could ward off everything from Necromancers to the pox, but Mavery couldn't Sense a single aura. Alain slowed as he eyed a stall laden with opulent rugs.

"Ah, you are a man who recognizes quality when he sees it!" the merchant cajoled. His gravelly voice was laced with a thick Maroban accent—a little *too* thick.

"Don't bother," Mavery muttered, giving Alain's arm another tug. "Those rugs are likely as authentic as that accent."

They continued to the next stall, though the wares were hardly an improvement. Mavery did nothing to hide her scowl as she briefly met the eye of a grocer who was charging fifty coppers for a single apple. She tried to ignore the blatant price gouging and instead focused on finding the source of the spiced meat.

It was a cart that sold Zakarzan street foods, the most enticing of which was a flatbread filled with curried lamb. Before she could retrieve her coin purse, Alain stepped forward and paid for both of them.

"I brought my own money, you know," Mavery said as the vendor began preparing their food.

"But coming here was my idea. Help yourself to anything you want."

She raised her eyebrows. "*Anything?*"

"Within reason." Alain smiled. "Consider it my thanks for persuading me to have more than books for company this evening."

The flatbread's smell alone—warm and earthy—was a refreshing change from the boarding house's usual fare of potato mash, onion gravy, and stale bread. Mavery took a bite, and her eyes widened at the deluge of flavors: the savory and slightly gamy lamb, the curry's subtle sweetness, the heat that lingered pleasantly on her tongue. Though Alain's teas hadn't quite refined her palate, she could now appreciate spices more exotic than cinnamon and clove.

All the picnic tables were occupied, so they continued to walk and peruse the other merchants' offerings while they ate. They passed by a busty woman carrying a tray of wineglasses.

"May I tempt you with a sample?" she asked.

They each took a glass containing barely more than a mouthful of red wine. Alain considered his with a swirl and a sniff before taking a slow sip. Though both the wine and the woman offering it appeared trustworthy, Mavery still waited until Alain encountered no ill effects, then threw back her own wine.

She realized at once why he'd sampled the drink with so much care. It was good wine. No, it was *excellent* wine, and it paired wonderfully with the flatbread. It was velvety on the tongue, with flavors too complex for Mavery to appreciate. She wouldn't have been surprised to learn this was the kind of wine the nobility drank with their everyday meals.

Alain, however, was not as impressed.

"It's adequate." He shrugged, and the wine merchant's smile stiffened. "The blackcurrant notes are too strong for my taste."

Mavery rolled her eyes. "Don't mind him. He's Dauphinian, so being a wine snob is in his blood—even when the wine is free."

Though she would have loved an entire bottle, she suspected Alain would argue it wouldn't be "within reason." They placed their empty glasses on the merchant's tray, then continued onward.

"What do you know of my family name?" Alain asked.

She considered his question as she swallowed her final bite of curried lamb. She wiped her hands on the insides of her coat pockets.

"Like most Dauphinian words, it has too many letters," she said.

He chuckled. "I won't argue with that. But beyond spelling?" He polished off his own flatbread, then produced a handkerchief to clean his fingers.

"Not a clue."

He gestured for her to follow him. "Let me show you something."

He led her out of the market. As they passed through the warding magic, the chill in the air returned, forcing Mavery to button up her coat again. She followed Alain around a corner and down a side street, where the botanical garden loomed in the distance, perched atop the slight hill. Mavery didn't have to ask where they were going; she knew it the moment she saw the storefront that was painted deep violet and glowing with warding magic.

They stopped beneath a lamppost directly across from Tesseraunt's Boutique. Its front window displayed mannequins dressed in exquisite gowns in the current fashion: ankle-length, form-fitting, with cinched waists and voluminous bustles. All were made from fabrics that were vibrant even at night. Mavery could only admire them from a distance, however; the shop was closed, all the windows were dark.

"I assume the wards are your doing," she said. Whereas the surrounding shops had only blue and gold auras over the doors and windows, the full spectrum of warding magic rippled across this building's entire façade.

"So long as my mother lives in the apartment above the shop,

I'll ensure this is the best-secured building in the district." He pointed up. "See that tiny window on the third floor? That's my childhood bedroom."

"Huh, I was certain you'd grown up in one of those manors a few blocks over."

Alain shook his head. "Far from it. I may be a wine snob, but 'Tesseraunt' is a peasant name. 'Weaver' would be the closest translation."

"Fitting, considering your mother's line of work."

"Yes, she comes from a long line of weavers, tailors, and the like. She started working in a textile mill when she was only eight years old—that was decades before Dauphine outlawed child labor—and when I was born, she was an apprentice seamstress."

In the midst of the revolution across the border, plenty of Dauphinians had fled to Osperland. But they tended to be nobles seeking refuge from the executioner's block; commoners like Alain and his mother tended to be the ones calling for those executions. Mavery watched him curiously as he continued to speak.

"When I was about nine years old, she befriended a customer who happened to be an aspiring wizard. Together, they developed a poison-warding fabric that earned the mage her wizard rank. One of the Elder Wizards was so impressed with the fabric, she paid my mother handsomely to design an entire Social Season's worth of ball gowns. With her newfound fortune, my mother opened this boutique and eventually sent me to Barcombe, in the hopes that I would one day become a wizard myself."

"So, we both come from working-class families," Mavery said. "That's the last thing I thought we would have in common."

"You come from a family of farmers, correct?"

She stared at him. When had she told him *that*? She struggled to recall a single time she'd mentioned her upbringing; it was a topic she rarely spoke about.

"The day we first met," Alain said, apparently sensing her confusion, "you mentioned something about a family farm."

"Right, I did." He'd remembered that little detail from so long ago? Her face burned despite the cold night air.

"What sort of farm was it?"

"An apple orchard, though we also raised hogs and chickens."

He grinned. "Ah, no wonder you were staring daggers at that one merchant."

"Fifty coppers for *one* apple!" she huffed. "That's worse than highway robbery!"

"Yes, I imagine highway robbery *would* be within your repertoire."

"Very funny." She crossed her arms, and his grin broadened.

"In any case, I'm already picturing our next project." He raised his hands and mimed an exaggerated ritual. "An incantation to ward off overpriced produce."

Seeing him struggle to contain his laughter at his barely half-decent joke, she held her hand to her mouth and failed to hold back a giggle.

Surely she wasn't...*giggling*?

She cleared her throat and came back to her senses. "What about your father?" she asked. As Alain stiffened, she added quickly, "Sorry, if that's a sore subject, you don't—"

"Not sore, just...delicate. All I know is that my father was a parish priest in the Church of the Dyad. In Dauphine, the Church outranks everyone—even the nobility. So, for a priest to have a child out of wedlock with one his parishioners...well, you can imagine the scandal that caused. That's why, shortly after I was born, Mother fled across the border with me. As for my father, I'm not sure what happened to him. She's always been mum on the details."

"That must've been difficult, growing up without a father."

"The earliest years were, from what little Mother has told me, and from what little I can remember." He gestured to the boutique. "But, as you can see, things eventually worked out for the better." With a shiver, he shoved his hands in his pockets. "Let's hurry back to the market before we both freeze."

They turned away from the shop. Though only the crest of the Night Market's dome was visible up ahead, the din of the crowd—and the music cutting through it—carried all the way down the moonlit street.

"Who was the wizard you mentioned earlier?" Mavery asked.

"The one your mother helped?"

Alain came to an abrupt stop. "It was…Nezima."

"Let me guess: being the reason for your mother's fortune is something she's always lorded over you. That's why you hate her so much."

"I don't—" he began. Mavery threw him a pointed look, and he sighed. "You're right, I *do* dislike her, but that's not the reason. The *real* reason is a story for another time, and one that would dampen the mood."

"Fair enough," she said. Her curiosity was far from quelled, but she would set the matter aside—for tonight.

Despite the cold, Alain continued down the road at a leisurely stride, and Mavery had to slow her pace to match his.

"So, if both your parents were Dyadists, are you also one?" she asked.

"Not in the slightest, despite my mother's best efforts. Besides, one can only return from the dead so many times and still believe in the afterlife—or higher powers, for that matter."

"Right, I'm sure you would've collected calling cards from the entire Pantheon by now."

He laughed. "Oh, I doubt any of them would be thrilled to see me, the number of times I've denied them another soul for the Beyond. But what about you? When you were a child, did your family also force you to weekly temple services?"

"Not weekly, but we made pilgrimage to the Temple of Messun at least once a season, to ensure the God of the Harvest protected our crops from demon-blight."

Alain scoffed. "Of course your crops would be protected from demons—they were driven out centuries ago!"

"And any Messunist would say that was proof that our prayers had been answered." Mavery shook her head. "One summer—I was thirteen at the time, I think—the last of my grandparents fell ill and passed away. Between the funeral and keeping up with the farm, we had no time to make our seasonal trip to the temple. When we still had our best harvest in years, I realized that all of it—the wassailing, the prayers, the pilgrimages—was a load of rubbish."

"Hold on, did you say 'wassailing'?"

"It's when you sing to the—"

"Oh, I'm familiar with that custom." A smile teased at the corner of his mouth. "I just can't imagine you singing to anything, much less *trees*."

She laughed. "Another reason why Messunism was never a good fit."

"Well, if more people used that same reasoning, perhaps all the Pantheonic churches would have less influence." They had now returned to the plaza. Alain stopped before the dome of warding magic and sighed. "Sorry, you wanted me to take a night off, and here I am, diving head-first into a theological discussion."

Mavery grinned as she nudged him with her elbow. "You can take a scholar out of his library…"

She stepped through the magical barrier, and Alain followed closely behind her. The Night Market was less crowded than before, but the festivities continued on, now with much shorter queues at the stalls. Mavery gasped as she spotted a familiar sight at one of them.

"I haven't had one of those in *years*!" she cried, pointing to one of Fenutia's signature pastries. Dozens of flaky layers formed a spiral shape that was roughly the length of her forearm and half as wide. The entire thing was encased in a thick, white glaze and dusted with powdered sugar.

"Good evening, sir," she said to the merchant in Fenutian. "How much costing, this is?"

Though Mavery had read plenty of the language over the past week, speaking it was another matter entirely. Despite her butchering of Fenutian grammar, the merchant—a stout, gray-haired man—gave her a broad smile.

"Normally, three potins each," he replied in Fenutian, albeit at a glacial pace. "But for speaking my mother tongue, you pay half."

Mavery relayed this to Alain, who balked at the cost.

"You did promise me *anything*," she said. "And trust me, these are so incredible, they're worth the cost ten times over."

"If you say so," he muttered as he handed the man a single note and fifty coppers.

Mavery had barely put any distance between herself and the stall when she could no longer resist. Hearing the crunch as she took a bite brought about a wave of nostalgia. Tasting the rich butter as it melted on her tongue, then ungracefully licking the cinnamon and sugar from her lips, brought about a second wave.

"It's called an *eenerharn*. Unicorn horn," she said, holding the pastry up to Alain. "Go on, try it."

He leaned forward and took a bite straight from her hand. She laughed. Though she had intended for him to take it from her, his method was definitely more efficient. From the corner of her eye, Mavery spotted an elderly couple shooting them disapproving looks, but she was too focused on Alain's reaction to the pastry to care. The longer he chewed, the more his eyes widened.

"You were right," he said. "That *is* incredible. I would've thought that was a Dauphinian pastry."

Mavery snorted. "Dauphine doesn't have superiority over *everything*, you know. I must have eaten my weight in these when I lived on the other side of the Merimar. They were far less expensive over there."

"Is that how you learned Fenutian?"

"Yes, although..." She narrowed her eyes at him as she took another bite. With her mouth full, she added, "Didn't you say it only requires sticking a sock in your mouth?"

"If only I'd known at the time how useful your Fenutian skills would be." Alain lowered his head. "In any case, I shouldn't have said that. I would like to know about your time in Fenutia, if you wish to tell me."

She took another bite as she considered his apology. As she swallowed, she decided to reveal a bit more about her past.

"Not long after I left the Dragons, I joined up with the River Watch. Thought I'd give mercenary work a shot. Mind you, I joined as a medic, not a soldier."

Alain looked up. "Ha, I knew it! I figured that was how you'd learned Soudremancy."

"Oh, no, I already knew a few healing spells by then." She thought of the stolen primer in her Compendium. "The Watch was so desperate for healers, they took me on even though I couldn't patch up more than a paper cut.

"But there was little need for me in the end. When the duke who'd hired the Watch showed up with a thousand militiamen, the other duke practically shat himself. They settled the border dispute before the ink on my contract even dried, but I ended up staying in Fenutia for nearly two years after that."

"If it was for the pastries, I don't blame you," Alain said. He gestured for her to hand over the *eenerharn*, then took a generous bite from what remained of it.

"It wasn't just the pastries. As is the case for many ill-fated decisions, there was a beautiful woman at the center of it."

"Are you talking about yourself?"

"Gods, no!" Mavery cackled as her heart thundered in her chest.

"Oh," Alain said. As he started to take another bite, he paused. His eyes widened, and now it was his turn to blush. "Oh, you mean..."

"I'm talking about Eryka, the barmaid who won the hearts of the militiamen but only had eyes for the medic." She pointed at herself, then frowned. "That was, until the civil war broke out two years later, and she refused to flee across the river with said medic."

"Do you know what happened to her?"

"No, I don't tend to keep in touch with old flames."

All except for one, but she wasn't about to speak of *him* tonight. Mavery lowered her gaze and fell silent as she ate the last of the pastry. Alain cleaned his sugar-dusted fingers with his handkerchief, then passed it to her. After she handed it back, he hesitated, fidgeting with the soiled cloth.

"So..." He cleared his throat. "Are you *exclusively* interested in women, or...?"

Her heart pounded again. "Er, no, I've taken lovers of all sorts. To put it more plainly, what's beneath someone's clothes has never mattered much to me."

He smiled. "That's yet another thing we have in common."

They held each other's gaze for a moment, until applause sounded nearby. Mavery realized they were alone; the remaining market-goers had crowded around some of the performers.

"Shall we go see what the fuss is about?" Alain asked.

"By all means," Mavery said, and followed him toward the source of the applause. It didn't take long to find what had drawn everyone's attention. Even the other entertainers had stopped their own performances to watch the show.

Alain weaved through the crowd, presumably seeking a spot where top hats and plumes wouldn't obscure the view. He found one near the front, but this section was still so dense, he and Mavery had to stand shoulder to shoulder.

Each of the performers controlled a ring of fire the size of a wagon wheel, which they tossed between one another. Every few passes, the rings split—first into six, then into twelve—and the crowd gasped each time. Yet, the performers juggled the enormous, fiery rings as though they were merely children's toys.

Mavery looked at Alain, half-expecting him to watch this flashy display of magic with a critical eye. But he was as transfixed as the rest of the audience.

The fire wielder in the center molded her rings into a whip, which then surged with white-blue flames. Her partners tossed her their rings, and she snagged each one with a crack of her whip.

How she had managed to make fire emit *that* sort of sound, Mavery pondered for only a second. She blinked, and both whip and rings vanished. In their place, a fiery serpent hovered above the stage. Together, the performers motioned as if casting a large net, and the serpent soared above the crowd. It twisted and writhed in a manner that was eerily realistic, illuminating the awestruck faces in orange light. A few screams of terror cut through the applause, and not all of them came from children.

As it swam closer, Mavery realized it wasn't merely a serpent but a *dragon*. Sculpted from fire were its bearded head, long snout, and tendril-like whiskers. Flames rippled along its body, creating the illusion of scales.

The dragon's jaws unhinged, and from its maw spewed a plume of bright yellow fire. As it swooped in close, Mavery briefly forgot herself. With a gasp, she grabbed Alain's hand. When she realized what she'd done, even the dragon's intense heat couldn't compare to what radiated from her own skin.

But before she could so much as mutter an apology for her impropriety—and here, in a place more crowded than the University's quad—Alain's fingers entwined with hers. She glanced at him. He was still looking ahead, but with a hint of a smile on his lips that she suspected had little to do with the show. As she returned her attention to the stage, she relaxed, nestling her fingers more comfortably between his.

They remained that way until the Elemental wielders dismissed their fiery serpent and took their final bow. Alain released Mavery's hand to add to the crowd's enthusiastic applause. She frowned, feeling a pang of loss, before joining in herself.

Twenty-Four

Alain hadn't seen this side of Leyport since he was a child. In the city's southwestern district—he couldn't even recall its proper name—few streets were paved with cobblestones, and lampposts were an even rarer sight. Moonlight filtered through the tattered linens spanning from tenement to tenement, casting patches of blue-white light over the garbage-strewn alleys. The carriage stopped in front of a dilapidated boarding house that Alain could only assume was similar to the one he and his mother had lived in once; he'd been too young to retain any memories of those days.

"So, this is where you've been staying," Alain said uneasily, peering through the carriage's window. His gaze passed from the boarding house's grime-streaked bricks to its barred—yet still cracked—windows on the ground floor. "It's...homey."

Mavery laughed. "Sure, for a hovel."

"Your word, not mine."

He opened the door, then hopped out of the carriage and onto the dim street. He turned to Mavery, offering her a hand.

She laughed again. "You don't need to do that. We're barely ten feet from the door."

"I know I don't need to." He inched his hand toward her. "But I want to."

She rolled her eyes, but then laid her hand atop his and allowed him to escort her the dozen or so steps from the curb to the top of the stoop. Here, the only light was the low flicker of the lantern hanging by the front door. But even these dismal surroundings couldn't detract from Mavery's beauty. Her eyes were vibrant as ever, her nose was slightly pink from the cold, she still had a trace of powdered sugar on her bottom lip...

Alain's thoughts were once again taking him down a path from which there would be no return, and so he instead forced himself to study the lantern. Its fuel source was not Elemental magic or even gas, but oil, as though this building were stuck in the tenth century. He doubted there was even a lick of magic on the entire city block, save for whatever Mavery used to secure her bedroom. She'd once mentioned that she'd started placing protective wards after awaking to a drunken brawl outside her window.

"I assumed your wages would afford something nicer," Alain said. "Perhaps I'm more out of touch with the local economy than I thought."

"Oh, I definitely can afford something better than this, but when I first arrived in Leyport, I had no plans of staying long-term. All I wanted was a place to rest my head."

"But those plans have changed, yes?"

She smiled. "They have."

"Then why continue subjecting yourself to *this*?" He pointed to the front door, with its dubious lock and rusty hinges. "You ought to live somewhere more comfortable, safer..."

She squeezed his shoulder. He glanced at her hand, then focused on a patch of dirt on the wall directly behind her. At least, he hoped it was only dirt.

"Trust me, Alain, this is a palace compared to some of the holes I've stayed in. Besides, I can handle myself."

"I know you can, but..."

I couldn't bear the thought of anything happening to you, was at the forefront of his mind. But he couldn't speak that thought aloud. Not after he'd already crossed so many lines tonight: agreeing to come out with her, revealing more about himself than he told most people, holding her hand in the middle of a dense crowd.

"It's really not so bad," she said. "I would give you the grand tour, but my landlady is very strict about her 'no men allowed' policy."

"I'll have to take your word for it, then." Alain suppressed a shudder as he gave their surroundings another cursory look. "Well, I suppose this is good night."

"I suppose it is," Mavery said, tucking a stray hair behind her ear. For a moment, they both stood perfectly still while expectation hung heavily in the air between them.

Alain had no choice but to let the moment pass. He clasped his hands behind his back and gave her a short bow before turning and descending the stoop.

"Wait."

He turned to her again. From the top step, Mavery peered down at him with a heavy brow.

"I've been meaning to ask..." She took a deep breath. "You've kept me around despite knowing about my past, despite knowing why I sought you out in the first place. Don't get me wrong, I appreciate it, but I've been wondering...*why?*"

Alain hesitated, recalling the words she'd spoken shortly after reviving him. In the days since, he'd replayed those words countless times:

I decided you were worth more to me than any potential score.

"Because, in the end, you chose *me*," he said. "That alone means more than you could ever realize."

She opened her mouth but seemed unable to speak—a sensation he knew too well. Before his own emotions got the better of him, he turned around.

"Good night, Mavery," he said over his shoulder, then climbed into the carriage. As the vehicle pulled away from the curb, he hazarded a glance out the window, but she was now too distant for him to make out her expression. The driver's clicking tongue cut through the clacking hooves and rattling wheels.

"You should've kissed her back there," he said.

Alain wanted to tell the driver that, while a not-so-small part of him was in complete agreement, he couldn't cross that particular line. He knew all too well that nothing good would come of it.

Furthermore, he wanted to scold the driver for eavesdropping on a private conversation. And in addition to *that*, he hadn't asked anyone for romantic advice—especially not someone who looked young enough to be one of Alain's first-year students.

But instead of articulating any of that, he shut the window between his and the driver's seats. He spent the rest of the trip home stewing over his thoughts in silence.

Twenty-Five

"This can't be everything," Mavery said.

Tristan, the arcanist on duty, had taken her to a corner of the University of Leyport's library that received few visitors, judging by the thick dust and cobwebs. The Sensing "section" comprised a single shelf, and from her thorough cataloging of Alain's library, she already knew many of these titles.

"You're telling me, out of a hundred thousand books, these are the only ones about Sensing?"

"I'm afraid so, Ms. Culwich," Tristan said. He was a lanky man with shoulder-length hair that had gone completely white. His clean-shaven face was a rare sight among the men on campus. "These are the only books on arcane hypersensitivity that have been deemed fit for scholarly research."

She wasn't sure she wanted to know what *that* was supposed to imply.

"Do you have any books by Enodus the Second?" she asked. "And Deventhal the...sorry, I can't remember which number he was. Whoever was the most recent—and a Senser."

"I can find that out easily enough." Tristan jotted down something in his notebook. "I should return within half an hour, if you don't mind waiting."

"That's fine." If it came down to it, she would spend the whole day here.

After Tristan stepped away, she pulled the unfamiliar books from the shelf, then carried them to the bench in front of the nearby window. Several stories below, people lounged about on the verdant quad as they took advantage of the warm afternoon. Most of them appeared to be students, though Mavery spotted the occasional black robe hurrying between the towers. Part of her yearned to be out there, rather than in the dustiest corner of the library, but she had work to do.

She turned her attention to the book on the top of her stack. Its spine emitted a worrying crack as she opened it, and a cloud of dust particles danced in the beams of sunlight. Coughing, she began reading the introduction.

> The first occurrence of arcane hypersensitivity is widely disputed, but historians agree that the terminology itself was first coined in a letter written by an unknown healer from the former Kingdom of Selona, now part of the Dauphinian Empire, in the year 452 of the Modern Era...

The rest of the paragraph was equally dry, and it became a blur as her attention wandered back to last night. She flexed her fingers at the memory of grasping Alain's hand. Her face warmed as she recalled how, instead of pushing her away, he'd laced his fingers with hers until the final applause. A pleasant chill ran through her as she remembered him asking about her romantic interests, and how he'd understood her answer in the way few others had. And then there had been that brief moment, after walking her to her front door, when she'd thought he would kiss her—and the disappointment she'd felt when he hadn't.

And why did you expect anything else?

Of course he hadn't. The man cared about following protocols and upholding decorum. Yet, between that moment last night and the look she'd seen in his eyes on the night of his resurrection, there was a part of him that *didn't* care about those things. As for whether he would allow that part of himself to take the lead…

Mavery looked up from the book and let loose a groan that echoed through the room. Somewhere in the distance, a voice responded with an indignant, *"Shh!"*

She was here to learn everything she could about Sensing. Yet, her eyes had scanned the opening paragraph at least three times, and she hadn't absorbed a single word. She pushed aside the less important thoughts—she could revisit those later—and forced herself to focus on reading.

As Kazamin had once said, some wizards viewed Sensing as pseudoscience. The wizard who had penned this book was among that crowd: his thesis was that all arcane hypersensitivity research was based on flawed methods. He would spend the next five hundred pages defending that claim. A waste of good paper, in Mavery's opinion. Not bothering to finish the introductory chapter, she set the book aside.

The rest of the books proved equally unhelpful. If they didn't seek to debunk Sensing's existence, they sought to trivialize its usefulness or overstate its dangers. While Mavery didn't love the side effects of her condition, she had never felt they were *life-threatening*, as some of these scholars implied. One scholar even argued that Sensers were possessed by demons, his primary evidence being a small sect of Sensers who claimed to communicate with them. Mavery was tempted to toss that particular book out the window.

By the time Tristan returned, the only thing she'd learned was that the wizarding community had little use for people like her. On a positive note, she was all the more motivated to help Alain finish his Sensing spell—and prove several generations of bastards wrong.

"All of Enodus the Second's books are housed at the University of North Fenutia, as none of them were ever translated into Osperlandish," Tristan said. "As for Deventhal the Fifth, the entirety of his oeuvre is on alchemy."

Mavery frowned. Alain had failed to mention that Deventhal had been an alchemist.

"He never wrote a single book about Sensing?" she asked.

"No, but I did find his autobiography. Perhaps you'll find something useful in here."

Tristan handed her a book that was surprisingly thin, as Mavery had expected a wizard to be exceptionally verbose when it came to writing about himself. She skimmed the first chapter, in which Deventhal recounted his early childhood. Her breath hitched upon finding a reference to Sensing on the second page, but her hopes were quickly dashed.

> In the spring of my fourth year, I developed a condition known as arcane hypersensitivity. My lifelong curse inflicted upon me great discomfort when casting even the simplest of spells. Thus became my primary motivation for dedicating my life to the study of alchemy, as opposed to spellcraft.

"Shall I take this down to the circulation desk for you?" Tristan asked.

"No, thanks." With a sigh, she handed back the book. "I doubt Deventhal will be much help."

"Then can I assist you with anything else?"

"Actually, yes, there's one more thing."

Mavery retrieved a scrap of paper from her pocket. Upon it, she'd written the strange phrase she'd seen in Enodus's spell tome: *ktonic magic*. Tristan took it from her and stiffened.

"Do you have any books on this?" she asked.

"No," he said curtly.

"Because they're already lent out?"

"Because that word is nonsense."

"Are you sure? You didn't even look—"

"Miss, I have served as the University's Head Arcanist for twenty-seven years. If such a thing existed, I would know of it." He narrowed his eyes. "Are you doubting my expertise?"

Mavery blinked at him. "No, of course not. I was only thinking, I found this word in one of Enodus's spell tomes—a transcription of it, anyway—so maybe it's Old Fenutian or—"

"It is not. It is a transcription error, nothing more." He straightened his posture, adjusted his robe. "Now, if you have no further questions, I have other patrons to attend to."

Tristan turned on his heel and disappeared around the end of the row, leaving Mavery alone with the shelf of useless books. It wasn't until his footsteps had faded completely, when she realized he'd taken the scrap of paper with him.

An hour later, after skimming through the remaining Sensing books, she exited the library empty-handed and with more questions than answers. Between the lack of information about her condition and Tristan's suddenly cold demeanor, she wasn't sure which was more concerning. As she crossed the quad, someone called out to her.

"Mavery! Wait a moment!"

She turned around, coming face-to-face with Nezima's curly-haired assistant.

"You're...Wren, was it?" Mavery asked.

"I sure am!" Wren gave her an enthusiastic two-handed handshake. "I was hoping to talk to you after Nezima's class the other day, but you left early. Is now a good time?"

Wren beamed a wide, toothy smile. There was no trace of her nervousness from the other day. No doubt a result of being away from Nezima—and Nezima's paperwork. A gust of wind sent Wren's robe billowing behind her, revealing an ample bust and curvaceous hips that brought to mind a certain barmaid from half a lifetime ago...

Mavery blinked. Alain was one thing, but now this woman? She needed to get a hold of herself before she lost all her non-magical senses.

"Er, sure," she said. "What did you want to talk about?"

"It's about Aventus. You see, I was his assistant for about three years, up until last Fervidor."

Mavery gave her a look of faint surprise, as if this were new information. Wren had resigned six months ago—a few months into Alain's sabbatical, as Declan had implied.

"He has you working on Finisday?" Wren asked.

"No, I came here for my own research."

"Oh, good. For a minute there, I was worried he was working you as much as he works himself."

"I take it he's always been that way."

Wren laughed nervously, then frowned. "Aventus is very passionate about his work, I'll give him that. But there's passion, and then there's *obsession*. Once he gets started on something, he'll forget everything else, even his own wellbeing. Especially when it comes to the...er..."

She trailed off, then chewed her lip as she looked away. Mavery stepped to the side to remain within Wren's line of sight.

"When it comes to *what*, Wren?" She crossed her arms. "You sought me out for a reason, so tell me."

Neldren had always told Mavery that, despite the prominent scar across her nose, she had a face more suitable for sweet-talking than intimidation. But from how Wren cowered under her hard stare, she was currently having no problem with the latter. Mavery sighed. Wren was a young scholar, not some tight-lipped thug who needed to be berated into submission. She unfolded her arms.

"Wren," she said with as much gentleness as she could muster, "I won't tell him anything, if that's what you're worried about."

Wren slowly uncoiled. Her hands continued to tremble, but she was able to meet Mavery's eye again.

"Sorry, it's just difficult to talk about." She leaned forward and, though there was no one within earshot, lowered her voice. "What has he told you about the Innominate Temple?"

"Not much, as he seems to have given up on it."

"Really?" Wren pressed a hand to her heart as her body relaxed. "Oh, that's the best thing I've heard all day! When I first started working for him, I thought the temple was just a little passion project of his, nothing he was ever serious about. That was until a year ago, when he made a research breakthrough that drove him absolutely *mad*."

Mavery frowned. "How so?"

"Two days later, he sent me and his other two assistants to the temple. Said we needed to 'strike while the iron was hot.' "

Mavery's stomach lurched. When Declan had told her that Alain's assistant had died on a research trip, he hadn't specified where. Surely Wren wasn't talking about the same trip.

"Don't tell me he actually sent you to *the Innominate Temple*."

Wren nodded.

"And the three of you went *alone*?"

When she nodded again, Mavery's head reeled. Between the hike through miles of wilderness, the overwhelming arcana, and the lethal traps that she herself had still never seen, the Innominate Temple was not a place someone visited on a whim. It was certainly not a place for someone like Wren, whom Mavery doubted had much experience investigating dangerous ruins. She would bet the same had been true of the other two assistants.

"What happened?" Mavery asked, though she already knew some of the answer and dreaded learning the rest.

Wren took a deep breath. "It wasn't easy. First, we wandered in circles for half a day. Just as we were about to give up, we found the godsforsaken place. It was *awful*. The magic was...was..."

"Strong enough to make you ill."

"Exactly." Her brown eyes widened. "Er, how did you know?"

"I've been there. Well, I've gotten close enough. But never mind that. What happened next?"

"We tried getting closer, then Conor triggered some hidden trap—a detonation ward, I think—and it killed him. It's awful enough that someone died, but the fact that it was *Conor* was even worse. He'd only been on our team for a few weeks, and gods, was he handsome. He had the most unusual eyes, and he—"

"Unusual in what way?" Mavery asked.

"Mismatched. His left eye was brown, his right was blue—or was it the other way around? Have you ever seen anyone with eyes like that?"

"No, can't say that I have."

Not in person, at any rate...

Wren blushed. "Anyway, Lorcan carried Conor back to the closest village. He got so shaken up over the whole ordeal, he resigned and left the wizarding community altogether. Last I heard, he'd moved to Durnatel and became a wardsmith for some bank."

"And then you resigned."

She nodded. "I didn't want to, not at first. But things weren't the same after that trip. Aventus became even more obsessed with the temple. He was so wrapped up in his research, he stopped leaving his apartment. I had to ask Professor Ward to help me with exams.

"Things only got worse after Dean Kazamin put Aventus on sabbatical. He'd go days without eating, without even getting out of bed. And then the drinking." She shook her head. "I hate that I resigned in the middle of all that, but... But being someone's caretaker wasn't what I'd signed up for."

Mavery recalled the state of Alain's apartment—and Alain himself—on the day they first met. To learn that he'd been living that way for *months* left an ache deep in her chest.

"Lucky for me," Wren continued, "Nezima was looking for another assistant and hired me on the spot."

Mavery snorted. Being used as a human satchel seemed the opposite of luck.

Wren shrugged. "I know taking that job was a bit of a setback. I graduated five years ago—at this point in my career, I ought to be assisting an independent wizard, not one still tied to the University. But I'll take grading term papers over being a caretaker any day, though I do sometimes miss getting paid—"

"Nezima doesn't pay you?"

"Wizards aren't required to pay their assistants; Aventus is one of the few that does." She furrowed her brow. "Didn't he review the Covenants with you?"

"I must've forgotten about that one. But if she isn't paying you, how do you get by?"

"I'm a Wincoff," Wren said, and Mavery resisted the urge to roll her eyes. Of course, someone connected to railroad barons wouldn't be concerned with something as arbitrary as *money*. "Speaking of Nezima, she runs a club for the women on campus—wizards and assistants alike. We meet every Middisday evening at a pub called the Lettered Gentleman."

Mavery raised her eyebrows.

Wren laughed. "She chose it primarily for the convenience, partly for the irony. You should join us! Come talk about your research, vent your frustrations, have a drink on Nezima; she always pays for everything."

Now that Mavery planned to stay in Leyport, it would be wise to make some connections in the wizarding community. Perhaps more friends, if she could manage it. At the very least, she could learn more about the enigmatic Nezima—for starters, why Alain disliked her so much.

"Thanks, Wren."

"Until then, take care of yourself, Mavery," Wren said cheerfully, but then her expression darkened. "And if Aventus ever brings up the Innominate Temple again, do yourself a favor and find any other wizard to work for."

Mavery frowned. "I'm not going to abandon Alain for 'any other wizard.'" Her frown deepened as Wren's eyes widened. "What?"

Wren flinched. Mavery's tone had apparently been more forceful than she'd intended.

"Nothing. Only, we worked together for three years and got along well enough, I suppose, but I never used his real name. Conor did, though. Strange..."

"What's strange?" Mavery demanded, but her question would remain unanswered. The clock tower atop the Great Hall chimed, announcing that it was four o'clock.

"I need to go," Wren said. "I hope you'll join us on Middisday. Remember: the Lettered Gentleman after final classes let out!"

With a smile and a wave, she bounded across the quad and into the library. Though Mavery hadn't learned much about Sensing today, she now had plenty more to think about.

TWENTY-SIX

When Alain reinstated his wards after his accident, he'd decided that locking the front door would be redundant. So long as Mavery gave a courtesy knock, she was free to enter as she pleased. The morning after her trip to the library, she rapped on the door, then opened it to find Alain amid another bout of pacing and spell-revising—mercifully, with protective wards in place.

"Good morning," he said, coming to a stop in the middle of the room. "How was your day off?"

"I did as you suggested and went to the library on my own."

His eyes brightened. "Did you learn anything interesting?"

She held back a laugh as she thought of her conversation with Wren. But she wasn't ready to press him on *that*.

"Not in the way I'd hoped. First, Kazamin wasn't joking when he said this was a niche field. The library has hardly any books about Sensing."

Alain nodded. "I should have warned you I already own every book that's worth the paper it's printed on."

"At least I got to see that for myself," she said with a shrug. "I then asked one of the arcanists about that word I found in your copy of Enodus's spell tome. He said there's no such thing as 'kay-tonic' magic, 'kuh-tone-ick' magic, however the hells you're supposed to say it."

"But you don't believe him."

She shook her head. "He didn't even bother looking into it. He turned defensive—hostile, even—like he was hiding something."

"Which arcanist did you speak to?"

"The Head Arcanist. Tristan, I think his name was."

Alain nodded. "I can only recall him acting in a similar manner once—when I inquired about Aganast—though I always assumed his disgruntlement had more to do with the stockpile of books I'd kept past their due date."

"But he still helped you with your research."

"He did." Alain considered this for a moment, scratching his chin. "Well, I doubt our understanding of that word will affect our progress with our spellcraft. Let's revisit it after the presentation."

Though he seemed unconcerned about Tristan, dread gnawed at Mavery's stomach. Before she could persuade him to reconsider, Alain spoke again.

"While we're on the topic of spellcraft, I'd say you're overdue for another Etherean lesson."

That lifted her spirits enough to put the matter to rest, at least for now.

For what felt like the thousandth time, Mavery repeated the incantation. A tendril of Ether manifested in the air, hovering a few inches above the iron coin on her palm. As she recited the words, the tendril slowly floated downward, wrapped around the coin and the single strand of dark hair lying atop it. Bolstered by her Etherean, the metal glowed. But then the Ether evaporated almost as quickly as she'd conjured it, and the metal dulled once more.

"I almost had it," she groaned. She placed the coin on the floor, then blew on her clasped hands. Outside, it was a pleasant spring day. Inside, she sat on the floor, back to the fire and shivering as if it were still the dead of winter.

Conjuring an orb of Ether had been as natural as breathing. Turning the coin into a basic compass had been more challenging, but she'd succeeded after half an hour of practice. After three hours of reciting *this* spell, however, the only thing she'd achieved was feeling like an icicle.

Alain had shown her an augmentation that, using a strand of his hair, would modify the compass. Instead of indicating north, the coin would glow when pointed in his direction. He'd made it sound so simple.

"You stumbled over the last two runes," he said. He stood a few paces away, holding his lecture notes, though he'd rarely referenced them at all that morning. It seemed Mavery had convinced him that the "practical" approach to learning Etherean was superior to his "tried-and-true" method. That was, until now.

"It's hard to enunciate when my teeth are chattering," she said, rubbing her arms as she continued to shiver.

Alain frowned. "Wait here."

He went to the bedroom and returned with the fur-lined faculty robe he'd put away until next winter. He crouched in front of her and wrapped the plum-colored fabric around her shoulders. While the robe didn't relieve the arcane chill coursing through her body, it took the edge off.

"Thanks."

She pulled the robe until she was completely shrouded in it. But she still continued to shiver; so, too, did Alain's frown persist.

"Are you sure you don't want the potion?" he asked.

"I told you, I won't always have it handy. I need to get used to spellcasting without it."

"I understand, but it's sweltering in here and you're half-frozen to death."

Though Mavery felt nowhere near warm, Alain's forehead glistened with sweat. He'd removed his vest and undone the top buttons of his shirt. He remained crouched in front of her, close enough for her to catch a glimpse of his bruise—now a deep brown—raise her fingers, place them against the hollow of his collarbone, and complete the healing process with a simple transfer of arcana. But she knew he'd never agree to it; he was still committed to letting his injury heal naturally.

You're just looking for an excuse to touch him...

She silenced that thought as Alain stood up.

"If half my students had half your talent, my job would be infinitely more enjoyable. You've made extraordinary progress considering you learned your first incantation just last week. You've earned yourself a break."

"I could say the same about you. Did you rest at all yesterday?"

"Yes, I had afternoon tea with my mother."

"And after that?"

"I didn't work on the spell tome..."

"*But...*"

"But I *did* make some adjustments to the anti-Sensing potion." Mavery pulled a face, and he chuckled. "If you can think of a better name for it, I'm all ears."

"Fine," she sighed. "Bring me the damn potion."

"Actually, I'll need to make a new batch, but it shouldn't take more than half an hour."

"Do you need any help?" She shrugged off the robe; it had made little difference. "Maybe getting up and moving around will do me some good."

"I've always treated alchemy as a solo endeavor." He smiled, and the slightest flicker of warmth stirred within her. "But I wouldn't mind some company."

He offered his hand, and she grasped it as he pulled her to her feet. They stood chest to chest for the duration of a few heartbeats—not long enough for Mavery to fully appreciate their closeness. Alain dropped her hand and turned toward the kitchen, leaving her even colder than she'd felt a moment ago.

"I hope you're not expecting a lesson," he said as he opened the kitchen door. "I know enough about alchemy to be dangerous, but not enough to teach it in any meaningful capacity."

"That's fine. Besides, I already know my way around a mortar and pestle."

"Then how about I leave that part to you?"

He retrieved his notebook from the table. It was the same one he'd used the day they visited the café, when he'd first thought of the potion. As she hovered over his shoulder, still rubbing her gooseflesh-covered arms, she glimpsed observations he'd made about her Senses, early drafts of the potion recipe, and a few sketches.

"Wait," she said. "Was that...?"

He sputtered something in protest as she reached forward snatched the book from his hands.

She paged through sketches of the herbs hanging in the kitchen, the birds that occasionally perched outside the sitting room window, the view of the Merimar from that same window. Then there was a series of the same human subject: reading, writing, drinking tea.

"Are these all of *me*?"

Alain's face flushed, which was all the confirmation she needed. He reached for the notebook, but she took a step back, taking it further out of reach. She was being childish, but she couldn't resist. She'd never given much thought to the contents of his notebook; his bouts of sketching and note-taking had simply become another of his quirks. Her heart fluttered as she wondered how often he'd been drawing her, studying her, without her ever realizing it.

"You've had your fun," Alain huffed. "Now, can you please hand it back?"

She relented. He continued searching for the recipe, but his shaky fingers struggled to turn the pages.

"You've nothing to be ashamed of," Mavery said. "In fact, I'm flattered."

"That's a relief, though it's difficult to not feel guilty whenever I devote even a few minutes of my time to art...if you can even consider this *art*."

"Why would you feel guilty about that?"

"Because it's been long ingrained in me that anything not directly related to my work is a waste of time."

Her heart sank as she remembered what he'd once told her about his painting hobby. "For what it's worth, *I* don't think it's a waste of time."

"Thank you." The faintest trace of a smile pulled at his lips. "I wish the rest of the wizarding community—especially those at the University—thought the same as you do."

"You really think none of your colleagues have hobbies outside of teaching and research?"

"Don't forget copious drinking. That's an age-old academic pastime." He gave a half-hearted chuckle that faded as quickly as it had arrived. "I can't say for certain, though I doubt many of them have time for it. That was certainly the case for me. My sabbatical was the first true break I'd had in years." He frowned. "Not that I was doing much relaxing."

He looked at his notebook, then out the window. Thanks to Wren, Mavery had a good idea of what his sabbatical had consisted of. She gently touched his shoulder, and he tore his gaze away from the window. His weak smile did little to ease her concerns.

"Can I ask you something?" she said.

"Of course."

"When I was rereading the Covenants last night, I noticed that there are many ways you wizards can retain your rank. Teaching is only one of them."

Alain nodded. "Yes, almost any contribution to scholarship counts. The High Council keeps it open-ended on purpose."

"Then why did you become a professor?"

"It was the first opportunity presented to me, and I didn't have much choice in the matter."

Mavery furrowed her brow. "What makes you say that?"

"Because Seringoth personally recommended me to the High Council. He might have been difficult to work for, to put it lightly, but he argued my case when the rest of the Elder Wizards thought I was too young for the job. I very well couldn't decline after that.

"Being young and not knowing any better, I thought professors spent most of their time in the classroom. Little did I know there was more to it than that: reading essays, administering exams, managing assistants, writing books, conducting research, crafting spells... Up until my sabbatical, I had little time for anything else—mundane hobbies, least of all." He gazed at his notebook again with a sigh. "We should start on the potion. At least alchemy is considered a 'respectable' hobby."

He showed her his latest version of the recipe. For a potion with such a profound impact on Mavery's Senses, it was relatively simple. It required only six ingredients, the most exotic of which were the powdered kutauss claws.

The first step was to create a sort of herbal tea to serve as the base. Alain's recipe required two herbs that even the most novice alchemist would recognize: fallowroot and feygrass. Bundles of them hung from the rafters. Mavery plucked off violet fallowroot petals and sapphire feygrass sprigs, shredded them into smaller pieces, then began to grind them with a mortar and pestle. Meanwhile, Alain set up a fireproofing ward—its aura was soft pink—around the perimeter of the kitchen.

"Let me guess," she said. "Fallowroot is to treat my headaches, feygrass is to treat my cold chills."

"Exactly. My first attempts included persilweed, but fallowroot is far more potent."

Persilweed was, as the name implied, a weed that grew rampant in the wilderness. Though it was most effective when brewed into a tea, chewing a few leaves would treat minor aches in a pinch. In large enough quantities, it was brewed into a contraceptive tea that was as effective as it was bitter. Mavery hadn't brewed it in over two months; it was difficult to say when she would need it again.

As she perished that thought, she drove the pestle into the bowl of the mortar with more force than was necessary. In what must have been record time, the fallowroot and feygrass became a fine indigo-hued powder. She tipped it into a saucepan, added a measure of water, brought the mixture to a boil, then removed it from the burner to steep.

With that settled, she went to see what Alain was doing on the other side of the kitchen. He was weighing out an ash-like substance on a set of brass scales.

"Powdered kutauss claws," he said. "We'll need to heat these with a torch."

Mavery peered into the container that stored the rest of the claws. It was almost empty.

"What are you going to do when you run out?" she asked. "Are you still avoiding Enid's shop?"

He stiffened. "I suppose I'll either need to find an alternative that's available through more...*legitimate* channels, or I'll need to make an exception. But that's a bridge to cross at a later date. Rest assured, I have enough to last through the spell presentation."

He swept the powder onto a piece of cloth, then tipped it into a calcinator—a shallow cast-iron bowl whose tall legs allowed for heating either from above with a torch, or from below with a candle. The powdered claws required the former method.

"Ever use one of these?" Alain asked, showing her the torch.

"No," Mavery said, "but I'll give it a go."

The main part of the torch was a brass chamber slightly larger than her fist. Embedded in the metal were gemstones with pink and black stripes. She attempted to feed a bit of her arcana into the chamber, but nothing came out of the torch's long, thin nozzle.

"Make sure your skin is in direct contact with the rhodonite," Alain said. "Here, wrap your fingers around it like this."

He stood behind her with his chest to her back. His hand covered hers, then guided her fingers to the smooth stone. But once her hand was in the proper place, he didn't pull his own away. Mavery became acutely aware of his breath against her neck, the warmth of his body behind her, the gentle pressure of his fingers slipping into the gaps between her own. Heart racing, she slowly turned her head to the side; with his cheek mere inches away, meeting his eye took no effort at all. His body froze with a sharp inhale, as though he'd suddenly realized what he'd done. They both spoke at once:

"Sorry," he said. "I, er, think—"

"Maybe you should handle this—"

"—you get the idea."

"—while I strain the herbs."

"Y-yes, that's probably for the best."

Alain removed his hand and took a half-step back. Mavery turned to her left at the same time Alain reached for the torch, and she walked straight into his outstretched arm. She tried moving in the other direction, only to bump into his shoulder. They exchanged nervous laughter as, no matter which direction they moved, they seemed destined to collide into each other. Alain took a full step back and remained still, allowing Mavery to finally slip past him. Face burning, she did so while lowering her gaze.

She returned to the stove, where the tea had cooled enough

to touch. She strained the liquid through a cheesecloth, using her bare hands to extract every bit of liquid from the clump of wet herbs. Each squeeze relieved a bit of her embarrassment, but plenty remained even after the herbs had yielded their final drop.

As she wiped her indigo-stained hands on a tea towel, Alain brought over the powdered claws. He sidled next to her and tipped the white powder into the herb-infused base. Once again, Mavery became acutely aware of how closely they were standing: their shoulders were barely an inch apart. Her Ether-induced chill was no longer a concern; the kitchen felt like an inferno.

"I should, er, go work on my translation," she muttered.

"All right," Alain said, nodding. "I'll finish up and bring you the potion in a few minutes."

Back in the sitting room, Mavery threw herself onto Alain's desk chair and allowed herself a single self-pitying groan before deciding she was being ridiculous.

Yes, she'd not only grown to enjoy Alain's company, she was drawn to this man like a moth to a flame. But she couldn't let his mere presence reduce her to a smitten schoolgirl. Now that she was an assistant in earnest, she had more important matters to worry about: the translation, the presentation, the strange word...

She was determined to take her job seriously, and that included not letting some condescending arcanist derail her research. And she was equally determined to not let some silly rules get between her and—

"Are you all right?"

She flinched at the sound of Alain's voice. She'd been so lost in thought, she hadn't heard him return from the kitchen.

"I'm fine," she said. "Just...thinking."

He placed a potion-filled teacup on the desk. "About the translation?"

He leaned against the desk, arms crossed over his chest in a way that suggested he was attempting to act casual in light of what had happened in the kitchen. Though Mavery's most recent behavior spoke otherwise, she was thirty-seven years old and had enough experience to recognize in Alain the same internal struggle she felt within herself.

"The Covenants, actually," she said. "I read nothing about how the High Council enforces those rules. When you become a wizard, do you swear a blood oath or—"

Alain laughed. "Blood oaths? Oh, those are just fairy tales."

"And how am I supposed to know that?" she scoffed. "Everything about wizards, the High Council... It's all so godsdamned cryptic."

"Sorry, I often take for granted what's common knowledge for wizards. To answer your question, when it comes to following the Covenants, we're completely on the honor system. If someone were to break a covenant, the High Council would only know if it's blatantly obvious, or if another wizard were to report a violation.

"As for the punishment..." He shifted uneasily. "Well, that depends. For something as banal as a dress code violation, the High Council will send you a sternly worded letter. Damaging a library book will earn you a small fine."

"And what about a more serious violation?" Her mouth began to dry, but she pushed ahead, forced herself to speak the words. "For example, if a wizard were to become romantically involved with an assistant, what would happen then?"

His eyes narrowed. "Why do you ask?"

She met his gaze and held it. "Just humor me, Alain. What would happen if something like that came to light?"

"That would depend entirely upon the whims of the High Council—"

"Tell me the worst-case scenario."

He sighed. "The assistant would face no formal punishment, save for the damage to her reputation following a scandal like that. As for the wizard, he would certainly lose his job at the University. And he would likely be stripped of his rank. That would mean no more research stipends, no more access to the universities' libraries, no more resurrections. The wizard would become, for all intents and purposes, an ordinary mage."

She laughed flatly. "You speak as though being an 'ordinary mage' would be a terrible thing."

"I suppose it wouldn't be, but losing one's rank is still a risk I wouldn't want to take. Er, hypothetically speaking, of course."

He looked away as color rose in his cheeks. Mavery couldn't recall ever knowing anyone who blushed as much as he did. It was one of the many things she found endearing about him.

"While we're engaging in hypotheticals..." She chewed her lip. "What if the Covenants didn't exist?"

Alain laughed nervously as he waved a hand. "Having romantic relations with *any* wizard is a recipe for disaster. Doubly so when it comes to the wizard standing before you. I can assure you, that's an idea not worth entertaining, even in hypotheticals."

Mavery frowned. "What do you m—?"

"I ought to go bottle up the rest of the potion." He nudged the teacup across the desk. "Drink up. We've plenty of work to do."

With that, he escaped into the kitchen. Though she wanted to follow him and press him further on what he'd said, she found herself unable to move. A heavy weight had settled on her shoulders, anchoring her to the desk chair.

He was right, much as it pained her to admit it. He couldn't risk his entire career for someone he'd known for not even two months. And now that she was committed to being his assistant—a job that was enjoyable, comfortable, *stable*—she wasn't about to risk losing that, either.

But what of the man in the paintings? Had Alain risked everything for *him*?

Mavery grabbed the cup of anti-Sensing potion. She tossed the black liquid down her throat, winced at its bitterness. Within seconds, the auras emanating from the front door faded. The potion had once again succeeded at dulling those Senses. If only everything else could be dulled just as easily.

TWENTY-SEVEN

As the week progressed, Leyport became caught in an endless storm, as if a petulant raincloud had parked itself over the city and refused to budge.

Middisday was an exceptionally gloomy day, made worse by Alain's sullen mood. Even though the High Council presentation loomed closer than ever, Alain seemed to have lost all motivation to work. He'd spent most of the day standing by the window, transfixed by the view that hadn't changed over the past three days: an ominously gray sky over a gray churning river.

Mavery, however, had devoted much of the day to learning a new incantation. The Sensing spell, once complete, would reveal the colors of the five primary types of wards: protective, detonation, resonating, soundproofing, and fireproofing. Out of the four types she had yet to master, she'd been most eager to learn the incantation for fireproofing.

She gripped the sides of a wooden box—the same one that had once been overflowing with Alain's mail—and recited the incantation again. It was only fourteen syllables but a touch more complicated than the others she'd learned so far. She stumbled over the final rune, almost forgetting to roll the 'r,' but the pulsation beneath her fingers told her the Ether had responded to her words all the same.

She gasped. "I think I did it!"

Even her excitement couldn't distract Alain from the window—or, more accurately, whatever thoughts were plaguing him. He continued to watch the downpour.

Mavery hoisted herself off the floor with a creak from her bad knee, and it continued to ache as she crossed the room.

"What's wrong?" she asked.

"Hmm? Oh, nothing," he said, finally acknowledging her for the first time in hours. She threw him a penetrating look, and he hung his head with a sigh. "Today is...not a good day."

"I can see that." She placed a hand on his shoulder. "Is there anything I can do to help?"

"No, it's nothing to concern yourself with." He cleared his throat. "Er, did you need something?"

"I think I managed the fireproofing spell. Come look."

Her hand trailed from his shoulder to his elbow. She pulled him away from the window and to the center of the room, where the box sat on the floor. She grabbed a match from the tea table. The scent of sulfur filled the air as she struck it. She dropped it in the box, and the flame extinguished with a tiny puff of smoke.

"Two down, three to go," Alain said, nodding, though his voice lacked a shred of enthusiasm. "Why don't we call it a day?"

Mavery glanced at the clock. "It's not even one-thirty."

"And yet, it seems you've already put in a full day's work."

"I could get back to practicing augmentations. I still haven't mastered the compass—"

"Don't worry about that. Leave the augmentations to me." He placed his hand against her upper back and nudged her toward the door. "Go on, take the rest of the afternoon off."

She shrugged away from his grasp. "Alain, what's going on? Are you worried about the presentation?"

He laughed humorlessly. "I'm *constantly* worried about the presentation, but no. This time, it's..." He hesitated, then gave her what she assumed was his best attempt at a smile. "As I said, it's nothing to concern yourself with. I'll be better come morning, I promise."

She met his gaze with another probing stare, though she knew any attempts to force the truth from him would be in vain. She could only hope her evening plans would prove more enlightening.

The Lettered Gentleman was a much higher-end establishment than Mavery had expected, though she probably should have known better, based on the name alone. The walls were paneled with dark-toned wood, and adorned with world maps, oil paintings of the University's towers, and other scholarly paraphernalia.

And, as the name implied, the patrons were predominantly male. Nearly all of them wore the plum robes that marked them as University faculty. Mavery could see no female professors as she surveyed the room. She didn't know what time classes ended for the day, so she'd left the boarding house at seven o'clock, immediately following the evening meal, though she now worried she'd missed Nezima's group altogether.

The air was thick with the slightly sweet and leathery aroma of cigar smoke. Mavery crossed the gleaming parquet floor to the equally gleaming bar along the right-hand wall. As she began to signal the bartender, a familiar face from the other end of the bar looked in her direction.

"You're here!"

Wren rushed over. Mavery raised her eyebrows, too startled to react further, when the younger woman threw her arms around her middle and pulled her in for a hug.

"Oh, I'm so glad you made it!" Wren said. The ale on her breath explained her overt friendliness.

"Er, glad to be here." Mavery patted Wren's shoulder before taking a step back. "I take it I'm not too late."

"No, no, not at all. Everyone comes and goes as they please. Selemin and Anneke arrived not even half an hour ago."

At least Nezima and Wren wouldn't be the only familiar faces.

Wren gathered up the four tankards the bartender had just finished pouring. Mavery offered to carry a few; from the way Wren was swaying, half the ale would end up on the floor. That freed one of Wren's arms, which she immediately hooked around one of Mavery's. Wren led her to a private room in the back of the pub, where there was no cigar smoke—only lively conversation.

The scholars were split between two tables, with assistants seated at one and professors at the other, and there were far more of the former than the latter. Most of them were still wearing their robes.

Nezima and Selemin sat at the professors' table. They were joined by two women Mavery didn't recognize. Before she could get a good look at either of them, Wren steered her to the assistants' table.

Wren passed around the tankards, then pulled up an empty chair and urged Mavery to take a seat. Upon doing so, Mavery understood the snide comment Nezima had once made about her age. None of the other assistants looked a day over twenty-five.

"Everyone, this is Mavery," Wren said. "Aventus's assistant."

Wren went clockwise around the table, pointing at each of the six women as she rattled off the assistants' names, wizards, and academic departments. All of it slipped immediately from Mavery's mind. Only Selemin's assistant, Anneke, stood out from the rest. With her straw-colored hair and thick spectacles, she looked somewhat familiar.

"I remember you," Anneke said dryly. "You once called me and my friends 'weirdos.' "

"Oh, right," Mavery said. "Sorry about that."

"When you walked in, I was *certain* you were a professor," said the mousy-haired assistant sitting beside Anneke. "How old are you?"

Anneke elbowed her in the ribs. "Gods, Nellie! Where are your manners?"

The group then returned to what they'd been discussing before: no less than three distinct conversations. Since Mavery had nothing to contribute to any of them, she quietly observed and caught fragments of crosstalk.

"First-years get worse every term."

"As if sixth-years are any better. Some couldn't so much as transmutate water into piss."

"—but the second reviewer said my writing 'lacked a distinctive authorial voice.' It was a godsdamned *literature review*!"

"Well, one of *my* reviewers recommended a dozen papers that have nothing to do with fabrication magic."

"—the meeting was on the day I went dress shopping in Durnatel. I told him I couldn't attend because I was on deadline."

"But aren't you *always* on deadline?"

"Exactly! So, I wasn't lying, was I?"

Mavery's attention then wandered to the other table, where Selemin's voice had risen above all the others.

"—pulled the funding for my research trip! He gave me some drivel about budgetary constraints, but Safiya reserved the train tickets a fortnight ago. No, I'll bet anything he's still mad about my Marya worshiper joke."

"The one you made at his Yvernal party?" asked a professor with sleek raven hair. "He wasn't even in the room at the time."

Selemin nodded. "One of his sycophants must have told him about it."

"Regardless, that was months ago!"

"Kazamin's memory these days may be faultier than a cracked bloodstone, but not when it comes to his precious Marya."

"I believe it," said a white-haired woman. "A decade ago, he denied an interdepartmental trip to a burial site along the southern border, on the off-chance any Maryans had been buried there. And that was merely an anthropological study; we had no intentions of exhuming any graves."

"He's always had difficulty separating his religion from his profession," Nezima said, shaking her head.

"You would know better than anyone," Selemin said. "Is it true that he's never been resurrected?"

"Yes, like all Maryans, he doesn't believe in interfering with death."

Selemin scoffed. "How the High Council considers him worthy of leading our department, when he's never even experienced all the perils of research—"

"If I remember correctly, *you* have never been resurrected," the dark-haired professor said with a smirk.

Selemin waved a hand. "Sure, but he's a Gardemancer, I'm a historian. What lethal dangers am I going to expose myself to? Paper cuts?"

Nezima laughed, and it took all of Mavery's resolve not to gape at her. Granted, Nezima's version of it was far from *mirthful*—it was no more than flat, clipped chuckles—but it was laughter all the same.

"How much do you need for your trip?" she asked Selemin. "Perhaps we can pool our resources."

"Much appreciated, but as I've done for the last three, I'll fund this one from my own pocket." Selemin took another swig from their tankard, then groaned. "Why can't he retire already? He's been dean for, what, a hundred years?"

"Forty-seven," the white-haired woman said. "Not that anyone is counting."

The professors laughed in unison.

Something prodded Mavery in the arm. She looked to her side and found Wren watching her with unfocused eyes. The scent of ale emanating from her was stronger than before.

"I said, 'How have things been with Aventus since we last spoke?' " Wren's speech was so slurred, Mavery barely understood her.

She chewed the inside of her cheek as she considered her answer.

"Complicated," she said at last.

"That's him to the letter!" Wren cackled, then her eyes widened. "Oh, no, I grabbed you before you had a chance to order a drink, didn't I?"

"Don't worry about—"

"Nonsense! What would you like?"

Wren attempted to stand, but her knees buckled. She clung to the back of her chair, which was the only thing preventing her from colliding with the floor.

Mavery stifled a laugh. "I would like *you* to stay put. I'll order my own drink."

As she rose from the table, Nezima called out, "Whatever you're ordering, put it on my tab."

"Er, thanks."

Nezima replied with a tip of her wineglass. Mavery continued to feel the professor's eyes follow her out of the room.

The pub had become much livelier, filled with even more patrons in University robes. Mavery had to shoulder through a small crowd to approach the bar. The cigar smoke had also grown thicker than ever; it lingered in the air like a dense fog, and the smell was so intense, it had lost all its pleasantness. Mavery peered in the mirror behind the bar and quickly identified the culprits: a group of male professors playing cards.

She caught the bartender's eye. He asked her for her order, much to the dismay of the men who'd been waiting in the queue. She assumed Nezima had accumulated an impressive bar tab, which was why the bartender was giving her preferential treatment. Not to mention she was the only woman presently at the bar.

As she waited for a glass of red wine, a chillingly familiar scent cut through the smoke: arcana-infused ash.

Her heart raced as she subtly glanced around the room. To her left, halfway down the bar, a man had just extinguished his cigarette that now smoldered in an ashtray. Mavery sighed, then chided herself for being so paranoid. Even if she *had* Sensed shadow magic, this room was filled with wizards. It could have come from any number of them.

"Your wine, madam," the bartender said.

She nodded in thanks as she took her glass. By the time she entered the back room, her heartbeat had returned to normal.

Most of the assistants were too busy gossiping to notice Mavery. Wren, however, had fallen silent. She stared at her empty tankard with a blank expression, much like how Alain had looked that afternoon. Mavery then recalled what Wren had told her only days ago.

She would bet a hefty sum that the ill-fated research trip had been exactly a year ago. She'd even wager that today marked the anniversary of their colleague's death. How had she not made that connection sooner?

"Over here," Selemin called out, patting the empty chair to

their right. As she doubted Wren was in any state to reminisce about the Innominate Temple, Mavery approached the professors' table.

"As you can see," Selemin said as Mavery sat down, "I'm the odd one out in this little drinking club."

"This is a *support group*," Nezima said, using the same tone she'd used when reprimanding her students. "And it is open to any scholar *not* of the male persuasion."

Drinking club, Selemin mouthed, then threw Mavery a wink before taking a swig of ale.

"It's good to see you again, Mavery," Nezima said.

"Likewise, and thanks for the drink."

"Think nothing of it." She gestured at the other two professors. "Have you met our colleagues?"

"I'm Rivalda," the raven-haired woman said, extending her hand. "Professor of Aumbremancy."

Mavery could have guessed this professor's innate School with ease. Rivalda had the ashen look of someone who, like most shadow-wielders, preferred to avoid sunlight whenever possible.

The woman sitting beside Nezima reached across the table and also offered Mavery a handshake. She was not only the oldest among the group, with her white hair and liver-spotted skin, there was a sagacity behind her crystal blue eyes that the other scholars lacked.

"Corenta, Dean of the Faculty of Faisancy," she said. "I've been at the University of Leyport longer than most of them have been alive." She inclined her head toward the assistants' table. "Rumor around campus is you're a Senser."

Mavery nodded. "The rumors are true."

"And Aventus's latest project is to develop some sort of Sensing spell," Nezima said.

News did indeed spread quickly at the University. Mavery took a long drink of wine. She wasn't sure how much of his research Alain would want shared publicly, but she could safely assume he'd want none of it shared with Nezima.

"I've been wondering, how did you and Aventus begin working together in the first place?" Nezima asked. "After all, no one from the University had seen him for the better part of a year."

In hindsight, this was a question Mavery should have seen coming, and one that she and Alain should have prepared an answer for. She took another sip of wine as she formulated a response that was as truthful as it was vague.

"I came to Leyport almost two months ago, looking for work, and we crossed paths. Once he found out I was a Senser, he got the idea for the spell and decided to take me on as his assistant. It was...serendipitous, I suppose."

"Quite serendipitous, considering assistants don't typically need to go about 'looking for work.' " Nezima peered at Mavery over the rim of her wineglass. "You told me you were in the midst of a career change. What were you doing before you came to Leyport?"

"Wardsmithing," Mavery said. It was also a job for "unlearned types," to borrow Alain's phrasing, but at least it carried a bit more prestige than wardbreaking.

Nezima gave an amenable nod, then appeared to ready another question.

"Can I ask *you* something?" Mavery said, eager to turn this interview around.

Nezima's lips drew into a thin line. "That depends. Is it about my heritage?"

Mavery blinked. "Do people often lead with that?"

"More than you can imagine," Corenta said.

"Some can't fathom the idea of a Nilandoren who isn't absurdly tall," Selemin said, shaking their head.

"Those are often the same people who can't place Nilandor on a map," Rivalda added.

To Mavery's surprise, Nezima was blushing slightly; there was a purplish undertone to her slate-colored skin.

"Well, no, it wasn't about that," Mavery said. "I once, er...*courted* a Nilandoren man, so I know a bit about the culture."

"How very worldly of you," Nezima said flatly. "In any case, I wouldn't be able to inform you of much on that matter. I am only *half*-Nilandoren, and I was born and raised in this very city." She drained her glass, then rested her forearms on the table. "So, what *did* you want to ask me?"

"I wanted to know more about your research. Alain once mentioned something about poison warding."

Nezima's embarrassment gave way to faint surprise. Thanks to the wine, it took Mavery a few seconds to recognize her blunder.

"Not even two months, and you've dropped his honorific. Curious." The corner of Nezima's mouth quirked into a smile. "He is correct: the bulk of my research has been on the convergence of Gardemancy and Alchemy. But I doubt whatever he told you was coupled with admiration and praise."

Mavery raised her eyebrows, and Nezima's smile broadened.

"Aventus has always harbored some resentment against me for subjecting my assistants to the hazards of poison research—hazards that *all* my assistants are made fully aware of upfront. It's a necessary evil, of course, as there's little use for warding against health tonics."

"Al—er, Aventus—also said his mother once helped you with a poison warding fabric."

"Yes, that was what earned me my wizard rank. Priscilla and I have remained good friends ever since." She settled back in her chair. "As a matter of fact, she told me about the most delightful chat she had with her son this past Finisday. He's positively smitten with some mystery woman; he could hardly stop talking about her."

"Is that so?" Mavery said as a warm tingling sensation washed over her. She raised her glass and took another long drink, hoping Nezima and the others would assume the wine was to blame for any sudden change in her demeanor.

"Do you have any idea who his new paramour might be?"

She lowered her glass and met Nezima's eye. "Not a clue. What he does in his spare time is his own business."

"Really? From what Wren tells me, the two of you are thick as thieves. Surely he would have told *you* something."

Mavery glanced at the other table, where Wren was now dozing in her chair. Had running into her outside the library been a coincidence, or did Wren's duties go beyond hauling around Nezima's paperwork?

"I think she misunderstood me," Mavery said. "We're on friendly terms. There's nothing more to it than that."

She raised her glass again, only to find that it was now empty.

"Please, have another drink on me," Nezima said. "And while you're at the bar, order another bottle of Maroban Cinsaut. The 1034 vintage, if they still have it."

"I owe her this round, Nez," Selemin said. They grabbed their empty tankard and pushed back their chair. "Besides, I could use a refill myself."

Mavery, thankful for an excuse to escape Nezima's scrutiny for a moment, followed Selemin back to the front room. The cigar-smoking scholars were gone, though their haze still lingered.

"I promise Nezima is usually more welcoming," Selemin said. "I don't know what's gotten into her lately."

Mavery shrugged. "I suppose even academics aren't immune to gossip."

They laughed. "That, my friend, is an understatement."

The two of them approached the bartender, who was in the middle of filling a dozen tankards for a group of men who appeared young enough to be students. Selemin, rather than standing while they waited, pulled up an empty stool.

"While we're on the topic of scholarly gossip," they said, "tell me more about that Innominate Temple theory Aventus has cooked up."

"Oh, that." Mavery sat in the empty stool beside Selemin. "He thinks the temple is tied to Aganast—or, at the very least, the Order of Asphodel."

"Can't say I've ever heard that one before. What's the connection?"

"I'm not sure. He was about to share that part of his research with me, but..." She thought back to how he'd snapped the journal shut and hidden it away. "Something came up. He told me this much: he thinks the temple wasn't used for worship."

"I reckon he could be on to something. The Order's meeting place was a little cabin about a mile or so from the temple's approximate location."

" 'Approximate'? What, does it move around?"

"Some would argue it does. But no, the magical protections wreak havoc on compasses and shroud the area in perpetual fog. You can't calculate the temple's coordinates, even by mathematical means, so it's impossible to place its exact location on a map."

"Huh…"

Perhaps Mavery's Senses hadn't been the only thing preventing her from reaching the temple all those years ago. Wren and Neldren were the only people she knew who had actually seen the temple in person. In Wren's case, it had been a result of sheer luck—or misfortune.

"I've never had any desire to go there myself, so that's the extent of what I know," Selemin said. "Going back to the cottage, the Church of the Dyad had it burned to the ground right after the Order was rounded up. Could be the members also used the temple—or *structure*, I should say—for their official business." They shrugged. "But until someone finds a way into that old ruin, we'll never know. And even then, it's hard to know whether those findings would ever see the light of day."

"What do you mean?" Mavery asked.

"We scholars can research anything we desire. But when it comes to *sharing* our findings, the High Council has final say on what's allowed in bookshops and libraries."

"I thought the arcanists controlled that."

They gave Mavery a pointed look. "And who controls the arcanists?"

At that moment, the bartender approached them.

"What can I get you ladies this time?" he asked.

"That's lady and *Chronicler*." Selemin fingered the hourglass pendant hanging from their neck.

"Beg your pardon." The bartender bowed his head. "Didn't realize you were clergy."

"Only a humble scholar, but close enough." Selemin pushed their empty tankard across the bar. "Another pint and a bottle of that Maroban something-or-other for Nezima's tab, if you would be so kind." They looked to Mavery. "You don't happen to remember what year she asked for?"

She smirked. "I thought *you* were the historian here."

They snorted, then waved a hand. "Oh, just grab something old and expensive. Wine is wine, as far as I'm concerned."

The bartender blanched at that sentiment. Shaking his head, he turned to the rows of bottles behind him.

"What about you?" Selemin asked Mavery. "Your next drink is on me."

She leaned over the bar. But instead of spotting a rare vintage, something in the mirror caught her eye.

Red hair and a familiar face.

Mavery blinked, and both had vanished. She took a deep breath, nearly choking on the lingering cigar smoke as she focused her Senses. Paranoia had not gotten the better of her after all; the scent of ash was not coming from any cigarette.

She slowly turned her head as she observed the room. In the corner by the front window, the shadows shifted unnaturally. The shrouded figure, knowing they had been spotted, was moving toward the door.

"Shit," Mavery muttered.

"Having trouble deciding?" Selemin asked. "See, this is why I stick with ale. Makes drinking so much more straightforward."

"Sorry, Selemin," Mavery said, mustering an air of cheerfulness, "but I'm afraid that drink will have to wait a little longer. I just spotted an old friend I haven't seen in ages."

"Oh? Why not invite them to join us?"

"I can assure you she's not the scholarly type."

"Ha! Fair enough," they said as the bartender passed them a fresh tankard. "Well, enjoy catching up with your friend. I'll get you that drink another time."

Mavery nodded. "Yes, another time."

She turned away from the bar and focused on the area by the entryway. The Sense of arcana-tinged ash was as strong as it had been a moment ago. Her target hadn't made it far, thanks to a line of professors who were stumbling out of the pub. The faltering shroud slipped behind the final inebriated scholar, and out into the street. Mavery followed closely behind.

Twenty-Eight

Maintaining a shroud was difficult enough while standing perfectly still in a dimly lit room. Being on the move made it infinitely more taxing—especially on a night like this, when the twin moons were full and bathed the city streets in their blue-white glow. The shroud faltered briefly as Mavery's mark passed through a patch of moonlight. It wouldn't be much longer before the spell failed entirely.

The rain had let up since Mavery had first arrived at the Lettered Gentleman, and a lamplighter was now illuminating the gaslamps. The mark, however, seemed to be in too much of a hurry to notice. They passed under a lamp. When the shadows dispersed beneath its warm glow, Mavery spotted that familiar mane of red hair once again.

"Ellice!" she cried. "Stop!"

Her former accomplice came to a halt, looked at her now visible hands, then glanced over her shoulder. Upon realizing Mavery was right behind her, Ellice swore loudly and took off at a sprint.

"Gods damn it," Mavery muttered.

She quickened her pace, and her knee protested immediately. She hissed through clenched teeth as her boots collided with the rain-slicked cobblestones.

Ellice rounded a corner and disappeared down an alley. Mavery continued her pursuit, but she couldn't ignore the electric pain shooting up her leg.

The younger woman was far more spry, with no old injuries slowing her down, and easily put several yards between herself and Mavery. At this rate, Ellice would reach the other side of the alley and disappear into the flow of traffic the next street over.

Mavery slowed to a jog, then stopped altogether. She breathed deeply, channeling her arcana. She pushed both hands forward—the ritual for a simple protective ward—and focused her gaze on a spot a few paces ahead of Ellice. A blue aura rippled through the air, spanning from building to building.

Ellice, unable to see the warding magic, ran straight into it. With a shriek that resounded through the alley, she bounced off the ward and landed on her back.

As she lay prone in the mud, Mavery caught up at last. Arcana pulsing through her fingertips, she loomed over the younger woman with a scowl.

"All right, you got me," Ellice groaned.

She raised a hand of surrender as she slowly sat upright, while her other hand rubbed the small of her back. She winced as she rose to her feet, then tried in vain to wipe the mud from the seat of her trousers. Ellice's normally pristine locks were now caked with grime, and Mavery wasn't above admitting that it was a pleasing sight.

"Fucking hells, Mave, you didn't have to hit me *that* hard."

"Try to run, and I'll hit you with much worse."

"Relax, I'm not going anywhere. Now, put your hands down and let's chat like proper ladies."

Mavery scoffed at the notion, but did as Ellice asked.

"Thank you," Ellice said with a curtsy. "Now, I'm sure you have questions—"

"You're damn right I have questions. What are you doing here? Did you follow me all the way from Burnslee?"

Ellice rolled her eyes. "Please, don't flatter yourself. Nel and I were just passing through on our way to Durnatel. Our payout from the Roven job was running low—"

"You burned through two grand in less than *two months*?"

And five hundred of it was mine, she thought as her arcana flared.

Ellice frowned. "Nel thought he could double it. Turns out, his Tribute skills aren't what they used to be."

Neldren's gambling habit had finally come back to bite him. It wasn't the extent of the punishment he deserved, but at least it was something.

"As I was saying," Ellice continued, "we were heading up to the capital to find work. We'd only planned to stay here for a few days, but then Nel spotted you in the Market District."

"When was that?"

"Three weeks ago. He followed you—and the rich bloke you were protecting—to a Dragon-owned apothecary."

Mavery's eyes widened. She *had* Sensed shadow magic back at the Cracked Pestle. Neldren had to have been lurking outside, watching through the window. He would never set foot inside any place affiliated with the Brass Dragons.

"So, you've been tailing me for weeks now?"

Ellice scoffed. "There you go again, flattering yourself. *No,* we've spent most of our time looking for work. Turns out, if you're not affiliated with the Dragons, finding it is next to impossible in this hellhole of a city.

"But *you* seemed to have landed yourself a nice little protection job. Once Nel got word that you were still around, he sent me to track you down. That's why I followed you to that pub. I assumed you were meeting with your buyer. Little did I expect to find you making friends with my old history professor."

"What did you overhear?"

"Nothing."

Mavery glared at her, and Ellice held up her hands.

"I swear it! I was keeping my distance, just in case my shrouding spell didn't work. I doubt anyone in there would've recognized me, but you know how it is—you can't be too careful."

"So, Nel told you to follow me so that we could, what, talk business?"

Ellice shrugged. "More or less. *He* wanted to do the talking, mind. He only wanted me to keep an eye on you tonight."

"Tailing people isn't exactly your strong suit. Why not send Itri? Better yet, why didn't he come find me himself?"

"Itri left just before we arrived here. He saw the ads Wincoff and Sons have been plastering in all the papers. Decided he'd rather break his back for the railroad barons than continue running with us."

Mavery could have sighed with relief. That kind of work wasn't luxurious, but at least the boy had managed to escape Neldren's clutches.

"Besides, Nel didn't know how receptive you'd be to a reunion."

Mavery scowled. "You can tell him to take his *reunion* and shove it up his ass. After what happened in Burnslee, I have nothing to say to him, and I want nothing to do with him."

"If you say so, but he's been whinging about 'clearing up some important details about the last time you saw each other,' " she said, curling her fingers for emphasis.

"*He shot me.* There's nothing to clear up."

Ellice's eyes widened, and Mavery swore she heard the faintest gasp escape the younger woman's lips. But then Ellice's expression hardened once more.

"So," she said, "you won't even pass along the name of your buyer?"

Mavery replied with another glare.

"Have it your way, then. If you change your mind, we'll be in the neighborhood. We're renting a room at the Salty Surling." She threw Mavery a wicked smile. "It's not much, but it's better than a dingy old boarding house."

Mavery's stomach plummeted.

"Be seeing you, Mave."

Ellice sauntered away and, with a flick of mud-streaked hair, vanished around the corner. Mavery remained in the alley, equal parts seething and on the verge of vomiting as dread morphed into panic. The man who had left her for dead was not only in Leyport, he had sent his underling after her. He wanted to *talk*. She doubted business and burying the proverbial hatchet were the only things on his mind. Worst of all, he knew where she lived—and he was staying at a tavern only two blocks away.

A clap of thunder sounded in the distance. Mavery had been so preoccupied with Ellice, she hadn't noticed the new batch of storm clouds that had rolled in, obscuring the moons. A raindrop wetted her hand. She looked up and another drop hit her cheek. Seconds later, the rain fell in sheets.

She raised her hand and conjured a blue veil above her head. Her protective ward deflected the raindrops as she returned to the main road and flagged down a carriage. On the way back to the boarding house, she chewed her nails ragged as her confrontation with Ellice replayed in her mind's eye. She worried that Ellice—or, gods forbid, Neldren—would be waiting for her on the stoop.

When she returned to the boarding house, there was not a soul outside, and only a handful of boarders on the inside. But it would be foolish to expect that to remain the case for long. Until Neldren burned through the final dregs of the payout, or Ellice finally convinced him to leave Leyport, Mavery would do everything she could to ensure their paths never crossed again.

Inside her bedroom, she wasted no time getting to work. At the bottom of her pack, tucked beneath her Compendium and lock-picking tools, she hid her savings. She now had over four hundred potins—almost as much as Neldren had stolen from her—alongside the antique coin Alain had given her.

Atop that, she filled her pack with her tiny collection of books and as many of her clothes as she could fit. She layered the rest over her current outfit, followed by her coat and assistant's robe. She sweat beneath the many layers, and she couldn't move her arms as freely as she wished, but this was no time to worry about comfort. After giving the room a final sweep, she slipped out into the night.

For three blocks, she walked with one hand aloft to protect herself from the downpour, until finally coming across a carriage that took her the rest of the way to Steelforge Towers. The horses trudged through the flooding streets, and the journey took nearly half an hour—barely faster than going by foot. If Neldren had spotted her leaving the boarding house, following her would take little effort.

Mavery was such an anxious mess, she forgot to conjure another protective ward as she exited the carriage, and she was dripping wet by the time she entered the lobby. She had never entered Alain's building at this time of night. Finding the front doors unlocked and no one at the front desk—not even the kutauss—did little to ease her concerns.

But once she reached the sixth floor and spotted Alain's wards, she sighed with relief. She hurried down the dimly lit corridor. The magic rippled as she reached forward and knocked on his door. Seconds passed with no answer. Mavery's heart raced. If he'd picked tonight of all nights to turn in early—

The door opened, revealing Alain dressed in his tartan dressing gown and pinstriped nightshirt, with his hair more mussed than usual. She was reminded of the day they'd first met. Only now, Alain's lips were stained purple, his gaze was slightly cross-eyed, and he reeked of wine.

"M-Mavery?" He blinked slowly, and his eyes widened as he seemed to realize she wasn't a drunken hallucination. "Gods, don't tell me it's morning already."

"It's still Middisday, at least for a few hours. I'm sorry to show up like this, but I didn't know where else to—"

"What's wrong? What happened?" he said quickly. The urgency of her words seemed to have pulled him from his stupor.

Despite wearing half her wardrobe, her body was trembling. She gave the empty corridor a sidelong glance. The rational part of her knew, had Neldren followed her here, he would have made himself known by now. But she was in no state to think rationally. She hated it with every fiber of her being.

"I... It's a long story."

Without needing further explanation, Alain pulled her into the apartment, closed the door behind them, and—though his wards rendered mundane locks unnecessary—slid the deadbolt into place.

The only light source was the fire, low and crackling, but it cast a comforting glow over the room. The familiar scent of leather and ink, interlaced with the metallic tang of warding magic, calmed Mavery's nerves.

She handed Alain her rain-soaked robe, which he draped across his armchair to dry by the fire. Her coat found a home over the back of his desk chair. She stripped off her three extra blouses, then tossed them in a corner to deal with later.

"First thing in the morning," Alain said, "I'm equipping your pack with a Transmutation spell. For now, make yourself at home."

Mavery crossed to the sofa, where she didn't hesitate to take a generous gulp from the wineglass on the tea table. Beside it were two bottles—one was empty, and the other was not quite half-full. Her second gulp drained the glass. As she refilled it, Alain lowered himself beside her.

"Tell me what happened," he said.

She took another long drink, followed by a deep breath. And then she told him everything.

Twenty-Nine

She began with how she and Neldren had first met. How, as a rookie member of the Brass Dragons, she'd been pursued down an alley by members of a rival guild. How she'd earned the scar across her nose while fighting them off, until a hint of ash had cut through the metallic scent of her own blood. And then, how her pursuers had fallen unconscious and her savior had emerged from the shadows.

She spared Alain the more sordid details of that night—namely how, in the midst of losing her virginity, she'd accidentally set fire to the bed—but for the better part of an hour, she relayed to him a truncated version of the years that had followed it.

Neldren had promised her a life where she would no longer find herself in the middle of petty guild squabbles. But her reluctance to leave the Dragons had been the first of their many disagreements that had left them going their separate ways. For nearly twenty years, she'd been in a holding pattern, with Neldren flitting in and out of her life for weeks, months, sometimes years at a time.

Mavery had spent so many hours sitting and watching Alain pace about this very room while spouting his ideas and theories. Tonight, she was the one to do the pacing while he gave her his undivided attention.

She recounted the Burnslee job, from its promising setup to its tragic end. When she told Alain of how Neldren had slashed Fennick's throat, Alain poured himself a very full glass of wine from what remained of the second bottle. When she explained what had happened later that same night, Alain looked ready to open a third. She concluded her story with her run-in with Ellice at the Lettered Gentleman.

"And then she alluded to the boarding house I've been staying at. So, you can imagine why I didn't want to spend another night there."

"Of course. Were the roles reversed, I would have done the same." Alain raised the wineglass to his lips, then paused. "You're certain Neldren has nefarious intent?"

"Yes... No?" She threw her hands up and sighed. "I don't know. Maybe he only wants to talk. Maybe he wants to work together again."

Alain raised his eyebrows. "Really? After all that happened between you?"

"We've reconciled after worse arguments. Granted, none of those involved one of us *shooting* the other."

At that moment, Alain took a very generous drink.

"Besides," Mavery added, "in our profession—*his* profession, I mean—you work with the most skilled people you know, even if you don't like them as people. But I'm never going back to that life, especially not for him."

With that, she reclaimed her seat beside Alain and gestured for him to pass her the wineglass. Speaking for so long had left her parched. The alcohol stung her throat on the way down.

"There's one part of your story that doesn't quite add up," Alain said. "After Neldren...did what he did...how did you wind up in the infirmary?"

"Some kind stranger saw me bleeding out and took pity on me?" She shrugged. "Your guess is as good as mine."

Alain hesitated before saying delicately, "Do you think it's possible *he* took you there?"

She furrowed her brow. "Need I remind you how he shot me, robbed me, and left me for dead?"

"I know, but didn't Ellice say he intended to clear up some details? Perhaps he had second thoughts."

She laughed coldly. "Neldren never has second thoughts."

She took another drink. When she looked at Alain again, there was an unfamiliar darkness behind his eyes that was as surprising as it was unsettling.

"If we ever cross paths," he said, "gods help me, I'll—"

"You'll what? Challenge him to a gentleman's duel? Write him a strongly worded letter?" She patted his hand. "I don't mean to disparage you, but Neldren isn't the type to play fairly."

"Perhaps...but the concept of having blood on one's hands is not completely foreign to me."

His words, and the dark tone with which he delivered them, gave Mavery pause. "What do you mean?"

He looked at her with unfocused eyes. He blinked, and the darkness seemed to pass. "Nothing. We ought to get some rest. The bed is all yours. I'll kip here on the sofa."

"Nonsense. I'm not putting you out."

"No one is putting anyone out. I am *offering* you the bed."

She shook her head. "As generous as that is, allowing me to stay here in the first place was generous enough."

"Shall we flip a coin over it?" Through heavy-lidded eyes, he smirked at her, and there was no doubt that he was still incredibly drunk.

"I'm staying right here. Full stop, end of discussion."

"Have it your way, then." He hoisted himself off the sofa, wavered a bit as he stood upright. "At least let me fetch you some linens."

While he stumbled into the storage room, she dug her comb and sleeping shift from her pack, then went to the bathroom to ready herself for bed.

When she returned, the last of the embers had burned out. Outside, thick clouds shrouded every trace of moonlight while rain continued to pour. The only light—a white glow that she recognized as Ethereal—peeked through the crack beneath the storage room door. Though Mavery could have conjured her own orb, she didn't need it; she knew this apartment like the back of her own hand. She followed the light through the pitch-dark sitting room.

She opened the door and found Alain sitting on the floor, his back to the wall and his orb of light floating overhead. His eyes were wide, his body completely still, as he stared at something directly across from him.

"Alain, what's—"

"Forgot to put away," he mumbled, "after you..."

She followed his gaze and realized at once what had left him so paralyzed.

"Here," she said softly, "I'll handle it."

After all, it was her fault the paintings had been uncovered in the first place. When he voiced no protest, she padded across the room and draped the paint-splattered tarp over the canvases, hiding away the man with the mismatched eyes.

Her efforts made little difference; Alain remained frozen, distant. She approached him slowly, then sank next to him on the floor. She raised her hand, hesitated before resting it on his shoulder. Though he didn't move, he didn't recoil from her touch.

"You don't have to say anything if you don't want—"

"No," he said quietly, with a slight shake of his head. "I don't *want* to, but maybe I *need* to."

The Ethereal light revealed his reddened eyes, his tearstained cheeks. Though he wasn't crying now, she wondered if that was how he'd spent his evening prior to her unexpected visit. Outside, the storm carried on. Rain pelted the roof while wind howled past the turret overhead. Further in the distance, thunder rumbled.

"He was very important to me," Alain said at last.

"I figured as much. Who was he?"

"Many things. My muse, my lover, and..." He sighed deeply. "My assistant."

Mavery nodded. "Conor, I presume."

"Yes." He looked at her. "How did you know?"

"Wren. I ran into her outside the library the other day. She told me about the research trip, and she mentioned something about Conor's eyes. I figured that couldn't be a coincidence."

"She never could resist an opportunity for gossip," Alain muttered, then hung his head. "No, I shouldn't disparage her. At least she was there when he passed. That's more than I can say for myself."

He pulled his knees to his chest, then rested his chin atop them, as though he were trying to make himself small enough to disappear entirely.

"I should start from the beginning," he said. "That is, if you're willing to hear it."

She answered with a nod and a squeeze of his shoulder.

"Conor and I first met two years ago this autumn, not long after Nezima hired him as her assistant. Though we'd only ever exchanged pleasantries in the common room, I was nothing short of infatuated with him. He was one of the most beautiful people I'd ever seen, and I attempted to capture his beauty in paint, to little success.

"That was, until I finally struck up the courage to ask him to sit for me. I assumed he would be like every other academic and belittle me for my hobby. To my relief, he was not only flattered, he agreed to be my model without hesitation.

"We met there"—he pointed at the trapdoor to his studio—"a few times per week, and we quickly struck up a friendship. All the while, my infatuation continued to grow, but I never acted upon those feelings."

"Because of the Covenants?"

He nodded. "And my own cowardice. I wouldn't have had a clue what to do or say. I'm sure it comes as no surprise, romance has never been my strong suit."

Mavery eyes widened in mock surprise, and he gave her a half-hearted laugh.

"One day, Conor told me how Nezima's latest experiment had gone awry. Her spell was supposed to negate a poison she'd developed. Instead, the spell backfired, and it nearly killed him. When he asked her to exempt him from being a test subject going forward, she told him if he couldn't handle the risks, he had no business seeking to become a wizard. And then she dismissed him on the spot."

"I take it that's why you don't like her," Mavery said.

He nodded. "I'd once held Nezima in high regard for being a prolific scholar, for everything she'd done for my mother. But after learning how she holds such little respect for her assistants, I lost all my respect for *her*.

"Shortly after Conor left Nezima's employ, he asked me for a job. I already had Wren and Lorcan; I could hardly afford a third assistant, but I could hardly turn him down in his time of need." He sighed as he rubbed his temples. "Conor then confessed that he'd harbored romantic feelings for me all along. I reminded him of the Covenants, but he insisted that he didn't care whether our courtship needed to remain secret; he wanted to be both my assistant and my lover. He made some quite, er, *persuasive* arguments."

His face turned scarlet, which told Mavery everything she needed—and a bit more than she *wanted*—to know. Alain cleared his throat.

"To the outside world, we were simply wizard and assistant. Behind closed doors, we were...much more than that." He winced. "I'm sorry, speaking of this must seem so crass, considering..."

Mavery smiled. "Considering what? Last I checked, friends were allowed to talk about their past lovers. Besides, after everything I just told you about Neldren, it's only fair."

"Right." He lowered his gaze. "Of course."

"So, how did you afford his wages?"

"I'm sure you noticed the dearth of magical trinkets around here. I paid him with whatever he could easily pawn. It was either that, or my life savings." He shrugged. "At least my affection for him never rendered me *completely* senseless."

Mavery's heart sank. Someone had gotten the drop on her long before she'd found that newspaper ad.

"I wish I could say it had all been worth it," Alain said, "but no matter how much I sacrificed, nothing was ever enough. Minor disagreements about research methods escalated into explosive personal arguments. Before long, I realized we had very little in common." He laughed darkly. "As it turns out, physical attraction alone does not make a sturdy foundation for a relationship."

Mavery nodded. "I understand that all too well."

"From the moment I agreed to our secret courtship, I don't

know, something in him changed. It's as though he became an entirely different person."

"Or, perhaps you were seeing the person he'd been all along."

"Perhaps," Alain sighed. "I wasn't happy, and neither was he. He tried to push my boundaries and make our courtship public. The tipping point was after we made a research breakthrough with the Innominate Temple. Conor and I went out to celebrate at the Lettered Gentleman. I hoped that being surrounded by our colleagues would deter him from doing anything rash.

"But, after a few pints, he threw his arms around me and tried to kiss me. I pushed him away, and I don't think anyone noticed, but we argued about it all the way back here, where we argued for hours. We said many hurtful things to one another. Things that can't easily be taken back."

He hesitated as his body became more tense, his breathing more shallow. Mavery grasped his shoulder again, bracing them both for whatever came next.

"Despite all that, Conor insisted...on becoming intimate." He took a deep gulp of air. "I tried to turn him down again, but that time...he..."

An ache settled in Mavery's chest, like a vise slowly squeezing her heart.

"You don't have to continue," she whispered.

Alain turned his head. His eyes glistened with tears that he was rapidly trying to blink back.

"Thank you, but I'm afraid the story doesn't end there," he said, then lowered his head again. "After that night, I couldn't remain with him, but he'd threatened to report me to Kazamin if I ended our relationship. And so..."

"The research trip."

He nodded. "I assume Wren filled you in on the details, save for the *real* reason why I sent them away."

"You felt trapped, and you thought that was your only option."

"Precisely. To Conor's credit, he never revealed my intentions to the others. Perhaps he also wanted some time apart." He paused. "Perhaps we both got what we wanted, thanks to my stupidity."

Alain's body shuddered as he let the tears fall at last. Without hesitation, Mavery threw her arms around his shoulders, pulled him into a tight embrace.

"His death was an accident," she whispered. "You can't blame yourself for what happened."

She brushed back his rumpled locks of hair, wiped away tears that had slipped down his cheeks. Before tonight, Mavery had hoped Conor's death had been quick and painless. Now, as white-hot fury kindled in her stomach, she hoped the bastard had *suffered*.

"Er, Mavery?" Alain said, looking at the floor.

Beneath her bare feet, tiny branches bearing green foliage had sprouted from the floorboards.

"Huh," she said. "I can't even remember the last time that happened."

Alain watched the branches with amusement. Then, his eyes widened. He pulled out of her embrace and looked away.

"What's the matter?" she asked.

He mumbled something beneath his breath. His gaze darted back to her feet as he flushed pink from neck to forehead.

She realized how, from knees downward, her legs were on full display. The rest of her was covered only by the thin cotton of her sleeping shift. It was little more than a shapeless sack that did nothing to reveal the contours of her body, but this was still the most exposed she'd ever been around Alain.

She'd spent a good portion of her adult life sleeping in shared quarters with strangers—a lifestyle that seldom allowed for modesty. And so, until this exact moment, she hadn't given her state of undress much thought. And neither had he, evidently.

"Sorry about that." She tugged the fabric over her bent knees, though she only succeeded at covering up a single inch of skin. "I didn't even think—"

"Don't apologize." Alain cleared his throat, though the flush in his cheeks lingered. "I did, after all, tell you to make yourself at home. I certainly can't fault you for following instructions."

She laughed, relieved that something had offered them a bit of levity. But, like all good things, it didn't last for long. Now that his nervousness had passed, Alain's expression darkened again.

"When Wren and Lorcan informed me of what happened at the temple, the first thing I felt wasn't sadness, not even guilt. Those all came later, and it's what drove me to confine myself to this apartment for months on end.

"No, the first thing I felt was...*relief*." He turned to her. "What does that make me?"

Mavery cupped his face between her hands.

"Human," she whispered. "It makes you human."

And then she embraced him again. At first, he remained frozen on the spot, his body tense against hers. But Mavery didn't let that deter her; she continued to hold him. His heart beat so rapidly, she could feel it thrumming through her own chest. Slowly, his tension began to ease. He wrapped his arms around her, letting them come to rest against the small of her back.

"Thank you," he whispered. His breath was heavy and warm against her hair.

"Of course. Now, I think we're both long overdue for some sleep."

Though the wine hadn't affected his ability to speak, the same couldn't be said about his ability to walk. Using the wall for support, she helped him to his feet. He swayed on the spot until she took his arm and slung it around her shoulders, then guided him to the bedroom. Mavery couldn't help but think of the last time they'd found themselves in a similar predicament. The next time she took him to bed, she hoped he would be fully present—and that it would be under better circumstances.

His orb of light, still tethered to his magic, had followed them. He made a fist, and Mavery blinked as her eyes adjusted to the sudden darkness. Rain spattered against the bedroom window, though with less fervor than before. It all but drowned out the soft rustle of fabric, the creaking of the bed frame.

As she began to turn away, Alain grasped her hand. Neither of them mentioned their argument about the sofa as he pulled her into bed with him. They said nothing about the Covenants as he draped his arm over her and pulled her closer, until her body was flush against his.

It had been months since she'd last shared a bed with someone in this way. Long enough to forget how much heat could radiate from another person's skin, how that could warm her more deeply than layers of blankets. She returned his embrace, and he clung to her more tightly. She stroked his hair, and he sighed deeply as his head fell against her chest.

The rain continued as they both drifted off to sleep.

THIRTY

When Mavery awoke the next morning, her first thought was that she was still dreaming. Outside, the storm had ceased. Pink clouds streaked across a steel-blue sky as the final stars blinked out of existence. Alain had rolled off her at some point during the night, but he hadn't run off to tweak potions or practice spells. He remained beside her now, fast asleep.

She shifted onto her side and studied the contour of his profile, the gentle rise and fall of his chest, the lingering wine stains upon his slightly parted lips. Whatever he was dreaming of, she doubted it had anything to do with research, or what he'd revealed to her last night.

No, this was real. And for once, he looked completely at peace. The sight alone filled her with warm levity.

Whatever she felt for him had progressed beyond friendship, beyond mere attraction. To deny that would be to deny the passage of time, the heat of the sun. But she now understood why he was reluctant to break the Covenants, why he struggled with the idea of being someone's lover again—especially if that lover was his assistant.

Regardless of whether he felt the same about her, she wouldn't force the matter; that would make her no different than Conor, as far as she was concerned. If Alain wanted to pursue this thing between them, it would be on his own terms. Until then, maybe what he needed wasn't a lover, or even an assistant. Maybe what he needed, above all else, was a friend.

Mavery slipped out of bed, careful to avoid shifting the mattress and disturbing him. Her sleeping shift provided little protection against the cool air. She shivered as her skin prickled with gooseflesh and the frigid floorboards numbed her bare feet. She made her way into the sitting room, where she relighted the hearth and dressed herself before stepping into the kitchen.

It had been years since she'd last lived somewhere with a private kitchen, and so her cooking skills were a bit rusty. At least she could still manage to fry up eggs and toast. Tea-making, however, proved more challenging. Though she'd watched Alain countless times, she'd never gone through the preparations herself from beginning to end. From his collection of tins, she chose a dark, peppery variety that left even her unable to sit still. Alain had become immune to that side effect, but Mavery decided it couldn't hurt; once he awoke, he would need every scrap of vitality he could get. She spooned into the teapot what she assumed was the correct amount of leaves, heated the water to what was probably the right temperature, and left it to steep while she worked on breakfast.

She had just finished frying the last of the eggs when Alain shuffled into the room, appearing close to needing another shot of resurrection serum. He mumbled something that sounded vaguely like "good morning," then sank into a chair. Mavery slid a plate of food in front of him, and he gazed upon it as though it were a priceless work of art.

"You didn't need to do all this," he said.

"You probably know a recipe for a hangover-curing tonic, but I figured this would be more appealing." She finished preparing her own plate, then took the chair opposite him. "Besides, I need it almost as much as you do."

He poured himself a cup of tea, took a sip, and winced.

"It's a tad strong," he choked, "but I can safely say I'm awake now."

Mavery dug into her meal with enthusiasm, breaking the golden egg yolks and sopping them up with her bread without any need for knife and fork. Alain still managed to eat with dignity, cutting his food into bite-sized pieces.

"So, about last night," he said hesitantly. "I remember our conversation in the storage room, but not much beyond that. Did we...?"

Mavery shook her head. "We only slept together in a literal sense, if that's what you're thinking."

"Right, I remember now." He gulped down another mouthful of tea. "Apologies. Last night, I crossed a boundary I shouldn't have."

"We both did. I'll take the sofa going forward. Better yet, maybe I should find my own place."

"You're welcome to stay as long as you need, so long as my mother doesn't come prying. She's the traditional sort who would take issue with an unwed couple living together." Alain froze, fork halfway to his mouth. "Er, not to imply we're a—"

"I know what you meant." She played it off with a laugh while her stomach fluttered. She began to take a bite of toast, then paused. "Hold on. Your mother would take issue with that? She had an affair with a *priest*!"

Alain shrugged. "She's always followed a 'do as I say, not as I do' approach to morality."

Mavery shook her head. She took a sip of tea and gagged. It was more than "a tad strong"; it was undrinkable. As she pushed her cup aside, Alain reached across the table and placed his hand over hers. His thumb stroked her knuckles, and Mavery was on the verge of melting into her chair. That light caress was more intoxicating than all the wine they'd shared the previous night.

"I also want to apologize for something else," he said. "The other day, when you pressed me about the Covenants, I should have told you how I'd courted an assistant before, and that it hadn't ended...on the most desirable terms, to say the least. But I was afraid you would judge me for what I'd done, that you would even hate me for it."

"I could never hate you." She turned her wrist, cradled his fingers with her own. "And I'm in no position to judge. Had your little accident happened when we first started working together,

I probably would have left you for dead and run off with your money."

He looked up, frowning. "Nonsense. You're too good of a person to do something like that."

She glanced away as a doubtful noise resonated from the back of her throat. Alain squeezed her hand.

"You *are*, Mavery. The way I see it, you're a good person who's been dealt an unfavorable hand, time and again."

"That's one way of putting it," she said, laughing flatly. But the sincerity in his voice compelled her to look at him again.

"I mean it. Last night, you could have left me to wallow in my sorrows, but you stayed with me. You listened to me." He smiled at her, though it didn't quite reach his eyes. "Before last night, I'd never told anyone any of that. I couldn't tell my other assistants the truth, and I certainly couldn't confide in any of my other colleagues."

"Not even Declan?" Mavery recalled the letter she'd come across. An ache settled deep in her chest as she realized Declan might have been the only one who'd attempted to visit Alain during his sabbatical.

Alain shook his head. "Declan is the sort of friend with whom you can share a pint, but not much beyond that."

He released her hand and returned to his breakfast. Mavery, however, had lost her appetite. The ache in her chest grew more acute as she thought of Alain completely alone, with no one to confide in as his entire life fell apart.

"I don't suppose you managed to stuff any formal attire in your bag?" Alain asked.

Mavery blinked, jostled from her thoughts. "Er, no, I can't say I did. Why?"

"The High Council has a strict dress code for presentations."

"Of course they do." She rolled her eyes. After coming across a covenant that detailed the differences between *royal* blue and *cobalt* blue, she'd skimmed past anything else pertaining to wizardly attire.

"I'm afraid you'll need to pay my mother a visit between now and the presentation."

"Does it *have* to be her?"

"You're welcome to try another dressmaker, but with the Social Season fast approaching, most are fully booked through the summer."

"Fine," Mavery groaned. "Your mother it is, then."

"I'll ask her to pencil you in as soon as possible." Alain gulped down the last of his tea, then pushed back his chair. "Until then, work awaits."

"Are you sure you're in the right state for it?"

"Oh, I've managed worse than this."

That did little to allay her concerns.

Mavery wasn't sure which was the more daunting task: translating centuries-old Fenutian, or painstakingly writing that translation in her best penmanship.

Her hand cramped after completing another long, meandering sentence. She dropped her pen on the desk and massaged her wrist—and then let loose a string of curses. The pen had left a large inkblot on the sheet of vellum, rendering the sentence she'd just finished unreadable.

"Are you sure you don't have a typewriter buried somewhere in that storage room?" she asked, looking over her shoulder.

"Unfortunately, no," Alain said. "And even if I did, the High Council wouldn't allow it."

"Don't tell me, in this day and age, they're actually still enforcing *that* covenant."

"I'm afraid so. All spell tomes must first be written by hand. Doing so makes for more careful spellcraft, and therefore makes one more appreciative of the process." Alain shrugged. "Or, so the Elder Wizards claim."

"Antiquated codgers," Mavery grumbled, then pointed at the tomes scattered across the tea table. "None of those were written by hand."

"Because these are reproductions. Not to mention, the High

Council didn't adopt the use of the printing press until the Second Reforms, long after that technology was first invented."

"Oh, I see." Mavery nodded. "Five centuries from now, when most of the world is writing with thoughts or some other nonsense, the High Council will *finally* get around to allowing typewriters."

Alain looked up from his book. "You know, in all the time you've spent arguing about this, you could have written another paragraph."

She crumpled her ruined leaf of vellum into a ball and threw it at him. Her aim was off, and it narrowly avoided the smarmy look on his face. He still flinched, though he did so with a hearty laugh.

"I'll take care of writing the final draft, if that makes things easier," he said.

Mavery looked at what remained of her work. A mere two pages had taken her most of the morning, as each errant drop of ink had forced her to restart, and her penmanship still looked no better than a child's scrawl. She'd wasted a small fortune in vellum and ink, but she wanted this to be *perfect.*

After spending so much time with Enodus's unfinished tome, she couldn't say she felt any personal connection to the long-dead wizard. Their Sensing abilities truly were all they had in common. Enodus had been born into a noble house—one whose family tree was abundant with mages. He had served as Court Wizard for three of North Fenutia's monarchs. Despite being so acclaimed in his homeland, Enodus's writings had never been translated. Mavery felt it was her responsibility to share another Senser's work with the rest of the continent. Having someone else do that work, even partially didn't sit well with her.

"Are you sure?" she asked. "You still have so much left to do."

"Actually, I think the incantation might be ready for a test run."

"Really?" Mavery raised her brows.

He nodded, though the look in his eyes belied the confidence in his words. He gestured for her to join him on the sofa, where he handed her the notebook he'd been using to draft the spell. Not even two weeks ago, she'd seen the runes as little more than a jumble of elegant lines and curves. Now, she could identify patterns that formed words and phrases. The lines of runes looked like stanzas, further cementing her view that incantations were like poetry. She doubted she had the stamina to attempt reading this spell aloud; it spanned three full pages.

"It's quite...*long*," she said. "It must take you several minutes to recite all this."

Alain sighed. "Two minutes and fourteen seconds, to be precise."

That was over twice the length of the incantation he'd used to shroud them in Ether—and that one had sounded exceptionally complex.

Mavery looked over the incantation again. This time, she noticed a series of fourteen runes that repeated five times in various places, though she lacked the fluency to know what purpose they served. She pointed them out to Alain.

"Each one of these will reveal ley lines," he said.

She pondered this for a moment.

"If I'm going about this correctly," she said, "Enodus's spell reveals all wards, but only casts them in Ethereal light."

"That's the first step. Then, my additions will cast the primary types of wards in their respective colors."

"Does Enodus's spell also work on ley lines?" When he nodded, she said, "They always appear silver to me, so not much different than Ethereal light. Why not take out all these repetitive sections?"

Eyes widening, Alain gaped at her. "Gods, how hadn't I thought of that before?"

He took back his notebook. While he patted his pockets, Mavery spotted a pen on the tea table and handed it to him. He muttered something that she interpreted as appreciation, then fell silent as he scribbled his revisions.

"I'd been so caught up in ensuring the spell was comprehensive, I'd completely neglected Venetum's Fifth Principle: efficiency. Well, this will definitely shorten it by a considerable amount." He snapped the notebook shut, then watched her for a moment as a smile tugged at his lips.

"Is something the matter?"

"Not at all," Alain said, then smiled fully. There was a glimmer in his eye that warmed Mavery in places that she dared not acknowledge at this exact moment. She forced herself to look away before she did or said anything foolish. To her immense relief, he asked, "Well, shall we give this a trial run?"

He rose from the sofa and began preparing the room, starting with adding a detonation ward to the slew of magic covering the front door. He assured Mavery it was harmless, but she kept her distance anyway. She then repeated the fireproofing spell she'd mastered yesterday, applying it to the wooden box before going to the kitchen and taking a dose of anti-Sensing potion. She would need to ensure any auras she saw were due to Alain's spell, not her innate abilities.

Finally, she retrieved the resurrection kit beneath the bed. It was only a precaution—one she hoped they wouldn't need. Alain had since replaced the vial of serum, and the stack of potins was much shorter than it had been before.

With everything assembled, they stood side by side in the center of the room, facing the front door as though they were anticipating a visitor to come bursting through it.

"Ready?" Alain asked, giving Mavery a sidelong glance.

She nodded. "Ready when you are."

He took a deep breath, then began reciting the incantation. Now that she was a little more familiar with Etherean, she better appreciated Alain's mastery over it. She closed her eyes as his words washed over her.

"—*shah rah ee-shah*—oh! Oh, gods!"

Mavery's eyes flew open, and she winced at the burst of Ethereal light emanating from the door. As her eyes adjusted, she gasped. The light came from more than magic alone: a small section of the door was on fire.

Alain's focus, however, was solely on his notebook. He frantically flipped between pages as he searched for the source of his error.

"I must have accidentally left in a few runes from Ardemin's Hue Shifting Augmentation. My blasted fault for using one from the Elemental School..."

Mavery ignored his ramblings as she snatched the fireproofed box from the ground—it, too, was aglow with white light—and bolted across the room. She slammed it against the door. The box jerked beneath her hands—she'd triggered the detonation ward—but it smothered the flames in a puff of black smoke.

Slowly, she removed the box. The fire had lasted not even a minute, and it had only left behind a scorch mark. Her heart continued to pound as she turned to Alain. Aside from clutching his notebook to his chest, he hadn't moved a muscle.

"I think I can prevent that from happening again."

She narrowed her eyes. "You *think*?"

"That *won't* happen again." He grimaced. "Give me a moment to make some adjustments."

Though his second attempt didn't result in any fires, it was also a failure. The wards glowed white, but the colors never appeared. After another round of revisions, every ward appeared orange, for reasons that left him completely baffled. His next attempt was a bit closer to the desired result, though the resonating wards appeared violet when they should have been gold. And after a dozen attempts, he only recited half of the incantation before the Ethereal light dissipated. His arcana was completely spent.

He tossed his notebook aside and tossed himself on the sofa with a drawn-out groan. He lay on his stomach, face pressed into the cushion.

"I shouldn't have let you transmutate my pack earlier," Mavery said. She picked up the notebook, smoothed the pages that had crumpled upon impact with the floor. "You shouldn't have wasted your arcana on me."

"None of this is your fault," Alain said, his voice muffled. He turned his head and gave her a pointed look. "And no spell I cast for your benefit will ever be a waste, I can assure you."

She smiled in spite of herself as she sat in his armchair.

"No," he sighed, "I should have known better than to attempt spellcraft after a night of heavy drinking." He rolled onto his back, gazed at the ceiling. "I think this room, this apartment, could also be playing a role. Too many reminders of my previous failures."

Mavery was inclined to agree. As far as she knew, he hadn't left his apartment in days. If confining himself to these small rooms for long periods of time was detrimental to his wellbeing, it might as well have the same effect on his spellcasting.

"Then maybe we need a change of scenery."

"I could request a classroom at the University," he said, then shook his head. "No, that likely won't be possible with final exams coming up."

Mavery looked out the window, where the sky had turned blue and cloudless. Finally, the season had taken a turn for the better.

"Actually," she said, "I have something else in mind."

THIRTY-ONE

After two months of living in the city, a walk in the forest was nothing short of exhilarating. Granted, Weywode Forest was still part of Leyport, just beyond the city walls. But it was far enough to be disconnected from the buildings, the grime, and—most importantly—the noise.

These thousand acres were the Duke of Leyland's personal hunting grounds; outside of hunting season, they were open to commoners. Mavery had escaped into Weywode Forest a handful of times during her first stint in Leyport. Unlike the rest of the city, this place had hardly changed over the years.

Everywhere she looked, she was surrounded by evergreen trees and verdant understory. Looking up, the sky was barely visible through the canopy of treetops. She breathed in the crisp air. There wasn't a hint of stagnant water, garbage, or horses.

Her body was stiff from having slept on the sofa last night, but she'd mentioned not a word of it to Alain. If she suggested feeling even the slightest discomfort, he would sacrifice his bed for her in a heartbeat, even though he needed a good night's rest more than she did. The deeper into the forest she walked, the more her muscles rejoiced at being allowed to stretch properly, to not feel the pressure of cobblestones beneath her feet. As she took another deep breath, her arcana pulsed beneath her skin, alert but not recalcitrant. She quickened her pace.

"Slow...down...please," Alain gasped.

She looked over her shoulder and realized she'd gotten a dozen or so paces ahead of him. With his gray hooded travel cloak and his staff, Alain looked more "wizardly" than ever. And that included looking old and feeble for a change.

"Sorry." Mavery stopped and waited for him to catch up. "Got a little overeager just now."

"That's...all well...and good," Alain panted. "But do keep in mind, this is a bit more strenuous than a stroll through the city streets."

He leaned against his staff as he caught his breath. Not even a quarter mile into this walk, and his forehead already glistened with sweat.

"Is your chest still bothering you?" she asked.

"Oh, no, that's now fully healed. My *legs* aren't used to this level of exertion."

Though he did plenty of pacing around his apartment, that hardly compared to an outdoor walk. And there had been many days lately when he'd remained sitting for hours on end. Until now, Mavery hadn't even considered how woefully out of shape he was, even for an academic.

"We can take a break—"

"No, let's press on," Alain said, "at a more *leisurely* pace, if you don't mind."

She smiled. "Of course."

Side by side, they continued onward. Mavery's fingers itched to close the small distance between them and take his hand. They'd only passed a handful of other people strolling along the trail, and they were now completely alone, but she kept her hands firmly at her sides. She'd crossed enough boundaries as of late: staying at Alain's apartment, sharing his bed. Though she'd rectified the latter, she'd made no progress yet on the former. And now, coming to this somewhat remote forest had been her idea.

Work was the reason for this excursion. So, she shifted her focus to searching for arcane resonances—potential anchors hidden among the underbrush—and alchemical ingredients that were easier to spot. Persilweed grew rampant here, as it did wherever there was a bit of soil and a hint of sunlight, but she was hoping to find something more noteworthy. A few minutes down the path, she stopped to point out a cluster of bushes at the center of a copse.

"I think those are drottberries," she said. "That's odd. I figured they'd be deeper in the forest than this."

She approached the copse at a light jog.

"We hardly have time for foraging," Alain called. "We only have a few hours of daylight remaining."

Mavery scoffed. "And whose fault is that? *You* were the one who insisted on running errands all morning, then took forever getting ready. Besides, I've noticed your stores are running low."

She slung off her pack and leaned over a bush to examine the vibrant red berries. Behind her, Alain sighed, then his footsteps and the thud of his staff grew closer.

"I suppose you're right," he said. "We might as well make the most of this trip, though I can't say I have any need for drottberries."

"They *could* be drottberries," she said, "or they could be baneberries. It's always hard to tell the difference."

"So, we will either reveal our deepest, darkest secrets—or we will suffer hallucinations and excruciating pain for hours before finally succumbing to death." He chuckled. "I can't say I'm willing to take that particular gamble."

Mavery opened her pack and peered inside, though the ambient light was too dim for her to differentiate anything inside the iridescent void. That was the downside of the Transmutation spell. She reached the entire length of her arm, from fingertips to armpit, inside the pack and fished around blindly. Her fingers brushed against paper, and she pulled out her Compendium. She put her pack aside and began flipping through the bundle of pages.

"I know I have something in here somewhere..."

Alain stepped closer until he was behind her shoulder.

"What's this?" he asked.

"I call this my Compendium of Knowledge. I can't believe I've never had a chance to show you until now. Ah! Here we are."

She turned to a section containing pages from an herbalist's field guide she'd pilfered over a decade ago. The paper was exceptionally worn, her notes in the margins so smudged they were almost indecipherable.

"Five-pointed leaves." She closed the Compendium with a sigh. "Baneberries."

"A shame," Alain said, "though I'm more interested in that book of yours."

She handed it over, then watched him slowly flip through the collection of mismatched pages. She appreciated his care, but the book only appeared more delicate than it actually was. The pages were bound together with thick, high-quality thread, and it had so far managed to withstand the test of time—and being jostled around in her pack.

"I started with some of my first-year textbooks from Atterdell," she said. "I then added other books I picked up in my, er, travels."

He raised a brow. "I presume the majority of them weren't purchased from a bookshop."

"You know me," Mavery said with a shrug. "I would cut out chapters and sections, based on what interested me the most at the time. What you see now is an effort two decades in the making."

Alain blanched. "Stealing books is one thing, but *defiling* them?"

She rolled her eyes. "They're far more useful in this state than collecting dust in some noble bastard's library. And it's not as though I had any better options. Until yesterday, my pack wasn't equipped with a Transmutation spell. I couldn't haul an entire library along with me."

As Alain continued skimming through the Compendium, Mavery caught a quirk of his eyebrows, a softening of his eyes, a slight upturn of his lips. His smile widened when he reached the most recent additions: the incantations he'd written during her Etherean lessons.

"This is remarkable," he said. "All this time, you've been curating a miniature library, like being your very own arcanist."

"I shouldn't have to." Mavery shook her head. "All this time, I've wondered why this knowledge is so easy for wizards and the wealthy to acquire, yet near impossible for everyone else."

Alain handed back the Compendium, and she returned it to her pack.

"The knowledge we keep in university libraries can be dangerous in the wrong hands," he said. "Best to leave it to those with years of education and training, who know how to use that knowledge responsibly."

She laughed. "Right, so you're saying there's *never*, in all of history, been a single wizard who misused that knowledge? That most forms of Necromancy, for example, were banned for the hells of it?"

He hesitated, and she gave him a satisfied smirk as he struggled to come up with a rebuttal.

"That's a fair point," he said, "but are you actually suggesting we allow common people unlimited access to arcane knowledge?"

"Why not? The way I see it, knowledge isn't good or evil—it just *is*. And like you said, only those with the proper training will know what to do with it, so why not make it accessible to everyone? Why hoard books away in universities—or in private libraries, for that matter?"

Alain frowned. Mavery knew they were both thinking of the apartment at Steelforge Towers, the room filled with books. While Alain had used a few tomes for his research, the vast majority of his collection likely hadn't been read in years. Mavery had even come across books with uncut pages. Was his library really any different than the one in Roven's manor, or the scores of others she'd robbed over the years?

They returned to the trail, but Alain walked only a few paces before coming to a sudden stop.

"Look!" he whispered, pointing to something further down the path.

Mavery gasped. She hadn't expected to find wild demonspawn so close to the city, but about a hundred yards away was a pair of kinchins.

They were feline creatures with the dark hair and red eyes of their fellow demonspawn. But to Mavery, they'd always looked like disgruntled balls of fur. Even full-grown kinchins, like the pair sitting a dozen yards away, were not much larger than bear cubs. Their lower fangs, too large for their mouths, protruded over their upper lips. Their whiskers and jowls drooped downward, giving their wide, squat faces looks of perpetual disappointment.

Alain's cloak rustled as he pulled his notebook from his pocket. His movements were slow and careful so as to not frighten the kinchins. Mavery kept her eyes forward, focused on the beasts; beside her was the energetic scratching of a pen. But the kinchins didn't notice a thing. The slightly smaller one—a female, presumably—had stopped to groom her mate, who looked displeased to be given the attention. Then again, kinchins *always* looked displeased, which was why Mavery found them so entertaining.

"Oh, this is amazing!" she whispered. "And to see two of them together outside of mating season..."

While most demonspawn traveled in packs, kinchins were solitary creatures. Once they reached adulthood and left their mothers' dens, they would pair up during their brief mating season but otherwise spent the remainder of their lives in isolation. This pair was an exceptionally rare sight.

Alain chuckled softly. "It all makes sense now."

"What does?"

"Your reaction to Enid's hellhound. I should have known you were a cat person all this time."

Mavery stifled a laugh, then peered at what Alain was recording in his notebook. He'd made a rough sketch of the kinchins. He was now working on a more detailed sketch of Mavery's profile. He stilled his pen once he realized she was watching him.

Somewhere off in the distance, a tree branch cracked and plummeted to the ground. A thud rippled through the forest, and the kinchins sprung onto all fours. Before sprinting away, they emitted screams that sounded like the cries of human children; every variety of demonspawn had at least *one* unsettling trait. They scampered into the underbrush and vanished.

Alain moved off the path and sat on a fallen log, where he resumed his sketching. Mavery sat beside him. Instead of hiding his work, he angled his notebook toward her. She inched closer to him, thrilled to not only be his subject again, but that he no longer felt compelled to keep this hobby private.

"I couldn't help myself," he said. "I've never seen you look at *anything* quite like that."

He added the final touches, then handed her the notebook. Even with rough pen strokes, he'd managed to capture her awe and delight from watching the kinchins. He waited patiently while she assessed his work, though his eyes were eager for her approval.

"I love it," she said, passing the notebook back to him. "And you managed that while you were working...technically speaking. I'd say that's proof that your hobby *isn't* a waste of time."

He smiled, then slipped the notebook into his pocket. He turned to her, and his gaze softened as it drifted from her eyes, down to her mouth. Mavery's breath hitched as everything—the breeze, her heartbeat, even time itself—seemed to go still.

But then Alain turned his head and stood up. "It's getting late, and we still need to find a suitable place to work on the spell. Let's get moving."

They found a small clearing deeper in the forest. Scorch marks in the dirt, flanked by a pair of logs, indicated it had been used as a camping spot somewhat recently. While Alain filled their canteens in the nearby stream, Mavery sat on one of the logs and bound together the persilweed she'd picked along the trail. Unfortunately, they'd found nothing else of note; the forest floor had been cleaned of Ether-sensitive stones, and the other alchemical ingredients were too poisonous to handle safely.

When Alain returned, they laid out everything they would need for the experiment: his notebook, a handful of anchors, a vial of anti-Sensing potion, a stopwatch, and a syringe pre-filled with resurrection serum. Same as yesterday, Mavery hoped the latter wouldn't be necessary.

She took a swig of potion while Alain set up the protective barrier. He'd stayed up half the night making revisions to the incantation, and he planned to practice it a few more times before the true demonstration began.

Though Mavery could Sense no violet auras, she could still detect a faintly flickering veil encircling the campsite alongside the gentle pulsation of magic in the air. Even with the potion, both seemed stronger than usual. Breathing in the pure forest air—rather than the stagnant, dusty air of Alain's apartment—must have cleared her head and sharpened all her senses.

Alain paced in a wide circle as he practiced the incantation. Mavery, meanwhile, tracked him with the stopwatch.

"Forty-three seconds," she announced after his fifth recitation. "That's your fastest yet."

He sat beside her on the log and took a generous gulp from his canteen. Even without the full effects of the Ether, simply practicing the incantation had been enough to leave him parched.

"Thanks to you and that brilliant suggestion you made yesterday," he said. "You may not have a conventional education, but you certainly think like a scholar." At that, she smiled. "Why *did* you leave university?"

"Oh..." Her smile faded as a dark cloud threatened to consume her thoughts. "It...wasn't by choice."

It had been years since she'd told anyone about this part of her past. As she considered whether to reveal it to Alain—if she was even *capable* of it—he placed his hand on her knee.

"Sorry, I didn't mean to pry. You don't—"

"There was a fire," she said softly. She recalled Alain's words from the other night. Though she didn't *want* to speak of this, maybe it was what she *needed*. She slipped her fingers in the gaps between his. "A few weeks after I started at Atterdell, a group of boys got drunk and wandered into my family's orchard. One of them got the bright idea to start a bonfire. You can guess what happened next."

Alain gasped. "Gods, that's horrible."

"It was the smoke that killed my parents and brother, not the fire." She laughed darkly. "A small blessing, I suppose, after I lost my family, the farm, *everything*. With no means of paying my tuition, I had to drop out and move in with my only remaining relative—my uncle, who hated magic so much, he forbade me from practicing it so long as I lived under his roof. He definitely wasn't going to spare a single copper to send me back to Atterdell."

Alain squeezed her hand. "He never...hurt you in any way, I hope?"

"Never physically. He was too afraid of my magic to lay a hand on me. But he made it very clear that I wasn't wanted—and my magic surges, even less so."

"I'm sorry. I can only imagine how awful that must have been."

Mavery shrugged. "I only lived there for a few months, and I wasn't forced to perform any hard labor. Not after a particularly gory incident involving the rooster." Alain's eyes widened, and she laughed halfheartedly. "I'll need several bottles of wine before I tell you *that* story. Let me put it this way: a broken mirror and sprouting floorboards are among the least damaging things my magic surges have done.

"Anyway, since my uncle didn't trust me around the livestock, he had me manage the bookkeeping. Every week, I'd make a few changes to his ledgers, skim a little off the top for myself, until I'd saved enough to strike out on my own. I suppose my life of crime began well before I got caught up with the Dragons."

"You were resourceful. I can't fault you for that."

Speaking about this had always brought about magic surges, which was why she tried to avoid doing so at all costs. At times, even *thinking* about it for too long had been enough. Now, there was no roiling arcana, no fire thrashing in her veins. Maybe enough time had passed, this chapter of her life no longer had that effect on her.

Or, maybe it had nothing to do with time, but with her present company.

"If you need a moment, the spell can wait," Alain said.

Mavery shook her head. "I'm ready. Let's do it now, before it gets dark."

She followed him to the center of the campsite. He turned his wrist to disable the barrier of protective wards, then turned to the page in his notebook where he'd written the incantations Mavery was to perform. She'd practiced them earlier that morning, under the same protections he'd just removed.

With the notebook in hand, she approached the nearest tree, placed her palm flat against the bark. She began with the fireproofing ward, as she'd succeeded with that spell twice already. The resonating ward, though more complex, came to her easily, as did the soundproofing spell. She rattled off the runes without stumbling over a single one. The anti-Sensing potion once again dampened the sensation of Ether, turning it into a cool but tolerable breeze.

And then came the detonation ward. At fifty-six syllables, it was the most complex of the lot, with the greatest consequence for failure. Her pulse quickened as she carefully spoke the incantation. In her head, she sounded less like she was reciting a poem and more like she was butchering a nursery rhyme.

Once the final syllable escaped her lips, she tore her hand away from the trunk as her heart continued to pound against her ribcage. Though she knew this was the same harmless ward Alain had used yesterday, she still didn't want to risk setting it off accidentally.

Speaking Etherean for longer than usual had rendered her mouth and throat cold, her tongue numb. She turned to Alain, whose broad smile warmed her by several degrees.

"You're a natural," he said as she gave back his notebook. "That was expertly done."

"Even the detonation ward?"

He shrugged as he paged through the book, returning to the Sensing spell. "If you made a mistake, I didn't hear it. And from the amount of magic I can feel in the air, the Ether didn't, either."

He took a stone from his pocket, then stepped away to place the augmentation that would replicate her spells to all the trees within a small radius. Without the potion, Mavery would have seen colorful tendrils spanning from tree to tree, encircling the campsite. Instead, all she sensed was fatigue from having expended so much of her arcana all at once. It would take her months—potentially years—of practice before she could match Alain's stamina for spellcasting.

"All right." He returned to her side and took a deep breath. "Here goes nothing."

He began the spell, and the Ether answered him immediately.

Light erupted all around them as if Alain had conjured a hundred pure-white orbs all at once. Mavery instinctively squeezed her eyes shut and threw up her arm. But then she slowly blinked her eyes open to watch the colors bleed in. Gold, violet, red, and pink swirled around the trees, turning the bark incandescent.

Though tears stung her eyes, she couldn't look away. She was as awestruck now as she'd been upon seeing Alain's tapestry of warding magic for the first time. It was then she realized: *she* had placed this magic. *She* had created this beauty.

Alain nudged her shoulder. "Don't forget to summon your protective ward."

This spell—the most natural of all—required only a raise of her hand. Under the effects of the Sensing spell, the ward appeared before her in a burst of white, then faded to blue.

"And now, for the augmentation," Alain said.

He turned and placed his palm flat against her protective ward. He spoke a brief incantation, similar to the first one she'd ever heard him recite. Seeing the magic up close confirmed what she'd suspected before: the base incantation alone was enough to reveal the ley lines. A thread of white light tethered itself to Mavery's ward and trailed to the stone in Alain's trouser pocket.

He then reached through the aura as easily as passing his hand through a stream of water, and touched his palm to hers. He hadn't told her *how* he'd planned to augment her ward, and so, this was a pleasant surprise. The magic rippled at his touch but did not falter.

"This is what you see?" he whispered. When she nodded, he shifted his hand slightly, interlaced his fingers with hers. "This is... Well, I actually can't find the words."

She laughed softly. "I'm glad to know I have that effect on you."

He smiled. "More than you realize."

A moment ago, the illuminated trees had enraptured her completely. Now, they were simply part of the background, all but forgotten. The only thing she could focus on—the only thing she cared to—was his face, cast in soft blue light.

Her ward rippled again as Alain took another step forward, crossing through it completely. Before now, she'd never fully appreciated how they stood eye to eye. It made it all the easier to see the flush of his skin, the desire in his eyes that matched her own. Her lips parted, but not a single breath escaped them as he leaned in and kissed her.

It was the softest brushing of lips—too brief for her to return the kiss, much less close her eyes and savor it. Alain broke away instantly, released her hand as he stepped backward. His eyes blinked rapidly, his skin was the reddest Mavery could ever recall seeing it—save for his knuckles, which were bone-white as he clutched his notebook to his chest.

"I-I'm sorry," he stammered, looking at his feet. "Forgive me, I don't know what came over me just now. I shouldn't have—"

Mavery lowered her hand, dismissing her protective ward, then grasped Alain by the lapel. He emitted a small gasp as she pulled him back toward her. Close enough for their breath to mingle, for her to sense the tea-and-parchment aroma that clung to his skin, as though it had long become a part of him.

"Don't you dare apologize," she whispered.

She drew him even closer and pressed her mouth to his.

THIRTY-TWO

Not only had he kissed Mavery, *she* was now kissing *him*—and more fervently than he ever would have imagined.

Alain's eyes closed as he lost himself in the gentle friction of her lips, the radiant warmth of her skin. She released his shirt, but only to allow her fingers to rake through his hair, along his temples, across his jawline, as if she sought to memorize every inch of him with her hands alone. The sensation of her exploring touch, coupled with the realization that her actions were driven by *desire*, was nothing short of bliss.

His own hands were still gripping his notebook. He tossed it aside, and it hit the ground with a soft thud, though he couldn't have cared less about seeing where it had landed. All he cared about was giving Mavery the kiss he should have given her over a week ago instead of leaving her at her doorstep like the fool he'd been.

With his hands now free, he cradled her face between his palms. She responded by trailing her fingers down his neck. He shivered, and she smiled against his lips before parting her own.

She took his upper lip between hers, gave it a gentle tug. A visceral sound resonated from the back of his throat. Her efforts to heighten the kiss awakened something within him, and any notion he'd had of kissing her with tenderness turned to mist. His lips moved against hers with a forcefulness that hadn't been there a moment ago, while his hands traveled down to her waist.

She brushed his lower lip with her tongue, and he answered by tilting her head back and deepening the kiss. The taste of her was as complex as a rare vintage, heady enough to leave his mind reeling. He was rewarded with a soft moan that made him fully aware of the warm desire that was pooling further down his body, threatening to strain the fabric of his trousers.

With a sharp inhale, Alain broke the kiss and opened his eyes. The Sensing spell had worn off, and so the forest had dimmed. Mavery's lips were still parted as her eyes fluttered open.

"Well..." he said. He doubted he could manage vocabulary more complex than that.

"Well," she echoed, and her smile brightened the world around them once again.

A moment passed while neither of them spoke. But instead of being wrought with tension or burdened with expectation, this silence was...*comfortable*. As he pulled her closer, her palms rested against his chest, his arms against the small of her back. He nestled his face in her hair, breathed her in as though he could fill himself with her very essence. He wanted nothing more than to continue holding her like this, with no worries about spellcraft, or covenants, or even the passage of time.

But that was not their reality; they needed to acknowledge what had just happened.

He sighed. "As much as I enjoyed that...it probably shouldn't happen again."

Mavery pulled back slightly, frowning. "If this is about those ridiculous Covenants—"

"Of course it's about the Covenants. And they're not 'ridiculous'; the High Council enacted them for a reason. Without any standards for decorum, the entire wizarding community would be...well, it would be complete *anarchy*!"

She snorted. "The entire world won't end over a kiss."

"Perhaps not the entire world, but my career might."

"Not if no one finds out about this—about *us*."

His stomach lurched. "You're not suggesting we try courting in secret? I told you what happened with Conor—"

She placed a hand on his cheek. "But I'm not him. I wouldn't dream of holding the Covenants against you." She smiled wryly. "Besides, you know I'm no stranger to keeping secrets."

"I..." He sighed again, closing his eyes as he leaned into her palm. "I don't know..."

"Then why don't I make this easier for both of us and resign?"

His eyes flew open. "Please, Mavery, don't sacrifice your career on my behalf."

She scoffed. "A 'career' that's lasted all of two months. Leyport's a large enough city, I can find work elsewhere." She looked downward. "Though, to be perfectly honest, I doubt I'll find anything quite as enjoyable."

"Then that's all the more reason to keep things as they are."

"But I don't *want* to keep things as they are. I want to be more than your assistant."

His instinct was to doubt her. Their kiss had been simply the result of getting caught up in the moment after a week of trials and failures. He'd warned her of what involving herself with him would entail. Yet, despite knowing the darkest marks of his past, she'd stayed. At this moment, she remained wrapped in his arms.

But if they went through with this, if they got caught...

"If I lose my rank, then what will I have?" he whispered.

"You'll still have your brilliant mind, for starters. Your good heart, your—"

"While I appreciate the compliments, you don't need—"

"Your *stubbornness*"—she jabbed his sternum with her index finger—"that's so relentless, I doubt losing access to *libraries* would stop you from doing anything."

He laughed. "I can't argue with that."

"You'll still have your passion for magic." The finger that had just prodded him now stroked his cheek, leaving behind a trail of tingling skin. "And a beautiful face, with a smile that's godsdamned *sublime*."

He smiled as heat trickled up his neck. "Hmm, I don't think those last two count as *scholarly* attributes."

She rolled her eyes. "There's that stubbornness again." She cupped his chin. "You will always be so much more than a scholar."

Her lips parted, and as she leaned closer, he was caught in a war between his heart and his mind. The former wanted to forget about the Covenants and kiss her again—and never stop kissing her. The latter knew this was no time to make any rash decisions. Her lips were a hair's breadth from his when he released her and slipped away.

He squeezed his eyes shut as he kneaded his temples, but nothing he did could temper the dilemma raging inside his head. And that wasn't even taking into account the work that awaited him in the days ahead. The incantation might have been a success, but he still needed to finish writing his report, then prepare the presentation itself—

Mavery touched his arm. It was enough to quiet his thoughts, if only for a moment.

"What do you think we should do?" she asked softly.

He turned to her, meeting her furrowed brow. "Perhaps...we should set aside these feelings for the time being, then revisit this conversation once the presentation is behind us."

Mavery sighed deeply. Her disappointment was palpable, but she nodded.

"All right," she said.

"For now, let's run through the spell again. We'll need to measure its area of effect, as well as its duration." He forced a smile, a vain attempt to add some levity. "I can't say I was paying attention to either the first time around."

They returned to Steelforge Towers two hours later, after running through the spell a half-dozen times. Though there was no more celebratory kissing, they did hold hands on the walk back through the forest, and they continued to walk hand in hand as they progressed down the corridor to Alain's apartment.

"What in the hells is *that*?" Mavery asked.

Rumbling reverberated through the corridor, followed by a high-pitched whine. Had they not been indoors, the racket could have been easily mistaken for a train. The further they walked, the louder it grew. It was suspiciously familiar, and Alain's suspicions were confirmed upon finding a man-shaped lump sleeping next to his front door.

"What's he doing here?" Mavery whispered.

There was but one way to find out. Regretfully, Alain released Mavery's hand and stepped forward.

"Declan, wake up!"

Declan replied with another bone-rattling snore. Alain nudged Declan's shin with his foot, and his colleague sprung awake in a fit of incoherent sputtering. He blinked, yawned as he reacclimated to his surroundings.

"You're back!" he said, then blinked again upon spotting Mavery. "Er, it appears *both* of you are back."

"What do you want, Declan?" Alain demanded.

"Bah! Is that any way of speaking to an old friend?"

"An old friend who only turns up unannounced whenever he wants something."

"I wouldn't need to resort to these measures if you checked your mail every now and again. Did you even *see* my most recent letter?"

Alain had been so focused on perfecting the incantation, he'd let his mail accumulate again; sending Mavery down to fetch it hadn't even crossed his mind.

"I'll take your silence as a 'no,' " Declan grumbled. "Well, you're right. I was hoping to ask you for a favor. Why don't we go inside and discuss this further?"

Alain looked to Mavery, who shrugged. With a sigh, he dismissed his warding magic to allow Declan entry, then unlocked the door for all three of them. Once inside, Declan wasted no time making himself at home: he plopped himself into Alain's armchair by the fireplace. He emitted a low whistle as he gazed around the room.

"I've never seen this place so *clean*!" he exclaimed. "This is Mavery's doing, I'll wager."

"It is," Alain said as he sat on one end of the sofa. Mavery took the opposite end, putting them at no risk of accidentally touching.

Declan nodded. "Yes, I sensed a feminine touch soon as I walked in."

Mavery snorted. "Being organized has nothing to do with femininity. If that were the case, then wouldn't every assistant—as well as every arcanist, for that matter—be female?"

"You got me there," Declan said with a hearty laugh. "Though a wizard with a knack for cleanliness is a rare sight."

"Somehow, I don't find that hard to believe."

"You don't know the half of it! Worst tower I ever saw, by far, had a—"

Alain cleared his throat. "I doubt you came here solely to discuss home decorating. What do you want?"

"Not in the mood for small talk, I see." Declan leaned back in the chair, rested his steepled hands atop his perfectly round stomach. "Final exams begin on Onisday. I was hoping you and your lovely assistant could help me with—"

"We can't. We're presenting to the High Council in a week's time."

"A spell presentation, yes?" When Alain nodded, Declan dismissively waved his hand. "This is, what, your third spell? Fourth? It'll be a walk in the park for a wizard like you!"

"I'm glad you have such confidence in me, but this will be my first time presenting before the Council in over two years. I need to be prepared."

"I understand, but the thing is..." Declan sighed deeply as he twiddled his thumbs. Alain braced himself for one of Declan's favorite tactics: the play upon one's guilty conscience. "Seeing as I covered some of your classes this term, a third of my students were originally yours. And since you're now stopping by campus again, I thought—"

"I'm sorry, Declan, but my answer is still 'no.' Our plates are too full."

"How many students do you have?" Mavery asked.

"Two hundred and thirty-three," Declan said.

Alain gawked at him. "Examining that many is going to take all week!"

"Three days, actually," Declan said. "I'm front-loading it,

starting with the first-years on Onisday."

"And you couldn't have given me more than *two days'* notice?"

"I tried! It's not my fault you can't be bothered to check your mailbox."

Alain knew, with the most difficult part of the spell complete, he could spare a few hours. But the University was the last place he desired to be, and he could scarcely think of anything less pleasurable than administering exams.

Out of the corner of his eye, he spotted Mavery looking at him, then Declan, then the tea table. She leaned over and picked up a pack of playing cards that, until this moment, Alain had forgotten about. They'd become well-worn during his sabbatical, after countless games of Patience.

"Declan, you don't happen to play Tribute?" she asked.

He chortled. "Do I play Tribute? Does a Dyadist worship the moons?"

She grinned. "Then how about I challenge you to a game? You win, and we help you with exams. I win, and we're completely off the hook."

Declan's mustache twitched, indicating a smile lurking beneath that mess of wiry red hair. He looked to Alain. "What do you say, lad?"

Alain sighed. "Fine."

The three of them relocated to the kitchen. Mavery cleared the table of alchemical supplies while Declan shuffled the deck. The two of them took the chairs at opposite ends of the table, leaving Alain to sit in the middle with nothing to do but watch as Mavery wagered three days of their lives.

"Durnatel rules fine by you?" Declan asked.

Mavery nodded. "Are there any others worth playing?"

"Oh-ho! I like this one," he chuckled as he began dealing cards.

From what little Alain could recall of the rules, each player began with a hand of five cards. They then took turns "paying tribute" to the other player by offering the highest card in their hand. In theory, the game was simple. In practice, the real skill was in tricking your opponent into believing the card on offer actually was your most valuable. After all, the winner was whoever ended the game with the best hand. These were only the basic rules; there were dozens of variations, including some that required actual money to be wagered alongside the cards. Although Alain could manage Patience well enough, anything more advanced was lost on him—especially when deception was involved.

For the first few rounds, Mavery and Declan exchanged cards rapidly but silently, occasionally drawing from the deck, while Alain struggled to keep pace. He soon gave up on following the game and turned to a pastime that made infinitely more sense: preparing a pot of tea.

When he returned to the table with three cups—extra cream and sugar in Declan's—the deck had dwindled considerably, and the game's pace had slowed.

"The best I can do is a nine," Mavery said, laying down a nine of clubs.

Declan grunted. "Oh, I know you can do better than that."

Mavery shrugged. "Take it, or draw."

Declan peered at her over his own cards. Mavery's expression remained flat, betraying nothing. With a groan, Declan took the nine of clubs and added it to his hand. In turn, he offered her a Lord of diamonds. Alain couldn't remember how much the cards with people on them—Wizards, Lords, and Priests—were worth. But he assumed Lords were valuable, as Mavery added it to her deck without comment.

"Why do you need Alain's help, anyway?" she asked, laying down a seven of spades. "Why not use your assistants?"

"Trying to distract me, are you?" Declan asked. Instead of taking Mavery's card, he drew from the deck. Mavery discarded the seven of spades. Alain assumed because Declan hadn't accepted it, the card was no longer in play.

"No, just making conversation."

Declan frowned. "I can't use my assistants because I don't have any."

"Why not?"

"Leona," Declan said, offering a Wizard of hearts.

"Who's Leona?" Mavery opted for the final card remaining in the deck. While Declan moved the Wizard to the discard pile, she laid her cards face-down and sipped from her teacup.

"Go on, lad, tell her," Declan said. He also put his cards aside in favor of tea.

Alain sighed, then turned to Mavery. "Leona was his last assistant and, briefly, his wife."

Mavery choked on a mouthful of tea. "You were *married* to your assistant?"

Declan nodded. "For about a month. We eloped in Maroba, thought we could keep it quiet from the High Council. As you can guess, something like that doesn't keep quiet for long. The High Council let me keep both my job and my rank, on the condition that I divorced Leona and never hired another assistant."

"When did that happen?"

"About twelve years ago." He shrugged. "It's not so bad. The 'no assistant' part, I mean. I've always favored teaching over research, though it would be nice to always have someone to help with exams and such."

Alain and Mavery exchanged a knowing look. While Declan gulped down his tea, Mavery drew a Lord of clubs from her hand and placed it in the center of the table.

"Ah, ah, ah!" Declan cried. Tea sloshed over the rim of his cup as he set it aside. "Didn't you just say you had nothing higher than a nine?"

"Er, yes, but then you offered me a Lord."

"I know for a fact it was a Lord of *diamonds.*"

"No, it was *definitely* clubs." She glanced at Alain, who raised his brows. Surely she didn't expect him, of all people, to corroborate her bluff?

"Leave him out of this!" Declan said, then narrowed his eyes. "You've been keeping a Lord from me all this time. We show our hands now, or you lose by default. Your choice."

Mavery sighed, then laid her cards face-up. Declan did the same and, after quickly tallying the cards beneath his breath, clapped his hands and laughed victoriously.

"Gods damn it," Mavery groaned, crossing her arms.

Alain peered at her cards. "You have two Lords, whereas he has only one. Shouldn't that make you the winner?"

Mavery shook her head. "One is black and one is red. That means they cancel each other out, so they're worthless."

"Durnatel rules," Declan said as he gathered up the cards. "And trying to offload one half of an unmatched pair is the oldest trick in the book."

"Sorry, Alain. I guess my Tribute skills have gotten a little rusty."

"If that was 'rusty,' I'd hate to play you after a few more rounds," Declan said. "Color me impressed. So impressed, in fact, I'll offer a compromise. Instead of all three days, what if you assist me only on Onisday? You can't argue that first-year exams, while maybe not the most painless, are definitely the most straightforward."

Alain looked to Mavery. "But your appointment—"

"Is at midday," she said. She reached beneath the table and gently touched his knee. Alain fought to maintain a neutral expression, though it was a miracle Declan didn't notice his heart pounding against his ribcage. "You help Declan. I'll be fine going alone."

Alain cleared his throat. "If you're certain..."

"Er, beg your pardon, but what appointment?" Declan asked.

"At Mother's. Mavery needs a dress for our presentation."

Declan chuckled, shaking his head. "Lad, if anyone can handle your mother, it's this woman right here."

Of course, *Mother* was the least of Alain's concerns. He'd agreed to accompany Mavery to the boutique and keep watch outside, just in case that scoundrel, Neldren, was still sniffing around the city. But Aumbremancers preferred nocturnal schedules, and men weren't allowed at the boutique during business hours. Alain hoped both of those factors would be enough to deter him.

"Well, this has been fun, but I must be off." Declan's chair scraped across the flagstone tiles. "Mind if I use the facilities? I'm about to piss like a racehorse."

"Yes, go ahead," Alain said. As Declan tottered out of the kitchen, he pinched the bridge of his nose and muttered, "And thank you for that *lovely* choice of words."

Mavery laughed. "I don't know why you complain about him

so much. Yes, he's a handful, but—"

"Him being a handful is *precisely* why I complain."

"Still, he seems like a good fellow. Why did you never tell him about Conor? I figure he would understand more than anyone."

"Because Declan couldn't keep *his own marriage* a secret. I doubt he'd be tight-lipped about—"

"Shit!" Mavery cried, making Alain jump a solid inch off his chair.

"What is it?"

"The bathroom!" she whispered. "When I took a bath this morning, I forgot to gather up my clothes—including my drawers."

Alain gasped. Not only from the horrific mental image of Declan stumbling upon Mavery's undergarments, but from the decidedly *not* horrific mental image of Mavery disrobing, then soaking in the bath. She must have done that while he'd been across town, arranging the appointment with his mother. Of course, it was within Mavery's right to make herself at home. And, of course, it was only natural for Alain's thoughts to meander in that direction while his lips still tingled from the memory of their kiss.

But this was no time for wanton thoughts. Alain cleared his throat—and his head.

"Let me handle this," he said.

He walked to the sitting room, and as he waited outside the bathroom, he formulated a cover story: Mavery had left her clothes in the bathroom after spilling a potion on herself. But wouldn't that imply she'd happened to have a change of undergarments with her?

Perhaps being truthful would be best. Mavery was only staying here temporarily, and their relationship was strictly professional. Then again, that was hardly a *truthful* statement, considering recent events—

His heart skipped a beat as the toilet flushed, then the tap ran for considerably less time than the healers recommended. The door creaked open, and Declan startled at the sight of Alain standing in front of it.

"Whatever you saw in there, I can explain," Alain said quickly.

Declan's eyes widened. "Er, yes, you definitely have some explaining to do." Every muscle in Alain's body clenched. Declan grinned. "Didn't anyone tell you broken mirrors are a bad omen? You ought to get a mender to come take a look at that."

Alain furrowed his brow, then remembered how the bathroom mirror was still cracked from Mavery's accidental magic surge. It had happened almost a fortnight ago, and Alain hardly noticed the cracked glass anymore. He sighed with relief as Declan clapped him on the shoulder.

"See you on Onisday, lad. Until then, behave yourself. Don't do anything *I* would do."

He nodded toward the kitchen, where Mavery stood at the threshold, then threw Alain an exaggerated wink. Alain's stomach plummeted as Declan left the apartment, whistling an upbeat tune.

THIRTY-THREE

The midday traffic was lighter than Mavery had anticipated, and so she arrived in the Garden District with plenty of time to spare. She decided to take advantage of the sunny, cloudless weather and peruse the main plaza before heading to Tesseraunt's Boutique.

Compared to the Night Market, the Onisday market was a dull affair. Only a handful of merchants had posted up shop today, and they made few efforts to attract the scattered market-goers. But there was no shortage of food merchants. They offered everything from fruit pies and fried dough, to seasoned nuts and spit-roasted meats.

Mavery's stomach growled at the pungent aroma of spices. As she'd never been to a dressmaker's before, she hadn't a clue if her appointment would finish in time for a midday meal—or even afternoon tea. Conventional wisdom would likely recommend against eating immediately before being fitted for a dress, but she wasn't about to face Priscilla Tesseraunt on an empty stomach.

She tracked down the merchant who sold the flatbread she'd enjoyed at the Night Market, then sought an empty table to sit and enjoy her food.

"You are a woman with exotic taste!"

Mavery turned, then frowned as she recognized something else she'd encountered at the Night Market.

"I hope your taste in the exotic does not end with food," the merchant said, gesturing grandly to the rugs draped over his stall. "May I interest you in one of the finest rugs from my homeland?"

The broad daylight revealed that, behind his kohl-lined eyes and colorful tunic, this man was no more Maroban than Mavery was—exactly as she'd suspected the first time she'd heard that terrible attempt at an accent. To darken his complexion, he'd slathered bronze makeup over his face, but he'd neglected to do the same to his hands. His true skin tone was pale and ashen, and he was missing two fingers on his right hand. Not to mention, though he was a head shorter than Mavery, his build was too lanky for a Maroban. There was something vaguely familiar about this man, but Mavery couldn't pinpoint what, aside from him being an obvious conman.

"Not interested," she said coolly.

He must have noticed her glancing at his hands, for he shoved them in his pockets. His eyes lingered on her face—her nose, to be precise. Up to this point, everyone Mavery had met in Leyport had been too polite to draw attention to her most visible scar. She'd all but forgotten how uncomfortable it was to be stared at while a stranger pondered what could have marred her face. She narrowed her eyes. In return, the man bowed his head politely, then cajoled an approaching couple.

Mavery found an empty bench a short distance away. The first bite of curried lamb sent a wave of warmth rippling through her body from head to toe. But that comfort dissipated as she realized she was being watched. Sure enough, the rug merchant's eyes kept darting in her direction. If he truly was a conman, he could stand to learn a thing or two about discretion.

Either he was sizing her up as a potential mark, or his intentions were even less savory. She had no desire to find out. Suppressing a shudder, she binned what remained of her flatbread, then continued to Tesseraunt's Boutique.

A bell chimed as she opened the door, but the hum of activity inside the shop quickly drowned it out. While the right-hand wall was lined with racks of dresses, each one more elegant than the last, the bulk of the room was dedicated to alterations. Seamstresses flitted across the shop floor with pins clenched between their teeth, arms laden with swaths of colorful fabric, tape measures draped over their shoulders and trailing behind them like capes. Their customers were all young women in various states of dress. Some wore puffy-sleeved ball gowns and were scrutinizing their reflections in the mirrors. Others had been stripped down to their chemises to have their measurements taken. With no men around, propriety hardly mattered.

Inside the waiting area were finely dressed women ranging from around Mavery's age to grandmotherly. Most of them were biding their time on the plush sofas, reading novels and fashion magazines. But one of them remained standing, arms crossed and foot tapping, as she watched the door to one of the dressing rooms.

A tawny-haired girl emerged from it, swathed in a gown that dwarfed her petite figure. Following closely on the girl's heels was a raven-haired seamstress who carried the gown's train with one hand while pinching the bodice closed with the other. And following on *her* heels was the woman who refused to continue watching from a distance.

"Please, Madam Fallstad, you must *wait*." The seamstress's tone indicated she'd uttered that phrase too many times today. She deposited the girl in front of a mirror, then spread her arms and ushered the other woman back to the waiting area.

"Mirabel is making her Society debut on Siddisday!" Madam Fallstad snapped. Like most noblewomen Mavery had ever encountered, her voice was grating, her tone insolent. "Her dress must be *perfect*."

"And it will be—if you allow me to do my work."

With a huff, Madam Fallstad lowered herself onto one of the sofas, clasped her gloved hands in her lap. The seamstress noticed Mavery lingering by the front desk.

"Do you have an appointment?" She nearly had to yell over the chatter from the shop floor.

"Yes, with Priscilla."

"*You* have an appointment with Madam Tesseraunt?"

In an eerily Priscilla-like manner, the seamstress's eyes roved over Mavery's outfit. Not wanting to look completely out of place, Mavery had worn her nicest blouse today, though she suspected her trousers negated the effect. The seamstress sighed, then flipped through the appointment book atop the front desk.

"She has nothing scheduled at this time today. What did you say your name was?"

"Mavery Culwich. Maybe it's under her son's name. He—"

"Sorry, did you say 'May-bree'?"

"Not to worry, Lydia. I understood her perfectly."

The seamstress flinched as Priscilla approached from behind. Alain's mother wore a high-necked, long-sleeved dress in deep violet. Mavery took the color to be a uniform of sorts, as all the staff wore similar shades.

"I'll see to Ms. Culwich while you see to Miss Worton's measurements," Priscilla said.

"But I'm already double-booked with Miss Fallstad and Miss..." Priscilla narrowed her eyes, and Lydia bowed her head. "Of course, Madam Tesseraunt."

She hurried back to Mirabel Fallstad, who seemed on the verge of collapsing under the weight of her voluminous dress. Priscilla turned to Mavery.

"This way," she said.

Mavery followed her across the shop floor. Instead of stopping behind one of the room dividers or inside one of the dressing rooms, Priscilla led her into the backroom. When she closed the door, the sounds of chatter quieted at once. Mavery tasted copper and noticed a sheen of violet over the door. She suspected the soundproofing, like the wards guarding the building, had also been Alain's doing.

Through the sheer curtain hanging in the window, sunlight cast a cozy glow over the small room. It was primarily used for storage: sewing machines, dress forms, and crates of fabric had been deposited here haphazardly. A full-length mirror leaned against the wall, and there was enough floorspace for a small round platform.

"Disrobe, but leave on your undergarments," Priscilla said, wasting no time for pleasantries.

Deciding there was no point in postponing the awkwardness, Mavery unbuttoned her blouse. She recognized the absurdity in how she hadn't yet stripped before Alain—that was a thought she'd only entertained in the privacy of a hot bath—but here she was, standing in her undergarments before *his mother*.

"This is a *slight* improvement over what you wore the first time we met," Priscilla said, giving Mavery's blouse a scrutinizing sneer.

Mavery fought the urge to roll her eyes as she handed Priscilla her trousers. Priscilla's frown deepened as she draped them, along with the blouse, over a chair.

"Do you own any petticoats?" Priscilla asked, then shook her head. "Silly question. Do you at least own a chemise?"

"Not unless you count my sleeping shift."

Her hard stare indicated that it did not. "Have you *ever* worn a dress?"

The last time had been when she and Neldren had stolen some formal attire from a laundry, then infiltrated an estate sale. Neldren had distracted the auctioneer with mundane questions about stamp collections and such, while she had tucked small heirlooms beneath her neckline, inside her gloves, under her skirts. It had been one of their most lucrative cons.

"On occasion," Mavery said. "I don't get invited to many formal events."

"Yes, I suspected as much. Now, up with you!"

Stripped down to her brassière, drawers, and stockings, Mavery stepped onto the platform. Priscilla wasted no time confronting her from all sides and angles with her tape measure. She jotted down numbers in a small notebook while talking to herself—a habit she'd passed down to her son, though her mutterings were mostly in Dauphinian.

"Just a hair over seven-and-sixty inches," Priscilla said after taking Mavery's height. "And with your measurements...yes, one of our standard sizes should fit you with minimal alterations. That is good. Thanks to Aventus saving things to the last minute, I will not have much time."

"Oh, you don't need to go through all that trouble."

Priscilla clicked her tongue. "No, the *trouble* will be my reputation if you leave my shop with a dress that is not a perfect fit. Stay there."

She returned to the main room with an eruption of sound, followed by an equally jarring return to silence when she closed the door behind her. She returned a moment later, carrying several dresses. Unlike the pastels and bold patterns Mavery had seen on the shop floor, these dresses had been dyed shades of emerald, burgundy, amethyst.

"Jewel tones," Priscilla said. "They are a bit dark for spring, but what matters more is how they suit your complexion."

To prove her point, she held up an emerald-colored skirt to Mavery's face. Indeed, the fabric made her green eyes appear more vibrant than usual. Priscilla then wrangled Mavery into a petticoat, followed by the skirt. She passed Mavery's arms through the sleeves of a cream-colored silk blouse, and came around to tie a large loose bow at its collar. Finally, she helped Mavery put on a bodice that matched the skirt. It had a sharp lapel, structured shoulders, and a dramatically cinched waist.

"There," Priscilla said, stepping away to let Mavery see her reflection. "A look suitable for meeting the Archmage."

Compared to the ball gowns flitting about the other room, this dress was simple—practical, even. But it was still the nicest garment she'd ever worn. The skirt swished in a wide arc as she turned to view herself from the side. The sunlight revealed gleams of gold and azure woven into the fabric; it shimmered like it was actually made of emeralds.

"It's perfect," Mavery breathed.

Priscilla shook her head as her fingers pinched and pulled the bodice in various places. "No, I must let out the shoulders and shorten the hem. *Then* it will be perfect."

Never had Mavery imagined herself owning something so elegant, much less made specifically *for her*. In the mirror, her eyes glistened with tears. Priscilla pulled Mavery into a hug that was stiff, one-armed, and too brief to reciprocate.

"Thank you," Mavery said. "How much do I owe you?"

"Let us say…five-and-twenty potins for the clothes—including the petticoat—and another five for the alterations."

Mavery gaped at her. She didn't know the first thing about fashion, but that figure sounded absurdly low.

"Consider it a special discount in exchange for everything you have done for my son. And I mean more than your help with his books and spells. I know you are very special to him."

Mavery's stomach lurched as she recalled what Nezima had said to her at the Lettered Gentleman.

"What did he tell you, exactly?" she asked. "And, better yet, what did you tell Nezima?"

"Aventus never mentioned your name, but I am no fool. Who else could it be but you?" Priscilla chuckled, then frowned. "Yes, I know I should have said nothing to Nezima, but can you blame a mother for being delighted to see her son *happy* for the first time in months, perhaps years? Not to worry, I will not speak of it again."

She gripped Mavery's arm, and the two women locked eyes for a moment. Mavery found in Priscilla's dark eyes the same warmth she had found in Alain's so many times. She hoped Priscilla didn't expect her to say anything, because she doubted she could find the words, much less speak them. Her throat had suddenly twisted itself into a knot.

So, she was beyond relieved when Priscilla patted her arm and promptly returned to business matters. She instructed Mavery to remove the dress and try on the others, as well as several pairs of dress boots. In the end, they both decided that the emerald dress was the winner. Priscilla pinned the dress in several places, and Mavery felt a bit wistful as she changed back into her ordinary clothes.

Priscilla placed a pair of lacquered boots inside a bag with *Tesseraunt's Boutique* stitched on the side.

"There is no charge for these, as they are from last year's collection," she said, handing Mavery the bag. "Genuine patent leather, so you had best begin breaking them in now."

Mavery doubted Priscilla would take "no" for an answer, so she accepted the bag with a nod. As she approached the door, she paused and turned to Priscilla.

"I've been curious about something. Why do you call your son by his wizard name?"

Priscilla stood with her shoulders back and chin raised. "Because no Tesseraunt has ever been a mage, much less a wizard. The day he earned that name was the proudest day of my life. I will never understand why he tries to hide his accomplishments."

"Maybe because he wants to be more than his accomplishments," Mavery said. "Maybe he just wants to be Alain."

Priscilla smiled, but her eyes lacked the warmth from earlier. "He will always be Alain, of course, but I will never let him forget who he has become—and everything he achieved to get there."

Mavery decided they would have to agree to disagree on that matter. She opened the door and returned to the chaos on the shop floor. It was somehow even busier now than it had been when she'd first arrived. Lydia, the seamstress from earlier, was now arguing about fabric swatches with a different noblewoman. Mavery stepped out of the boutique and returned to a world that felt leagues more sane.

Outside the shop, she leaned against the wall and peeked inside the bag. The boots were so glossy, her reflection stared back at her. With a shrug, she decided to take Priscilla's advice and exchanged her regular boots for the new pair. The stiff leather pinched her toes, and the heel was a bit higher than what she was used to, but they were bearable.

Carrying her old boots inside the bag, she headed back to the main plaza. As she walked down the tree-lined street, the shadows grew darker, the air more frigid. She peered up at the sky, but it was the same as it had been earlier: blue and cloudless.

She stopped walking. When she looked down, she gasped. Her blood turned to ice.

Thick tendrils of shadow swirled at her feet, like mist lingering after a storm. The air reeked of ash and arcana.

"Oh, shit."

She ran.

THIRTY-FOUR

The world darkened around her as she sprinted down the cobblestone street. It was as though night had fallen early, but there were no moons to light her path. She could no longer see the trees, the buildings, the sky. Everything had become lost to the shroud. She wanted to cry for help, but she couldn't tell if there was anyone around to hear. Anyone other than the last person she wanted to see.

She ran with all the grace of a newborn calf, her feet screaming in agony from the too-tight boots. She wanted to rid herself of the bloody things, but she couldn't afford to stop.

The distance between the boutique and the market was not even a block. She had to be close by now. Once she returned to the market, she would be safe. The area would be too open, too sun-bathed for even a master of Aumbremancy to cast it all into darkness.

She continued running forward, but the arcana-infused shadows caught up with her. A tendril snaked up her leg like a dark, intangible rope. She tried to shake it off, but the more she struggled, the more it persisted. Another quickly followed, coiling around her other leg, then her midsection and arms.

She needed to dispel the shadows. The incantation came to mind automatically. But when she opened her mouth to conjure an orb of Ether, the shadows caught in her throat, burned her lungs. Choking on their acrid taste, she couldn't manage so much as a whisper.

The shadows engulfed the final inch of her exposed skin, and then her stomach lurched as she became weightless, one with the black void.

Three heartbeats later, her feet met solid ground again. The shadows dissipated, but the world around her was still dim. From what she could tell, she was in an alley. And judging by how briefly she'd been within the shroud, she couldn't have been transported far.

"Hello again, Mave."

Her breath caught in her lungs as she froze, then slowly turned toward the voice she'd expected but nonetheless dreaded to hear. Standing behind her was the man who had put a bullet in her stomach two months ago.

Neldren had shaved his goatee, and the scars marring his slate-colored skin were now on full display. One of them appeared fresh. He was wearing the same longcoat he'd worn the last time they saw each other, though it had gained several new patches.

He took a step forward.

"Don't!" Mavery cried, reflexively summoning a protective ward.

"Relax." Neldren raised his hands, fingers spread and palms facing out. "I know how this looks, but I *do* come in peace."

She scowled at him through the blue veil.

"It's like Ellice told you: I just want to talk. I reserved us a table at a café around the corner. I figured if I brought you straight there, it would cause a scene, and I wanted to do this properly. After all, word around town is you're a regular in the Garden District these days." His gaze flicked downward. "Nice boots, by the way."

"Fuck you."

He sighed. "All I'm asking for is five minutes. I know I don't deserve it, but give me that, and you'll never see me again. I swear."

Neldren Rel'Selayne was a master of deception; he'd taught her everything she knew about that art form. Yet, there was something in his voice that gave her pause: a modicum of sincerity. Only someone who knew him as she did would recognize it.

"Five minutes," she said stiffly. While she didn't trust the bastard—far from it—she had to admit she was curious enough to humor him.

He inclined his head. "Follow me."

Mavery kept her ward aloft all the way down the alley. They rounded the corner, and before them was a small café much like the one Alain had once taken her to. But this one had a spacious patio with a front-row view of the botanical garden, whose glass roof gleamed in the sunlight. They were still in the Garden District, just down the road from the boutique.

A dozen café patrons chatted quietly, drank tea, read newspapers. A few risked glances in Mavery and Neldren's direction but otherwise paid them no mind. It was little wonder; Neldren's presence signaled that, while he didn't belong here, he was someone best left alone.

He gestured to an empty table. Mavery dismissed her ward, then took a seat in one of the wrought-iron chairs. In front of her was a porcelain cup filled with what looked like an exceptionally dark tea. Its aroma was earthy, somewhat burnt. Had it been Alain offering her this unfamiliar drink, she would have tried it without a second thought. But she was not about to trust anything from the man who'd seated himself across from her.

"I took the liberty of ordering for you," Neldren said. "It's called coffee, made from tiny beans from the Isles. The Dauphinians are so mad about this drink, they went to war with Maroba just to get their hands on those beans. At least, that's what the bloke behind the counter told me."

"Fascinating," she said flatly. "So, how did you track me down?"

"My old friend Vilk. Remember him?"

She shook her head. Neldren had scores of "old friends."

"Then maybe you'll remember that night a few years back, when I played twelve games of Tribute with you practically sitting on my cock the entire time. He sat across the table from us, lap notably empty. Even if you don't remember Vilk, he definitely remembers *you*."

Mavery couldn't remember the man's face well enough to pick him out of a crowd, but she *could* remember the way he'd leered at her all night. Her skin prickled at the memory.

"Oh. *Him.*"

"We reconnected not long after I arrived in the city. Vilk's current scheme is selling fake rugs to rich tossers who don't know any better. He mentioned seeing you the other night."

Her breath caught in her lungs as she recalled the merchant she'd spoken with earlier—the man with the bronze makeup and the fake accent. The hand with the missing fingers was the same one that had drawn cards and thrown down coppers until the small hours of the morning. And when that hand had tried to grope Mavery's breast afterward, Neldren had threatened to snap off its remaining digits.

Every muscle in Mavery's body clenched as Neldren reached inside his coat pocket. But he revealed only a bloodstone. He gave it a playful shake before slipping it back in his pocket.

"I told him to send me a signal if he ever saw you again," he said. "And, as luck would have it, I didn't have to wait long."

Mavery frowned. "That's one minute gone, so get to the point. What do you want?"

"First, I have a gift."

He reached into his other pocket, pulled out a dagger, and laid it on the table. It was the same one Mavery had lost back in Burnslee. Its hilt was carved from ivory, and a floral pattern was etched in its golden sheath.

"Take it," Neldren said.

"What's your game?"

"No game. Just returning what's yours."

The dagger wasn't *hers*, technically speaking. She'd never been able to afford a weapon like this, not even at the height of her thieving career. She'd stolen it years ago from a noblewoman during a carriage robbery.

She snatched the dagger and slipped it in her bag before Neldren had the chance to change his mind. Oddly, she felt no safer with it in her possession again.

"I had every intention of returning it to you," Neldren said. "I only held onto it because I knew the healers would confiscate it."

She blinked. "You...*what*?"

"How do you think you got to the healers in the first place?"

"So..." She tried to swallow, but her mouth had gone dry. "So, you took my knife after dumping me on their doorstep?"

He sighed. "I didn't *dump you on their doorstep*. I made sure they found you, then waited outside the infirmary for two hours while you were in surgery. Once I knew you would live, I went back to the inn, gave Ellice and Itri some bullshit story about how you'd slipped on a patch of ice." He hung his head. "I was too ashamed to admit what I'd done."

"You think I'm stupid enough to believe all that?" Mavery demanded, her voice low with barely contained rage.

Neldren looked up, frowning deeply.

"I barely slept at all that night, so first thing in the morning, I snuck back into the infirmary. You were still unconscious, but I was determined to wait around until you woke up. I had to keep to the shadows because I doubted the healer they'd assigned you would've been happy to see me, the way she ranted about vagabonds. Right bint, that Emma was."

Mavery's stomach roiled, but this time, shadow magic had nothing to do with it. Alain had been right after all: Neldren *hadn't* left her for dead.

"Once the village caught wind of"—Neldren's eyes shifted, then he lowered his voice—"our *job*...that miserable little place became infested with bulls. I had no choice but to leave before I could explain myself."

"Explain what, exactly? You tried to kill me but then felt guilty about it?"

"I never wanted to *kill* you, Mave. I was already in a right state over Fennick and how he'd almost cost us the score. When you walked out, something in me just...snapped. But even in the moment, I didn't want to see you dead. That's why I didn't aim for any vital organs."

"Oh, how *considerate* of you," Mavery said with as much bitterness as she could muster.

"Look at it from my perspective. You come back after dropping off the face of Perrun for almost a year. I allow you to rejoin my crew, even though I had every right to turn you away. I then snag us the best job either of us had seen in ages." He accentuated each point with a jab of his finger against the tabletop. "Even after all that, you *still* walked out on me again, all because I took care of a minor hiccup in the most efficient way I could."

She glared at him. "You would call murdering a man in cold blood 'a minor hiccup'?"

He scoffed. "Is it really *murder* when the man already has both feet in the grave? Besides, why do you care? You barely knew the bastard."

"It was the principle of it, Nel. A principle I thought we both shared." She dropped her voice; their argument had prompted some glances in their direction. She leaned forward, placed her palms flat against the table. "We never kill for profit—even if it makes the job more 'efficient.'"

Now that she knew the truth of that night, the man sitting across from her wasn't charming or conniving. He'd all but admitted that shooting her hadn't been an act of malice, but the equivalent of a child throwing a tantrum. Why had she been so afraid of him? With newfound resolve, she barreled ahead.

"So, what's the point of all this? After giving me my dagger and a cup of whatever this shit is, you hope that, in return, I'll come running back to your bed? Is that it?"

He snorted. "Hardly. I've moved on. So have you, from what Vilk told me. That bloke you were cozying up with at the Night Market...was he your lover, or just another mark?"

"That's none of your godsdamned business."

Neldren chuckled. "Lover, then. We'll see how long that lasts." He sipped from his cup as Mavery narrowed her eyes.

"What's that supposed to mean?"

He blinked at her, then threw back his head with barking laughter. A few of the nearby patrons shot him dirty looks. As his laughter subsided, he took in her incredulous look, and a similar one spread across his face.

"Well, fuck me twice on Finisday! You really don't know, do you?"

"Know what?"

"At the first sign of conflict, you toss aside your lovers like a broken plaything, then you're off to find a new one. This is what you've always done, Mave. You and that fickle heart of yours."

Her blood and arcana flared in unison. "*I'm* the fickle one? After all the times you've left me over the—"

Porcelain rattled as Neldren slammed his fist on the table. Mavery flinched. The couple sitting at the table closest to them scampered away.

"No, Mave. It was always *you* who left *me*! The first time, you snuck off in the middle of the night after I told you to leave the Dragons. You returned six months later, only to leave again when we disagreed on how to split our cut for a job—"

"You wanted a finder's fee, even though *I* was the one who—"

"Then, when you got tired of playing house with that Fenutian girl—"

"She left me to go fight in a godsdamned *war*!"

"In any case, you slithered your way back into my bed again."

Mavery laughed coldly. "From what I recall, you didn't hesitate when you slithered your way back into *me*."

"It's been the same thing over and over *and over* again since the night we first met." He shook his head. "Do you even remember how many times you've left?"

"I don't—"

"Eight times, Mave." He pounded the table again. "You've left me eight *fucking* times in eighteen years! Admit it: you've only ever seen me as your backup plan."

This time, she did not flinch. She clenched her fists, set her jaw. "Don't you dare put the blame on me. Not when you always welcomed me back with open arms—just like you did three months ago."

"You're right, I did. I was an idiot then, but—"

"Sir, you're causing a disturbance to the other guests," said the constable who'd just approached their table. Though he appeared a pustule-faced schoolboy, his tone was authoritative and laced with contempt. "I must ask you to leave."

Mavery crossed her arms and threw Neldren a smirk.

"That goes for you, too, ma'am," the constable said. "I have half a mind to fine you both for unvirtuous conduct. Lucky for you, I'm feeling generous today."

"Lucky for *you*, mate, I was just leaving," Neldren said. With a teeth-aching scrape of metal against stone, he pushed back his chair. Mavery expected him to disappear into the shadows, but he walked westward—the same direction she was headed, unfortunately. She pushed back her own chair and gathered up her bag.

"Bloody gray-skins," the constable muttered.

Neldren sauntered down the street, keeping to the tree-lined side where the shadows were most abundant. Mavery silently cursed his slow pace, though she was unlikely to get around him. They'd sat at the café long enough for the blisters on her feet to fully develop, and this new bout of movement rubbed her skin raw. At least it distracted her from her other bodily aches.

"Reminds me of old times," Neldren said, not bothering to turn and look at her as he spoke.

"Which part? Arguing in public, or getting kicked out of the local watering hole?"

"Didn't the two always go hand in hand?"

"True," she said, and they shared a laugh.

"Though I don't remember ever getting booted from a 'watering hole' as posh as that one."

"First time for everything," Mavery said, wincing. The pain had grown intolerable. She leaned against a tree, prised off her right boot, and nearly cried out from relief. As she changed back into her well-worn boots, Neldren approached.

"Didn't you say you were leaving?" she asked. She finished tying her laces, then peered up as he loomed over her.

"After all my talk about doing things the 'proper' way, I never actually got around to it." He extended his hand. "Mave, I'm sorry for everything that happened back in Burnslee."

Mavery eyed his hand skeptically as she stood upright. "You'll need to be more specific than that."

"I'm sorry for letting my anger get the better of me, for shooting you, for taking your cut—"

"And losing my cut."

"Fuck, she told you about that?" He pinched the bridge of his nose and sighed. "I'm sorry for being so shit at cards, I lost your cut. And, last but not least, I'm sorry for skipping town before I had the chance to apologize when it mattered the most. I mean it, Mave. If I could go back to that night, I would do everything differently. By the Five-Eyed Mother, I swear it on the memory of Selayne Fel'Danla."

"But you're not religious, and you *hated* your actual mother."

"Like I said, I'm trying to do this proper."

"Fine." She rolled her eyes, then gave his hand the most cursory shake. "Apology accepted."

This was far from the first time they'd reconciled, though something about this one felt different. *Final.* She thought back to every disagreement that had led to every breakup. Whether by happenstance or by following rumors that carried his name, she and Neldren had always had a knack for finding each other again. He'd always been the one constant in a life where nothing was permanent. But there had been some truth to his words back at the café. Neither of them could give what the other desired most. For Neldren, someone who could give him loyalty through feast and famine. For Mavery, someone with whom she could avoid famine entirely.

"And *I'm* sorry for making you feel like a backup plan all these years."

He shrugged. "Looking back on it, we were never a good fit. Like...trying to use a key in the wrong lock. Every time we were together, it was like filing off another tooth until we were left with a skeleton key. Eventually, we made it work, but only after causing a lot of irreversible damage."

For a brief moment, Mavery found herself unable to speak. "That was surprisingly poetic, coming from you."

"What can I say? Now that it's just me and Ellice, I've had to get better about using my words." He glanced away as a somewhat sheepish look spread across his face. "After she learned the truth of what happened that night in Burnslee, I'd never seen her so furious. And that's saying a lot. Bringing you to the café, giving you a proper apology... All of that was her idea, actually."

Mavery raised her brows. "Really? I thought she hated me."

Neldren shook his head. "It was never personal; she only hated how I went back to my old ways the minute I saw you across that tavern a few months back. But now that all of that's behind us, would you consider joining up again? Strictly as business partners this time."

"You're joking."

"I'm not. Look, I'll be frank." He hung his head, crossed his arms. "Since losing you and then Itri, it's been a struggle. Ellice's talents and my contacts have only gotten us so far. Our crew could really use a wardbreaker, and I can't think of anyone better than—"

"No."

He looked up. There was a desperation in his eyes that she'd not seen in a very long time. "Think of the bigger picture, Mave. We head to a place where a single guild doesn't control everything. Durnatel, for instance. Just imagine, in a city like that, all the money we could—"

"I'm out, Nel."

Annoyance flickered across Neldren's face. There had once been a time when Mavery would have let this man convince her to do almost anything. Now, the only thing she desired was to return to the apartment filled with teacups, alchemical supplies, and old books—and the man who she'd decided was more precious to her than any amount of money.

"I'm not going back to that life," she said. "I'm trying to build something of a new life here in Leyport."

"Does this 'new life' involve your Night Market companion?" When she nodded, he raised an eyebrow. "Must be one hell of a bloke, to convince you to stay in fucking *Leyport*, of all places."

"He is," she said, and her face warmed.

"I see." He frowned. "Well, I need to go. I've got some other debts to settle before leaving town."

Neldren turned on his heel and vanished into the shadows, leaving behind only a faint scent of arcana-tinged ash.

Thirty-Five

A bronze-skinned girl entered the classroom—and immediately stumbled over her own two feet. She regained her composure long enough to cross the room, then stopped in front of the table where Alain and Declan were seated. With her lanky figure and wide eyes, she looked closer to twelve than seventeen—how did each first-year manage to look younger than the last?—and her entire body trembled as she waited. Alain had half a mind to fetch a bin before she vomited over the hardwood floor. He couldn't blame her for being nervous; when he was a student, practical exams had always left him in a similar state. Though being on the other side of the table wasn't much of an improvement.

Declan cleared his throat, then issued the prompt that he'd recited so many times, Alain was bound to hear it in his sleep tonight:

"Miss Zireen, to your left is a chest that I've warded with a standard arcane lock and Berimur's Electrostatic Augmentation. Using only Gardemancy spells, retrieve the item inside the chest. You have two minutes, starting now."

Declan turned over an hourglass. For the first few seconds, Miss Zireen remained frozen on the spot. Then, as though she finally remembered why she was here, she rounded on the chest and grabbed the padlock. She emitted a yelp of pain; evidently, she'd missed the "Electrostatic" part of Declan's instructions. Alain shook his head as he scribbled a note on Miss Zireen's scoring card.

She attempted a spell, and Alain grimaced as she stumbled through the incantation. As her spells proved ineffective and the grains of sand continued to fall, she grew more frustrated. Meanwhile, Alain continued to record demerits. With only a few grains remaining in the hourglass, she recited a final incantation, then screamed.

Alain looked up. The chest had erupted in green flames.

It would have been a startling sight, had she not been the eighth student today to set fire to the chest. Six students had turned it invisible, three had resorted to kicking it, two had transmutated it into stone, and one—a student who was seemingly immune to Elemental magic—had managed to pick it up and chuck it across the room. Miss Zireen was the first to conjure *green* fire, though she wouldn't receive points for originality.

She hopped from foot to foot as she wrung her hands. With a grunt, Declan pushed his chair back, rounded the table, and hovered his hand a few feet above the flames. He chanted an incantation that extinguished the fire without so much as a puff of smoke. Fortunately, no damage had been done. Unfortunately, Nadya Zireen had failed her exam quite spectacularly.

"I'm so sorry, Professor Ward," she said in a trembling voice. "I don't know what happened!"

"Not to worry, Miss Zireen," Declan said. "Accidents happen to even the best mages. You were on the right track with that counterspell, but at the end you used '*cha*' instead of '*kha.*' A very common mistake."

He guided her to the door, wished her well with a friendly pat on the shoulder, then returned to the table. He slumped into his chair with another grunt. All the while, Alain had been writing his evaluation, which now spilled onto the back of the scoring card.

"Why did you tell her she was 'on the right track'?" he asked as he continued to write. "Not only was that an *abysmal* performance, she was supposed to use only Gardemancy spells. That last incantation she attempted was from the Elemental School. I would have deducted five points for that, had she any points left *to* deduct."

Declan sighed. "You know, lad, a little positivity now and then doesn't hurt."

"That's certainly not how I was taught."

"Remind me, who taught *your* first-year Gardemancy class?"

"Cadavan," Alain said. Though Cadavan exclusively taught advanced courses these days, his reputation continued to strike fear into the hearts of the University's youngest students. Even most of the faculty tried to avoid crossing his path whenever possible.

Declan shuddered. "That explains it. You ought to try my approach with your own students. Maybe then they'll take a shine to you."

Alain bristled, laying down his pen. "Judging by the number of assistantship applications currently sitting in my mailbox, I'd say I'm liked well enough."

"Oh, lad, I can assure you they don't like you for your *personality!*"

Declan clapped Alain on the back as he roared with laughter. Alain attempted to ignore him as he stuffed his scoring sheets into his satchel.

"How many do we have left?" Declan asked once his laughter subsided.

"She was the last one."

"About time! I love teaching, but by Selesta's sagging left tit, do I *loathe* exams."

Alain agreed with the sentiment, though in less blasphemous terms.

"After we tidy up the room," Declan said, "why don't we wander over to the Lettered Gentleman for a couple of pints?"

Alain stifled a groan. He'd already spent the past eight hours in Declan's company. Going to the pub would add another hour—or more. At this point, the only place Alain wanted to be was in his own sitting room, and the only company he desired was Mavery's. The thought alone made his chest ache.

"I really ought to be going," he said. "I need to work on—"

"Right, right, your presentation. We'll make it one pint, then.

It's the least I can do to thank you for your help today. Besides, it's been ages since we last went out together."

Knowing Declan, accepting the invitation would be less of a hassle than attempting to decline it.

Alain sighed. "All right. But only one pint."

While this wasn't the exact table Alain had shared with Conor on that dreadful night, it was close enough. Simply being here was enough to bring about memories that Alain had no desire to ponder for too long. He took a careful sip of his ale. The moment the liquid hit his tongue, bile churned within his stomach. Declan had ordered him a dark, bready ale—not the same one Alain had drunk the last time he patronized this pub, but it was close enough. He lowered his tankard and pushed it aside.

Declan chugged from his own tankard, then wiped the foam from his mustache. "Oh, don't look so dour. Compared to the fourth-years' research papers I have to tackle tomorrow, today was painless."

"If you're asking for my help with those—"

"No, no, you helped plenty today. So much, in fact, I'd say I now owe *you* a favor."

Alain held back a scoff. That was a line Declan had uttered countless times. Holding him to it was another matter entirely, as he tended to conveniently forget promises made over pints of ale.

Declan rubbed his hands over his face. "Gods, what on Perrun possessed me to give those fourth-years a *twenty*-page minimum? It's times like this I wish I had an assistant again." He threw back the rest of his ale, then slammed his empty tankard on the tabletop. "Speaking of assistants, what's the story with you and yours?"

"Er, what do you mean?" Alain asked as the back of his neck warmed.

"You know very well what I mean."

"I swear, I haven't the foggiest." Alain raised his tankard and feigned a sip, attempting to avoid Declan's eye.

"Come off it, lad. Your lies are shakier than a virgin in a brothel." Declan leaned across the table, lowered his voice a notch. "Unless you've got an unusual taste in fashion, those were *her* knickers in your bathroom. You've made the beast with two backs, haven't you?"

Alain flinched, and ale sloshed up his nose. "By the gods, Declan!" he sputtered. His heart raced as he glanced around the room, though none of the other faculty seemed to be paying them any mind. Even so, Alain also lowered his voice. "I can assure you, nothing of that sort happened between us."

"But *something* of *some* sort happened. And I doubt your eagerness to run home has anything to do with your presentation."

"What gives you that idea?"

Declan laughed. "Lad, I'm over twenty years your senior and I've had three wives. I understand romance better than you do."

Alain wanted to argue how having three *ex*-wives provided evidence to the contrary, but he held his tongue.

Perhaps Mavery was right: he should go easier on Declan. After all, the man had cared enough to attempt to visit Alain during his sabbatical. Even Kazamin had only ever managed to send the occasional letter that was well-intentioned but nonetheless dripping with disappointment. Declan's actions, as far as Alain could tell, had been purely out of concern for someone he considered a good friend.

"All right," Alain said. He rested his elbows on the table and leaned in. "If you must know, we kissed, but nothing happened beyond that."

"Who initiated?"

"I hardly see how that's relevant."

"Trust me, lad, it's of the utmost relevance."

Alain sighed deeply. "I did."

"And she reciprocated?"

"Yes." His heart thrummed as he recalled the softness of Mavery's lips, the warmth of her breath, the eagerness of her touch. "Most enthusiastically."

"Tesseraunt, you sly dog!" Declan said with a grin. Though his tankard was empty, he raised it and clinked it against Alain's.

"We violated the Covenants!" Alain hissed as a wave of heat crept up his neck. "This is no cause for celebrations!"

Declan waved a hand. "Bah! Even those cadavers on the High Council have broken a covenant or ten. If you don't believe me, I've an island off the coast of Zakarza I'll sell you."

"But—"

"Look, lad, you'll find no judgment from me. Leona and I were a pair of fools who acted on a whim, without sparing a thought for the consequences. You, on the contrary, do *nothing* on a whim, and you could stand to spend *less* time thinking about consequences. If you want my advice—"

Alain didn't, but he doubted he would have much say in the matter.

"—forget about the Covenants. It's clear as day that woman makes you happy; her name alone is enough to turn you into a grinning fool."

Had he been *that* obvious? The heat, now concentrated in Alain's face, refused to subside.

"See?" Declan chuckled. "There you go again! So, follow your heart and pursue her. After everything you went through this past year, you deserve a little happiness."

"Declan, I..."

He couldn't find the words to tell Declan that pursuing his assistant had been the catalyst for that miserable year. That, while he knew Declan was right, he couldn't risk repeating that same mistake.

But *would* it be the same mistake? Mavery wasn't Conor. To mention the two of them in the same breath was to disparage her, because she was a better person than him in every conceivable way. Someone like Mavery didn't deserve to be hidden away like some shameful secret. A single minute with her made Alain happier than all his years of teaching combined.

At that moment, Alain knew what he needed to do.

Declan sighed. "I should've been a better friend when you needed me most."

"Nonsense. You were going through a divorce."

Declan snorted. "My *third*, and for a marriage I'd finished mourning a long time ago."

"Well, regardless, you did plenty. You covered my exams when I couldn't leave my apartment. You attempted to visit me when I was at my lowest point. Though I wasn't receptive to it at the time, I appreciate it. Truly."

Declan reached across the table and gripped Alain's shoulder. His eyes were misty, and for a second, Alain wondered if he would actually shed a tear. But then Declan's gaze fixated on Alain's tankard.

"Are you going to finish that?"

"It's all yours," Alain said, pushing it toward Declan. He would need a clear head when he returned home this evening.

THIRTY-SIX

Mavery winced as the liquid burned her tongue. She knew she'd let the water get too hot. She placed the mug on the tea table to cool, then settled for pulling a blanket around her shoulders and curling herself into a tight ball on the sofa.

The moment she returned to the apartment, she'd kicked off her boots and discarded her brassière. Yet, discomfort persisted. She was tempted to throw caution to the wind and pour the entire mug of scalding liquid down her throat. It couldn't hurt any worse than her feet, her lower abdomen, her head.

It was tempting to blame all this misery on Neldren. But no, he was only to blame for the headache—and, arguably, her blistered feet. The other aches had started this morning, with the arrival of her monthly courses.

As she readjusted, seeking a more comfortable position, the door opened. Alain entered with a broad smile and more vigor than she'd expected from someone who'd been conducting exams all day. But upon seeing her, his smile faded and his shoulders slouched.

"What's wrong?" he asked.

"Nothing."

"Liar." He closed the door behind him. "One, you look completely out of sorts. Two, you're doing that hair-tucking thing you do whenever there's something vexing you."

Mavery glanced at her right hand, which hovered beside her ear. That old habit had become so second-nature, she'd long stopped noticing whenever she repeated it. Evidently, Alain had caught on. Her stomach fluttered at the realization, but even that couldn't distract her from the dull ache in that general area. She glanced at the mug. Tendrils of steam continued to rise from it, so her special tea was likely still too hot to drink. She sighed.

"I take it your afternoon was worse than mine," Alain said. "I hope my mother wasn't too hard on you."

"No, your mother was fine. Well, 'fine' by her standards." She looked at the dagger lying beside her mug. "I had a run-in with Neldren."

"*What!?*" Alain cried, then rushed to her side. "How did that happen? Are you all right? Did he—"

She placed her index finger to his lips, quieting him. He grabbed her hand, held it to his chest as his eyes filled with concern. She explained how her encounter in the market had led to Neldren's ambush outside the boutique. The longer she spoke, the more Alain's face paled, the more tightly he clutched her hand.

"I knew I shouldn't have let you go alone," he said.

She shook her head. "I was fine...surprisingly. You were right, by the way. He was the one who took me to the healers that night. He never wanted me dead; he was frustrated about all the times I'd left him over the years, and so—"

"And so he *shot* you for it? And I thought academics were a vindictive bunch."

"I know what he did was extreme, but he apologized for it. He even returned this to me." She pointed to her dagger. Alain's eyes widened at the sight of the weapon, though its blade was hidden within the elegant sheath.

"You believe he was sincere?"

She nodded. "He seemed remorseful enough, and we both made amends that were long overdue. After all that, I don't think he'll come looking for me again. Though, as I once guessed, he offered that I join his crew again."

"You can't be serious!" Alain sputtered. "Please tell me you turned him down."

"Of course I did! Why would I give up all of this"—her free hand gestured at the room before coming to rest on Alain's cheek—"to go scrounging for coppers with the last person in the world I want to be around?"

He smiled as he leaned into her hand, then pressed his lips to her palm. The kiss was so light, yet so intimate, a swell of emotion rushed through her. Mavery swallowed hard, tamping it down long enough to speak.

"Now that Neldren's no longer an issue, I suppose there's no reason for me to continue hiding away here."

"I can think of *one* reason," Alain said, his breath warming her skin.

"Oh? And what's that?"

He turned his head, met her gaze. "I want you to stay."

"I..." The swell of emotion returned, stealing her voice. She cleared her throat. "I would like that—quite a lot, actually—but are you sure? What about the Covenants?"

"Right, the Covenants." He took both of her hands in his. He fell silent for a moment, gazing downward at their joined hands as his thumbs caressed her knuckles. "I suggested we talk about this after the presentation. I know that's only five days from now, but I don't want to wait. I've made my choice."

She held her breath as she waited for him to continue. He looked up, and his eyes were filled with warmth, sincerity.

"I've decided I'm going to resign from the University."

Mavery gaped at him. "Alain, you can't—"

"I can, actually." He smiled. "Trust me, this is not a decision I'm making lightly. And it's hardly a new idea. There were several times during my sabbatical when I considered giving Kazamin my resignation. Assisting Declan with exams today reminded me of what I've always known: I was never cut out for this line of work, I simply chose the first one that was presented to me."

"But if you're not a professor, what will you do?"

"I don't know," he said with a shrug, "but without the expectations that teaching brings, I will finally have the freedom to explore what I *truly* enjoy: the pursuit of knowledge itself. The thrill of asking questions, of delving into research, of seeing an experiment come to fruition—even if it's unsuccessful, or the results are not what I had hoped for.

"Because that's the beauty of it: there's always something new to learn, even from failures. And we will never know everything there is to know about spellcasting, about the Ether, about the universe. There is some comfort in knowing there will *always* be a thrilling new discovery somewhere out there."

Mavery found herself enthralled by his words—as she found herself whenever he spoke so passionately.

"Whatever you discover," she said, "I want to be by your side for all of it."

"Nothing would make me happier." He squeezed her hands. "And, since that pesky covenant only applies to professors, you can be by my side as my assistant—and as the woman I'm courting. Er, assuming that's still something you want."

She smirked. "As if you even need to ask."

He laughed. "Well, one should never assume. Then that settles it. After we present the Sensing spell, I'm going to meet with Kazamin and hand in my resignation. In the meantime..." He gave her a coy smile. "I see no reason to delay the courtship part."

He drew her in, and their lips met in a gentle caress. His fingertips combed through her hair, guided her head back to kiss her more deeply, though he lacked the fervor he'd shown back in the forest. But Mavery matched his slower pace, allowed herself to savor the simple pleasure of their connection. She couldn't remember the last time someone had kissed her so tenderly, without any need to hurry. Because neither of them was going anywhere.

A firm tug of his robe sent her to her back, his weight on top of her. The sudden change of position forced them to break the kiss. She opened her eyes at the same time he did, and they exchanged a laugh.

He lightly kissed her forehead, then placed a more lingering one on the scar across her nose. It didn't matter that this mark was a permanent reminder of the night she'd met Neldren; he gave that part of her as much reverence as he'd given her lips. She sighed as he moved downward, placing a kiss on one corner of her mouth, then the other, before continuing to her jaw. He pushed aside the blanket, her collar.

"Oh…" She shivered as his lips brushed the crook of her neck. Then his fingers fumbled with the top buttons of her blouse, and her eyes widened. "*Oh!* Er, wait a moment."

Alain pulled back. "Is something wrong?"

"Your timing," she groaned, then sat upright. "If only you'd come to this decision yesterday, before I started my courses." She sighed. "I'm afraid anything beyond what we just did is out of the question for the next few days."

"That's a relief. Er, not your courses, I mean." He blushed. "For a minute there, I was worried I'd been too presumptuous." He took her hand, gave it a reassuring squeeze. "I don't mind waiting a little longer. In the meantime, how are you feeling? Is there anything I can get you?"

Smiling, she kissed his cheek. If only she could show this man her appreciation in *every* way she knew how…

"You're sweet to offer, but there's no need. Not when I have *this*." She leaned over and retrieved her mug. The liquid no longer appeared scalding, but the stoneware was warm against her palms. Alain sniffed the drink—and gagged.

"Gods, what *is* that!?" he coughed.

"An old remedy for aches and pains: a cup of fallowroot tea, the juice of a lemon wedge, a pinch of cinnamon, and a shot of whiskey."

"Yes, the whiskey was apparent." He waved a hand in front of his face as his eyes watered. "Does it at least help?"

"Immensely. The taste isn't half-bad, either, though I won't be disappointed when I no longer have to drink this every month. Until then… Cheers to you, Lavestra." She raised the mug toward the ceiling before taking a large gulp. She winced as the liquid burned all the way down—she'd poured the whiskey with a heavier hand than she'd intended—but the few seconds of discomfort were worth the immediate relief it brought to her aching muscles.

"Lavestra?" Alain asked. "I'm no theologian, but isn't Illara the Goddess of Fertility?"

Mavery laughed flatly. "I promise you, this is entirely within the Goddess of Afflictions's domain." She began to take another sip, then paused. "But speaking of fertility, I ought to prepare some persilweed tea for when all this passes."

"Oh...that won't be necessary," Alain said. When she raised an eyebrow, he cleared his throat before continuing, "Not long after I became a wizard, I underwent a procedure involving a rather complex infertility spell that's part Soudremancy, part Transmutation. I'll admit, it was quite painful—"

She threw him a pointed look.

"Though not as painful as childbirth, of course!" He laughed nervously. "I'd say the majority of wizards have taken advantage of this procedure, as the majority of wizards would rather not have children."

"The Covenants definitely didn't mention *that*."

"Er, no, they wouldn't. The procedure is voluntary, but it's not exactly a topic that comes up in polite conversation."

"This procedure is effective?"

He nodded. "Completely. And irreversible."

"Huh..."

As she drank more of her whiskey-tea concoction, Mavery pondered how, over the years, she'd run the gamut of contraceptives: herbs brewed into bitter teas, sheaths made from questionable animal parts, the tried-but-seldom-true method of consulting lunar charts. Never had she heard of an infertility spell. It had to be yet another privilege the wizarding community kept to itself, but it was a fortunate one nonetheless.

"I take it you never wanted children," she said.

Alain shook his head. "Like most wizards, I wanted to focus fully on scholarly pursuits. Besides, I can barely handle first-years. Could you imagine *me* trying to care for a *child*?" he said with a nervous laugh. "That, er, won't be an issue for you, I hope..."

She put her tea aside, then cupped his face between her hands. "Not in the slightest. I'm glad that's yet another thing we agree on." She smiled wryly. "You know, I may be on my courses, but there are *other* things we could do."

"Oh?" His eyes widened. "What did you have in mind?"

She shrugged off her blanket, tossed it to the floor, then straddled him. Grasping his shoulders, she pushed him deeper into the sofa until she was peering down at him. In reply, his hands came to rest on her hips. When she pressed her mouth to his again, her desire was more wanton. She wasted no time before sweeping her tongue across his lips, parting them, delving into his mouth. From how his tongue passionately stroked against hers, to how his fingers pressed firmly into her skin, it was clear that his desire hadn't quelled. The longer they continued, the more she felt his arousal stiffen beneath her. She lowered a hand, palmed the stiff fabric of his trousers. He moaned into her mouth, which she took as an invitation. But when her fingers tugged at his waistband, he turned his head, breaking the kiss.

"You don't...have to," he gasped. He took a deep breath. "I won't be able to reciprocate, so—"

"So? I still want to, unless that's not something you'd enjoy."

"Oh, no, I definitely would. It's just..." He sighed. "Sorry, this is a novel concept to me."

She leaned back, sinking onto his lap. "What do you mean?"

He fidgeted with the hem of her blouse as he avoided meeting her eye. "In my experience, what I wanted always came secondary. On occasion...it was never even a consideration."

Her fingers brushed his cheek while her heart ached for him. He continued to look away, as if embarrassed by his confession, and her heart wrenched even more. Though she couldn't rectify the past, she could see to his desires in the present—and in the future.

"I promise, pleasuring you will be a pleasure in and of itself." She lowered her lips to his ear and whispered, "So, tell me what you want."

For a moment, the only sound was his heavy breathing, coupled with his pounding heartbeat.

"I want you..." He hesitated, wet his lips. "I *need* you to touch me." Though it came out as a whisper, she was close enough that his voice reverberated through her.

She readjusted her position to watch his face as she slipped her hands between their bodies again. Desire had darkened his eyes to the deepest black, and his gaze remained fixed on hers as she slowly unbuttoned his trousers. His lips parted as she loosened the final button, freeing his erection. She trailed her fingers down his length, relishing the smooth skin and the firmness that lay beneath it. With a gasp, he closed his eyes and tilted his head back. She curled her fingers around him, and a low groan resonated from his throat. The sound was undeniably his voice, but so heavy, so sensual, that a wave of warm arousal rippled through her own body.

"Like this?" she whispered as her fingers returned upward.

A nod was all he could manage; words now seemed beyond him. With the pad of her thumb, she drew small, slow circles against his tip. A ragged gasp urged her to keep going. Meanwhile, his hands slipped beneath the hem of her blouse. She shivered as his fingers skimmed her bare skin, sighed as he cupped her breasts, moaned as he stroked her firm nipples.

They continued this intimate exploration of skin against skin, saying through touch what words alone could not convey. Their breaths converged, their sighs echoed through the room before culminating in a visceral moan as her touch brought him over the edge. His body shuddered as he pulled her close, buried his face in the crook of her neck. Though he didn't speak, the hot tears against her skin told her that he'd experienced not just a release but *catharsis*.

Later that night, as she drifted off to sleep—no longer alone on the sofa but in his bed, wrapped in his arms—she thought of how none of this felt temporary. How she was no longer *trying* to build a new life for herself.

At last, she'd found something permanent.

Thirty-Seven

Their presentation was the day after final exams, and so the University of Leyport's campus was warded off to everyone but faculty. Mavery waited for Alain by the gate, feeling a bit anxious. The presentation had nothing to do with it; she and Alain had run through it countless times over the past five days. Nor did her new dress; it fit her like a glove. Rather, her discomfort came from the strong magic thrumming against her skin.

The gate was enshrouded with hundreds of thin silver ley lines threaded around the blue cords of the protective ward. Never had she seen so many augmentations tied to a single spell; she assumed each ley line corresponded with a faculty member who was allowed passage. Beyond the warding magic was a scarlet aura—a fabrication spell that Mavery assumed powered the gate itself. The air was thick with a scent she could only describe as burning metal.

Footsteps approached. She turned to find a well-dressed man walking down the sidewalk. When he came a few steps closer, her breath hitched upon realizing that well-dressed man was Alain. For once, he was wearing clothes that fit him properly: a black dinner jacket with an ivory cravat tucked into a matching waistcoat. The style was a little old-fashioned, and the satchel over his left shoulder certainly clashed with it, but this was the most put-together she'd ever seen him.

Tucked under one arm, he carried the leatherbound spell tome he'd picked up from the bookbinder's while Mavery was at the boutique, picking up her dress. He stopped a few paces from her and froze as he took her in from head to toe. As his gaze lingered where the bodice accentuated her hips and waist, he also seemed to momentarily forget how to breathe.

"Gods, you're stunning," he sighed.

"You can thank your mother for that," Mavery said as warmth flooded through her.

"It's not just the dress," he said. "I thought you were stunning from the moment we first met."

"Really?" She raised her eyebrows. "Even when I was covered in dirt and bloodstains?"

"Yes, even when you were…" He blinked. "That was *blood*?"

"I'd been shot only a few days prior, remember?"

"Right, of course," he said with a nervous laugh. "Well, dirt and blood aside, my initial thought was that Declan had played some sort of prank on me, that he'd sent you to lure me out of my cave after his own attempts had failed."

Mavery smiled as she wondered what antics he and Declan had gotten into before his long sabbatical. She assumed most of those had been one-sided.

"You look quite dashing yourself," she said.

He returned her smile. "It's a shame we'll have to cover all this up." He opened his transmutated satchel and pulled out a bundle of black cloth: her assistant's robe. "The University's dress code still applies."

She frowned. "Then why bother with the formal attire in the first place, if we're just going to wear these sacks?"

"Some archaic tradition, no doubt. Here, hold this for a moment."

He passed her the spell tome, then pulled out his own robe. The tome's cover was black leather with silver filigree; it could have been mistaken for a mundane book. But when she opened it, seeing her own name on the title page made it more precious to her than even the rarest tomes in the University's collection.

"An Incantation to Simulate the Aura Detection Effects of Ar-

cane Hypersensitivity on Basic Gardemancy Spells," she read. "The name doesn't exactly roll off the tongue."

"It's only a placeholder. Once our spell goes through peer review and the High Council approves it for public use, I'll give it something snappier. Perhaps I'll name it after you: 'Culwich's Aura Illuminator'...or something to that effect."

"I think 'Sensing Spell' will do just fine," she said, though the idea made her heart race.

She donned her own robe while Alain passed through the magical barrier. Hinges creaked as the front gate swung open autonomously. He turned around and, with a slight bow, extended his hand to her as if inviting her to dance. She laughed as she took his hand, and he pulled her through the warding magic. It left her with a slight chill running down her spine and a sharp pang in the center of her forehead. This magic was much more powerful than the spells that protected Alain's apartment.

Their apartment, she reminded herself. Another shiver passed through her—and this time it had nothing to do with magic.

The portal room's magic was as prominent as it had been the first time Mavery stepped foot in this place. The air pulsated with arcana and brushed against the back of her hand like a gentle breeze. They stopped in front of the largest portal; THE HIGH COUNCIL OF WIZARDS was engraved in the silver frame.

"Are you ready?" Mavery asked.

"Not in the slightest," Alain said, "but I don't have much of a choice, do I?"

She gave his shoulder a firm squeeze. He took a deep breath and stepped forward. The vaporous substance rippled, and his body flickered for a moment before vanishing entirely. Once the portal stilled again, Mavery followed him.

And then the world ripped in two.

Arcana pounded against every bone in her body, blackened her vision, wrenched the air from her lungs. White-hot pain ripped through her head as though it were being cleaved in half. She hadn't taken the anti-Sensing potion today; she'd seen no need for it, as their spell worked as intended and their trip would be brief. But she doubted it would have made any difference. Never had she felt such a powerful concentration of magic all at once. She could barely breathe, her thoughts could focus on nothing but pain.

And then the sensation passed. Her non-magical senses returned one by one, beginning with her vision. The lighting in this room was warmer, its walls even taller than the room she'd just left. She had no memory of falling, but she was now on all fours. Her fingers gripped the fibers of a plush cobalt blue rug. She gasped, and her lungs ached as they refilled with air.

"Are you all right?" Alain asked. He was kneeling beside her, rubbing her back.

"That was...unpleasant," she gasped.

"Stepping through a rift in the Ether always is," he said gravely.

She attempted to stand up, but her head reeled and she promptly found herself on all fours again. Alain offered her a hand and helped her to her feet. Her bad knee buckled beneath her, and she swayed on the spot, using Alain's shoulder for support as she regained her balance.

"Hold still," he said.

He produced a handkerchief and delicately blotted it beneath her nose, across her lip. When he pulled the fabric away, it was stained with blood. She'd been so overwhelmed by the portal magic, she hadn't noticed she was bleeding. Luckily, nothing had soiled her new dress or, more importantly, the spell tome. Alain retrieved it from the floor.

"Are you certain you don't want the anti-Sensing potion?" he asked.

"A bit late for that, isn't it?"

"I mean for the trip back." He handed her the spell tome, then retrieved a vial of dark liquid from the outer pocket of his satchel. "I came prepared."

"Gods, I could kiss you right now," she sighed.

He smiled. "There will be plenty of time for that later—and *more.*"

Mavery's eyes widened at his boldness. But she then noticed they were completely alone. Unlike the room they'd just left, this one had no attendant. Alain offered his arm. She slipped her hand in the crook of his bent elbow, and they left the portal room together.

They proceeded down a long curved corridor lit with arcana-infused sconces. The walls and floors were gray stone, though the carpet runner dampened their footsteps. The only decorations were portraits of former Archmages. Aside from their differing skin tones and beard lengths, the subjects of these paintings were largely interchangeable: elderly men wearing dark blue robes.

They approached an arched window. Mavery stopped and gasped at the view of Montesse, the capital of Dauphine. Here, the sun was lower than it had been only moments ago; dusk was approaching. Once she'd recovered from the shock of crossing half the continent instantaneously, she was awestruck by the sheer scope of the largest city she'd ever seen. Montesse had to be at least ten times larger than Leyport. It seemed to stretch on forever, with rooftops sprawling beyond the horizon. The High Council's tower loomed so high above the city, the people milling about on the streets were mere pinpricks. The sight of it made Mavery's head reel again—along with her stomach. She took a step back from the window before she became sick.

"Why do wizards insist on having such absurdly tall towers?" she asked, rubbing her temples.

"It harkens back to the classical understanding of magic, when the Ether was believed to be not an intangible force but a physical layer of the atmosphere. Wizards thought that properly attuning oneself to the Ether required being as physically close to it as—"

"One of these days, I'm going to introduce you to the concept of a rhetorical question." She rolled her eyes. She risked another glance out the window and winced.

"You're not partial to heights, I take it."

She shook her head.

Alain leaned his back against the window, crossed his arms, and smiled. "And yet, you still sought out a wizard."

She smiled back, appreciating the distraction from the unsettling view. "If you think I would've let a silly little fear of heights stop me, you don't know me at all."

"Oh, I'd never think that for a second."

His gaze dropped to her lips, sending a trickle of heat up her neck. No, they definitely couldn't risk doing anything risqué *here*, of all places. She cleared her throat.

"Besides," she said, "I'm fine so long as I have a landmark to ground myself. Where's the Dauphinian Academy of Magic? Can we see it from here?"

"I'm not sure," Alain said, glancing over his shoulder. "It might be on the opposite side of the city, come to think. I attended a conference there once, but I took the portal."

"So, you've never actually visited Montesse?"

"As in seeing the sights, traveling for pleasure? No, I've never had the time."

"Then maybe we should make that a priority."

He laughed. "Dauphine may not be the ideal spot for a holiday, considering the rebellions."

"Somewhere else, then," Mavery said. "Maroba, Nilandor, the Isles, anywhere. Say the word, and we'll go."

A wistful look crossed his face. But it passed within seconds, and he stepped away from the window. "As lovely as that sounds, first things first: let's get this presentation over with."

Arm-in-arm again, they continued down the corridor until they reached a chamber. Before them, a larger-than-life painting of Archmage Seringoth hung over the fireplace. He looked much like the Archmages before him, with aged skin and a long white beard that matched his hair. His blue-gray eyes had an intensity that, even in paint, compelled Mavery to avoid his gaze.

On the left side of the room was a set of double doors that shimmered with a soundproofing ward. Running the length of the wall was a wooden bench, and upon it sat a familiar pair of women.

Alain froze.

"Hello, Aventus."

Nezima gave him a benign smile. Sitting beside her was Corenta, the dean of the Faisancy Department, whom Mavery had met at the Lettered Gentleman over a week ago.

"Nezima," Alain said with a stiff nod that matched his tone. "I didn't know you also had a meeting with the High Council today."

"Yes, Corenta and I are presenting a research proposal."

"Together?" Alain asked, his arm tensing beneath Mavery's hand.

"Consider this the first of what we hope will be *many* collaborations," Corenta said. Her blue eyes peered at him over her spectacles.

Nezima looked to Mavery. "We missed seeing you on Middisday."

"Oh, sorry about that," she said. Alain gave her a sidelong glance, but she kept her eyes focused on Nezima. "We were working on our presentation."

Among other things that had kept our hands and mouths occupied...

"Of course. Any scholar knows how demanding these presentations can be." Nezima smiled as her gaze shifted downward. A chill prickled the back of Mavery's neck upon realizing that her and Alain's arms were still linked. "Mind if I take a look?"

Nezima was referring to the spell tome, she realized with relief. Alain nodded, and Mavery handed Nezima the tome. In exchange, she handed Alain a scroll of parchment. As his eyes scanned the page, a small contemptuous noise sounded from the back of his throat. Mavery peered over his shoulder.

WHERE ETHEREAL MEETS PRACTICAL:
A NEW PEDAGOGY FOR THE MODERN AGE

———

As mundane technological advancements such as the locomotive engine continue to see exponential growth, it is critical for arcane scholarship to avoid rendering itself obsolete. The traditional pedagogical standard relies on a theoretical approach to magic. However, this—

Before she could read any further, the double doors burst open. Out came a dark-skinned man in rust-colored robes, trailed by his young assistant. The wizard ranted in a language Mavery didn't understand—Zakarzan, she assumed—and chucked his spell tome into the fireplace as he stormed out of the chamber. The assistant uttered an incantation, plucked the singed tome from the fire, and ran after the wizard.

The bald man who now stood in the doorway looked old enough to be a wizard himself, though his black robes indicated he was an assistant. He turned to Nezima and Corenta, then spoke to them in Dauphinian. From what Mavery could gather, the High Council was ready to see them.

Alain rolled up the parchment. His expression was flat, and he said nothing to Nezima as he handed it back to her.

"Good luck," Mavery said, hoping that would allay some of the awkwardness.

Nezima nodded. "Thank you, though I believe we will have little need for it."

The High Council's assistant guided the two women into the presentation chamber, then closed the door behind them.

"What did she mean by 'we missed seeing you'?" Alain asked.

"Oh, that. She has a club that meets at the Lettered Gentleman."

"I know of it. Don't tell me you were drinking with *them* last week. I know for a fact you failed to mention that little detail."

She scoffed. "*Who* I was with didn't seem relevant. But yes, I was with them—Wren invited me—though I can't say I enjoyed myself. Not with Nezima prying about our relationship, thanks to your mother's slippery tongue."

"I never mentioned your name."

"But anyone with a lick of common sense could put two and two together. Your mother knows we're more than colleagues, and Nezima is definitely suspicious."

Showing up together just now, arms linked as though Alain were escorting her to a ball, likely had done little to quell those suspicions. But she didn't mention this to Alain, who was looking a bit green in the face. He rushed over to the bench and sat with his hands clenched into fists, knees bouncing.

Mavery sighed, then sat next to him. She placed her hand on his knee, knowing that she was taking yet another risk, and that he would likely mention something about decorum. Yet, he took her hand with a tight, almost painful grip.

"After today, you won't have to worry about Nezima or anyone else from the University ever again."

"I'm not worried about them," Alain said in a quiet voice. "I'm—"

The door opened again—slowly this time. In one swift movement, Mavery and Alain released each other's hands, then shifted in their seats to put a few more inches of space between them. Mavery folded her hands in her lap, atop the spell tome.

Nezima and Corenta's presentation had lasted not even five minutes, but judging by their satisfied expressions, theirs had gone much more favorably than the Zakarzan wizard's.

"Best of luck to *you*," Nezima said. As she honed her gaze on Alain, her lips formed a sly smile. "When we reconvene this autumn, I suspect our department meetings will include some *industrious* discourse."

Without another word, she and Corenta left the room together, then disappeared down the corridor.

"Well, that wasn't the least bit cryptic," Mavery muttered.

Before Alain could respond, the Council's assistant addressed them in heavily accented Osperlandish.

"Aventus the Third and Madam Culwich, the High Council will see you now. Please follow me."

The High Council of Wizards' bench was so high off the ground, Mavery had to crane her neck to spot the wizards looming silently from above. Archmage Seringoth was seated at the center, flanked by the eight Elder Wizards who each represented one of the Schools of Magic. All but Seringoth wore hooded robes that completely obscured their faces. Mavery was reminded of judges presiding over a courtroom. But this windowless round chamber had no seats for a jury, nor an audience. There was only a marble podium in the center of the room. Apart from a few Ethereal orbs hanging overhead, the room was shrouded in darkness. To Mavery's eyes, the only hint of color was a flicker of violet over the soundproofed walls.

Footsteps echoed as she and Alain crossed the stone floor. Once they reached the podium, Mavery handed him the spell tome, then took his satchel and retreated a few steps. He wouldn't need her for the first part of his presentation.

Alain avoided gazing upward, as if making eye contact with any of the Elder Wizards would shatter his already fragile resolve.

"Welcome back, Aventus the Third," Seringoth said. Despite his advanced age, there wasn't a trace of feebleness in his voice; it resonated through the chamber like the pealing of a church bell. "Per your written request, this presentation will be conducted in Osperlandish to accommodate your assistant. However, the High Council requests that your assistant attain basic fluency in Dauphinian prior to your next presentation."

The Archmage looked to Mavery, and she suppressed a shudder. She now understood why Alain refused to look upward. To be under that man's employ—and his piercing stare—for nearly three years... The thought alone turned her stomach.

"Today, you will present an original spell in the School of Gardemancy," Seringoth said. "You may begin when ready."

Alain nodded, then cleared his throat as he opened the spell tome. Mavery hoped the High Council was too high up to notice his trembling hands. But when Alain spoke, his voice carried through the room clearly, unwaveringly.

"Arcane hypersensitivity—or Sensing, as it is referred to in the common parlance—is a hereditary condition that allows mages to detect magic in ways that are impossible for even the most highly trained wizards.

"This condition is exceptionally rare: in the past century, there have been only fourteen known Sensers across Tanarim. The formal study of Sensing is equally rare, as the general consensus among the wizarding community is that the centuries-old practice of attuning oneself to the Ether is sufficient. But, I argue, why continue limiting ourselves? Seeing magic as Sensers do would be a tremendous boon to our understanding of every School of Magic, beginning with Gardemancy."

This garnered a few murmurs. Seringoth raised his hand, and the Elder Wizards fell silent. Alain continued, undeterred.

"Today, I am presenting to the High Council an incantation that will not only reveal the auras for the basic types of Gardemancy spells, but will differentiate them by color. This is based on the work of Enodus the Second, a Senser who left his own aura-detection spell unfinished upon his death in 804. I have completed the spell using techniques based on Venetum's Principles, as well as an adaptation of Ardemin the First's Hue Shifting Augmentation."

He extended an arm toward Mavery.

"To begin the demonstration, my assistant, Ms. Culwich, will perform basic resonating, detonation, fireproofing, and protective wards. I will then perform my spell to reveal the auras of her wards, as well as the soundproofing wards surrounding this room."

He turned to Mavery and nodded before stepping away from the podium. She'd recited the incantations so many times over the past week, she'd memorized even the detonation ward. When she completed the final incantation with the numbness of her tongue that she'd grown accustomed to, the podium was aglow with red, pink, and gold auras that the Elder Wizards couldn't yet see. She then raised her hand and summoned a protective ward.

Alain began the spell that he had likewise practiced scores of times, though Mavery had yet to grow tired of hearing it. Her heart soared as she watched his performance. Because, at the end of it all, wasn't this meeting just a spectacle?

While light flooded the room from the podium to the walls, she spared a glance at the Elder Wizards. Most of them were focused on taking notes, but some watched Alain intently. That included Seringoth, who peered at his former assistant over his steepled fingers.

At last, Alain finished speaking Etherean. He walked around the podium, gesturing to the wards as he spoke.

"Blue for protective wards, red for detonation, gold for resonating, pink for fireproofing, and violet for soundproofing." For the latter, he gestured at the shimmering walls. "These colors are based on the observations of my assistant, a Senser who came into my employ two months ago. Her observations are consistent with the ones documented by Enodus and other Sensers before her.

"Up close, we can study the subtle differences between the wards, and how they interact when combined. We can also see the ley lines of augmentations, and trace them to the locations of their anchors. This incantation would serve as the baseline for more complex spells that can reveal the smell and taste of magic as experienced by Sensers. This is but the beginning to understanding magic in ways that only a select few have ever experienced it."

He stopped pacing and stood with his hands clasped behind his back. Mavery dismissed her ward and mimicked his pose.

She hadn't expected the wizards to fall over themselves in adoration, but she'd hoped for at least some polite applause. Instead, there was silence interspersed with hushed whispers and shuffling papers. With each passing minute, Alain's shoulders sank a little deeper, his neutral expression shifted more toward a frown. Was it normal for the High Council to go *this* long without asking a single question?

Mavery flinched as, without warning, a male Elder Wizard's voice cut through the chamber like a gunshot.

"What would be the practical applications for this spell?"

Alain cleared his throat. "Within the spell tome, I discuss at length some of my theories pertaining to its—"

"I did not ask you about *theory*. I asked you about *practicality*." As the wizard leaned forward, his hood shifted, revealing a dour face framed with dark, bushy eyebrows. "Have you even performed this spell outside of a controlled environment?"

"Yes, Elder Lythandus. Before today, I performed it many times without protective wards in place."

"You have performed it on wards that you or your assistant did not place?"

"With the exception of the soundproofing wards in this room, no, sir, I have not."

His answer sparked some low grumbling from at least half of

the High Council. Their voices were predominantly male, but the next Elder Wizard to address Alain directly was a woman.

"This spell, you intend to let *anyone* use it?"

She had a haughty manner of speaking that had nothing to do with her Dauphinian accent. A high-ranking noblewoman, if Mavery had ever heard one. Furthermore, the twin moon pendant around her neck marked her as a follower of the Church of the Dyad. She had to be the Elder Wizard representing the Soudre-mancy School.

"Yes, Elder Thedonus. Anyone with a wizarding ed—"

"Then how can you be certain it won't be used for nefarious purposes? This seems a dangerous spell to release into the wizarding community, given the political unrest here in Dauphine. I can only imagine what would happen, were this spell to fall into the hands of those *treacherous* anti-Royalists—"

"Elder Thedonus," Seringoth said sharply, "how many times must I remind you to refrain from voicing political opinions in the presentation chamber?"

"My sincerest apologies, Archmage." Her tone was decidedly insincere and unapologetic.

"Elder Thedonus does raise a valid point," said another male wizard. "Aventus, how would you ensure that this spell does not pose any security risks?"

Alain wrung his hands as he opened and closed his mouth, but seemed no longer able to speak. The High Council's disgruntlement grew louder the longer Alain failed to articulate a response. Mavery's heart raced. She had to do something before he fell apart entirely.

She stepped forward.

"Excuse me."

If anyone on the High Council had heard her, they were choosing to ignore her.

She cleared her throat. *"Excuse me!"*

At last, the nine wizards ceased their muttering and looked at her. Their expressions ranged from faint surprise to utter repulsion. She was probably breaking a dozen of their sanctimonious covenants, but it was too late to do anything but forge ahead.

"If I can lend some of my expertise—"

"And what *expertise* would that be?" another of the male wizards snapped, as if Mavery had insulted his manhood and spat in his face.

"Before becoming Aventus's assistant, I worked as a freelance wardsmith. I know firsthand the importance of protecting the lives and valuables of Tanarim's highest-ranking citizens."

Flattering the nobility soured her stomach more than the half-truth about her former profession.

"Continue, Ms. Culwich," Seringoth said.

"This spell would be completely impractical for would-be thieves and spies. First of all, the incantation itself is quite complex; only a mage with advanced Etherean training would be able to pull it off. Secondly, the spell has a range of..." She looked to Alain.

"Approximately thirty feet," he said.

She nodded. "Not only that, the spell permeates walls and other barriers. And as you can see for yourselves, anyone within the spell's range will be able to detect the wards—not just the spellcaster. It would draw too much attention to someone who's trying to rely on stealth."

The wizards resumed talking amongst themselves, but their overall tone seemed slightly less hostile, with more nodding than before. Mavery gave Alain a sidelong glance.

"Thank you," he whispered.

"Of course," she whispered back.

Seringoth cleared his throat, and in unison they snapped their attention back to the High Council.

"Ms. Culwich, have your Sensing abilities been evaluated by a Mystic?"

Mavery raised her brows. That was not the question she'd been expecting.

"Er, no—"

"That's entirely my fault, Archmage," Alain interjected. Rather than looking directly at Seringoth, he looked straight ahead, focusing on the speckled granite of the High Council's bench. "I didn't think it would be worth the trouble."

"You didn't think confirming the authenticity of one of your primary sources would be 'worth the trouble'?" Seringoth asked flatly.

"N-no, Archmage, I misspoke. I only meant that I had no reason to doubt my assistant's authenticity, based on my own observations. Therefore, I didn't think burdening the Mystics would be worth the trouble."

"Elder Yuriva, as Tanarim's highest authority on the School of Mysticism, what do you make of this? Would confirming whether a mage has arcane hypersensitivity be a 'burden' as Aventus claims?"

"Not at all," replied the serene voice of the woman sitting on the far right end of the bench. "As a matter of fact, I could perform an evaluation right now. It would take but a few minutes."

"Precisely as I suspected." Seringoth turned to Mavery again. "Ms. Culwich, if you would please follow Elder Yuriva into the antechamber."

As the Mystic descended the stairs behind the bench, Mavery looked to Alain. His face was even paler than usual.

"I'm sorry," he whispered. "I should have listened to Kazamin and had you evaluated right from the start."

"I'll be fine," she whispered back, hoping she sounded more confident than she felt. She knew the stories from Neldren and countless others who had been unlucky enough to be interrogated by Mystics. None of those stories were pleasant. She tried to push all that from her mind as she crossed the chamber and met Mystic Yuriva at the bottom of the stairs.

"Right this way, Ms. Culwich," she said. She placed her hand to the stone wall, and a section of it shifted aside, revealing a wooden door. She opened it and gestured for Mavery to enter first.

THIRTY-EIGHT

The cold, windowless room was even more austere than the presentation chamber. It contained only nine chairs—each large enough to be a throne—arranged around a long table. Orbs of Ethereal light hung near the ceiling, bathing the room in an oppressive onslaught of pure white.

"Have a seat," Yuriva said, extending her bony hand.

Mavery took the chair closest to the door. With their ornate carvings and lack of cushioning, these chairs were designed to be luxurious but not comfortable. The unyielding wood forced her to sit with a rod-straight back, but that was no matter. A little discomfort would keep her on her guard.

Yuriva picked the chair directly across from Mavery. The Elder Wizard was the oldest person Mavery had ever seen. Her black eyes were rheumy, her wrinkled and liver-spotted skin was the same shade as an overcast sky. As a Nilandoren, she had to be decades older than Seringoth.

"Have you ever undergone questioning by a Mystic?" Yuriva asked. Her accent was Dauphinian. She had either been born on this continent like Nezima, or she hadn't lived in her motherland for quite some time.

"No, but I'm aware of the process...more or less."

Yuriva smiled sagely. "Then this should take no time at all. I will ask you a few preliminary questions to establish a baseline. Please, relax and answer to the best of your ability."

Instead of relaxing, Mavery probed the depths of her mind for every scrap of training from the Brass Dragons. While this wasn't the same as resisting the effects of truth serum, she assumed the same principles would apply. She cleared her mind of all thoughts, and focused solely on the woman across the table. Mavery's own thoughts became the least appealing thing in the world. What mattered most was attempting to memorize Yuriva's face: every wrinkle, every blemish, every strand of white hair peeking out from under her hood. She would let the Mystic glimpse her Sensing abilities and nothing more.

"What is your name?" Yuriva asked. There was not a trace of emotion in her voice.

"Mavery Culwich," she replied in an equally flat tone. She focused on a mole on Yuriva's left cheek.

"What is today's date?"

"The sixth of Verdure, 1041."

"From which country do you hail?"

"Osperland."

"When did you first develop arcane hypersensitivity?"

"Not long after I first developed magic." Mavery focused on Yuriva's thin, dry lips.

"How old were you then?"

"Four, maybe five."

Mavery blinked and, despite herself, a memory appeared in her mind's eye. She was sitting on her mother's lap, in the kitchen of her childhood home. Her mother's face was blurred, partially obscured in shadow, the finer details lost to time and the faultiness of memory. The most vibrant detail was a ribbon of blue swirling around them—an inchoate protective ward. Mavery grasped at it with her tiny hands, aware that she had conjured the magic but not yet aware that only she could see it. Mum wrapped her arms around Mavery, murmured something in her ear. The specific words had also been lost to time, but they left an impression of comfort.

This was one of Mavery's earliest memories—if not *the* earliest—and one she hadn't thought of in years. A knot formed in her throat.

The room smelled of baked apples, fresh hay, and...flowers?

No, that can't be right. Mum never kept fresh-cut flowers around the house; pollen always made her sneeze.

Mavery forced her attention on the background, searched for an element that hadn't been conjured by her own mind. Her eyes trailed along the whitewashed wall. Its texture shifted unnaturally. She focused on that spot and glimpsed Yuriva's features embedded within the plaster. Mavery gasped as Yuriva's eyes flew open, locking with hers. The memory dissipated. She returned to the antechamber, with the real Yuriva watching her from across the table.

What the fuck just happened?

"Language," Yuriva chided. "I was simply observing your memory, though few are able to detect me so quickly. Have you ever received Mysticism training?"

"No."

"Curious. Let's try something else. Focus your attention on my right hand."

Yuriva raised it and produced a protective ward. Mavery smelled copper, now interlaced with that floral scent again. As she watched the ephemeral blue aura, her head throbbed. She touched the back of her head, though that did nothing to ease the discomfort. It felt as though an invisible hand were massaging the deepest folds of her mind, in a place she could neither see nor touch. Impulsively, she squeezed her eyes shut, tried to force out the intrusion.

"This will all be over much sooner if you cooperate," Yuriva said.

"What are you doing to me?"

"Seeing through your eyes."

Mavery acquiesced with a sigh. She opened her eyes again, then winced at the sudden intensity of Yuriva's protective ward. She grit her teeth as she tried to ride out the probing sensation.

It was clear when the spell ended: the floral scent faded, the throbbing in her head subsided. She rubbed her scalp again, though she knew the Mystic hadn't physically touched her.

"There," Mavery said flatly. "Are you satisfied?"

"Such impatience," Yuriva said in that serene voice that Mavery now found irritating. "I detected an air of distress just now. Is that something you often experience?"

Mavery scoffed; *distress* was a bit dramatic. "Only with very powerful or prolonged magic. To help with that, Al—*Aventus*—made a potion that dulls my Senses."

Yuriva's eyebrows raised slightly, betraying her otherwise stoic demeanor. "Describe this potion."

"How is that relevant?" Mavery asked.

"Answer the question, please."

She automatically recalled her most recent memory of the potion: about an hour ago, after stepping through the portal.

"Are you certain you don't want the anti-Sensing potion?"

"A bit late for that, isn't it?"

"I mean for the trip back."

The scent of flowers made her stomach lurch. Yuriva was watching on, and Mavery couldn't let the Mystic witness how that conversation had played out. She willed her memory of Alain to freeze in place, pinching the vial between his fingers. That bought her a few seconds to card through her memories for one that was less incriminating.

She thought back to the morning he'd revealed the potion to her. The teacup filled with the viscous, black liquid. The taste as it slid down her throat—bitter, with that hint of bergamot. Alain standing before her, waiting.

"Do you feel anything?"

"No."

"Try looking at the door."

The past version of herself gasped. Then, she was across the room, examining the rippling effect where colorful auras had been only a moment ago.

The floral aroma persisted. Yuriva was still here...somewhere. Mavery turned around and searched the room. As this memory was more distant than the previous one, her surroundings were a blur of mismatched furniture, stacks of books, piles of loose papers. Her gaze roved over it all, seeking a detail that didn't belong.

"Where did you go?" she asked, both in her mind and out loud.

Yuriva snapped her fingers, and the memory faded. The Mystic's lips formed a thin line—not quite a frown, but far from a smile.

"Why did you change to a different memory?" she demanded.

Mavery shrugged. "You asked me to describe the potion. I thought you'd prefer to see a time when I actually drank it."

Yuriva narrowed her eyes. She opened her mouth at the same time the door opened.

"Elder Yuriva," said the assistant from earlier, "the Archmage wants to know if you've finished your evaluation."

"Yes, Darvis." Yuriva's joints creaked as she rose from her chair. "I'm ready to report my findings to the rest of the Council."

She left the room without asking Mavery to follow.

"You may return whenever you are ready, Madam Culwich," the assistant said. He began to close the door, but Mavery hoisted herself off her own chair. Her tailbone ached almost as much as her head.

"I'm ready now." Not only to leave this room, but to put all of this—the presentation, the Elder Wizards, and their tower—behind her.

Back in the main chamber, the podium was no longer imbued with warding magic. Upon seeing her approach, Alain sighed, his relief apparent even from a distance. He began to extend a hand toward her, then seemed to think better of it. Instead, he formed a tight fist that he held to his side. Seringoth's voice rang through the chamber.

"Well, Elder Yuriva, what is your verdict?"

"Aventus's claims are true," she replied without a shred of enthusiasm. "What I witnessed just now was what I witnessed when I evaluated Deventhal over sixty years ago. Ms. Culwich does, indeed, have arcane hypersensitivity."

Seringoth looked to Alain. "It seems you are most fortunate. Leave your spell tome on the podium and follow Darvis into the waiting room. He will collect you when the High Council's deliberations are complete."

According to the clock in the waiting area, only half an hour had passed, but it felt as though they'd spent half a day in that chamber. Darvis closed the door, leaving Alain and Mavery alone.

"I can't thank you enough for stepping in," Alain said. "I think you impressed the High Council enough to overlook what they normally would have considered an outburst."

"I had a feeling assistants don't typically speak at these things."

"Not unless an Elder Wizard addresses them directly, and that rarely happens. Also, I'm sorry again for that spur-of-the-moment evaluation with Elder Yuriva."

"I can't say it's something I ever want to repeat, but it wasn't so bad."

"Oh, you must tell me *everything*!"

As he dug out his notebook and pen, he explained how Mysticism was an esoteric subject, even for wizards. Innate Mystics were exceedingly rare—though nowhere near as rare as Sensers—and only those who'd been trained at the College of Mystics were allowed to practice this School.

So, Mavery spared not a single detail as she recounted Yuriva's questioning. He only stopped recording notes when she told him how she'd veered Yuriva away from a memory.

"You don't suppose she suspects anything about us, do you?" he asked, somehow looking even paler than he'd appeared during the presentation.

Mavery shook her head. "More than anything, she seemed annoyed that I was able to derail her procedure."

The doors to the presentation chamber opened. As Darvis reentered the room, Alain rose from the bench.

"Is the High Council finished already?" he asked.

Darvis hurried past without a word, clutching a roll of parchment. His footsteps echoed down the main corridor as he jogged out of sight.

"I suppose not." Alain shrugged, then sat down again. "I

would have been surprised if they were. Spell tomes usually take a bit longer to review."

Darvis returned fifteen minutes later, now with a second roll of parchment. He again said nothing as he crossed the room and returned to the presentation chamber. The soundproofing ward prevented any sound from escaping, and the chamber was too dim for Mavery to glimpse the Elder Wizards.

She and Alain continued to wait. Kindling crackled in the fireplace, the wall clock ticked as the minutes dragged on. Mavery lost track of how many times Alain paced the room. Eventually, her muscles began to stiffen and she joined him, though she quickly regretted it. The eyes of Seringoth's portrait seemed to follow her no matter where she wandered.

When an hour had passed, Alain stopped by the hearth and stared into the flames. He chewed on a fingernail.

"This is the fourth spell I've presented to the High Council." His voice quavered as he spoke. "Deliberations have *never* taken this long."

"I'm sure everything will be fine," Mavery said, though she doubted her own words. Her stomach groaned. "You didn't happen to pack any food?"

Alain shook his head. "No, but I know a spell for that."

"You what?"

He ripped a blank page from his notebook. A chill passed between them as he spoke a rather complex incantation. Mavery knew it was twenty-eight syllables without needing to count; she'd picked up on the rhythm of speech he always used for incantations of that length. The paper glowed white for a second, then dulled again. Though it still looked like an ordinary sheet of paper, it had become as firm as hardtack.

"Transmutated grain," Alain said, his voice slightly less tense. "It's perfectly safe to eat."

Mavery laughed. "It reminds me of that old folktale—the one about the demons who learned to talk to humans by eating their books."

"I suppose every folktale has some basis in truth, but this is only a Transmutation spell. Nothing demonic here, I promise."

Mavery took a small bite from the corner and nearly choked on it. The grain was flavorless, but its texture was unbearably gritty. She wished she had something—anything—to wash away the sensation of sand coating her tongue.

"It's more appealing as a slurry," Alain said. "Add a bit of water, and it becomes something like porridge."

She wrinkled her nose. Anything that could be described as a "slurry" sounded even *less* appealing. With a hard swallow, she choked down the grain.

"Sounds like you're speaking from experience," she said.

Alain's shoulders sagged. "When you arrived in Leyport, I'd gone nearly a month without leaving my apartment at all. When my real food ran out, I sacrificed a few notebooks and survived off this."

"For almost a *month*?"

He nodded. "It will ward off starvation, but it's not intended to be eaten over extended periods."

"Gods, that sounds awful." Mavery's heart sank. Upon seeing him for the first time, she'd assumed he had been ill. She'd been correct, in a sense.

"At the time, I considered it a fitting addition to my self-inflicted punishment."

She touched her hand to his cheek. "I hope you never have to think that way again."

With a weak smile, he placed his hand over hers.

The door to the presentation chamber opened. They both flinched, and Mavery jerked her hand away as her heart raced for multiple reasons.

"The High Council has completed its deliberations," Darvis said. Nothing in his voice indicated he'd noticed their impropriety.

Alain looked to Mavery, then took a deep breath. As he turned to follow Darvis, she tossed the rest of the transmutated grain into the fire.

THIRTY-NINE

Halfway across the presentation chamber, Alain froze.

The spell tome lay atop the podium.

The previous three times Alain had presented a spell, the High Council had taken the tome, created copies for peer review, and stored the original in its archives. They'd never returned the original to him. Perhaps they'd changed their process at some point in the past two years.

Or, perhaps Alain had *failed*.

He approached the podium cautiously, like an animal trying to avoid ensnaring itself in a trap, as a tempest of dread churned within his stomach.

Seringoth's voice resounded through the room.

"Aventus the Third, after much deliberation, the High Council has decided that your spell lacks the scientific rigor necessary to proceed to the peer review phase. Your spell requires significant revisions, based on these recommendations.

"Firstly, you must remove any and all references to Enodus the Second's 'Sensing Spell,' as this tome is no longer in circulation. That includes the entirety of the translation of his treatise. Second—"

"Ex-excuse me, Archmage," Alain said, avoiding Seringoth's

eyes. He knew speaking out of turn could worsen this already volatile situation, but surely he'd misunderstood. "How is that possible? I viewed it myself at the University of North Fenutia less than a month ago."

"Arcanist Dolokir recently deemed it unfit for scholarly research, on the grounds of it being an unfinished spell. Now—"

"How recently?" Mavery interrupted. Alain could hardly blame her for breaking decorum—not after they'd just disparaged her primary contribution to the tome. Muttering rippled across the High Council's bench, but she stood firm. "When, exactly, was it removed?"

Seringoth shuffled some of his notes. "The twenty-third of Pluviose."

Two days after her trip to the library. One day after she'd spoken of her encounter with Head Arcanist Tristan. Alain had dismissed her concerns, insisted they would revisit that topic after the presentation. If only he'd known at the time they would be nearly a fortnight too late.

"Aventus, Ms. Culwich, the sooner you let me proceed without interruption, the sooner we can all be on our way." Seringoth shuffled his papers again. "Secondly, while you dedicated a lengthy portion of the discussion section to the spell's theoretical implications, you failed to identify a single *practical* use. As it stands, this spell is little more than a parlor trick."

Mavery clenched her fists, and Alain could nearly feel the heat emanating from her skin. But he couldn't find it within himself to share her rage. Rather, he stood still as a statue, hands clasped behind his back, as he let the Archmage's deluge of criticism wash over him.

"To rectify these shortcomings, you must conduct a rigorous field experiment. Test the spell on any Gardemancy spells of your choosing, so long as they were not cast by yourself or your assistant, then present your findings to the High Council in one week's time. Inside the tome is a portal pass for your follow-up presentation. Fail to appear, and your rank will be rescinded immediately."

Alain dared to look up. He wished Seringoth's gaze contained simmering fury, or even utter contempt. Either would be preferable to what he found instead.

Regret.

"To speak frankly, Aventus, the High Council is most disappointed in your performance today. A wizard of your fortitude ought to be capable of more sophisticated spellcraft—especially following a year-long sabbatical. Consider the follow-up presentation as a one-time courtesy."

The Archmage fell silent as he returned his attention to his stack of papers. Though he'd spoken on behalf of the High Council, Alain knew the truth behind Seringoth's words: the disappointment was personal. For a moment, Alain remained frozen on the spot, unable to say or do anything. He felt like a boy of twenty-three again, the first time he'd failed to meet his mentor's expectations.

Seringoth looked up. He raised his brows, as if surprised to see Alain still standing there. "Unless you have any further questions, you are dismissed."

Alain swiftly tucked the tome under his arm, slung his satchel over one shoulder, and turned for the double doors. Behind him, fabric swished and heels clacked across stone as Mavery hurried to catch up.

He remained silent as he retraced his steps through the waiting area and down the corridor, pausing only once he'd returned to the portal room. He handed Mavery the vial of anti-Sensing potion, then turned toward the University of Leyport's portal. She grasped his shoulder.

"Alain, wait."

He stopped and turned to her, though all he wanted was to keep moving and get away from this place.

"For what it's worth," she said, "I think you did an amazing job."

He shrugged, then said flatly, "If only that was worth anything to the High Council. Come on, let's go home."

"But wasn't the plan to visit Kazamin next?"

"I'm afraid the plan has changed."

He readjusted his satchel, then stepped through the portal.

It was said that, in the seconds preceding death, one's entire life would flash before one's eyes. In Alain's case, he thought of nothing from his past. His thoughts focused solely on the present.

And the present was pain.

His body erupted in acute, white-hot agony. It originated in his chest and spread in waves to his extremities. Bones, blood, muscle, skin… Every inch of him, inside and out, was on fire.

The pain vanished as everything turned to darkness.

Then, after what could have been either a second or eternity, light returned.

He lay on a metal table in an unfamiliar room. He sat up. The air was cool and somewhat damp against his skin. A dull ache pulsated from deep within his chest. He looked down and found himself undressed from the waist up. An incision—raw, violent pink—bisected his torso, from an inch above his navel to the center of his breastbone.

"Idiot boy."

He flinched at the familiar voice, then looked to his right, where Seringoth sat in a chair. Behind him, a surgeon rinsed his blood-stained hands in a sink. But there were no healers present, nor were there any surgical instruments lying about. The walls were lined with jars containing organs—hearts, lungs, livers, kidneys—suspended in viscous liquids. The room was still enough for Alain to detect a faint undulation of arcana in the air.

This was not a surgeon's operating room, but a Resurrectionist's chamber.

"I told you to leave that section of the incantation alone," Seringoth said. "Yet, you, an assistant scarcely three months graduated from university, thought you knew better than an Elder Wizard."

Alain opened his mouth, readying an apology, but no sound escaped his lips. His lungs had shriveled, his vocal cords had turned to dust.

Seringoth leaned closer. His face contained no relief in seeing his assistant returned from the dead. His eyes were as cold as a midwinter sky.

"By every right, you should have died today as a result of your imprudence," he said in a low voice. "Instead, I chose to give you a second chance, as I know there is great potential within you. But understand that, by bringing you here, I have violated the Covenants. This is a matter I do not take lightly, and one that I will never repeat. I have paid the Resurrectionist handsomely for his silence, and you will speak of this to no one. Do you understand?"

Alain nodded, and Seringoth rose from his chair.

"Good. Do not make me regret this decision."

"Alain?"

He turned his gaze from the window—it was a cloudless, sunny day, as though the weather itself were making a mockery of his failure—and toward Mavery. Though the carriage he'd hired had a spacious bench, she sat close to him, resting her hand against his cheek.

"Alain, where we you just now?"

The first time I died.

"What was that?" she asked.

He blinked, not realizing he'd spoken aloud. He cleared his throat. "Er, nothing. I was only...lost in thought."

"Obviously. Do you want to share any of those thoughts, or are you going to continue keeping me in the dark about why you abandoned the plan?"

He sighed. "Now is not a good time to hand in my resignation. Think of how it would look, further abandoning my duties immediately after delivering the High Council a mediocre spell—"

"Mediocre?" Mavery scoffed. "You took a spell no one had touched in two hundred years and completed it in *two weeks*. You're a brilliant scholar, despite everything those assholes said back there."

He gaped at her. "They're the greatest wizards of our time!"

"And who decided that? The Elder Wizards themselves?" Mavery frowned. "Don't tell me you believe that bullshit excuse for removing the spell tome."

"I don't," Alain said without hesitation, much to his own surprise. It was the truth, though he could only admit it to Mavery. He'd never be so brazen as to speak those words before the High Council. "There are scores of incomplete spell tomes in the University of Leyport's archives. I know every arcanist weeds their collection based on their own criteria, but—"

"The *arcanists'* criteria, or *the High Council's*? I'll bet you anything this has something to do with that magic Enodus mentioned."

She ground her knuckles into her forehead, and Alain knew this discomfort had nothing to do with her Senses. Not directly, at any rate. He wrapped his arms around her and pulled her close. At least the two people sitting in this carriage knew that Enodus's spell tome had once existed. They still had Alain's transcription and Mavery's translation.

But what good were those now? Even if they discovered what "ktonic magic" was, what could they possibly do with that knowledge? Throughout history, there'd been scholars who'd gone rogue and attempted to publish their research without the High Council's blessing. Their names had been remembered—but only to serve as a warning that there were far worse punishments than losing one's wizard rank.

"All this time, I was hoping I could spare you one of the pitfalls of being a scholar," Alain said softly.

Mavery replied with a frustrated groan.

"And now," he said, "just when I thought our work was complete, we have this field experiment to address. In the past, a theoretical analysis had been sufficient. Granted, I last presented a spell over two years ago. No wonder Kazamin encouraged all that peer review."

"Which you never finished."

"Between the potion and the spell, I didn't have the time." He shook his head. "That's too often how it goes."

Mavery loosened herself from his embrace. As she drummed her fingers against her chin, Alain could almost see the gears within her brilliant mind turning, formulating a new plan.

"At least the field experiment should be simple enough," she said. "We could stop by the provincial courthouse, test the spell there. I know for a fact that place is overflowing with wards." Alain arched his eyebrows, and she shrugged. "It's a popular place for thieves."

"I assumed *competent* thieves would know how to avoid ending up in court."

She smirked. "No, competent thieves know how to avoid ending up in *prison*. I can assure you, this former thief never spent much time there."

He laughed, but it flattened as he recalled Seringoth's words from nearly an hour ago—and over a decade ago.

There is great potential within you...

A wizard of your fortitude ought to be capable of more...

Do not make me regret this decision.

Mavery's idea would be fine if Alain could get away with the bare minimum. But this afternoon's events proved that he needed to do more than that.

He needed to do something *extraordinary*.

FORTY

The moment they returned home, Alain made a direct path for the storage room. He opened crates and rummaged through their contents, muttering to himself while Mavery watched on from the doorway. Though Alain had managed to speak to her on the trip home, he'd quickly returned to his thoughts. Whatever plan he'd hatched in silence, he was now putting it into motion.

Not only had the High Council's verdict derailed his plan to resign from the University, their *other* plans for the evening now seemed postponed indefinitely. Having her work scholastically shat upon certainly hadn't left Mavery in a celebratory mood. A long, hard nap was the only bedroom activity that interested her at this particular moment.

"No, not here," Alain grumbled. "Where *are* those blasted things?"

"What are you looking for?"

"My old journals. I moved them here ages ago, but I forgot exactly where I—aha! Here they are!"

He brought a stack of journals into the main room, dumped them on his desk, and lowered himself into his chair. Without another word, he began to read.

Mavery took one of the journals—the same one he'd shown

her during the first week of her assistantship. When Alain didn't protest, she turned to the final entry, and her blood chilled upon seeing a name that had become hauntingly familiar. She now understood why Alain had prevented her from reading this before.

SIDDISDAY, 20 PLUVIOSE, 1040

At long last, Conor discovered the breakthrough we needed! He came across a letter written by Aganast, acting as the head of the Order of Asphodel. Beneath his signature was an odd symbol that matches the one depicted on the Innominate Temple's pediment. I will reproduce it here. This could be proof that the temple is connected to Aganast, the Order, or both.

I'm already fast at work planning a research trip for this summer. Before we conduct an on-site investigation, we should start with interviews across Dyerland Province. Local villagers may have information that cannot be found in the University's library. I plan to meet with Kazamin on Onisday to discuss fund

I must cut this entry short, for Conor is insisting we go out for a pint. And now he is standing over my shoulder while I write, as he so often enjoys doing. Yes, my darling, I agree that a discovery like this is cause for celebrations!

She tried to avoid thinking of how their "celebrations" had ended, and instead focused on the symbol Alain had sketched in the margin. From a distance, it appeared to be a six-pointed star. She looked closer and noticed how those points were thin and slightly rounded—an asphodel flower.

She closed the notebook and returned it to the stack. Alain was still absorbed in his reading. She glanced over his shoulder, and the word "temple" stuck out to her like a beacon.

"Alain, what are you planning?" she asked cautiously.

"With a single field experiment, I can kill two birds with one stone: prove to the High Council that I'm still capable of more than 'parlor tricks,' and prove that our spell is viable. So viable, in fact, it can help with something no scholar has ever accomplished."

"I take it you're not planning to pop over to the courthouse."

He shook his head. "Were these normal circumstances, I would see no problem with that plan. But I need to give the High Council something far more impressive. I need to—"

"Crack the Innominate Temple."

He closed his notebook and turned to her. "Yes."

"But they've only given you a week for this field experiment."

"Which is all the more reason why I need to act quickly."

"Alain—"

"The fact of the matter is, it's too late for me to begin a new project from scratch, so I've no choice but to pick up an old one, and I've made more headway on the temple than anything else."

"But why go to these lengths to prove yourself to the High Council?"

"You don't understand—"

"I think you'll find I'm *plenty* capable of understanding," she said, crossing her arms.

He hung his head. "I didn't mean it that way."

He pushed back his chair, rose to his feet, grasped her by the shoulders. As his fingers trailed down her arms, she unfolded them and allowed him to take her hands. In his eyes, Mavery couldn't glimpse the spark of rapid-fire inspiration. Rather, his thoughts seemed more akin to water circling a drain.

"For my entire life—before I was a wizard, or even an assistant—there have been lofty expectations placed upon me. Expectations that few others are subjected to. Trust me when I say, if there were another option, I would seize it in a heartbeat. But I know that I failed Seringoth today, and only through extreme measures will I regain his favor. Besides..." He sighed. "I can't help but feel as though everything has been leading to this. I have an obligation to finish what I started, for Conor's sake."

"Whatever you do, *don't* do this for him," Mavery said as her stomach twisted into knots. "Don't do this for the person who—"

"I know what he did, but even that didn't warrant a death sentence. If I complete my research, then at least his death won't have been in vain. I owe him that much—"

"You don't owe him a godsdamned thing!"

"That's not for *you* to decide!" Alain snapped.

Mavery recoiled, releasing his hands. For a moment, she simply blinked at him, unable to voice a response. His hands clenched and unclenched into fists as he gazed downward.

"I'm...I'm sorry." His voice was quiet, strained. "I know cracking the temple won't bring him back, it won't change the past. But I *must* try to finish what I started. If not for him, then for myself."

Mavery sighed. "Fine. When are we going?"

He looked up. "*We* are not going anywhere. This is something I must do alone."

"Like hells you will! You've never even been to the temple."

"Neither have you."

"I've gotten close enough to know that going it alone would be suicide. The temple is the least of your worries. Can you handle yourself against wild demonspawn, highwaymen, navigating the *real* wilderness? This won't be a cozy little hike outside the city walls."

"I know, and that's precisely why you shouldn't come with me."

"No, that's precisely why I *should* come with you."

"But you're..." He raked his fingers through his hair as his gaze darted between Mavery's face and the far corners of the room. It finally settled on the kitchen door. "I need...something...help me think."

He turned and headed to the kitchen. Mavery began to follow him, but a full day in her new dress boots had done a number on her feet. A single step was all she could manage before unlacing the boots and tossing them aside. Hiking up her skirt and ignoring the ache from her fresh blisters, she hurried toward the clatter coming from the kitchen.

"I swear," she muttered, "if you've maimed yourself on another cup..."

When she entered the kitchen, he was rifling through his collection of tea tins as though his life depended on choosing the right one. Mavery heaved a sigh that was tinged with both frustration and relief. She came to his side, lowered his hands, and took them in hers.

"Talk to me," she said. "Tell me what you're thinking about."

He uttered a single nervous laugh. "I'm afraid that would take all night."

"Then we'll stay up all night if need be."

He smiled, though his eyes were misty. "Even when I'm an utter mess, even when I plan to barrel straight toward uncertain death, you refuse to leave my side." His left hand slipped from her grasp and traveled upward to rest against her cheek. "What did I do to deserve someone like you?"

His fingertips traced the scar across her nose, trailed down her other cheek, brushed her lower lip. She leaned into his touch, eager to feel his mouth against hers, but she could tell there was more he wanted—*needed*—to say. His dark eyes were filled with enough adoration to render her breathless.

"I keep thinking back to my accident...how you revived me." He leaned forward, rested his forehead against hers. "Ever since that night, you've brought me back to life in countless ways. I love you, Mavery. You've become so precious to me. So much so, I can't let you join me on this trip, not when there's such great risk involved. How could I, when I can't bear the thought of losing you?"

"And what if *I* lost *you*? If you died out there alone, whether at the temple or on the road to it, what would I be left with?" She cupped his face between both hands. "I love you, too, but I want to love more than the memory of you."

He leaned back slightly as his eyes widened. "I...hadn't considered..."

"Of course you hadn't." Smiling, she shook her head. "Somehow, you're both the most intelligent and the most foolish person I've ever known. And yet, I wouldn't change you at all."

At last, he pulled her in, bridging the space between them. His lips were firm and unyielding against hers, as if he sought to pour every emotion into a single kiss. She skimmed her fingers through his hair, prompting a tremor that forced his body to relax slightly, his lips to part. As their kiss slowed to an indolent caress, he wrapped his arms around her, clung to her long after their lips broke apart.

She didn't love the prospect of going back to the Innominate Temple, and she loved the reasons for this excursion even less. But she loved *him*, and she would remain by his side; she had no intention of breaking that promise.

"Now," she whispered, "will you stop being a martyr for one godsdamned minute and let your assistant *assist* you?"

He nodded, then released her. His face was flushed, his eyes bloodshot. He rubbed the latter with the heels of his palms.

"What do you suggest?" he asked.

"First of all, how long will it take us to get to the temple?"

"Two days to get to one of the nearby villages. Then, it's a matter of tracking down the temple. The magical protections make it impossible to pinpoint its exact coordinates."

Mavery nodded, recalling how Selemin had once told her the same. "What kind of magic do you think is behind that?"

"It's likely an obfuscation ward—an exceptionally powerful one, at that. Our spell won't denote them by color, but I doubt that would make much difference; obfuscation wards are far from my area of expertise."

"Then I suggest we find an expert. Who at the University specializes in those wards?"

Alain laughed. "Someone who just so happens to owe me a favor."

Part Three

The Arcanist

FORTY-ONE

"**Y**ou want to go *where*!?"

Alain stopped in front of the fireplace. Though it was unlit, his forehead was slick with sweat. He'd paced the length of Declan's sitting room no less than fifty times while recounting everything that had happened that afternoon, from the disastrous spell presentation to the plan to set out for the Innominate Temple. He'd even shared his theory about the temple's ties to Aganast and the Order of Asphodel.

From his armchair, Declan stared blankly at Alain. He clutched a glass of whiskey, though he hadn't taken a single sip during Alain's rambling and pacing. Beads of condensation dripped down its sides.

Alain sighed. "I know this sounds a bit mad—"

"A bit!" Declan bellowed an incredulous laugh. "I understand wanting to prove your worth to the High Council, but there must be an easier way to go about it."

"Exactly what I said," Mavery muttered from the other armchair. Declan had also offered her a glass of whiskey. Not only had she accepted it, she'd already drank half of it.

Alain turned to the bookcase beside the fireplace, and drummed his fingers on one of the bare shelves. For a professor,

Declan owned a surprisingly small number of books.

"This isn't about what I *want*," he said quietly. In fact, few things in his life had ever been about what he wanted. "You don't know Seringoth like I do. He expected more from me today, and I failed to meet his expectations."

"Sounds like your mind is made up, then," Declan said. "But I'm struggling to see why you're asking me for help."

Alain turned to him. "I have another theory: it's possible that the temple is protected by an obfuscation ward. Seeing as you invented the Diversion Ward—"

"That was twenty-five years ago, lad. And since then, my career has been confined to classrooms and taprooms." He chuckled as he patted his stomach, then took a swill of whiskey. "You're more suited for field work than I am. At least you have youth on your side."

Alain's shoulders sank. At this moment, he felt anything but youthful.

"Could someone else in the Gardemancy Department help us?" Mavery asked. "Selemin might not know much about wards, but they seemed pretty knowledgeable about—"

"No." Alain shook his head. "I'm not trusting anyone from Nezima's inner circle."

Declan scratched his mustache. "You know, this is the sort of thing you'd typically contract out."

"I can't," Alain said. "I need to conduct the field experiment myself."

"Not the 'experimenting' part, I mean the 'finding the temple' part. A few years ago, Ferikar over in Transmutation paid someone to investigate this very same temple. The lad he hired didn't find a way in, but he did manage to get around the traps unscathed. Got within ten feet of the place—at least, that's what Ferikar claimed."

Mavery stiffened briefly before throwing back her glass, draining every last drop of whiskey.

"I reckon someone like that could guide you to the temple," Declan said. "It might set you back a couple hundred potins, but it's better than blindly wandering all around Dyerland Province for days on end. I'll see Ferikar at the graduation ceremony tomorrow evening. I'll ask if he remembers the name of his contact."

"I can't wait until tomorrow evening," Alain said. "The High Council has only given me a week to complete the field experiment."

"Then the best I can do is write you up a scroll or two. Though, without knowing the specific types of obfuscation wards you're up against, I don't know how helpful they'll be."

"At this point, I'll take any help I can get."

Declan hoisted himself out of his armchair and lumbered over to the desk in the far corner. After a few moments of scribbling, he returned with a rolled-up sheet of parchment.

"This is a counterspell for my Diversion Ward. It's a long shot, but whoever was behind that temple might've also figured out a way to trick you into turning back the way you came." Declan handed Alain the parchment, then clapped him on the shoulder. "Take care of yourself, lad." He nodded to Mavery. "Her, too. I want both of you to come back in one piece."

"Thank you, Declan," Alain said.

He and Mavery left the townhouse but lingered outside on the stoop. It was now dusk, and a lamplighter was making his rounds.

"Well, it was worth a try," Alain said. He opened his satchel, tucked the scroll into the transmutated pouch.

Mavery offered no counterargument. She crossed her arms as she chewed on a hangnail. She'd been unusually quiet since leaving Steelforge Towers. Alain had attributed her silence to her reservations about his plan, but he now suspected she was formulating a plan of her own.

"Do you have any ideas?" he asked.

She blew out a long stream of air, then turned to him. The dark look behind her eyes tightened the knot in his stomach.

"I do," she said. "But I don't think you're going to like it."

The Salty Surling was a grimy, weather-beaten shack near the docks. The sign above the door was, like the clapboards, coated in green mildew. It depicted a red-eyed, raven-like bird singing drunkenly as its talons clutched a tankard of ale—an oddly whimsical image for a place like this. Grizzled dock workers shuffled past. Like the air, they reeked of rotten fish and even less savory odors Alain dared not fathom.

Mavery ran her fingers through his hair—an act he would've found calming under different circumstances. Alongside his baggiest trousers, his most understated shirt, and his gray travel cloak, this was the final touch for his "common laborer" guise. He felt somewhat exposed without a waistcoat, but Mavery insisted it would defeat the purpose of fitting in.

"There," she said. "Now your look no longer screams, 'please come pick my pockets.' "

"Is that a possibility?"

She shrugged. "Anything is possible in a place like this. Just keep your wits about you, don't make eye contact with anyone, and let me do the talking."

Alain tried to voice a reply, but all he could manage was a weak groan of disbelief.

"Trust me, I'm as thrilled about this as you are, but Neldren's been to the temple before. I've no doubt he's the same 'contact' Declan told us about. Like it or not, we need him if we want to find this temple as quickly as possible."

"You're certain he'll accept your offer?"

"We may be desperate, but seeking me out like he did means he's even more desperate. So long as there's money on the table, he'll at least listen." She cupped Alain's chin between her fingers. "You don't have to do this. I can handle him on my own."

"I know you can, but we're in this together."

She smiled, then kissed him on the mouth. His eyes widened at her unabashed display of affection—and in *public*, no less. But the odds of encountering anyone from the University here were less than zero, and a kiss was probably among the least lascivious things to happen in this corner of the city. So, he kissed her back, and his stomach fluttered at the sheer *freedom* of it.

She pulled away entirely too soon and smiled at him again.

"Ready?" she asked.

He nodded. She turned to the door, and its rusty hinges squealed as she opened it. Night had fallen hours ago, and the pub was swarming with laborers and vagrants alike. The ambiance in the Salty Surling made even the most raucous nights at the Lettered Gentleman look like temple services. Gruff voices jeered and spouted profanities over card games and pints of sour-smelling ale. Smoke from cheap tobacco created a thick haze. Mavery had brought her dagger along, and she kept her fingers against its hilt as she crossed the uneven gray floorboards.

Alain followed her advice and ignored meeting anyone's eye, though he was tempted to seek out the source of a wolf whistle aimed in her direction. His blood flared, but he kept his gaze fixed on Mavery's back. She strutted through the room, head high and undeterred by her surroundings.

It then occurred to Alain that, until two months ago, this was the sort of place she frequented. For the first time, he was seeing her in her element.

She came to a stop near the back of the room.

"There he is," she muttered. "And in his natural habitat, no less."

Gathered around one of the tables were three men in the midst of a card game. Alain knew at once which one of them was Neldren, and not because he was the only Nilandoren at the table. He was undeniably handsome, with long, dark hair and a sharp, stubble-lined jaw. His commanding presence penetrated the crowded room. Alain could see why Mavery had been so infatuated with this man.

But this man had also shot someone he supposedly cared about.

A petite young redhead was perched on his right knee. She spotted Mavery from across the room, shot her an acidic glare, then leaned over and whispered in Neldren's ear. He whipped his head around so swiftly, the redhead nearly lost her balance.

"Well, look who's decided to grace us with her presence," he said. "Sorry, mates, afraid I must quit while I'm ahead."

His announcement was met with grumbles and curses. But Neldren ignored them as he laid down his cards and gathered up his winnings—more coppers than potins—and nudged the young woman, who rolled her eyes before sliding off his lap.

They relocated to the closest thing this pub had to a private corner. Neldren and the young woman sat together on one side of the table; Neldren draped his arm over the back of her chair. Alain gathered his resolve before it depleted entirely, then sat beside Mavery, who'd claimed the chair directly across from Neldren.

"And you've brought a friend," Neldren said. He extended his hand. "Neldren Rel'Selayne."

"Alain Tesseraunt," he replied stiffly.

Neldren's palm was callused, his grip firm. It was a mercifully brief handshake. Had it lasted any longer, Alain would be tempted to make this man *truly* answer for putting a bullet in Mavery's stomach. The young woman—Ellice, Alain presumed—eyed Alain with suspicion but made no effort to introduce herself.

"So, to what do we owe the pleasure?" Neldren asked.

"The last time we spoke, you suggested we work together again," Mavery said.

"I did."

Ellice glared at Neldren. "I told you to *apologize* to her, not recruit her!"

He kept his eyes on Mavery. "I take it you've found a job."

"I have, as a matter of fact."

"Who's your buyer?" His eyes flicked to Alain. "Him?"

"No, I am."

Mavery glanced behind her shoulder before extracting an envelope from the inside pocket of her coat, then slid it across the table. Neldren's eyebrows raised as he peeked inside. Ellice eagerly craned her neck.

"Five hundred potins," Mavery said in a low voice. "All accounted for."

He closed the envelope but placed his hand over it instead of passing it back to her. "If you're willing to share your newfound wealth, consider me interested. All right, what kind of job are we talking?"

Mavery exchanged a sidelong glance with Alain. "A few years back, you took a job for a wizard at the University of Leyport. We'd like to hire you for that same job."

He flashed her a wicked smile. "You'll need to be more specific than that." There was a particularity with which he phrased that sentence, as if sharing an inside joke.

Mavery sighed. "The Innominate Temple."

Neldren's smile flattened. He fell silent as he and Mavery exchanged another knowing look. Ellice glanced between the two of them, confusion etched on her brow.

"What's the Innominate Temple?" she asked.

"It's—" Mavery began.

"A godsdamned nightmare of a place," Neldren said. "Cursed, if you ask me."

"It's not *cursed*," Alain scoffed. Neldren and Ellice turned to him with mild surprise. Heat trickled up his neck at the sudden attention, but he pressed on. "What you encountered was an exceptionally strong concentration of magic—obfuscation and detonation wards, to be precise—though *any* School of Magic would produce the same effect. It's simple Etherean magic. Well, not to imply that magic that's been in place for over five centuries is *simple*. What I mean is, curses are superstition; the magic protecting the Innominate Temple is anything but."

Neldren gawked at him. "Er, right... Who did you say you were, again?"

"Someone who's been researching this ruin for the better part of a decade. Call it a pet project, if you will."

Neldren sniffed. "Right, *research*. I take it you've never seen the place for yourself."

"No, I—"

"And that's where you come in," Mavery interjected. "We need a guide and, as you can see, we're willing to pay handsomely for one."

"Not handsomely enough." He pushed the envelope back across the table. "No deal. I'm surprised you'd even want to go there, considering—"

"I know what happened last time. But that was years ago, and now I know what to expect."

"And you think that's going to make any difference? Forget it.

I'm not risking my arse for another wizard."

Alain blinked. "How did you...?"

Neldren laughed. "Mate, I pegged you as one of them the minute you opened your mouth. You sound just like the wizard who hired me last time around. He also had all sorts of fancy words and research, and you know what they amounted to? *Fuck all.*"

Scowling, Mavery snatched up the envelope and pushed back her chair. "Come on, Alain. I should've known this would be a waste of time. We'll stick with our original plan and do it ourselves."

As she stood up, Neldren's smugness dissipated. "Wait. You're not seriously going it alone?"

"Why not?" Mavery said. "You may not have any faith in his research, but I know that if anyone can find a way past the warding magic, it's this man right here." Though Alain knew this was part of Mavery's tactics, just as they'd rehearsed on the trip over, his heart fluttered at that sentiment all the same. "And, as his reasons are purely academic, he'd be more than willing to share whatever is inside the temple."

Neldren snorted. "Whatever's *inside* that place is likely as cursed as the outside."

"Wait," Ellice said, her eyes lighting up. "Are we talking about treasure, or...?"

"No one knows," Mavery said before Neldren could interrupt. As she sat down again, she kept her expression flat, but Alain was close enough to notice the corner of her lips arcing into the faintest hint of a smile. "For centuries, this place has baffled wizards and historians. Nel's but one of scores of people they've paid to investigate, but no one's ever been able to find a way inside. Alain thinks the temple has ties to a Necromancer from the sixth century."

"Necromancers?" Neldren groaned. "Oh, fantastic! Then it's *definitely* cursed!"

"As I said before," Alain muttered, "it's not—"

"Come on, Nel," Ellice said, "don't tell me you've lost your sense of adventure."

"Only when it comes to that place."

"You have to admit this sounds better than sitting around and waiting for Vilk to pay us—if he ever pays us. This is the first *real* job we've had in weeks, with a *real* payment right in front of our eyes."

Neldren frowned as he muttered to himself. Ellice gazed at him with pleading eyes, a slightly pouted lip. Alain wondered if Mavery had ever used that same look; his stomach soured at the thought.

"Fine," Neldren sighed. "We'll help, but make it five hundred *each.*"

Mavery gawked at him. "A thousand potins? What do I look like, the Dragons' guildmaster? And what is *she* going to do?"

"I'm sure I'll find a way to make myself useful," Ellice said coolly.

"We're a crew," Neldren said. "You hire both of us, or neither of us."

The money she'd brought to this meeting comprised nearly her entire savings. She'd insisted on using her own funds, as recruiting Neldren was her idea. A thousand potins was an extravagant cost for field research, but Alain would pay any price if it helped him secure his wizard rank.

"Deal," he said. "Half now, half later, if that works for you."

Mavery turned to him. "*What?* No, Alain, don't—"

"It's all right." He reached beneath the table, took her hand.

"Excellent," Neldren said, gesturing for the envelope. Mavery hesitated before sliding it back across the table. He seized it and tucked it in his coat pocket, denying her the opportunity to change her mind. "So, when are we heading out?"

"As soon as possible," Alain said. "First thing in the morning, if we can manage it. To make a long story short, we need to get there and return to Leyport within a week's time."

Neldren nodded. "I'll get in touch with some of my contacts, should be easy enough to find someone who can provide us fast and cheap transport out of—"

The end of his sentence was drowned out by an argument that had erupted on the far side of the room. The shouting was largely incoherent, but Alain gathered that one man had accused another of cheating at cards. In response, the man chucked a glass at his accuser's face. His aim was an entire foot off, and the glass hit the wall in an explosion of brown liquor and sparkling shards. Alain flinched. Someone else grabbed the glass-thrower by the collar and slammed him against the table. Wood splintered with a resounding crack that made Alain nearly fall out of his chair. The bartender bellowed something at the three men, but his voice was quickly lost amid the fervor of a crowd that now craved a tavern brawl.

"We'll meet you by the train depot at dawn," Mavery said, nearly shouting over the commotion.

With their business settled, she grasped Alain's hand and pulled him away from the table. They reached the pub's back door as chairs began flying across the room.

FORTY-TWO

As Mavery stifled a yawn, she regretted suggesting they reconvene so early. As she failed to suppress a second yawn, she doubted a few more hours would have made much difference. She rarely got a full night's sleep before a job, and this one was no exception. Her mind had been too restless. By the time she'd packed and taken inventory of their supplies, the stars had begun to fade.

Alain had spent last night doing much of the same. He'd gathered every book that could be of use—a feat he'd achieved in record time, thanks to Mavery's cataloging system—and then he'd spent the rest of the night with his nose buried in those tomes. Even now, waiting on the curb outside the train depot, he held one of his research journals inches from his face. An orb of Ether bobbed overhead; the early morning light was too dim for reading. His other hand gripped his wizard's staff, which was barely keeping him upright.

"You brought the rest of the anti-Sensing potion?" he asked without lifting his eyes from the page.

"Right here," Mavery said, patting the outer pocket of her pack. A single small vial was all that remained of the last batch; they hadn't had time to secure more kutauss claws to brew another. It was enough to subdue her Senses for merely an hour, so she would have to save it for when she was desperate.

"And the anchors?"

"*Yes.*"

"And what about the res—"

She plucked the journal from his hands. "As I said when you asked me an hour ago—and an hour before that—I checked the list three times. We have everything we could possibly need."

"Sorry," he sighed. "It's been years since my last research trip, and I've never had one with such serious consequences for failure."

"Everything will be fine." She caressed his cheek, letting the pad of her finger trail along the edge of his beard, where the coarse hair met smooth skin. "But you need to stop fretting and get some rest."

"With luck, perhaps I can take a nap on the train. Speaking of which, it should be departing soon. Where is—"

Several sets of hooves clacked on the cobblestones. In unison, Mavery and Alain turned toward the noise. A stagecoach, led by a four-horse team, slowed to a stop beside the curb. The vehicle itself was larger than the city carriages, though not by much. Its sides were painted deep maroon, and it bore no transportation company's insignia. Neldren's face peered at them through the paneless window.

"This is your idea of 'fast and cheap'?" Mavery demanded. "A private stagecoach?"

"The route I've planned will put us on a direct path to Dyerland; we'll get there a half-day faster than if we took a train up to Durnatel. And, believe it or not, our driver drove a hard bargain." He extended a hand through the window, gestured to the driver. "Allow me to introduce you to Vilk's half-brother's youngest nephew, an up-and-coming businessman in his own right."

The driver was a slip of a thing, with a face bearing more freckles than facial hair. He appeared even younger than Ellice.

"Evrard Gainour, at your service," he said. He removed his pageboy cap and bowed his head, revealing a heap of mousy curls.

"That's a Dauphinian name, if I'm not mistaken," Alain said.

Evrard nodded. "We Gainours were raising horses long before my great-grandda crossed the eastern border."

"Look at that: a pair of Dauphers!" Neldren said. "If that's not fate, I don't know what to tell you."

Mavery narrowed her eyes at Evrard. "How did you acquire this coach?"

"I didn't steal it, ma'am, if that's what you're asking." His tone was polite, though his voice quavered slightly. "It's an old mail coach. I bought it at auction late last year with my own savings, spent all winter fixing it up. I'm hoping to start my own transportation service. You'll be some of my first customers."

"See? Perfectly legitimate." Neldren opened the door. "Now, are you coming, or are you going to stand there all morning?"

Mavery frowned. Traversing the countryside with an inexperienced driver at the helm wasn't the most reassuring plan, but they didn't have the luxury of time to devise a better one. She nodded to Alain, readjusted her pack, and climbed into the coach. Neldren offered a hand, but she ignored it and made use of the handholds. She took Alain's staff and satchel, then gave Alain himself a hand.

"Thank you, my love," he said softly, and Mavery's heart skipped a beat. Though he'd used that term of endearment several times between last night and this morning, she was still growing used to it.

The coach had appeared larger from the curb. With four passengers—one of whom was well north of six feet tall—and their effects, the interior was cramped. Mavery sat across from Ellice and had to angle her legs to prevent their knees from touching. Alain sat directly across from Neldren. The latter stared at the former with his arms crossed.

"Ready?" Evrard called from the driver's seat.

"Ready," Neldren said stiffly.

Evrard cracked the reins. The stagecoach pulled away from the curb and took off toward the city's southern gate.

"So, *you're* the reason Mave decided to stay in Leyport," Neldren said, peering at Alain.

Alain started. "Er, yes, I suppose I am."

"You know, I had my suspicions last night, especially when you left the pub hand in hand, but I didn't want to assume—"

"Why does it matter?" Mavery snapped. "Didn't you tell me

you'd moved on?"

"I have." His eyes flicked at Ellice, who'd been throwing him a warning look the entire time. Her pink cheeks and clenched jaw suggested she was struggling to hold her tongue. Neldren's gaze settled on Mavery again. "It matters because I thought you'd do me the courtesy of telling me I'd be partnering up with your current lover."

"Well, sorry for leaving out that detail." After parting ways in the Garden District, she'd assumed they would go about this as adults. Evidently, he still had a few bones to pick from the carcass of their former relationship.

"It's funny," Neldren said. "When I told her to 'go fuck off with the wizards,' I didn't think she'd take that *literally*."

Alain scoffed. "Were those your parting words as you left her in the infirmary with a bullet in her stomach?"

"Gods, are you really going to bring that up?"

"Yes, I *really* am."

Neldren rolled his eyes. "I already apologized!"

Mavery touched Alain's shoulder as she muttered in his ear, "As much as I appreciate it, I'd also appreciate not letting things come to blows while we're confined to this carriage for the next couple of days."

Neldren barked a laugh. "If it comes to that, you can bet on a short fight—especially if *that's* all he brought along." He pointed at Alain's staff. "Aren't those staffs supposed to have magical gems?"

"Staves," Alain mumbled.

"Come again?"

"The plural is *staves*. And this one did, until about a year ago."

At the crown of Alain's staff, branches entwined like spindly fingers that normally would have clutched an Ether-sensitive gem. He gazed at it forlornly, then looked to Mavery. He didn't need to say a word for her to know the missing gem had been one of the many things he'd sacrificed for Conor.

"So, it's just a useless stick."

"*Nel...*" Mavery groaned.

He held up his hands. "I'm only saying, with him being a

wizard and all, I'd expected him to bring along some powerful artifacts."

"Artifacts alone wouldn't help us," Alain said. "A gem would only amplify my own arcana, which I already have in abundance, rest assured."

Neldren cocked an eyebrow as he eyed Alain from head to toe, as though skeptical that someone of Alain's stature could hold an abundance of anything.

"Oh, just whip out your cocks and measure them already, why don't you?" Ellice said.

"Mother help me if I have to rely on him and his *arcana* to save my arse."

Alain set his jaw as he flashed Neldren an icy glare. "With any luck, it won't come to that."

"For fuck's sake, we're not even out of the city yet!" Ellice said, throwing up her hands. "Why don't we all attempt to tolerate one another's company *in silence*?"

"Now, there's an excellent idea," Neldren said. He shot Alain one final glare, and his expression softened as he turned his attention to Ellice.

"That, at least, we can agree on," Alain said beneath his breath. He opened his pack, pulled out one of his books, and resumed his reading. From her own pack, Mavery retrieved a book—a detective novel she'd picked up ages ago but had set aside to prioritize the spell presentation. With a sigh, she leaned her head against the window frame and began to read.

The rest of the day progressed in near silence. Alain and Mavery kept to their books while Neldren and Ellice played cards. It made for a painfully dull day of travel, but at least there were no more arguments.

Around dusk, they stopped in a thoroughfare town along the Royal Turnpike. But finding a place to rest and change horses proved easier said than done. The first inn they came across refused

to rent rooms to an unwed couple, and their rates were too exorbi-
tant to justify individual rooms. The next one turned them down
on the basis of having a Nilandoren among them. In the end, they
were forced to settle on what had to be the town's most ramshackle
inn, but it had cheap rooms and a less discriminating innkeeper.

They finished checking in as the final dregs of dinner were
being served. Alain opted to take his bowl of gristly stew and
heel of day-old bread up to his room, claiming he'd come across a
potentially useful incantation he wanted to memorize. The other
four—Neldren had invited Evrard to join them—gathered around
one of the long tables in the dining room.

As Neldren and Ellice taught the young driver the finer points
of Tribute, Mavery was reminded of a similar evening at a similar
inn. In fact, this place was like a larger version of Seringoth's Rest,
down to the watery ale and the portrait of some long-dead Archmage hanging on the wall. Like that night over two months ago,
Mavery longed to be among different company. Unlike that night,
no one protested when she rose from her chair and left the room.

FORTY-THREE

Alain was stretched out on the single bed, his back against the headboard and a thick book propped open on his chest. He read it in the warm glow of the oil lamp on the bedside table. His pounding head and aching body begged him to get some rest. Yet, he continued to read.

Earlier that afternoon, he'd read about an obfuscation ward to create a dense fog. The spell had been developed in the fourth century, so with any hope, it would be similar to the one protecting the Innominate Temple. Using Declan's scroll as a baseline, he could reverse-engineer this obfuscation ward and create his own counterspell. But that would require—

A knock at the door interrupted his thoughts. The ward he'd placed only protected him from faulty spellcasting; it did nothing to dampen the sounds coming from inside or outside his room. He wished he'd taken the time to place a soundproofing ward. The walls in this inn were nearly as thin as its mattresses, and all these interruptions were making it difficult to concentrate. A heated argument had erupted from one of the rooms down the hall. But worse still was his travel companions' uproarious laughter. The sound of Neldren's voice was especially grating on Alain's last frayed nerve.

"It's me," said Mavery's voice through the closed door. "Are you still awake?"

Well, there was at least *one* sound he didn't mind.

"Yes," he said. "Come in, it's unlocked."

The door swung open, and the air rippled as Mavery passed through the protective ward. He could only imagine this room was similar to her former accommodations at the boarding house: cramped, dusty, and with furniture that favored function over comfort. Though Mavery was likely as road weary as he was, she was nonetheless an exquisite sight. Too exquisite for this dingy room.

"Are you planning to come back downstairs?" she asked.

"And be further lambasted by your former lover who very clearly despises me? No, thank you. I can think of better ways to spend my evening." He gestured to his book. "This, for instance."

"I know he's an ass, but it's not personal. His line of work has left him with a poor opinion of wizards as a whole."

"I'll keep that in mind the next time he throws an insult in my direction." Alain turned a page. "Go on, don't let me ruin your fun."

She snorted. "Yes, I'm having a rip-roaring time with Neldren, Ellice, and their soon-to-be newest accomplice." She took a step forward, closed the door behind her. "I'd much rather spend my evening with you, assuming you don't mind the company."

He looked up from the book with a smile. "I will never turn down your company. Come here."

She locked the door and kicked off her boots before clambering over the foot of the ramshackle bed. With every movement, the wooden frame creaked, the mattress rustled. How Alain missed his bed filled with cotton and reinforced with box springs. And that was to make no mention of the plush blankets and feather pillows.

He shifted, wincing as a lump prodded his ribcage. "It's awful, isn't it?"

"A bit," she said, making a similar expression as she settled between his body and the wall. She peered at his book. "What are you reading?"

He began to explain his plan for creating a counterspell, but after a few sentences, her eyes glazed over. Her gaze lingered on a point in the vicinity of his mouth.

"I've completely lost you, haven't I?" he asked.

"I caught maybe the first half. For what it's worth, I do love watching you talk, even when I'm not following a word of it."

Her eyes met his, and a carnal gleam indicated that spellcraft was the furthest thing from her mind. Taking the hint, he put the book aside, then turned until they lay face to face. He brushed aside a lock of hair that had fallen across her eye, caressed her face as he'd done while lying together on a far superior bed.

"Thank you," he whispered.

"For what?"

"For convincing me to not make this journey alone. What I did last year was a mistake, but going it alone would have been equally foolish. You were right. I do need your help. And, loath as I am to admit it, I may even need Neldren's—"

"Shh." She placed her index finger on his lips. "No more talking about him, or spells, or even the temple. In fact..." She shifted closer, until the tips of their noses were barely touching. "I'm not much in the mood for *talking*."

He smiled. "What a coincidence. I'm not in the mood for that, either."

He drew her in for a kiss that began soft and slow. The moment his tongue slipped into her mouth, her hands began to roam. Over these past days, they'd explored each other's bodies while fully clothed and beneath bedsheets. Tonight was the first opportunity to see what they'd only imagined.

One of her hands cupped his chin while the other trailed the length of his spine, grasped his arse, and gave it a firm squeeze. He emitted a moan of surprise, then wrapped an arm around her waist and drew her closer. Their arms entangled while their fingers sought every inch of exposed skin. One of her hands meandered to the front of his shirt. She pulled the fabric free from his waistband, and he shivered as her fingers brushed his bare stomach. But when her hand slipped into his trousers, they both paused.

"Oh," Mavery said. "Seems you're not ready yet. Well, not to worry..."

She wrapped her fingers around his length as she resumed

kissing him. But her efforts proved ineffective; he remained as soft as before.

Damn it...

He squeezed his eyes shut as he focused on Mavery's touch, hoping he could manifest a great surge of arousal, that he could will every drop of blood to flow where he needed it most. But it was no use. It never was when his body was this fatigued, his mind this full. Mavery's free hand rested on his cheek, and behind his eyelids, he saw brief flashes of Vara's disappointment, Conor's frustration. He feared what he would see this time when he opened his eyes.

"I'm sorry," he said. "I can assure you, this has nothing to do with you. I find you incredibly desirable. It's—"

"Alain, it's all right."

He opened his eyes at last. Mavery's gaze was soft, and though she wore a slight frown, it seemed more out of concern than frustration, or even disappointment.

"I understand," she said. "It's been a rough couple of days. Maybe we should both turn in for the night, get some rest."

"Yes—I mean *no.* I need this. I need to..."

I need to know I'm adequate. As adequate as the man downstairs, at any rate.

She sighed. "Is this because of Neldren?"

His eyes widened. If he didn't know any better, he would think she was a Mystic. Perhaps his thoughts truly were that obvious.

"How did you...?"

She laughed softly as she stroked his cheek. Though her touch was feather-soft, it left his skin scorching. "He tends to have that effect on people. But I'll let you in on a little secret." She leaned closer, whispered, "Whatever we do together, I know it's going to be wonderful. Because it's *you* I want, not him."

Gods, did he love her. He wanted to give her what she'd already given him several times over. He didn't care if she couldn't return the favor.

He kissed her firmly, catching her lower lip between both of his. As he tried to deepen the kiss, she pulled back.

"We don't have to," she said. "Only if you want—"

"I do. And don't worry, I'm going to enjoy this as much as you will." He smiled. "Well, *almost*."

He guided her onto her back, then made short work of unbuttoning her trousers, sliding them and her drawers down her legs, tossing both to the floor. That he'd once become flustered at the sight of her bare calves seemed preposterous now. Here she lay before him, exposed from the waist down, and his only desire was to touch every inch of her.

He began by following the curve of her calf. His touch was lighter than air as it skimmed across her bad knee. But he then applied more pressure to her thigh, to fully appreciate the firm ridges of her muscles, the soft curve of her hip. She gasped as his fingers moved inward, lingering on her inner thigh. When he reached the point where her thighs joined, her eyes closed with a soft moan. That sound would have been enough to bring him close to the edge, had his heart and the rest of his body been on the same page tonight—or in the same book, for that matter.

He hadn't bedded a woman in years, but it didn't take long for old instincts to return. He started with slow, methodical strokes. Each blissful sigh that escaped her lips urged him to go a bit faster. When he slipped a fingertip inside her, her breath hitched.

"*Yes*, just like that," she breathed. "I want you inside me."

He leaned down to kiss her as he obliged, starting with a single finger. When he added a second, she whimpered while clutching the bedsheets.

"Should I place a soundproofing ward?" he whispered, his lips close enough to graze hers.

"No," she whispered back. "Don't stop."

He nodded, then continued his intimate caress. When the pad of his thumb brushed the most sensitive part of her, she arched her back and released another moan; this time, it echoed through the room. Her hand then traveled downward to meet his. At first, he worried he'd touched her incorrectly. But as they locked eyes, he realized she wanted them to work in tandem: her fingers drew small circles while his continued to glide in and out of her.

They quickened their pace together, sharing the same labored breaths. She writhed beneath him, rolling her hips to allow him to touch her more deeply. He did so without hesitation, relishing how her slick warmth enveloped his fingers, how she trembled around him as she reached her peak. When she began to cry out again, he leaned down and smothered her orgasm with a kiss. Her voice resonated through his body as his pace slowed, helping her ride out the wave. Only then did he ease out of her.

She lay beside him, cheeks flushed and chest heaving as she recovered from her euphoria. All of this had been *his* doing, he realized with a touch of pride—and relief.

He raised his hand, gazed at his fingers. On impulse, he slipped one into his mouth. Her taste—sharp but with an undercurrent of sweetness—was so undoubtedly *her*, his eyes closed as a moan sounded from the back of his throat.

"All this time, I'd been wanting to taste you," he said, his voice low and rough. "Next time, I'm going to *savor* you."

He opened his eyes to find her staring at him, mouth agape. A chill ran through him. Had he come on too strongly just now? Of course, not every woman found pleasure in that sort of thing. Perhaps he'd presumed too much.

But then she grasped him by the shirt and pulled him down into a kiss that was all heat and ferocity. Her lips and tongue were clumsy, her fingers pulled at his hair. He kissed her back, though he struggled to keep apace.

No, if anything, he hadn't come on strongly enough.

When she palmed the front of his trousers, she once again found only slackened fabric. She broke the kiss and took a desperate gulp of air.

"Even after all that," she gasped, "still nothing?"

He sighed. "I'm afraid so. But rest assured, I *thoroughly* enjoyed watching you come undone." He placed a soft kiss to her forehead. "The next time we share a bed, I promise we'll do much more than this."

"The next time we share a bed, it had better be large enough for two." She winced as she readjusted her position. "And more comfortable."

"Yes, that will be nonnegotiable," he said with a laugh, then sealed that promise with another kiss.

FORTY-FOUR

If Neldren, Ellice, and Evrard had overheard any noise from Alain's room the night before, they made no mention of it the following morning. The second day of travel continued how the previous one left off, the only difference being that Neldren's fiery temper had cooled to icy indifference. He remained silent until around midday, when he consulted his map and instructed Evrard to exit the Royal Turnpike and take a back road.

"Are you sure about this?" Mavery asked as they entered a dense forest.

"You want to get to the temple and back in under a week, right?" Neldren said. "This is faster than continuing down the Turnpike. It's the same route I took last time."

She gazed out the window, feeling no more reassured. If not for the dappled sunlight on the forest floor, she would have thought night had already fallen. The Turnpike had been wide enough to accommodate traffic in both directions. Here, the way was so narrow, there was barely enough room for the horses to trot two abreast. Instead of well-packed dirt, most of the ground was covered in dead leaves and loose silt. And instead of following a maintained path, Evrard had to guide the horses around roots and rivulets.

About a mile in, they encountered a felled tree branch blocking the path. With Ellice's mending magic and Neldren's muscle, they rolled the branch off the path within seconds. Ellice sauntered back to the coach and wore a smirk as she reclaimed her seat.

"I told you I'd make myself useful," she said, then leaned out the window. "Are you coming, Nel?"

"Hold on," he replied. "While we're stopped, I might as well take a piss."

Mercifully, he chose to relieve himself behind a tree that wasn't within Mavery's peripheral vision—or within earshot of the stagecoach. A moment later, he returned at a jog while buttoning up his trousers.

"Shit," he said. "We're about to have company. Highwaymen, from the looks of it, and they're coming in fast."

"*Highwaymen!?*" Evrard cried. There was no window between the coach's interior and the driver's seat, so Mavery could only hear his voice. "I've heard stories of them, and not good ones. Oh, gods..."

"Damn it, Nel," Mavery groaned. "I knew this forest was a bad idea."

"Relax, both of you." Neldren closed the carriage door as he walked past, then hoisted himself onto the driver's seat. "You especially, boy. Keep a calm head and let me take the lead. Now, do we have somewhere to stash our valuables?"

"The...the..." Evrard gulped. "The bench closest to us, there's a compartment beneath it."

Ellice got on her hands and knees, then pushed on a wooden panel that appeared only decorative. "Found it," she said. The panel moved aside, revealing a compartment barely large enough to fit all of their packs. Once those were secured, she popped the panel back into place.

"Good," Neldren said. "And since even the wizard isn't dressed like a dandy—"

Alain scoffed.

"—let's hope they'll assume we don't have anything worth stealing. But, seeing as you're hauling four passengers, I reckon they'll try to swindle you into paying an outrageous toll. Unless you've got a couple of human-sized compartments hidden back there, I'm afraid it's too late for the others to run off and hide."

Alain's eyes widened.

"I have an idea," he said. He grasped Mavery's hand, closed his eyes, and began to whisper something she couldn't quite catch. From the chill trickling up her spine, she had her suspicions. Ellice cocked an eyebrow at him.

"Look, I understand wanting to say your prayers," she said, "but I doubt the gods are going to be much help."

Mavery leaned close enough to catch bits of the incantation Alain was reciting. It was intimately familiar. She turned to Ellice.

"Take my hand."

"What?"

"He's not praying, he's casting a spell that's going to turn us invisible, more or less."

" 'More or less'?" Neldren called from out front.

"Trust me on this."

She extended her hand to Ellice, who skeptically raised a brow before taking it. As the sound of galloping horses drew closer, Alain, Mavery, and Ellice's bodies turned incorporeal and glowed with Ethereal light—just as Mavery's had on that sunny afternoon outside Steelforge Towers. She could only hope Alain had enough arcana to keep them veiled until the highwaymen finished their business.

"Unbelievable," Ellice gasped. Her voice was a distant echo. "Can they hear us?"

"No," Alain said, "but I've modified the spell so that we can still hear them."

"Should you need an anchor, I'm right here." Mavery intended to squeeze his hand, but as their bodies were completely weightless, she felt nothing. She looked to Ellice again. "Don't move."

"Wasn't planning on it," she muttered.

Evrard continued to breathe shallow, rapid breaths, despite Neldren's mutterings about the importance of remaining calm. Mavery turned her gaze to the window, where a trio of highway-men came into view.

Their leader, riding a bay horse, was a Nilandoren man with skin the color of rain-slickened shale. It was impossible to place his exact age, but his salt-and-pepper beard and thinning hair suggested he was older than Neldren. Flanking him on a pair of roan horses were a man and a woman who had to be siblings, if not twins; they shared the same shade of chestnut hair and sharp features. The woman, like their leader, wore a shoulder holster bearing a pistol. The man had a longbow slung over his back.

"Afternoon, *deydan*," Neldren said.

"We're not in the Motherland, *stranger*," the leader said sharply. He stopped his horse beside the driver's seat. "We're in *my* woods, and I've never seen either of you before. What's your business here?"

"Just passing through."

"With an empty coach?"

"We're—"

"I'd like to hear it from your partner." He narrowed his eyes at Evrard. "Tell me, boy, what are you doing here?"

"We're...we're passing through, just like he said," Evrard stammered. "We have a customer to pick up in, er...in Archstone."

"Do you, now?" The leader leaned forward, resting his hands on the pommel of his saddle. "You see, ever since I became the toll collector of these woods, I've made it my business to know all the stagecoach drivers in this corner of the province. So, explain to me why, instead of hiring a local, your 'customer' would hire a pair of strangers who're almost a half-day's journey away."

Beside Mavery, Alain's body reappeared for a split second before turning incorporeal again. Her breath hitched, but none of the highwaymen so much as glanced inside the coach; they were focused solely on Evrard.

Alain's transparent eyes squeezed shut, and his brow furrowed. The spell had run its course, and he was now prolonging it with his arcana. Mavery recalled the toll this had once taken on his body, though he'd been sleep-deprived after a long day of spell practice.

"I received the job in the mail, I didn't question it. Er...*sir*," Evrard said. Though his voice trembled, he was doing better than Mavery had expected. "How much is the toll? Whatever it is, we'll pay it and be on our way."

The highwayman chuckled. "Much as I appreciate your eagerness to cooperate, I can't let you go that easily. There's been a lot of smugglers through my woods as of late, so we'll need to search your coach." He flashed Evrard a wide smile; a patch of sunlight illuminated a gold-capped canine. "A routine inspection, is all."

The woman brought her horse closer to the carriage. She peered through the window, and her gaze swept past the three Ether-veiled figures without a second glance. Then, her eyes widened.

"Looks like they've got a wizard's staff in here," she said.

Alain hissed through clenched teeth. His staff wouldn't fit in the secret compartment, so he'd left it lying on the floor. Evidently, the coach's dim interior was no match for the highwaywoman's keen eye.

"That old thing?" Neldren said. "It's just my walking stick."

"Then you won't mind if Kella takes a look," the leader said.

"By all means," Neldren replied flatly.

The woman, Kella, slung herself off her horse. She was tall, muscular, with the weathered look of someone who spent most of their life in the sun. She opened the door and reached for the staff. Her fingers came within inches of Ellice's foot.

She picked up the staff, sniffed it deeply as if she were sampling an oversized cigar. Then, she opened her mouth and licked it, leaving a six-inch trail of saliva on the wood. Alain uttered a sound of abject disgust.

"Genuine ebonwood. Definitely a wizard's staff," she said, then peered at the crown. "Hold on, it's missing one of those magic gems."

"Gem or no gem, where did someone like you find a wizard's staff?" the leader demanded. "If you're a wizard, then I'm the Duchess of Dyerland."

"Dunno what to tell you, mate, other than you're making a big stink over a walking stick," Neldren said with an indifferent shrug in his tone.

"Don't bullshit me. Where did you stash the gem, and what other stolen goods are you hiding in there?"

"As my partner told you, we're just passing through."

The leader's eyes darkened. "Search the coach. Tear the godsdamned thing apart if you have to."

Kella tossed Alain's staff back inside the coach and grabbed the handhold next to the door. As she began to pull herself up, she vanished—along with everything else. The world plunged into darkness as the smell of ash permeated the air.

"*Go! Now!*" Neldren shouted.

Cloaked in Ether and immersed within Neldren's summoned shadows, Mavery couldn't see or feel a thing around her. Reins cracked, wheels rattled. Kella yelped, followed by a heavy thud in the dirt.

"Bast, get the mage!" the leader yelled from somewhere in the distance.

On all sides, horses panted, hooves thundered against the dirt path. To Mavery's right, something zipped through the air, followed by a dull *thunk*.

"Fuck!" Neldren cried. "Bastard shot me!"

"*Nel!*" Ellice screamed, but her voice was trapped in the veil of Ether.

All at once, the shadows dissipated. Mavery blinked as her eyes readjusted to the light. The carriage was moving at a breakneck speed, though the male twin—Bast, the leader had called him—had managed to keep apace with it. Outside the right-hand window, he lowered his bow as his horse slowed to a canter.

"The shadows!" Evrard said. "They're gone!"

"Godsdamned kutauss poison," Neldren groaned. "Can't use my magic. Don't look at *me*! Focus on the road and keep driving."

Alain extended his left hand. It became corporeal again, and Mavery worried that his arcana was also failing. But then he placed his palm flat against the nearby wall and began to chant Etherean beneath his breath. Once again, his hand turned invisible—and so did the section of wall beneath his skin. Like a slate being wiped clean, the carriage vanished, beginning with the corner closest to Alain and spreading toward the front.

Alain commenced a new string of syllables with a slightly altered rhythm. The driver's seat vanished, though it somehow still supported Neldren and Evrard. They appeared to hover six feet above the ground.

"What the…" Neldren said, peering downward. He clutched his right arm, which had the shaft of an arrow sticking out of it. Blood dripped between his fingers, spattered the dirt directly below him. He fumbled with something at his hip, then raised his injured arm with a glint of silver. He tried aiming his pistol at the approaching highwaymen, only to lower his arm again with a hiss of pain.

Alain furrowed his brow. His gentle whispering had turned to strained muttering. Yet, the veil seemed unable to reach Neldren and Evrard.

"Ellice, grab Nel," Mavery said. "His coat, anything you can."

Still clutching Mavery's hand, Ellice stretched her free arm upward. Just as Alain's had done a moment ago, her hand reappeared long enough to grab the hem of Neldren's coat. It wasn't skin-on-skin contact, but it was enough. The veil overtook him, too.

A shot rang out. The coach had outrun the highwaymen, so they'd resorted to opening fire.

"Nel, grab Evrard and don't let go!" Mavery cried.

Neldren groaned as he released his injured arm and grasped Evrard's shoulder.

Another gunshot ripped through the forest.

A bullet passed through where the Evrard's chest had been corporeal not even a heartbeat earlier.

Mavery looked to Alain again. He shuddered as he focused on extending the veil to the reins, then each of the four horses. But not once did she feel a pull against her arcana. He was channeling everything he had into this single spell.

"What in the ever-loving fuck?" the leader cried. "They're gone!"

Mavery looked down. Though Alain's spell hadn't healed Neldren's wound, his blood had turned incorporeal and no longer left a trail. The coach's wheels and the horses' hooves had also stopped leaving tracks.

"Stop the carriage," she said.

"Are you out of your godsdamned mind?" Neldren barked. "They'll close in on us!"

"Again, just trust me."

Whether he actually did trust her, or he was simply following the first order he was given, Evrard pulled the reins. The stagecoach gradually rolled to a stop.

As Mavery had hoped, the highwaymen didn't notice. They continued onward for a dozen or so yards before the two men stopped. Kella pressed on, charged past them at a full gallop. But when she realized she was the only one still giving chase, she yanked her horse to a halt.

"Come on!" she called to the other two. "They must be hiding in the shadows."

"But I shot the shadow mage," Bast called back.

"They must've had another one hiding in the carriage. Check the shadows again."

"I did! I don't know what made them disappear, but it ain't shadow magic."

"Then they must've kept going. If we hurry, maybe we can catch up and—"

"And *what*?" the Nilandoren snapped. "For all we know, they're out of the woods—and out of our jurisdiction."

"But—"

"If you want to try collecting a toll in Corryn territory, be my guest," the Nilandoren said. "But it'll be your funeral."

"It ain't worth it, Kel," Bast said. "They're long gone."

They both turned their horses around and trotted down the trail.

"Can't believe I wasted an arrow on those bastards," Bast grumbled.

Kella continued to linger in the center of the road. She gazed at the path ahead while her horse grunted indignantly. Finally, with a growl, she turned and followed the others. She led her horse through the center of the carriage, passing directly through Mavery's incorporeal body.

Alain's breathing was labored, his body trembled as he held the veil in place. Much too slowly, the hoofbeats and disgruntled voices faded.

"They're gone," Neldren announced at long last.

"Ellice, let go," Alain rasped.

She released Neldren's coat. All at once, everything—from the vehicle to the horses—turned solid again. Had Ellice not moved her hand, it would have become fused within the coach's inner wall. The horses squealed at the sudden change, and the coach jostled as its wheels settled into the dirt. Out front, Neldren roared incredulous laughter while Evrard began to sob. Ellice opened the door, flung herself out of the coach, and swung up onto the driver's seat.

Alain swayed on the spot, and Mavery realized their hands were still joined. While his lay limply in hers, she'd been clutching his with a painful, white-knuckled grip. She released him, shook out her aching hand. He peered at her through half-closed eyes as he chuckled.

"And Elder Lythandus once described that spell as 'wholly impractical.' "

He then pitched forward and collapsed on the floor.

FORTY-FIVE

Alain ran through a dense forest, stumbling over roots hidden in the underbrush. He pushed aside a branch, revealing a grove with what appeared to be a stone mausoleum at its center. All around were ominous gray clouds, as if he were in the eye of a thunderhead.

He strode forward. But he made it not even three paces when his foot caught on something solid. His stomach lurched, and the wind was knocked from his lungs as he collided with the ground. He picked himself up, brushed the dirt from his trousers, then turned to see what had made him fall.

A body, long dead, lay facedown in the grass. He knew he ought to leave it alone. The mess of auburn hair was enough to tell him the corpse's identity, but his muscles were already moving of their own accord. He crouched down, rolled the corpse over.

The skin was tinged with gray, the mismatched eyes lifeless. But the perfect, full mouth contorted as Conor's corpse spoke to him, just as it had countless times before, in dreams like this one.

"You didn't even have the gall to come to my funeral. Shameful."

Alain released the corpse and bolted upward.

Conor propped himself up on his elbows, shook his head. "I always knew you were spineless."

"You're wrong."

"Am I?"

Conor rose to his feet. Alain peered up at the statuesque figure, forced himself to once again confront the achingly beautiful face that had haunted his dreams over the past year. Because Conor was beautiful, even in death. Even with cruelty behind his eyes and hollowness in his expression.

"But I knew so much about you," Conor said. "I knew about your mother's wealth, and how you were so eager to share it. After all, you were one of the few at the University who actually paid their assistants."

"Not this again," Alain groaned as his hands formed fists.

"I knew all the gossip, too. How you'd always been so dedicated to your work, it had cost you colleagues, friends, even a betrothal."

"Stop it!"

"You would be the last person on Perrun to admit it, but beneath that stoic façade, you were desperate for a friendly word, a lover's—"

"SHUT UP!"

Alain lunged forward, reached up, seized Conor by the throat. His skin was as cold and unrelenting as stone.

"I never wanted you to die," he said through clenched teeth. "Your death was an accident. It was not my fault."

"Is that what Mavery told—"

"Keep her name out of your mouth!" Alain's knuckles paled as he tightened his grip, yet he left no indentation on Conor's throat. "You have no right to speak her name."

"That may be, but you know deep down she'll never know you as I did. She'll never love you as I did."

" 'Love'?" Alain spat. "You never loved me. You only saw me as someone you could exploit."

Conor opened his mouth. But this time, when Alain clenched his fist, the apparition choked on its words.

"You've said enough, and I'm no longer listening."

A hairline fracture formed beneath Alain's hand. It snaked up Conor's throat, erupted into a web of fissures across his face. Conor's entire body crumbled, leaving Alain with only a fistful of dust. He unfurled his fingers and let the breeze carry away the remains. With Conor gone at long last, he turned toward the temple again.

But there was no temple, no forest. Only a dark, endless void.

"Oh, darling, you can't get rid of me that easily."

Though he couldn't see Conor, his voice was everywhere—ringing inside his head and surrounding him on all sides. Alain began to run, but something cold and unyielding grabbed him around the middle. He couldn't move. His feet sank into the loam. The taste of decay filled his mouth as he was pulled down, down, down...

He awoke drenched in sweat, his heart hammering in his throat. He eyelids fluttered as he regained his bearings. The double bed he lay upon comprised the majority of the unfamiliar room. A light breeze drifted through the open window, fluttering the patchwork curtain and filling the room with the scent of fresh pine. Somewhere nearby, a clock ticked softly.

He'd been dreaming. Yet, there was still decay on his tongue, a weight against his body.

Mavery was asleep beside him, atop the quilt and fully clothed. Her arm was wrapped around his, and she clutched a damp rag in her hand. Beside her was a stack of papers bound together with thread—her Compendium of Knowledge, she'd called it. It was open on a page taken from a Soudremancy textbook: an overview of arcana deficiency-induced comas. As Alain reached for it, she stirred. Bleary-eyed, she raised the rag to her mouth to cover a yawn, then gasped.

"You're awake!" She threw the rag aside, then threw both of her arms over his torso. "Gods, you had me so worried."

He put the Compendium aside and returned her embrace, though his arms felt as though they were made of lead. His entire body felt that way, in fact—save for his mouth, which was drier than a desert's worth of sand.

"How long was I unconscious?" he rasped.

She peered at a clock on the bedside table. "About thirty-two hours."

He couldn't remember the last time a single spell had left him incapacitated for that long. Luckily, only a little more than a day had passed. They could still investigate the temple, albeit on a tighter schedule than he would have liked.

He raised his left hand to summon a protective ward. A faint wrinkle in the air indicated that he was successful, but even this most elementary of spells left an acute ache deep within his marrow, much like walking on a broken bone that hadn't fully healed.

Mavery grabbed his hand and forced it downward, dismissing his ward. Of course, she'd very clearly seen what he'd done.

"No magic," she said. "At least, not until you've made a full recovery. Don't over-exert yourself."

He sank into his pillow with a sigh. He considered telling her that she didn't have to play healer. Despite what her Soudremancy texts may claim, he'd been through this enough times to know that being able to perform *any* magic meant he was nearly fully recovered. But, if he was being honest, he didn't mind being fussed over—and especially not if she was the one doing the fussing.

"All right," he said. "No magic."

"Can I get you anything?"

He attempted to wet his lips, but his tongue was too parched to accomplish even that. Without his needing to ask, Mavery rolled off the bed and poured him a glass of water from the pitcher on the bedside table. Alain shifted to a seated position, then gulped it down as if it were the most wonderful thing he'd ever tasted. He handed Mavery his empty glass, which she promptly refilled.

"What happened after I passed out? Is everyone else all right?"

She nodded. "More or less. Ellice had to drive the carriage for a bit. Evrard was so shaken up over the ordeal, he cried for nearly an hour, poor thing. Last I saw him, he was in the taproom downstairs, a few pints deep and reconsidering his entire stagecoach idea.

"After I made sure you weren't injured, I healed Neldren's arrow wound, though I couldn't do anything about the kutauss claw poison. We got him to a healer as soon as we arrived here last night."

"And 'here' is...?"

"Archstone, a village a few miles west of the temple. Evrard's brother, Benard, runs this inn. He was so grateful that we helped Evrard, he gave all of us rooms free of charge."

Alain winced. "That's too gen—"

"I know. I offered him money, but he refused." Mavery sat on the edge of the bed and smiled warmly as she brushed a sweat-soaked clump of hair from his forehead. He blinked slowly at her touch. "You were *incredible* yesterday. I still can't wrap my head around how you pulled off that spell."

He chuckled. "Neither can I, truth be told, and it will likely take weeks before I can repeat it—assuming I even remember how. I improvised most of those modifications. I knew if I could extend the spell to another person, it stood to reason that I could extend it to multiple people. The odds of pulling it off in a moving vehicle seemed nigh on impossible, but..." His face grew warm, and he tried to hide it by taking another long drink of water.

"But what?" Mavery asked.

He looked up with a sheepish smile. "You were with me."

"But you didn't draw from any of my arcana."

He shook his head. "I didn't need it. Your presence is all the assurance I need that there's no such thing as impossible odds."

She smiled broadly as she cupped his face, then pressed a soft kiss to his mouth. But it was exceptionally brief. She pulled away with a grimace.

"No offense, love, but your breath is..."

"Like death?"

"You said it, not me."

He laughed. "Yes, lying comatose will do that to a person."

After a hot bath, a beard trim, and a mouthful of tooth powder, Alain was ready to rejoin the living. But his legs were still weak. He slowly descended the stairs, leaning on both Mavery and his staff for support. The latter, she assured him, had been cleaned thoroughly.

This establishment's taproom was boundlessly more inviting than the Salty Surling, or even the Lettered Gentleman. The scent of fresh-cut wood filled the air; the pub tables and spindly stools, untouched by age or heavy use, seemed to be the source. The floors were polished and unmarred. Evrard tended a bar stocked with gleaming bottles. He spotted Alain and gave an enthusiastic wave.

Through the windows, a red-orange sunset streaked the sky. Dinner service was well underway, and the local villagers filled the room with laughter and lively conversation. Along the far wall, a familiar face looked in Alain and Mavery's direction. Neldren rose from the table as they approached.

"At last, our hero returns!" he cried, arms outstretched.

Alain bristled as he expected Neldren to follow that up with a sarcastic remark about wizards needing their beauty rest, or something along those lines. Rather, Neldren strode forward, clasped a hand on Alain's shoulder, and pulled him into a hug. Alain was so shocked, he clung to his staff to avoid tumbling to the floor. Neldren gave him a few firm pats on the back before releasing them, then held out a hand.

"A thousand thanks for yesterday," he said. "Turns out, I was wrong. At least *one* wizard is capable of saving a hide that isn't his own."

Alain eyed his hand cautiously, expecting this newfound cordiality to be a ruse. Mavery stepped between them.

"Believe it or not, he's been singing your praises ever since I took that arrow out of his arm."

"Only because you were too busy to do it yourself," Neldren said. Alain flinched as Neldren's elbow nudged his ribs. "Did she mention how she barely left your side since we arrived in town? We had to force her downstairs this morning to eat something."

At that, Alain's stomach grumbled. His only sustenance since leaving the last village had been the spoonfuls of broth Mavery had managed to slip down his throat. For the first time in ages, he had an appetite—and it was *ravenous*.

"Give him some room," Mavery said, taking Alain's arm and guiding him to an empty table. "And a plate, while you're at it."

Tonight's offering was chicken paired with lumpy gravy, undercooked dumplings, and carrots that had been boiled within an inch of their lives. The innkeeper, Benard, provided a complimentary bottle of wine that could have been mistaken for cooking sherry. But, for once, Alain couldn't care less about quality. He devoured an entire plate of food, then asked for another, all the while being a terrible conversation partner. But Mavery seemed amused as she ate her own beige dinner. He was halfway through his second plate when Neldren and Ellice approached their table.

"So, are we still heading to the temple?" Neldren asked.

Mavery frowned at him. "Can we talk about this later? He's been awake all of two hours."

"It's fine," Alain said, placing his hand over hers. "We ought to plan our next steps, seeing as my recovery put us behind schedule."

"No, mate, my 'shortcut' put us behind schedule," Neldren said. "If we'd continued down the Royal Turnpike, we would've made it to Archstone only a few hours ago."

"I can't believe you, of all people, failed to account for high-waymen," Ellice said, rolling her eyes.

"Last time I passed through this province, those woods were Corryn territory. How was I supposed to know there'd been a change in—"

"Enough!" Mavery groaned. "Regardless, the fact of the matter is, the temple is a three-mile hike from here, and Alain is in no shape for that."

"Not at this precise moment, but I'll be much better come morning."

She turned to him with a frown. "You want to go *tomorrow*?"

"What choice do I have? Best-case scenario: we complete the field experiment tomorrow, then we have another two-day journey back to Leyport. Not accounting for further delays, we'll be arriving home the night before the presentation, with scarcely a moment to spare."

She sighed. "If you're sure."

"I am." He squeezed her hand. "We'll leave in the morning. The earlier, the better."

"Excellent," Neldren said. "Let's meet here at first light."

"First light?" Ellice grumbled. "Oh, for fuck's sake..."

"Best make it an early night. Be mindful to avoid too much drink and *strenuous* activities."

He threw Mavery an exaggerated wink. In reply, she narrowed

her eyes and flicked her nose at him, which prompted one of his barking laughs. He slung his arm around Ellice's shoulders, and the two of them proceeded upstairs.

Alain blinked. "Wait. Are they...?"

"Who knows," Mavery said, raising her glass. "But he *would* be the type to replace me with a younger model. Bastard..."

Their hands remained joined as they drank their terrible wine. There was no need for conversation when her thumb brushing his knuckles spoke volumes. The only downside of their silence was that there was nothing to distract him from his thoughts, which included scattered echoes from his dream.

She'll never know you as I did.

Alain took another sip of wine as he tried to silence that one. Though, he had to admit, there was some truth to it. As much as he and Mavery had shared with each other over these past months, he was acutely aware of the things they *hadn't* yet shared.

He watched her over the rim of his glass. He didn't believe in luck or fate, but for this clever, caring, all-around *brilliant* woman to enter his life, and for her to love him as he loved her... Well, that was almost enough to make him a believer.

"What is it?" she asked.

A heady warmth flowed through him, and it had nothing to do with the wine. He lowered his glass with a smile.

"You know, my arcana isn't the only thing that's been restored."

FORTY-SIX

T hey'd hardly closed the door when they were on each other, kissing with all the finesse of inexperienced adolescents. The darkness, paired with the cheap wine, made their movements clumsy. They fumbled about, kicking off shoes, loosening belts, bumping into furniture as they managed to maintain their connection. As Alain's tongue slipped against hers, Mavery reached behind her back, searching for the bedside lamp. A quick infusion of her arcana cast the room in soft golden light.

She sighed as Alain's lips skirted across her jaw, down her throat, until the collar of her blouse prevented him from going any lower. He pulled at the top button, then paused. Mavery's eyes fluttered open, meeting a look of desire mixed with hesitation.

"Are you sure?" she asked. "If you still need to rest, I understand. We can—"

"I want this—I want *you*—more than anything." He bowed his head. "I'm only thinking of how it's been a long time, and my last was...memorable, but for all the wrong reasons."

She tilted up his chin. "Then why don't you lead the way?"

He nodded. "So long as you're also sure."

She smiled. "Of course."

He smiled back, then held up a finger. "There's one last thing I need to attend to."

"And what's that?"

He turned to the nearby wall. A verse of Etherean, paired with a rush of magic that cooled her flushed skin, answered her question. The walls and ceiling became veiled with violet auras—a soundproofing ward. Though Alain voiced no discomfort, he winced as he turned to her again.

"There," he said. "Complete privacy."

She sighed. "I thought you agreed to not cast any spells tonight. I could've done that."

"I know, but I wanted you to save your voice."

She raised an eyebrow at him. "Are you expecting me to wake the entire inn again?"

He cupped her chin, then kissed her deeply. When he pulled back, his smoldering look made her shiver with excitement.

"No, my love." He spoke with the low, rough voice he'd used the other night. "With what I have planned, you would wake the entire *village*."

She grinned as fiery desire surged through her body, and then his lips were on hers again. He unbuttoned her blouse, slipped the fabric from her shoulders, down her arms. As she worked on his shirt, her mind briefly returned to the moments before she'd revived him. Her fingers were as frantic as they'd been that night, but now only desire guided her movements. She removed his shirt, then pulled down his trousers. Their discarded garments pooled at their feet, save for her brassière, which she tossed aside after unhooking it.

They took a moment to gaze at the parts of each other that had remained hidden before now. His body was slender, more bone than muscle. Her skin was not as taut, her breasts not as pert, as they'd once been. But when their eyes met again, the look behind his told her that he'd found not a single flaw. Likewise, his body was one she was eager to experience.

In the dim light, his scars were barely visible, but their locations had long become ingrained in her memory. Her fingertips traced the one down the center of his torso, and he sighed as she placed a tender kiss to the one above his heart. A token of appreciation for the warmth of his skin, his quickening pulse.

His sigh deepened as she left a trail of light kisses along his collarbone, then up the side of his neck, until their lips reconvened at last. His erection nudged her hip. As she'd done before, she wrapped her fingers around his cock, rubbed her thumb against his tip. His soft moan gave rise to her own pleasure, now pooling between her thighs. But before she could make a second pass down his length, he placed his hand over hers, stilling her.

"Should you continue like that, I'm afraid I won't last long at all." He leaned closer, pressed his mouth to hers. "And I want *you* to come undone first."

She smiled against his lips, and he guided her onto the bed, where she nestled herself against the pillows. Before joining her, he paused to take in her nude figure at this new angle. His eyes roved over her body from head to toe.

"You're beautiful," he said.

"So are you." She extended a hand. "Now, get over here."

He didn't hesitate to take her hand and crawl on top of her. He lowered his body until it was merely inches above hers. Even that small gap was enough to render hers cold, yearning for his skin to slip against hers again.

She shuddered as his warm mouth caressed the crook of her neck, his hair tickled her collarbone. Deep beneath her wave of desire, she recognized the too-familiar sensation of arcana rearing its head. This time, it was in the form of electric chaos.

Gods, no. Not now...

Mavery needed to focus her thoughts, control her arcana before it rose to the surface. Better yet, tell Alain to wait until it was completely spent. But then his lips traveled down the valley between her breasts, and those thoughts faded to the back of her mind. He took one of her nipples in his mouth, teased it with his tongue, and she could no longer remember what she'd been concerned about in the first place.

He moved lower, leaving a trail of light kisses on her stomach, her navel, her hip. His hands grasped her thighs, and she sighed with delight as she watched his face vanish between them. He continued where the trail left off, placing a kiss to her inner left thigh, then her right. At a torturously slow pace, each kiss descended a bit lower than the last, progressing a bit closer to the joining of her thighs.

And then—*finally*—his lips brushed against her clit, and she threw her head back with a moan. Her arcana roiled as his tongue encircled her, parted her, thrust inside her. She shuddered, then focused on her breath, trying to calm the electricity coursing through her veins. Yet, how could she focus on anything but his tongue when it was nothing short of *bliss*? His languid strokes, followed by vigorous circles, were warm and slick against her already warm and slick skin. She envisioned him reciting an elaborate incantation composed specifically for her, to transmutate her into a breathless, unraveling mess.

He stopped and pulled back slightly. Though she knew he likely needed a brief respite, his absence was nonetheless agonizing.

"Should I continue?" His breath warmed her sensitive skin, causing her entire body to quaver.

"Gods, yes," she sighed.

Her voice reverberated through the room when his tongue reunited with her clit. She was thankful he'd taken that moment to place the soundproofing ward.

She reached down, entwined her fingers in his hair. A gentle tug made him groan, the vibration of his lips made her writhe against his mouth. She pushed her hips forward, and each stroke of his tongue became hotter, more forceful than the one before it.

And then, there it was again. As another flick of his tongue brought her to the edge of her climax, arcana crackled beneath her skin. She looked to the ceiling, focused on the violet tendrils dancing across it as she tried to calm the oncoming surge. But arcana and pleasure had become one and the same; she could no longer differentiate the two. Her toes curled, her back arched.

Wait...!

She tried to shout a warning, but all she could manage was a drawn-out moan as her orgasm, alongside a swell of electric energy, rippled through her.

Alain yelped, and Mavery bolted upright. She grasped him by the arm a split-second before he pitched backward off the bed.

Mercifully, her arcana had subsided as quickly as it had broken free, and she avoided shocking him a second time.

Both of them sat back on their heels, facing each other, as their hearts pounded and chests heaved in unison. Their eyes met, and they exchanged breathless laughter.

"Are you all right?" she asked.

"I'm fine," he said as he rubbed his lips. "I can only imagine that's what kissing a lightning rod during a thunderstorm would feel like."

Though she was relieved she hadn't harmed him, her heart continued to hammer against her ribcage. Her stomach clenched with the guilt from easily losing control again.

"Gods, I'm so sorry. I can't remember the last time I had a magic surge during sex."

"Well!" he chuckled. "If I was responsible for *all that*, I ought to take it as a compliment."

"You should." She reached up to brush a lock of hair from his eyes. They closed as her fingertips lingered against his temple. "Once again, you prove to be incredible."

"I'm glad you think so. I rather enjoyed that." He opened his eyes again. "For clarity's sake, I meant the amorous congress between your thighs, not the less-than-amorous brush with electrocution."

She laughed.

"Your arcana, it's...?"

"Lying dormant. We can keep going if you're—"

Before she could even complete the suggestion, he cupped her face between his palms and pulled her into a deep, intense kiss. Her taste lingered on his tongue, her scent on his skin.

Her hand wandered downward. She was surprised to find that he was still hard, and she wondered if the shock had actually *added* to his arousal. He moaned into her mouth as she resumed stroking him. A moment later, he broke the kiss. His brow furrowed as he seemed to struggle with holding himself together.

"Should I savor *you* now?" she asked.

He shook his head. "Not this time. Let's move to the 'grand finale,' so to speak."

Together, they moved back to the center of the bed. As before, he bestrode her as she nestled her head against the pillows. He shifted his hips and pressed his tip to her entrance, but his aim was slightly off-center. He muttered something that she gathered was frustration with being a bit out of practice.

"Let me," she whispered, then slipped her hand between their bodies.

He emitted another deep groan as she wrapped her fingers around him. They sighed in unison as she guided him inside her, their bodies becoming the most connected they'd ever been.

He leaned down to kiss her cheek, her jaw, her neck. Her eyes fluttered shut at the softness of his lips, his hair brushing her face, both now heightened with the sensation of being completely filled by him. A low whine escaped the back of her throat as he began to move, his slow friction rekindling her arousal. She opened her eyes and pushed back his hair, uncovering a gaze that was completely drinking her in.

Her hand traveled to the nape of his neck, and she pulled him down into another kiss. She teased his tongue, a mirror of the movements he made easing in and out of her. His pace was slow, gentle, cautious. Perhaps he wanted to savor this for as long as possible, or perhaps he was uncertain of how far he could push himself tonight.

She broke the kiss and leaned back. From the strained look on his face, she could tell he hadn't been exaggerating before. It wouldn't be long before he reached his own release.

Together, they found a new rhythm. She met each of his thrusts with a tilt of her hips. He groaned as her fingers raked down his back. She gasped as she arched her own back, allowing herself to take him more deeply. The longer they continued, the more erratic his breathing became.

He came undone with a final thrust, a guttural moan against the side of her neck, a full-bodied shudder. His arms trembled, yet he managed to keep himself upright.

"See?" he gasped. "I told you I wouldn't last long."

"Oh, hush. I still enjoyed every minute of it."

He slipped out of her, then lay at her side. He pulled her

toward him, and she rested her cheek against his chest. They remained like that for a while, absently caressing each other. His fingers ran down her back as hers drew circles against his chest hair.

"Whatever awaits us tomorrow—"

She cut that sentence short with a kiss. "Let's not talk about tomorrow. Not yet."

"I know I shouldn't ruin the moment, but..." He sighed as he pulled his arms more tightly around her. "But I love you, and whatever awaits us tomorrow, I promise I will do everything I can to ensure no harm comes to you."

"I love you, too, and I promise the same."

His eyes—dark, warm, brimming with adoration—met hers. From that point forward, they had no need for words. They let their bodies continue the conversation deep into the night, until they once again collapsed in each other's arms, pleasantly spent, and the final tendrils of warding magic dissipated.

FORTY-SEVEN

Though they woke before sunrise, Mavery and Alain remained in bed until they could no longer delay the inevitable. When they headed downstairs, the sun had fully risen, and Neldren and Ellice were halfway through breakfast. The taproom was largely empty, but the scent of fried meat wafted from the kitchen.

"So much for meeting at first light," Neldren said. He looked to Mavery and Alain's entwined hands, then snorted. "No need to explain why you're late."

They joined Neldren and Ellice at the table. Benard brought out plates piled high with toast, stewed beans, and sausages, as well as a pot of tea that smelled identical to the bergamot-laced variety Alain brewed every morning. Apparently, that was custom for anyone of Dauphinian descent.

Once again, Benard held up a hand when Mavery brought out her coin purse.

"Saving Ev was payment enough," he said, then chuckled. "Though, if you lot actually find a way into that ruin, I may change my mind on that."

"What do you mean?" Alain asked.

"Archstone is the closest village to the Innominate Temple. We get all sorts passing through here, whether they think they'll be the ones to crack it, or just want to take a gander." He shook his head.

"Strange idea for a holiday, if you ask me, but the tourists keep business steady during the warmer months."

"Oh," Alain said, lowering his head. "I'd...never considered that."

"In fact, one such adventurer stayed here a few days before you arrived," Benard said, scratching his beard. Aside from his facial hair and a smattering of fine lines, he was the spitting image of his younger brother. "Come to think, he didn't stop through here on the way back. Hope he's all right."

A patron from across the room signaled Benard, who excused himself with a bow of his head.

Neldren pushed his empty plate aside, brandished his map, spread it across the table.

"The temple is somewhere around here," he said, jabbing a section of the map that depicted the pine forest on the village's outskirts. "I did some scouting yesterday afternoon. It's the same as it was five years ago: all wild land, no roads. Good news is, we won't run into any more highwaymen. Bad news is, it won't be the easiest hike. But, so long as we keep a decent pace, it'll only take an hour or so."

Mavery gave Alain a sidelong glance.

"I can manage it," he said.

"Then hurry up and eat," Neldren said. "Let's head out before the day gets away from us."

After breakfast, Neldren led the group eastward, out of the village and into the surrounding forest. At first, there was a sem-blance of a path: a thin strip of dead, flattened grass that snaked between the tall pines. But that soon became lost among the wild grasses and brambles. This was nothing like the cultivated trail in Weywode Forest. Despite what Alain had said, it was evident that he hadn't yet fully recovered, and that the hike was taking more of a toll on him than he wanted to let on. He clung to his staff as he picked his way across the forest floor. At least his transmutated satchel wasn't weighing him down.

Though Neldren and Ellice were determined to forge ahead, Mavery didn't mind falling in step with Alain's sluggish pace. Her muscles were still pleasantly sore from last night—and earlier that morning. Besides, since their trip to Weywode Forest, she'd been eager to return to the wilderness. The crisp air and gentle breeze left her refreshed, her arcana humming pleasantly. Yet, even that couldn't keep her from thinking of what awaited them at the end of this hike. She took Alain's hand, gave it a firm squeeze.

"Everything will be fine," he said. "My satchel is filled with every scrap of research I've gathered over the years, and then some. We couldn't be more prepared for this."

"You say that now," Neldren called from several yards ahead. "Just wait until you see it in person."

The next time Neldren spoke, it was to estimate that they were a mile from where he'd first encountered the temple. Raw arcana lingered in the air, a faint but steady pulse, like the field music of an army they were advancing upon. Even from this distance, it was enough to leave a dull ache behind Mavery's eyes. She dropped Alain's hand and rubbed her temples.

"Are you all right?" he asked.

"I'm fine."

She squeezed her eyes shut as she continued to walk, then swore under her breath when she stubbed her toe on something in the underbrush. But the throbbing in her head quickly drowned out that pain. Through her half-closed eyes, she noticed Alain watching on with concern.

"Really, I'm fine," she said. "Let's keep going."

She tried to instead focus on the rustling of the wind through the tree branches, the steady rhythm of their footsteps, the intermittent thud of Alain's staff. But with every step that brought them closer to the temple, the magic grew more oppressive. It was worse than she remembered. They had to be much closer than she'd gotten during her first excursion through these woods.

Before long, mist lingered in the air and her pace slowed to a crawl. A bit further, and that mist became a dense fog, white-hot pain ripped through her skull. She dropped her pack at her feet, then leaned against the closest tree.

"It's beginning to affect me, too," Alain whispered as he rubbed her shoulders. "Should I fetch the anti-Sensing potion?"

"Not yet," she gasped. "Only one dose."

"Mavery, you don't need to suffer like this."

"I know. But need...to see...temple first."

He sighed. "All right. When you *are* ready to take it, just say the word."

She nodded. Though she appreciated his concern, it did little to quell the pounding inside her head. She continued to lean against the trunk, breathing deeply. She closed her eyes as she attempted to ground herself, focusing on the tenderness of Alain's touch, the rough bark beneath her fingertips, the chill of the forest air, the scent of pine laced with it...

She pushed herself away from the tree and snatched up her pack. But a new wave of arcana hit her like a wintry gale, piercing her skin and leaving shards of ice embedded in her bones. Alain caught her before she crumpled to the ground.

"Gods, this magic," he gasped. "I've never felt anything quite like it."

You're telling me, she thought, as speaking required too much effort.

Alain offered her his staff, and she clung to it as he helped her to her feet. With one of his arms around her shoulders, they pressed onward.

A few minutes later, Ellice, too, gasped and clutched her head. Neldren, however, continued on as though this were a perfectly normal forest, untouched by powerful ancient magic. Mavery had always judged him for being so weakly attuned to magic that wasn't his own. For once, she envied him.

The final leg of the journey stretched on interminably. They inched their way across the forest floor while being battered on all sides by invisible forces. The fog continued to thicken, and it was impossible to see more than a few yards ahead. At last, they passed through a dense copse, and Neldren came to a halt.

"Gods, I hate this fucking place."

Even he could no longer ignore the magic, but Mavery was

too miserable to find even a modicum of satisfaction from it. She feared that simply cracking a grin would turn her violently ill.

"This is it," Alain breathed. His fingers gripped her upper arm. "We're here."

It took the last shred of her willpower to open her eyes fully.

Just beyond the trees was a column of green light that stretched from the ground to far above the tallest treetops. The sky swirled with thick gray clouds that completely obscured the sun. The ambient light must have come solely from magic.

As Mavery's eyes adjusted—and as she fought a wave of nausea while attuning her Senses—she realized there was something strange, something *untamed,* about this magic. Rather than pulsating gently, the green-hued ward thrashed like rapidly boiling water.

But that was all she could take in. Gazing at the magic for even a moment proved too much for her Senses. Alain's staff slipped from her hand as she collapsed on all fours. Pain erupted from her bad knee, and as she opened her mouth to scream, she vomited the remains of her breakfast into the grass.

"Mavery!" Alain cried.

She was about to warn him to stand back, but nausea overcame her again, which had the same effect. She continued to heave until only bile remained. Wiping her mouth on her sleeve, she eased herself upright, coming to rest on her heels.

"I'll take the potion now," she muttered. "Front pocket."

Alain retrieved the vial within seconds. She downed it in a single gulp before her stomach could protest. The magic was so powerful, even the potion couldn't eradicate its effects. But her headache subsided enough for her to think and see clearly again. Before, the green aura had been an impenetrable curtain; now, it was a translucent veil.

Within it was a circular clearing where the grass was brown and shriveled, as though nature itself couldn't withstand the strange magic. The clearing sloped gradually upward, and atop the desolate mound stood a stone building with a pointed roof. The temple itself was much smaller than Mavery had expected; it was barely larger than the mausoleums she'd seen in noble families' cemeteries. From this angle, the temple appeared to have a single entrance: a three-pointed archway. Etched into the pediment was the asphodel emblem from Alain's notebook.

She tore her eyes away from it to look to her left. Ellice sat in the grass, clutching her head, while Neldren paced and surveyed the area. To Mavery's right, Alain sat with the Sensing spell open across his lap. Mavery retrieved her canteen from her pack, swilled water to remove the taste of vomit.

"It's green," she said softly.

Alain looked up from the spell tome. "Come again?"

"The magic around the temple is green."

He tapped his chin. "What shade of green, exactly?"

"Light green." She sipped from her canteen as she gave the aura another look. "Sage."

"If I'm not mistaken, you've Sensed that exact color before."

Her mind was too addled to recall anything at the moment. Alain rummaged through his pack and pulled out one of his many notebooks. She peered over his shoulder and recognized the notes he'd scrawled on the day they'd first met, when she'd described the wards that had guarded his door.

"You associated sage green with my Diversion Ward—or Declan's, rather. This confirms it: the temple is protected with an obfuscation ward. Declan's spell included an augmentation from the Mysticism School. But, even by themselves, obfuscation wards are exceptionally complex magic. So much so, they always require an anchor, and all anchors will have—"

"Ley lines." Mavery's eyes widened. "Our spell will reveal those."

"Precisely. If we can trace the ley lines to their source, we might be able to disable the ward. We'll need to be prepared to destroy the anchor if necessary."

"What are you two blathering on about?" Neldren asked.

"We've determined that the temple is protected by an obfuscation ward, most likely anchored to an Ether-sensitive mat—"

"In *Osperlandish*, if you don't mind."

"We might be able to get past the warding magic," Mavery said. "But first, we need to track down what's powering it."

FORTY-EIGHT

The more distance they put between themselves and the temple, the more its effects receded. Alain led the way this time, with the Sensing spell anchored to the iron coin he'd once given Mavery.

She thought back to the time Alain had diverted her from his storage room. But now, instead of sending them around an apartment, the ley line took them through woods that were even more dense than the ones they had just traversed.

They walked for nearly half an hour, until they reached the remains of a small cabin. Most of its stone walls had crumbled, and it had no roof. Scattered all around the area were tall plants bearing six-pointed white flowers.

"Asphodel," Mavery said.

"You're right," Ellice said, giving the white petals a closer look. "Strange, I thought these grew further south, closer to Maroba."

"Then someone must have planted them here."

Mavery recalled what Selemin had told her: the Order of Asphodel's meeting place had been a cabin in these very woods, and the Dyadists had burned it to the ground. Though that had happened centuries ago, she could swear the scent of burnt wood lingered in the air.

"This place must have belonged to the Order," Mavery said.

"Indeed," Alain said, pointing at what remained of the longest wall. Carved into the crumbling hearth was that same flower symbol from before. Unlike the one on the temple's pediment, this one had worn away with time; little more than an impression remained.

Alain crouched beside the ley line and pushed aside a tuft of grass. At first glance, the ley line simply ended. But upon taking a closer look, Mavery realized it sank beneath the dirt, in what had once been the center of the room.

"It's a shame we didn't bring a shovel," Alain said.

"No, but we *do* have a mender," Mavery said.

They both turned to Ellice.

"All right," she sighed. "Let's see what we're dealing with."

She lowered herself onto the ground and pushed up her sleeves, then closed her eyes and placed her palms flat against the dirt. Mavery's small dose of potion had worn off, and so she Sensed saltwater in the air, though more faintly than when Ellice had created a hole in the fence at the Roven estate. Mavery realized that Ellice was simply probing the ground, trying to determine what lay beneath it. Ellice's brow furrowed as her fingers gripped the dirt.

"There's definitely something buried down there." She opened her eyes again. "At least six feet deep."

"A body?" Neldren asked.

"No, it gave too much resistance to my magic. It's inorganic—maybe some sort of metal."

"The anchor," Alain said. "Can you dig it up?"

She frowned. "This amount of dirt is going to be heavy, which means it'll require *a lot* of magic. Probably more than I have to spare, if I'm being honest."

Mavery turned to Alain. "Did you bring any extra anchors?"

"Only the sort that would help with the spell's longevity or area of effect. What she needs is something that will amplify her arcana." He sighed. "If only I still had my gems, or if I'd thought to bring a potion..."

"What if she used one of us?"

"Using another mage as an anchor?" He considered it for a moment, then nodded. "Yes, that should work."

As he stepped forward, Mavery threw out her arm, stopping him. "You're still recovering, or have you already forgotten?"

"I'm all but fully recovered, which means I have plenty of arcana to spare."

"But what if you end up too drained to destroy the anchor, not to mention deal with whatever is inside the temple?"

Alain scoffed. "I hardly think a simple Faisancy spell will—"

"I'll do it," Neldren said.

The other three turned to him in unison.

"Seeing as how my magic's been useless so far." There was an edge of bitterness to his voice. He lowered himself beside Ellice, then sat back on his heels. "What do I need to do?"

"The majority of it will be Ellice's doing," Alain said. "You'll simply need to maintain physical contact with her for the full duration of the spell."

"You say that like it'll be a challenge." Neldren smirked as he placed a hand on Ellice's knee. Mavery fought the urge to vomit again.

"Ellice, you'll need to focus on drawing from his arcana. Imagine illuminating a lamp, but in reverse. It's an advanced technique, so don't be disappointed if you're not successful—"

The scent of saltwater filled the air so strongly, Mavery thought for a second that she'd been transported to the sea. A section of ground directly in front of Ellice fissured, then rose in the air and landed off to the side with a soft thud.

"On the first try," Alain finished flatly. He looked to Mavery. "Well, it seems you're not the only fast learner around here."

Ellice continued to clear away the dirt, one square foot at a time. Sweat beaded across her forehead, her cheeks turned the same color as her hair. Neldren wavered slightly as Ellice's arcana began to feed off his, but never once did he let go of Ellice's knee. He even placed his other hand on her lower back as he muttered something beneath his breath. Rare words of encouragement, Mavery assumed.

Before long, there was a deep hole in the ground and a towering pile of dirt beside it. Ellice raised her hands, and the anchor was lifted from its resting place. Mavery gasped. It was the largest slab of copper she'd ever seen, roughly the size of a coffin. Blinding silver light flooded the immediate area.

With a groan, Ellice lowered her hands and ended the spell. The anchor plummeted to the ground with enough force to rattle the cabin's remaining walls. Neldren and Ellice collapsed backward in unison. If her spellcasting hadn't completely drained the arcana from both of them, it had certainly come close. They lay in the weeds, breathing heavily, as Alain began examining the anchor.

Once Mavery's eyes adjusted to the light, the ley line itself came into focus. Whereas most were threadlike, this one was as thick as rope. It fizzled with wild energy, much like the magic that shrouded the temple. Alain closed his eyes as he hovered his hands above it.

"Odd," he said. "I can feel the Ether...and something else."

"Necromancy?" Mavery asked.

He shook his head. "No, even the most heinous forms of Necromancy are Ethereal in nature. *This* magic is from no School I'm familiar with."

Mavery came to his side, closed her eyes, and focused her Senses. At once, she recognized the Ether caressing her like a soft breeze. But as she continued to focus, she detected another force that was chaotic, yet solid. Like a wild animal tugging on a leash, it reminded her of how her own arcana felt just before a magic surge. She breathed deeply, filling her lungs with an aroma that she'd mistaken as coming from her physical surroundings. Now, she realized that she'd been Sensing this strange magic ever since arriving at the cabin.

When she opened her eyes, Alain was holding a book she assumed he'd retrieved from the small library in his satchel.

"Could you Sense it?" he asked.

"Yes, it smells like a forest fire and..." She paused to attune her Senses again. "And soil after a rainstorm, strangely enough."

"Petrichor."

She nodded. "I've never Sensed anything quite like this. What do you think? Can you work with it?"

"Only the part that is undoubtedly Gardemancy. As for this other magic, I'm not sure." He scratched his chin for a moment, then shrugged. "I think the most straightforward solution is to destroy the anchor."

Neldren sat up. "Hold on. That amount of copper is worth a small fortune! You're not actually going to destroy it?"

"It's either that, or we camp out here until I can fully study this magic and determine which School it's from. And even then, I'm not entirely certain I'll be able to disable the spell itself."

Neldren and Ellice exchanged a look. Mavery could see their collective wheels turning, calculating exactly how much the anchor was worth, and dreaming of the luxuries they could afford with such a score.

"If *you* would like to take a stab at the strange, all-powerful magic, be my guest," Mavery said.

She stepped aside and gestured at the anchor. As she suspected, Neldren remained seated. Even if his arcana had been at its full capacity, she doubted he would be that reckless.

"Fine," he grumbled. "Just seems like a waste..."

"All right," Alain said, clearing his throat. "Mavery, you'll want to take a step back."

She did so, and he kneeled beside the copper slab. He placed the pad of his index finger against a tiny section that the ley line didn't touch, then rattled off a long incantation. Mavery shivered as the Ether brushed against her skin; Alain's spell contained no trace of that dark, wild magic. The copper glowed, then an acrid stench filled the air as it transmutated into gray stone. The ley line dissipated, taking the silver light along with it. The world grew suddenly dim, the scent of burning wood and petrichor faded to the aroma of pine.

Alain swayed on the spot, clutching his stomach, but the sensation seemed to pass quickly. Taking Mavery's hand, he rose to his feet and brushed the dirt from his knees.

Neldren sighed with the melancholy of watching a loved one pass away.

"Don't worry," Ellice said, patting his knee. "With any luck, whatever's inside the temple will be just as valuable."

He laughed coldly, unconvinced.

FORTY-NINE

When the temple came into view again, it was no longer enclosed within the water-like wall Alain had seen earlier, and he suspected Mavery no longer saw the sage-hued aura. The temple now appeared an innocuous building that had been tucked away in the forest and long forgotten. The fog had lifted, and the sun shone directly overhead, bathing the clearing in sunlight.

The Transmutation spell had successfully destroyed the temple's external defenses. Alain could only hope that any magic *within* the temple had also been disabled. He now carried a bone-deep ache that flared with every step he took, and he doubted he had the strength to pull off anything more complex than a protective ward. Fortunately, the Sensing spell was still anchored to the coin in his hand.

He recalled a time during his first year at university, when he'd managed to get his hands on a Transmutation primer. Those spells were intended for sixth-year students, but his curiosity had gotten the better of him. He'd attempted the most basic of Transmutation spells: instantaneously turning water into vapor. At twenty-eight runes, the incantation was longer than any he'd learned in his classes at that point. After reciting the incantation in his head a dozen times, he'd spoken it aloud.

On his first attempt, the water in his cup had vanished. But before he could revel in his success, he'd passed out.

The next thing he'd known was awaking in the University's infirmary three days later, with violent nausea and a personalized note from Chancellor Lythandus, informing him that his next foolish stunt would earn him academic probation.

As Alain approached the clearing, he felt a bit like his seventeen-year-old self again. Only now, there was more than his transcript at stake.

"The Sensing spell only has a radius of thirty feet," he said. "Stay close."

With Mavery and her Senses leading the way, just in case there was any magic the spell couldn't detect, they trudged through the grassy clearing and toward the smaller clearing that was devoid of life. Dotting the landscape were corpses in various stages of decay: rabbits, squirrels, and other small creatures that had wandered too close.

"Trap up ahead," Mavery announced.

Alain approached, then pushed aside a thistle with the butt of his staff. Beneath it was a red aura anchored to an Ether-sensitive stone embedded in the dirt. Alain wondered how many more detonation wards had been buried here, how many innocents had been killed or maimed over the years.

They continued onward until the other three groaned in unison. Mavery stopped, hunching over as though she were about to be ill again.

"Oh, gods, is that what I think it is?" Ellice said, pinching her nose.

"It is, sorry to say," Neldren groaned.

Alain turned to them. "What is it?"

"How do you not smell *that*?" Neldren cried, pointing at a large dark object in the grass nearby.

"Years of alchemy experiments have made me immune to most—"

He froze as he realized the object was a corpse. Auburn hair flashed before his eyes, then he blinked. No, *this* corpse had black hair. Alain's stomach lurched at how the left leg had been blown apart at the ankle. The foot lay several yards away. The rest of the body was stomach-side down, bloated from lying in the sun, but it was still in the early stages of decomposition—a few days, at most. Even the wildlife hadn't yet picked it apart.

"This has to be the bloke Benard told us about," Neldren said, shaking his head. "Poor bastard must've triggered one of those blasting wards."

Detonation, Alain thought, but he lacked the capacity to do anything but stare at the corpse as Mavery's hand slipped into his.

"It's not him," she whispered.

"I know," he whispered back. "But gods...knowing now what happened, seeing it in person." He closed his eyes and breathed deeply.

She squeezed his hand but said nothing more. He doubted there was anything she *could* say.

Alain opened his eyes, cleared his throat. "Let's keep moving."

"Finally," Neldren muttered.

They left the corpse behind and encountered no more traps as they approached the innermost clearing. They climbed the slight hill, their boots crunching on dead grass, and finally stood before the temple. The archway was nearly three feet off the ground, but there were no steps leading up to it.

Neldren, being the tallest, pulled himself through the opening first, then helped each of the women up. Alain waited, practically trembling with anticipation as the place he'd researched for years was now merely feet away. He all but threw himself at Neldren's proffered hand. Once his feet were on solid ground again, Alain pushed aside the slight strain on his arcana and conjured an orb of Ether. He directed it toward the pitched ceiling, and the white light revealed...

Nothing.

The Innominate Temple was a plain stone room. Aside from the entrance, it had neither doors nor windows. It contained no treasures, no iconography, not even a single plaque explaining its purpose.

Alain was too shocked to say anything. So, too, were Mavery and Ellice, judging by their slackened jaws. Neldren, however, threw back his head and laughed. The sound was almost deafening as it reverberated through the small high-ceilinged chamber.

"After all this," he said, wiping tears from his eyes, "it's fucking *empty*! Looks like someone beat us to the punch and kept the treasure all to himself."

"No," Alain whispered, shaking his head. "Those wards, that strange magic... No one could get through that unscathed."

"But *we* did. Apparently, someone else did, too. I'll bet they got past the wards, looted the place, and reset the defenses."

"What about the anchor?" Ellice asked. "They left all that copper to guard an empty building?"

Neldren shrugged. "Stranger things have happened."

"This can't be right," Alain muttered.

For centuries, this place had eluded the continent's best scholars. Until not quite an hour ago, it had been shrouded in some of the most powerful magic Alain had ever seen. All that effort for what was, effectively, a Necromancer's storage shed that had long been cleaned out?

"No, there must be more to it than this..."

Mavery appeared to agree. She began running her hands over the walls. When that proved fruitless, she gazed upward, searching the ceiling for answers. Alain followed her gaze but could see only his orb of light against a backdrop of gray stone.

"Watch it, Mave!" Neldren cried.

Alain turned to see Mavery standing with her back to Neldren's chest. Neldren had her by the shoulders, steadying her. She looked down at her feet, then gasped. She pulled herself out of Neldren's clutches and got down on all fours.

"*Now* what are you doing?"

"It's a fabrication!" she said, sweeping her hand in a broad arc across the floor.

Ellice leaned over and placed her hand beside Mavery's. "She's right. I'd know that feeling anywhere."

Alain approached, bringing his orb of light closer. In the dead-center of the floor was a round stone that was slightly offset from the rest. It was rimmed with a thin band of metal. Iron, from the look of it. A faint pulsation emanated from it. It had the rhythmic quality of a Gardemancy spell but at a more rapid tempo.

"Our Sensing spell only works on warding magic," Alain said. "That's why only Mavery can see it. What kind of fabrication do you think it is?"

Ellice shrugged.

"Only one way to find out," Mavery said. She pressed her palm flat against the fabrication, furrowed her brow as she fed it a bit of arcana. The fabrication itself did not change, but the walls trembled.

"Oh, gods, it's a trap!" Ellice cried. "The whole godsdamned building is going to collapse!"

Mavery pulled back her hand, and the trembling stopped.

"Wait a minute..." she said.

She fed the stone more arcana, and the building shook again, more forcefully this time. Ellice shrieked. The floor now vibrated as well. Alain looked out the archway.

"It's not collapsing," he said. "We're *ascending*!"

The more arcana she fed the fabrication, the higher in the air they rose. Alain knelt beside Mavery and placed his hands on the fabrication. His arcana, combined with hers, sped up their ascent. As the ground vanished, Mavery emitted a low groan and honed her attention on the fabrication. Alain recalled that she had a fear of heights. She'd revealed that only days ago, when they were in the High Council's—

He gasped.

"What is it?" Mavery asked.

Before he could answer, the building jerked to a halt, then the fabricated stone rattled beneath Alain's palms. It slid to one side, disappearing into a slit within the floor, and revealed a stone spiral staircase. It was too dark to see how far it descended, but there was no doubt another level—likely several—below this one.

Alain took Mavery by the hands. He shook with excitement as he beamed at her.

"Have I mentioned lately how brilliant you are?"

"No, *you're* the brilliant one," she said. Despite her apparent unease, she smiled back. "You were right: the Innominate Temple isn't a temple."

He nodded. "It's a wizard's tower."

FIFTY

The spiral stairs led to a tiny room that appeared to be a dead end. But then Mavery Sensed a swarm of buzzing red auras: another fabrication spell. This one came from a pressure plate embedded in the stone wall. She pushed it, and the wall swung open into a large chamber. With the flick of his wrist, Alain sent his orb of light ahead of them.

The chamber was sparsely furnished with a four-poster bed, a trunk at the foot of it, a wardrobe, and a single chair. If this was a wizard's tower, this had to be the wizard's living quarters, though it was evident no one had actually *lived* here in a very long time. The air was stagnant, and everything was blanketed in dust. Though the furniture remained standing, the linens upon the bed and tapestries upon the walls were so threadbare, they looked as though a gentle breeze would be enough to disintegrate them. The floor-to-ceiling windows had become so caked in dirt from remaining belowground, no natural light shone through. At the far end of the chamber was a door that glowed with blue and silver auras.

But there were no personal effects, nothing to identify the tower's previous owner. The wooden trunk seemed the most promising place to find answers. Alain tried to lift the lid, only to discover that it was secured with a padlock bearing a green patina.

"Can one of you scrounge up your lockpicking tools?" he asked.

"No need," Neldren said.

He shouldered past Alain and brandished his pistol. Alain flinched, but instead of firing a shot, Neldren struck the butt against the padlock. The clang of metal on metal made Mavery's ears ring. After the second strike, the lock snapped in half and clattered to the floor. Neldren holstered his pistol with a grin.

"Now, what treasures did this wizard go through so much trouble to hide?" He raised the lid and frowned. "Books. Why did I even ask?"

He and Ellice stepped away, no doubt to search for something more worth their while. As Alain carefully reached for one of the books, Mavery conjured her own orb of light. She brought it close enough to read the embossed lettering on the cover: *A Treatise on the Ktonic Magicks*. The author was—

"Aganast," she gasped.

"And there's that word again," Alain said.

The two of them exchanged a look.

"Well, what are you waiting for?" Mavery nudged his shoulder. "Open it!"

"I will, but with caution. These books are centuries old."

She nodded, though she still huffed impatiently as Alain took his time opening the cover. The book reeked with the musty stench of vellum—*real* vellum, not the cotton-based imitation that modern books were printed on. Many of the pages contained colorful illustrations of winged beasts. They looked more suitable for a book of fairy tales than a scholarly treatise. She attempted to read over Alain's shoulder, but it was written in an old form of Osperlandish. That, combined with the blocky lettering, made the text difficult to parse at first glance.

There were still plenty more tomes to investigate, so Alain placed this one aside. Following his lead, Mavery extracted another book and handled it as though it were a newborn babe.

"Aganast also wrote this one," she said. "*The Burden of the Senova*. What's a 'Senova'?"

"Not a clue. He coauthored this one as well: *The Ninth School*."

"*Ninth* School? I thought there were only eight Schools of Magic."

"Perhaps it's referring to wizarding schools. The coauthors' names look familiar. I'll bet you anything they were members of the Order of Asphodel."

"Either the wizard who owned this tower was a very dedicated fan, or Aganast wasn't the humble sort."

"*Or*, Aganast wanted to ensure his work didn't fall into the wrong hands. Let me see your pack."

Mavery raised her eyebrows at him.

"Mine is already filled with my own books," he said, but she continued to stare at him. "What's wrong?"

She shook her head as she laughed softly. "Pilfering first edition books like a common thief. If I didn't know any better, I'd say I've rubbed off on you."

Alain shrugged. "I highly doubt Aganast is going to mind. Now, help me gather these up. I want to study them more closely once we return to Archstone."

"What, this décor isn't cozy enough for you?" Neldren called from the opposite end of the room. "I thought wizards and towers went together like bread and butter."

Alain turned to him, then startled. "What are you doing!?"

Neldren was prising a candelabra off the wall, while Ellice was stuffing her pack with candlesticks.

"Collecting our payment," Neldren said. He gave the candelabra another tug, and it clattered to the floor. "Didn't you and Mave promise to share any treasure we find in here?"

Alain rubbed his forehead and sighed. "All right, but remember: anything of *academic* value is—"

"All yours, mate, mark my words."

Aside from the books and silver, there appeared to be nothing else of note within this room, but that didn't stop Neldren and Ellice from searching every nook and cranny. Alain and Mavery returned to moving the books to her pack. There were only eighteen in total, but if this small collection shed any light on the mysterious "ktonic magicks," then it was more valuable than an entire tower's worth of silver.

With the living quarters now thoroughly picked through, the group headed to the door. Its protective ward was permanently anchored to the silver doorknob. With the Sensing spell still active, the blue and silver auras were visible to all four of them.

Neldren whistled. "Well, I'll be godsdamned."

"It's beautiful," Ellice breathed. "So this is what magic looks like to your eyes?"

"More or less," Mavery replied with a shrug.

"And this ward is child's play," Alain said. "With any luck, we'll find more sophisticated magic downstairs."

"Don't sound *too* eager, now," Neldren grumbled.

Alain broke the ward with little more than a wave of his hand, though Mavery noted how he turned away, attempting to hide his pained expression. The door's hinges creaked as he pulled it open. With his orb of light guiding them, they descended single file down another narrow, winding stairwell.

At the bottom of this one was a room so cavernous, even Alain and Mavery's orbs combined couldn't illuminate the entire space. The far corners remained completely shrouded in shadow. Unlike the living quarters, this room contained no windows. The walls were covered in bookshelves that stretched from floor to ceiling, though many of the lower shelves were bare. Upon the floor were piles of books that Mavery assumed had fallen during the tower's ascent.

Alain took a step forward.

"Wait," Neldren whispered. He grabbed Alain by the sleeve and pulled him back. "I felt something in the shadows just now."

"Can you see what it is?" Ellice whispered.

He closed his eyes, and a faint scent of ash lingered in the air as he probed the darkness. Their surroundings were so quiet, Mavery's ears began to ring again. After an excruciatingly long moment, Neldren opened his eyes and shook his head.

"My magic's too spent to see anything, but I can tell we're not alone. Keep quiet and tread carefully."

Alain gripped his staff. Mavery's and Ellice's hands hovered close to their blades. Neldren's rested on his pistol. As they crossed the room, even the softest steps sounded like thunder against the stone floor, until they reached a section that was covered with an old rug. Though it was as tattered as the linens upstairs, it dampened their footfalls all the same.

A large desk sat in the center of the room. The papers on top were covered in dust, yellowed with age, and splattered with hardened wax from candles that had burned down to their holders. There was also a journal splayed open on its final entry.

4 Nivose, 534

It has been five months since I fastened myself inside my tower with only Nox for company. Were it not for my commitment to this journal, I would have long ago lost count of the days and given to madness. That none from the Order has followed my instructions and dispelled the wards, I take as the gravest omen.

To leave, we might well run afoul of the Dyadic lunatics. Yet, should I remain here, my larder will run dry within a fortnight and this wretched place will become my tomb. I must convince Nox to

The entry ended there, unfinished.

"This was Aganast's journal," Alain whispered. "I recognize the handwriting from the letter Con..." He took a deep breath. "From one of his letters."

"He spent five months in this place?" Mavery whispered back.

"Reminds me of my own confinement."

"At least you had sunlight."

"At least he had company."

She looked at Alain, but he only gazed at the journal. He tucked it in the outer pocket of his satchel, where it wouldn't be jostled around with the much heavier books. He then riffled through the loose papers on the desk.

"Oh, you bookworms will love this," Neldren said wryly. Despite his warning about staying quiet, his voice wasn't far off from its normal volume. "Come over here and take a look."

Alain turned to Neldren and gasped. He and Ellice were re-moving books from the shelves, opening them, and promptly toss-ing them onto the mound of books at their feet.

"I always figured some wizards were full of shit about all the books they claimed to read," Neldren sneered. "Look, this library is full of fakes! All covers, no pages."

Mavery plucked the book from his hands before he could toss it aside. To her eyes, the pages still existed, though not in any form that was readable. They hovered like wisps of dark smoke from a recently extinguished fire. She caught the same aroma that she'd Sensed back at the cottage. She looked closer. The pages were made of some sort of untamed black arcana.

"They're not fake," she said. As she described what she Sensed, Neldren and Ellice gawked at her. Alain had produced a notebook and pen, and he listened on while scribbling feverishly.

"Sounds like they were transmutated," Alain said. "But into what, exactly? And for what purpose?"

Mavery shrugged. "I've never seen anything like it. Your guess is as good as mine."

Alain grabbed a book from the pile at Ellice's feet. Just as she and Neldren had done, he opened it, tossed it aside, then grabbed one from the shelf. With each book he discarded, he became a bit more agitated. All of the pages had been transmutated into the same strange substance.

Mavery searched the other shelves and found plenty of books that had been spared the fate of the others, though she couldn't discern any reason why. It certainly hadn't been for their entertain-ment value. One row was devoted to tax codes that were so ancient, they'd been obsolete even in Aganast's time. Another consisted of a half-century's worth of farmers' almanacs. And another housed dozens of copies of a Dyadic devotional for children. All of these books had been printed on cheap paper, not vellum or parchment. Judging by their publication dates, these had to be some of the earliest mass-produced books on the continent.

"Don't mourn these books too much, Alain," Mavery said. "Nothing here is even remotely related to magic."

"Why would a wizard fill his library with so many useless books?" Ellice asked.

She and Neldren looked to Alain, who shrugged. "Just because I'm a wizard, doesn't mean I can explain every other wizard's eccentricities. Perhaps we'll find an answer downstairs."

The next level down contained another library. Here, *every* book had been cleared from the shelves and lay strewn across the floor in heaps of smoldering arcana.

The smell made Mavery's empty stomach sour. While the other three crossed the room, she hung back and leaned against one of the barren shelves. She breathed deeply, clutching her stomach in an effort to calm it. After today's events, she could stand going without magic for a few days, if not longer—an idea she'd never imagined herself entertaining.

Alain, noticing she'd lagged behind, doubled back.

"This strange magic is doing a number on you, isn't it?"

"That's putting it lightly," she said through bared teeth. "What about you? How are you holding up?"

"Me? Oh, I'm fine." He placed his hand on her shoulder. "Just worried about you, is all."

She frowned. "Don't lie to me, Alain. You're a terrible—"

Across the room, the shadows shifted. Her breath hitched, and Alain's grip on her shoulder tightened.

"What is it?" he whispered.

"I thought I saw something just now."

She raised her hand and sent her orb to where she'd glimpsed movement. But as her light dispersed the shadows, it revealed only another tower of discarded books.

"Nothing," she said.

"I wouldn't be too certain about that. Let's stay close."

She nodded, and they walked side by side to join the other two. Once again, by instinct, her right hand stayed close to the sheathed dagger on her left hip. Alain clenched his staff, knuckles whitening. They rejoined Neldren and Ellice, who were picking through the books.

"Bad luck," Neldren said. "No pages in these, either. All these books are worthless."

"Shh!" Ellice whispered. "Over there—something's moving."

Mavery *hadn't* been seeing things. She didn't know if that made her feel better or worse.

"Let's move," Neldren said, "and hope we find a way out of this godsforsaken tower."

With him leading the way, they left the library and descended what would have been another pitch-dark stairwell, if not for the twin orbs of light. There wasn't a single candelabra attached to the walls.

Mavery had expected to find yet another library, but they instead entered a high-ceilinged kitchen. Living in isolation for long stretches of time wasn't the only thing Alain and Aganast had in common; the kitchen also doubled as an alchemy laboratory.

A few steps from the stairwell, Alain stumbled.

"What in the—"

He brought his orb of light closer, then yelped. A pile of bones lay at his feet.

"Well, *that's* a great omen," Neldren said.

Alain prodded the remains with the butt of his staff. Then, to Mavery's horror, he bent down and rifled through them with his hands.

"Are you out of your godsdamned mind?" she hissed.

He prised a ring from one of the finger bones, then showed it to her. She recoiled. It didn't matter that the flesh had long since decomposed; the ring had still come straight from a corpse.

"It's the Order of Asphodel's emblem," Alain said. "See these grooves? I think he used it as a stamp."

Mavery nodded as her disgust subsided. "What do you think happened to him? Starved on his way back from the empty larder?"

"That, or he crossed paths with whatever was skulking about upstairs," Neldren said.

"Gods, don't even hex us like that," Ellice groaned.

Alain pocketed the ring. Together, he and Mavery investigated the rest of the room. The tables were piled high with alchemy equipment, though it was all too old to be of any use, too tarnished to be of value even to a collector. Likewise, the contents of the glass jars were in various stages of decay, if they hadn't perished entirely.

"I think this is the way out," Neldren said.

He pointed to an iron door that was barred from the inside. All four of them gathered around it. Neldren gripped the bar, then groaned and grit his teeth as he tried to force it upward. Despite his efforts, the bar wouldn't budge.

"Damn thing's rusted to shit," he muttered.

"I should have just enough magic to mend that," Ellice said, "but it'll take me a minute or—"

A low, guttural growl ripped through the room. Though it sounded like some sort of animal, there was an otherworldly quality to it. Goosebumps covered Mavery's skin. Ellice squealed, then clapped her hands over her mouth.

They all remained frozen by the door. With the slightest movement of his hand, Alain sent his orb to the far side of the room. It revealed a sight that sucked the air from Mavery's lungs.

"What on Perrun is *that*?" Ellice whispered, voice trembling.

Perched atop one of the cabinets was a giant catlike beast that could have been mistaken for a panther. Its sleek tar-black fur melded into the darkness. But its leathery wings—currently folded against its body—and piercing red eyes marked it as some variety of demonspawn, though it was unlike any Mavery had ever seen. This monstrosity made even the most bloodthirsty hellhound look like a harmless pup. With a rumbling snarl, it bared its long razor-sharp fangs.

If this beast had been locked up in this tower with Aganast...

And if Aganast had been a demon sympathizer...

Mavery's blood chilled.

This was no demon*spawn*.

This was an actual *demon*.

It spread its broad membranous wings and launched off the cabinet. As it descended upon the four humans, Alain lunged forward.

"Quickly, Ellice!" he yelled. "I'll hold him back!"

He pushed his free hand out at the same time he arced his staff overhead. Mavery winced as an overwhelming scent of copper permeated the air. She choked on the taste of metal, as though her entire mouth had filled with blood. She then looked up and gasped. With only a ritual—without voicing a single syllable of Etherean—Alain had encased the four of them inside a shimmering blue dome.

The walls shook and glass jars rattled as the demon landed on the floor. It retracted its wings and raised one of its great paws. At the end of it were obsidian claws almost as severe-looking as its fangs. It swiped at Alain's ward. The magic fractured for a split second before repairing itself.

"Oh, shit!" Ellice cried.

"Focus on the door, not the beast!" Neldren snapped.

"What do you think I'm trying to do?"

With a roar, the demon swiped at Alain's ward again. The force of it, combined with Alain's already weakened state, made him stumble. His ward began to splinter like a broken mirror. Mavery leapt beside him, conjured her own protective ward, and raised her palms to the blue dome. Her magic slithered through the gaps, reinforcing Alain's.

The demon paused and tilted its head to the side. It seemed to understand what Mavery had just done. Instead of lifting its paw again, it retreated back a few steps. It pivoted its body, then threw a muscular shoulder against the ward. The magic fractured again, now becoming a vast spiderweb of fissures. The ward wouldn't hold much longer. Fear coursed through Mavery's veins, along with a rising tide of fiery energy.

"Hurry up!" she yelled over her shoulder.

"I'm trying!" Ellice yelled back.

Mavery couldn't blame her for panicking. It was taking every bit of her focus to keep her ward aloft while her arcana thrashed beneath her skin. Perhaps a surge would be useful against a centuries-old demon. But she couldn't control what the surge did once it escaped her body. It was likely to ricochet off the ward and back into her own face—or Alain's.

The demon lunged again, using its body as a battering ram. This time, even more of the magic chipped away.

Mavery grit her teeth as she channeled everything she could into the ward. She spared a glance at Alain. His teeth were also bared, his forehead glistened with sweat, his arms trembled as he struggled to keep them raised.

She looked forward as the beast charged the ward for a third time. She braced herself for the inevitable impact.

The force of the demon's body shattered the ward. The blue aura dissolved into mist.

With nothing left in its way, the demon focused all of its ire on Alain. It once again raised its paw, black claws bared and gleaming.

"*No!*" Mavery screamed.

For a split second, her very blood was on fire. As arcana blazed through her, she raised her arm, pointed her fingers at the demon. A bolt of white-hot magic escaped her fingertips, shot through the room, grazed the beast's shoulder. Apart from a clump of singed hair, her magic surge didn't seem to leave any lasting damage, but it was enough to distract the demon. It turned its attention away from Alain—and onto her.

The demon looked at her like a predator sizing up its next meal.

She took that brief pause as her opportunity to drop her pack and sprint toward the stairwell. Behind her, Alain yelled with a guttural ferocity unlike anything she'd ever heard from him.

She glanced over her shoulder to see him swing his staff and hit the demon's singed shoulder. The beast didn't so much as look at him as it flexed its wings. One hit Alain squarely in the chest with enough force to send him stumbling backward. He collided into a cabinet with a pain-stricken groan.

Mavery wanted to scream, but she couldn't afford to do anything but run.

She took the stairs two at a time. When she reached the top and reentered the lower library, her lungs were on fire. Each step brought about a jolt of pain from her bad knee.

Panting, she searched the library for a place to hide. Distracting the demon had been her only goal, so she hadn't planned what to do next. She fled to the farthest corner, then huddled behind a large pile of books. She flicked her wrist, sending her orb of light to the opposite corner of the room. While being shrouded in complete darkness would be ideal, she needed at least some light to know when the demon returned.

That quickly proved to be the best course of action. True to its catlike form, the demon was completely silent as it crested the stairs.

It paused. Its eyes glinted like rubies as they swept the library. *"There is no need to hide, young mage."*

Mavery blinked. Had the demon just...*spoken* to her?

No, she was hearing things. Exhaustion and overexposure to magic had finally driven her mad.

The demon crossed the room at a leisurely pace.

"Fear not, for I will not harm you. You are Senova—same as Master Aganast."

The voice was a gentle purr, not the bone-chilling growl from before.

This had to be a demonic trick, just like in the old folktales. She clenched her fists, dug her nails into her palms—a bit of pain to keep her wits sharp. She doubted she had anything in common with a Necromancer and demon sympathizer.

The beast stepped closer. It had found her hiding spot, but it hadn't charged after her. In fact, it could have easily overtaken her on the stairs, but it had allowed her a head start.

Slowly, she turned and met the demon's gaze. Its red eyes were still unsettling, but gone was the fierceness she'd seen downstairs. The beast cocked its head as it eyed her with the curiosity of a housecat, despite being at least ten times the size of one.

"You can Sense arcana, can you not?"

Never once did the demon's jaws move. She heard its voice only in her mind. And she once again smelled that strange arcana: burnt wood and petrichor, the aftermath of fire and rain. It was now stronger, more concentrated, than the aroma emanating from the discarded books.

The demon took another step, then stopped. It was close enough that Mavery could reach out and touch it. She should have been trembling in fear, watching her life flash before her eyes. And yet...

"Aganast was a Senser, too?" Mavery whispered.

The demon inclined its head. *"Senser, Senova... Call it whatever you prefer, for they are one and the same."*

She remembered something she'd discovered in the University's library weeks ago: one scholar's claim that Sensers were possessed by demons. She'd dismissed it outright, but what if there'd been a modicum of truth to it?

"You mean Sensers are...*connected* to dem—?"

"*NO!*"

The demon roared aloud at the same time its voice pealed inside her mind. She flinched, clutching her temples.

"MY KIND ARE NOT DEMONS. WE ARE—"

An explosion resonated through the room. Mavery flinched again and covered her ears. Her mind flooded with memories of a frigid night, her stomach clenched from a phantom pain.

She had enough presence of mind to watch the creature turn on the spot as it roared at the intrusion.

Another shot fired. Then a third.

The creature whimpered before collapsing to the floor. It lay on its side, fur saturated with black liquid in the area where Mavery imagined its heart would be. Its body shuddered as it drew a ragged breath, then stilled.

It was dead.

The ringing subsided. Her gaze drifted from the creature's body to the smoking pistol in Neldren's right hand.

"Godsdamned beast. Bullets were too good for it." He looked at Mavery, and his gaze softened. "You all right, Mave? Did it hurt you?"

She regarded the creature's corpse as its final words echoed in her mind.

My kind are not demons...

"No," she whispered. "It didn't."

"Good. Ellice finally cracked the door. Your wizard's a little bruised—his ego more than his body, I'll wager." Neldren holstered his pistol and offered his hand. "Now, let's get the fuck out of here before something else tries to kill us."

FIFTY-ONE

As Mavery stepped through the open door, the midday sun blinded her. She closed her fist and at last extinguished the light hovering above her palm.

"Watch your step," Neldren said.

She took his hand again, and he helped her down the two-foot drop from the tower's door. The ascent had fractured the ground and felled several trees on the outer edge of the forest.

Ellice was leaning against the tower's exterior, arms clutched around her midsection. Upon seeing Neldren, she became a blur of red hair as she launched herself at him. She threw her arms around his neck and pulled him down into a hard kiss. Mavery raised her brows. Even Neldren seemed taken by surprise, but he quickly recovered and returned her kiss with wild abandon. When Ellice pulled away, her face was nearly as red as her hair.

That was yet another mystery solved.

"Gods, when you ran after that *thing*, I thought you were dead!"

"Oh, come now," Neldren said with a smirk. "You know it'll take a lot more than that to kill me."

"Where's Alain?" Mavery asked.

The two of them turned to her with blank looks, as if they'd already forgotten she was still there.

"He went off to sulk," Ellice said, rolling her eyes. "Go look around back."

Mavery shouldered her pack and took off at a slow jog—her aching body could manage no more than that—and found Alain on the other side of the tower. He trailed his hand over its stone exterior as he paced back and forth, muttering to himself.

"Alain!"

He turned around. He dropped his satchel, tossed his staff aside, and ran toward her. They collided in an embrace. Alain clung to her tightly, his face pressed against her hair.

"I heard the gunshots," he said, his breath warming her neck. "Did he...take care of the beast?"

She nodded. "It's dead."

He sighed with relief. "I'm sorry for failing you back there. I should have told you I was weaker than I was letting on. My magic was useless against that—"

She pulled back. "You were anything but useless! You destroyed the anchor and disabled the wards. Not only that, your theories about the temple, about Aganast, were correct."

"All fair points," he said. "But I failed to protect you. I wish I could have done more in that regard."

She placed her palms to his cheeks, angled his face until he looked her squarely in the eye. "Alain, I don't need your magic, or your protection. I only need *you*."

She realized she'd been holding back tears. She let them fall freely as Alain gave her the warmest smile he'd ever given her. He raised his hand to her cheek, dried it with a slow swipe of his thumb. He leaned forward, lips parting—

"Well, this has been fun," Neldren said.

Alain froze, and Mavery suppressed a groan as Neldren came sauntering over. Ellice clung to his waist, looking none too eager to leave his side anytime soon.

"Now that the job's done, we'll be taking our leave." He extended a palm. "The other half of our payment, as we agreed."

Ellice hissed something at Neldren, who mumbled in return. But Mavery was too preoccupied with wiping away her remaining tears and rummaging through her pack to make sense of their bickering. She pulled out the old sock in which she'd hidden the five hundred potins, along with the syringe of resurrection serum. It was by some miracle that she hadn't needed to use the latter today.

She held out the wad of cash to Neldren. For a second, he stared at it hungrily. But then his eyes flicked to Ellice, and that hunger faded. He sighed.

"Keep it."

Mavery blinked at him. "What?"

"Consider us even. Besides, all this silver we collected should fetch a fair price." He tipped his head to Mavery, then Alain. "Until we meet again."

"Let's hope we don't," Ellice said, though there was no malice in her tone. Her lips pulled into a smile as she looked to Mavery, who was too flummoxed to respond.

"Oh, you never know," Neldren said. "This continent is only so big."

He slung his arm around Ellice's waist, and they parted without any additional fanfare. Once they vanished into the pine forest, Alain broke the silence with a heavy sigh.

"I, for one, am glad he didn't decide to dole out another round of hugs."

"That *was* rather odd, wasn't it?" Mavery said, then looked at the cash that remained in her hand. It had been almost as odd as him turning down a payment, but perhaps she'd underestimated his willingness to change. Why he could only do that for *Ellice*, a woman half his age, Mavery would never understand. But she put that thought to rest as she returned the money to the sock.

Alain peered up at the tower. "Now that *that* business is settled, we ought to give the tower another sweep."

"Dare I ask why?" Mavery groaned.

"Because the High Council will soon arrive to claim what's theirs."

Mavery's eyes widened as realization struck. "Not *that* covenant."

He nodded. "I'm afraid so."

"Fucking hells..."

She couldn't recall the precise wording, but any wizard who discovered an arcane archaeological site was required to turn it over to the High Council. That covenant explained why so many wizards sought out contractors. Not exclusively to avoid getting their hands dirty, but to take advantage of a loophole. Paying a mage for hire a small fortune for a useful ruin was preferable to letting the Elder Wizards seize control. Mavery had been so preoccupied with other matters—most of which had centered on not dying—it had slipped her mind.

"But we cracked this together," she said, "and I'm not a wizard—"

"But you were performing your duties as my assistant, so you also forfeit your ownership rights." Alain shook his head. "Had Neldren and Ellice not been so hasty to leave, that would've made matters a bit less straightforward. Not that I wanted to partake in more negotiations with them. In any case, we ought to get started now, while we still have time."

"You speak as if the High Council will swoop in at any moment. How will they even know?"

"Just look around." Alain gestured at the cracked ground and toppled trees. The top of the tower was likely visible from Archstone—or even further out. "It won't be long before they receive word of a significant arcane disturbance in this area. I wouldn't be surprised if they already have.

"If Aganast took these measures to hide his research, I'm not about to turn it over to the High Council. At least, not until I've gotten the chance to read his writings for myself."

"What about the creature? Aganast's remains?"

He shrugged. "I'm not too concerned about either. The books are our most valuable resource."

Mavery chewed her lip as she once again recalled the creature's dying words. If it hadn't been tricking her—if it truly wasn't a demon—she had come so close to discovering something about her abilities. But now she'd lost that resource forever.

Unless...

She reached inside the sock and pulled out the syringe.

"Will this work on something that's not human?"

Alain gawked at the syringe, then blinked at her. "Mavery, my love, are you suggesting you want to *revive* that demon?"

She nodded. "This is going to sound mad, but just before Neldren shot it, it spoke to me in my mind, like a Mystic but...different. It—*he*, I think—told me that Aganast was a Senser, that there's a connection between my magic and demonic magic. Well, not exactly. He said he wasn't a demon, but he died before he could explain."

Alain stared at her, mouth slightly agape.

She sighed. "I know I must sound insane—"

"Not at all." He grasped her by the shoulders. "I believe you. I only hesitate because the resurrection serum has limitations."

"Right, it has to be administered within an hour."

"Not only that, as the vital organs grow older and therefore weaker, resurrection becomes less viable. This creature is at least five centuries old. Even if the serum works on its species, it may not work on one so ancient."

"But we won't know until we try."

He nodded. "Where, exactly, did Neldren shoot it?"

"In the heart, I think."

Alain frowned. "That's far from ideal. Besides, if any bullets are lodged in its heart—or any vital organ—you would revive it, only to have it die again within minutes."

"Then I'll make sure to remove the bullets first."

Though she spoke matter-of-factly, she knew her plan was deranged—and potentially suicidal. But if this creature could tell her anything of use, then it would be well worth the attempt. Alain's eyes searched hers. A few times, his jaw quivered as though he were about to posit another warning, another caveat, but he said nothing. He took a deep breath, then smiled.

"If this is truly what you want," he said, "then I'm with you."

She leaned forward and pecked him on the lips. The kiss was too brief for her liking, but time was not on their side.

"Come on, we need to hurry."

She seized her pack and headed back to the tower's front door, taking care to avoid tripping over exposed rocks and uneven ground.

"Er, say you *do* need to remove any bullets," Alain said as he followed closely behind. "How are you planning to do that?"

Mavery's fingers slipped against the matted fur. From the floor, she'd recovered two of Neldren's bullets that had missed the creature entirely, so she needed to search for only one. Even with an orb of light directly beside her, it was hard to differentiate the creature's blood from his flesh and fur. It was all various shades of black on black on black. But then her finger slipped into a small divot—a bullet hole.

She dug her finger in deeper. Behind her, Alain groaned at the squelching sound. Her fingertip brushed against metal.

"Found it," she said.

When she removed her finger from the wound, her skin was coated in tar-black blood. She grabbed the pliers Alain had found among Aganast's alchemy supplies. She probed the bullet hole again, but the bullet itself was lodged between two walls of flesh that were beginning to grow stiff.

"Damn, it's in there tight." She put the pliers aside as she pondered what to do next. At most, she had ten minutes until the serum would be useless. "Say I were to cut the wound open, make it larger. Would the serum heal that, too?"

"Er...yes," Alain said weakly. "It will return the body to its pre-death state. That was why I had a fractured sternum, even after you revived me, as that injury occurred *before* I suffocated. Mere seconds before, I'll wager, as the serum is quite precise in that regard. Fascinating history behind its development, too, now that I think on it..."

Mavery knew his rambling was to distract himself from how she was about to perform impromptu surgery on a creature that may or may not be a demon. Perhaps *autopsy* was the correct word, seeing as how the creature was already dead. Or, perhaps they needed to invent a new word for a situation as absurd as this one.

She unsheathed her dagger. As she sliced into the creature's chest, Alain bolted to a corner of the room and retched.

"I would've thought you'd have an iron stomach, considering you've had your own chest sliced open... Remind me again, how many times was it?"

"Three," Alain said gravely. "But I never had to bear witness to that procedure. It's the advantage of being, well, dead."

Mavery snorted as she laid down her dagger, then widened the wound open with her fingers. She could see a glint of metal peeking out from the heart. Instead of giving in to disgust, she treated it as picking a rather complicated lock. She held the wound open with one hand as her other worked the pliers and prised out the bullet. She then tossed both pliers and bullet aside.

As she'd done once before, she grabbed the syringe and plunged the thick needle into the heart, dispensed the serum while counting to thirty, then pulled out the emptied syringe. She got to her feet and backed away, just in case the creature turned violent upon awakening. Alain joined her at her side, hands half-raised and prepared to summon another protective ward.

And then they waited.

Seconds passed, then a full minute, and the beast remained as lifeless as before. After another minute passed with no change, Alain lowered his hands.

"It appears the serum doesn't work on these creatures," he said, touching her shoulder. "I'm sorry."

Mavery sighed.

"We still have Aganast's books, not to mention his journal," he said. "If he was a Senser, as the creature claimed, perhaps we'll find our answers in there."

She nodded, then stepped forward and kneeled beside the corpse again. Acting on impulse, she gently stroked the creature from the crown of his head, down to where his wings joined his shoulders. In this state, he was nothing more than an oversized cat taking a nap. His fur was much softer than she'd expected, despite the rigid muscle beneath it.

Her hand stilled as she gasped. The incision she'd made with her dagger was smaller than she remembered. The serum *was* healing the beast, albeit very slowly. Maybe it needed more magic to speed up the process.

She placed her palm against the broken skin and channeled a little of her arcana, performing the same spell she'd once used on Alain's hand. The wound glowed with a turquoise aura that quickly faded.

"No. " The voice in her mind was barely a whisper. *"Paper. "*

"What?"

The creature did not speak again. But his torso rose and fell in the tiniest increments. She pulled her hand away and considered whether she'd heard the creature correctly. She looked around the room at the piles of books that had been reduced to nothing but leather covers and...

Arcana.

"Grab a book!" she cried. "Find one that still has its pages."

Alain's staff clattered to the floor as he sprung into action. Mavery focused on the creature while Alain opened tomes and tossed them aside.

"All of these have been transmutated," he said. "I could try upstairs—"

"That'll take too long. Bring me my Compendium. It's inside my pack."

Mavery resumed stroking the creature's fur. His body was less stiff, a few degrees warmer. But he was still too close to death for her liking.

Alain handed her the bundle of papers. She ripped off the front page.

"All right, I have paper," she whispered to the creature. "What do I need to do?"

One of his front paws twitched—a movement so subtle, she almost missed it entirely. She pressed the paper to the pad of his foot and held it there. The paper turned black and shriveled, as though it had been set on fire. And then it faded into the same dark mist she'd already seen countless times within this tower. The air smelled of smoldering wood and damp soil.

"Amazing," Alain breathed. "The book-eating demons weren't simply folktales."

Mavery didn't have the presence of mind to debate whether

what the creature was doing counted as *eating*. Though his breaths were less shallow, she knew he still teetered precariously on the edge between life and death.

"*More,*" his voice echoed through her mind.

She ripped out another page and repeated the process. Then another page, until she was ripping out full sections of her Compendium at a time. Gone were the herbalism field guides, the illustrations of healing spell rituals, the biographies of ancient wizards. They all turned to black vapor, but she was too focused on her task to mourn the loss.

With every scrap of paper the creature consumed, a bit more of his life force returned, his wounds stitched back together more quickly. A cloud of thick, dark arcana formed above them.

She gave the beast the final pages—the incantations Alain had written during her lessons—and all that remained in her hand was the thread she'd used to bind her Compendium together. She was preparing herself to ask Alain to fetch more books when the beast opened his eyes. Red irises gleamed in the Ethereal light and met her gaze.

"*Where is the one who killed me?*"

"Don't worry," she said softly. "He's long gone."

"*And his staff of thunder?*"

"Staff of...? Oh, you mean his gun. Also long gone."

The beast slowly raised his head, then rolled from his side to his stomach. Mavery moved back—not out of fear, but to give him more space. Though his final words had been fueled by anger, they hadn't been directed at her. She couldn't say the same about Alain. The beast looked behind Mavery's shoulder and at last noticed the other human in the room. He growled; Alain gasped.

"Easy, now," she said. "He's a friend."

The beast continued to eye Alain with suspicion. Alain, to his credit, took a step forward but only made it as far as Mavery's side when the beast growled again.

"Y-yes," he sputtered. "You can tell him we're all friends here."

"He says—"

"*Though the wizard cannot speak with me, I understand him.*"

"You understand Osperlandish?"

"Verily, though you and I require no common tongue to communicate. Our arcana connects our thoughts."

Mavery relayed this to Alain.

"Fascinating," he said. "And, er, I apologize for bashing you with my staff before."

The creature tilted its head. *"Bashing?"*

"It means to hit—" Mavery began.

"I know the meaning of the word. His 'bashing' was no more than the nibble of a flea."

Mavery decided to not repeat that part. The creature raised himself off the floor, rested on his haunches, and looked at Mavery again.

"That spell you used on me..." He grimaced, flashing his knife-like teeth. *"Soudremancy does not agree with my kind."*

"What *is* your kind, exactly?"

"Ktona. In your tongue, it means, 'from below.' "

"Kuh-*tone*-ah," Mavery repeated. "So, ktona are not at all related to demons?"

She winced as the creature growled. *"Ktonic magic comes from belowground. Your churches spread lies that ktonic magic comes from deep below. The hells."*

As Mavery repeated what the creature—the ktona—had said, a faint scribbling resounded through the room. She turned to find Alain huddled over his notebook again.

"Don't mind me," he said, pausing only to wave his pen. "Just eagerly recording evidence of the churches' misdoings."

The creature grunted. *"I had mistaken him for a church-sanctioned wizard. 'Twould seem I was wrong."*

Mavery nodded. "We don't belong to any churches."

"What are your names?"

"Mavery, and this is Alain. I assume you also have a name."

"Noxanthyan, but Master called me Nox. You may do the same."

He rose, then stretched his back. He stumbled upon taking his first steps, but regained more control of his muscles with each one that followed. He paced around the room, then ascended the stairs to the upper library. Mavery rose to her feet and placed her hand on Alain's shoulder. He flinched at her touch. Though the ktona had proven friendly, Alain was no less anxious.

"I think we can trust him," she said.

"*You* can. You saved his life, after all. If I didn't know any better, I'd say you've just earned yourself a lifelong companion."

She smiled. "That reminds me of someone else I know."

Alain returned her smile, but it faltered as he watched the stairwell. "As for me, I'm half-expecting him to come charging down those stairs and give me another swift wing to the chest." He rubbed the spot where his head had collided with the cabinet downstairs.

Instead of returning in a rage, Nox descended the stairs at a trot. In his mouth, he carried a small book, which he placed at Alain's feet. Alain hesitated, then slowly bent over and picked it up.

"*Master's first journal,*" Nox said, "*from when we first sought refuge in this tower. The one you pilfered from his desk was his second—and final—volume. How long has it been since that final entry?*"

"About five hundred years," Mavery said. "I assume your master died not long after that."

"*Yes.*" Nox's ears flattened as he hung his head. "*That same day, I had chided him for carelessly wandering about the tower without sufficient light. He tumbled down the stairs. My arcana was incapable of saving him.*"

Mavery hadn't expected to learn that a notorious Necromancer had succumbed to such a mundane death. It would have been somewhat funny in any other context. But Aganast's early demise meant that Nox had been completely alone for over five centuries.

"*I can sense your concern. For my kind, a century is akin to a decade.*"

"Still," Mavery said, "that's an awfully long time to be alone. And without seeing the sun."

"*Oh, to see the sun again. Did you manage to open the door?*" When she nodded, his tail swished. "*Then let us leave this place.*"

To watch Nox run in circles on the cracked, sun-bathed ground, it was hard to believe he'd been the fearsome beast that had attacked them not even two hours ago. He lapped the tower while Mavery and Alain watched on.

Nox gained a bit more speed with each lap, and the scent of his arcana permeated the air. He ventured into the grass, and Mavery's heart leapt as he neared one of the detonation wards.

"Wait!" she cried.

Nox bounded over an Ether-sensitive stone. But instead of setting off the trap, the red aura vanished. Mavery jogged closer, then gasped. The stone had transmutated into the same vaporous substance as the books and her Compendium. She tried to touch the stone, but her fingers passed straight through it.

"Did it disappear?" Alain asked.

Mavery shook her head. "I think he feeds on it, just like he did with the paper."

Nox seemed to notice her surprise. He stopped his frolicking and trotted over.

"This is ktonic magic. Whereas humans must draw arcana from the Ether, ktona draw arcana from stones, plants, any natural resource that is connected to the ground. As a Senova—Senser, in your tongue—you are capable of both. Does your magic not feel stronger here, surrounded by ktonic sources?"

Nox was right: her magic *had* always felt stronger whenever she was in the wilderness. She'd felt that way earlier that morning—and back in Weywode Forest. That explained why she'd always hated cities. She'd always blamed the filth, the crowds, the endless noise. But maybe there had also been a subconscious reason for it all along.

"That makes sense," she said, "but I've never drawn magic from stones or anything like that."

Nox cocked his head to the side. *"Never?"*

"What about anchors?" Alain asked. "That sounds like a similar process to me."

"More than similar—the very same. How else did wizards learn

to harness the power of natural resources?"

"Wait, so anchors are actually ktonic magic?" Mavery asked. When Nox nodded, she furrowed her brow. "Then why did the churches say that your magic—*our* magic, rather—came from the hells?"

Nox uttered a noise that sounded eerily similar to cold laughter. *"Because once the churches and wizards leeched every last bit of knowledge from my kind, they discarded us, enslaved us, bred us with more subservient creatures. The Senova, being the only ones who communicate with ktona, were tasked with keeping us obedient. This was the way of Tanarim for centuries, until Master and his Order sought a different path."*

"What was the Order of Asphodel, exactly?"

"A group of twelve Senova that sought to liberate the ktona. They encouraged my kind to rebel against our enslavers."

Mavery gawked at him. She was so stunned by his words, she forgot to interpret them for Alain.

"What?" Alain asked, tugging on her sleeve. "What did he say?"

"The Order...they were Senova, Sensers. That means..." She gasped. "That means there were once a dozen Sensers, right here, all at once!"

"A dozen in Master's Order, yes, but there are hundreds across Tanarim." He cocked his head. *"You find this surprising?"*

After Mavery repeated Nox's question, Alain answered, "*Incredibly* surprising. There might have been hundreds of Sensers when you and Aganast went into hiding, but those numbers have dwindled significantly over the past five centuries. Mavery here is one of the few Sensers currently living. I wonder..." He looked skyward with a laugh. "All along, the subjects most shrouded in rumors and secrecy—Sensing, the Innominate Temple, the Order of Asphodel—all shared a common thread..."

"What happened to the Order? Why did none of them disable the tower's defenses, as Master had planned?"

Mavery frowned. "I'm sorry, Nox. They were all executed."

Alain recoiled as Nox growled, baring his teeth. After regaining his composure, Alain turned to Mavery. "We still need to give the library another look. It won't be long until the High Council arrives."

"The High Council of Wizards?" Nox arched his back and hissed. This time, even Mavery flinched. How easily she'd forgotten that this creature, though highly intelligent, was still a beast. *"You cannot allow Master's books to fall into their hands! Not the books he kept to sustain me, but his life's work. He stored those precious tomes in the bedchamber."*

"Don't worry," she said, "we already found those. Is there anything else in the tower we should grab before the Council arrives?"

"Master's remains. At long last, he ought to receive a proper burial."

Mavery inwardly shuddered at the thought of touching that pile of bones, but then she nodded. "We'll handle it. You ought to hide in the forest until—"

Nox's wings retracted into his body, and he shrank to a quarter of his original size. Instead of an imposing winged beast, he now appeared a miniature panther—or an overgrown housecat. His eyes, however, retained their crimson glow.

"Master called this my familiar form."

Mavery blinked at him. "Er, yes, that should work. If anyone asks, we'll say you're some sort of demonspawn."

Nox sneered. *"You would compare me to one of those abominations?"*

"It's either that, or let the Elder Wizards take you away."

He gave a low growl—in this form, he sounded as intimidating as an angry kitten—but then trotted away and resumed stretching his muscles for the first time in over five hundred years.

Alain volunteered to handle Aganast's remains. The trunk in which Aganast had stored his life's work became his coffin. Alain and Mavery, each carrying one end of the trunk, followed Nox into the forest, back to the cabin blanketed with asphodel. Nox instructed them to place the trunk in the same spot where Ellice had exhumed the anchor and then buried it again. Now that they lacked both a shovel *and* a mender, Mavery wondered how they would manage "a proper burial."

As Nox approached the trunk, the air filled with the aroma that she now knew was ktonic magic. Slowly, the trunk sank into the ground. White petals fluttered in the breeze, like hundreds of tiny heads bowing in reverence.

Mavery had expected Nox to deliver a eulogy, or to spare a few moments to mourn. But once his spell was complete, he turned back to the tower in silence. She supposed he'd had plenty of time to grieve his master's death; this burial was simply a long overdue formality.

She and Alain were also silent as they followed the ktona. Not that there was much they *could* have articulated. If her head was reeling from all these revelations, she couldn't imagine how Alain felt.

When they returned to the tower once again, Mavery finally appreciated the grandeur of the ruin they'd uncovered. In the early afternoon sun, its shadow just barely touched the trap-laden field. Beneath the mud and substrate were gray stone and a glimmer of stained glass windows. Once the next rainstorm washed away all the grime, Aganast's tower would be not quite as stately as the towers at the University, but it would be an impressive sight all the same.

"It's a shame you have to hand this over," she said. "You uncovered it. You ought to decide what happens to it."

"It is," Alain said with a nod. "Alas, I'm duty-bound."

"What do you think they'll do with it?"

He shrugged. "If a ruin has ties to someone of importance, the High Council usually preserves it as a historical site. But seeing as we've removed everything that would identify *this* tower's owner, they'll probably destroy it. I doubt any of the Elder Wizards will want to keep it for themselves."

"What about you?"

Alain looked at her. "Me?"

"Would *you* want to keep the tower for yourself?"

He laughed. "And do what with it, exactly? Surely you're not suggesting we *live* here?"

"Gods, no! But once you resign from the University, you'll no longer need to confine yourself to Leyport. Not to mention, you'll need a new project. Why not let *this* be it?"

She gestured at the tower, then realized her hands were still covered in Nox's blood. As Alain pondered her idea, she pulled her canteen from her pack and wet her hands. The dried blood on her skin washed off easily enough, but the black gunk beneath her fingernails proved more stubborn. She couldn't wait to return to the village and spend the rest of the afternoon in a hot bath.

Before she could daydream about that, a clap of thunder sounded in the distance. A second later, Mavery's head erupted in pain. She recoiled as a powerful wave of arcana crashed against her, reverberated through her bones. Somewhere nearby, Nox hissed. She didn't need their connection to know he felt the effects as strongly as she did.

"A portal spell," Alain said. "The High Council is here."

FIFTY-TWO

With Nox at their side, Alain and Mavery crossed the field and approached three robed figures. The one leading the way was a tall man sporting a long white beard. Though Mavery couldn't see his face from this distance, she recognized him by his bearing alone.

"The Archmage himself decided to pay us a visit."

"So it seems," Alain said. "I'll handle this."

"Are you sure?"

He nodded as he squeezed her hand, then released it and walked forward. Seringoth trudged through the grass, flanked by two of the male Elder Wizards. His intense gaze left an uneasy feeling in Mavery's stomach, but knowing he hadn't brought the Mystic along was a small comfort.

"Archmage," Alain said, bowing his head. "What brings you to this corner of Osperland?"

"I believe you already know the answer to that question," Seringoth said tersely. "Late this morning, the High Council received word from Highillen University about an unusually high surge of arcane activity, followed by a half-dozen reports of an earthquake in this area—the first in over a century. We could not let such reports go without a thorough investigation." Arms crossed, he turned to the tower. "So, Aventus, it appears you are the one responsible for cracking the mystery of the Innominate Temple."

"Yes, Archmage, though it seems the 'temple' was a wizard's tower all along." He chuckled weakly, then cleared his throat. "And I couldn't have done it without Ms. Culwich's help."

Seringoth and the other two wizards spared Mavery a split-second glance before returning their attention to the tower. Mavery suppressed a scoff.

"Have you investigated this tower?" Seringoth asked.

"Most thoroughly, Archmage. Using the same Sensing spell we presented to the High Council last week, we located the anchor that had powered its protections, and we disabled the fabrication that had buried the majority of the tower underground.

"Unfortunately, there is nothing of note inside, other than a long-abandoned library. None of the books identify the tower's original owner, nor do they appear to have any scholarly merit."

Mavery held her breath as she expected Seringoth to call Alain's bluff. At her feet, Nox batted an insect. Either he wasn't at all interested in this conversation, or he was fully committed to pretending to be an innocuous familiar.

"That will be for the High Council to decide," Seringoth said. "As stated in chapter five of *The Covenants of Wizarding Decorum,* the High Council will now take custody of this ruin. Your work here is complete."

"Of course, Archmage. We'll be on our way." Alain bowed his head, turned on his heel.

"Hold on," Mavery said. Alain blanched as he came to her side. "What will the High Council do with this tower?"

"Whatever the High Council deems is necessary," said one of the Elder Wizards. From his condescending tone and thick eyebrows, Mavery recognized him as the wizard who had chided Alain about the Sensing spell's "practicality."

"Care to be a little more specific?" Mavery asked.

"What are you doing?" Alain whispered in her ear.

"Finding you a new project," she whispered back. "It's worth a shot."

"As with any newly exhumed historical site, the High Council will begin with a full inventory of the tower's contents," said the short, sepia-skinned wizard to Seringoth's left. He spoke with a Maroban accent. "Any books and artifacts of scholarly significance will be given to the High Council's arcanists for safekeeping. If what Aventus claims is true, and this tower bears nothing of note, then the structure will be destroyed."

"Destroying something this large will require, what, a dozen menders?" Mavery asked. "Why go through all that trouble when someone could simply take it off your hands?"

"That 'someone' being *you*, I presume." The wizard with the thick brows sneered at her. "What could a mere mage possibly want with a wizard's tower? Would you even know what to do with such a thing?"

Mavery smirked. "Oh, I have it on good authority that a 'mere mage' is perfectly capable of handling a wizard's *tower*."

Alain sputtered something that he promptly stifled with a cough. As Eyebrows opened his mouth, Seringoth took him and the other Elder Wizard by the shoulders. The three of them stepped a few paces away, then spoke in heated whispers. Mavery and Alain exchanged glances. Nox watched the Elder Wizards with suspicion, ears lowered and fangs bared.

A moment later, the three wizards returned.

"The High Council is open to your suggestion," Seringoth said. "Given this tower's age and condition, it is unlikely to be of any scholarly use. Allow us to conduct a thorough investigation of its contents and seize immediate ownership of anything with scholarly merit. Agree to this, and the tower will be turned over to you."

Mavery narrowed her eyes. "And when would that be?"

"No less than one year, as is standard practice."

"Three months," Alain said. His tone was surprisingly firm, though he avoided meeting Seringoth's eye. "Agree to complete the investigation by the end of the summer, Archmage, and we have a deal."

Eyebrows scoffed. "Why, you insolent—"

Seringoth raised a hand. "Calm yourself, Elder Lythandus." He looked to Mavery. "Ms. Culwich, will you allow Aventus to negotiate on your behalf?"

She nodded. "He can take it from here."

The Archmage turned to Alain. "Why do you wish to expedite the investigation?"

Alain gave Mavery a brief glance before returning his gaze forward. He clasped his hands behind his back while keeping his head high—respectful but nonetheless assertive.

"My reasons are my own, Archmage." He met Seringoth's eye. "Wouldn't you agree that a wizard of my *fortitude* ought to have a more robust space for conducting experiments and housing his library?"

Mavery's stomach fluttered with fondness—alongside more wanton feelings—but she bit the inside of her cheek, forcing herself to retain her composure.

"Understandable," Seringoth said. "What I fail to understand is why a professor at the University of Leyport would want a tower that is located over two hundred miles from campus."

"As I said, Archmage, my reasons are my own."

He and Seringoth held each other's gazes. Under normal circumstances, Mavery would take the moment of silence to appreciate the sun's warmth upon her skin, the gentle breeze, the serenade of birdsong from the nearby woods. Instead, the air was thick with tension, and all she could focus on was Alain, somehow holding firm beneath Seringoth's penetrating stare. After a long moment of silence, Seringoth spoke again.

"Very well. Should this tower prove to be of no use to the High Council, it will be turned over to you in three months. Until then, we look forward to your follow-up presentation on Siddisday."

"Thank you, sir," Alain said with a slight nod. "If I could make one final request... Could I get all of this in writing?"

A quarter hour later, Alain's agreement with the High Council was committed to parchment, and he and Mavery were on the journey back to Archstone. They had Nox in tow, the tower at their backs.

When they were deep enough in the forest that the Elder Wizards wouldn't overhear them, Mavery shook her head and laughed.

"I can't believe you lied to the High Council," she said. "To *Seringoth*."

"Technically speaking, I didn't outright lie."

"You told them there was nothing inside the tower!"

"Precisely. There was nothing in the tower. *On our persons*, on the other hand..." He met her raised brows with a sly smile. "What can I say? You *have* rubbed off on me. Besides, my little half-truth is nothing compared to what the High Council has hidden for centuries about Sensers, about ktonic magic."

Never had Mavery expected him to be so brazen.

Never had she found him so desirable.

She would have thrown herself at him, had her body not ached from head to toe, inside and out. After today's events, she yearned for a hearty meal, a long bath, and an even longer nap. And she could tell that Alain's desires aligned with hers. The further they continued through the forest, the more his pace slowed—and it had been far from brisk to begin with.

"What do you think happened to the rest of the ktona?" Mavery asked. "Do you think they were all killed?"

"Many of my kin spoke of seeking refuge in Nilandor," Nox said. *"The High Council and the churches held no power there."*

Mavery repeated this to Alain, and he nodded.

"There may be some ktona left in Tanarim," he said, "but I'll bet most of them are in Nilandor."

"What do you think, Nox?" Mavery asked. "Should we try tracking down your kin?"

But Nox did not answer. Now that he was safe from the Elder Wizards, he had returned to his bestial form. He soared overhead, a dark blur against the sun-dappled treetops.

This would be his last opportunity to spread his wings for a few days. Since they couldn't risk the High Council discovering Nox, he would journey back to Leyport with Mavery and Alain tomorrow. He would find a new home in Weywode Forest—at least until hunting season began.

On the trip home, Alain would prepare his presentation, and

after meeting with the High Council again, he would finally announce his resignation to Kazamin.

Beyond that, it was impossible to say what awaited them; even Aganast's tower wasn't a certainty. But as Mavery slipped her hand into Alain's, and his fingers entwined with hers, she decided she didn't mind a bit of uncertainty. Whatever the future held, they would face it together.

FIFTY-THREE

As Alain sat in Kazamin's library—not at the University, but in his home—he considered how this space was unlike any wizard's library he'd ever come across. The room was roughly the size of Alain's sitting room, and it contained just as many books. But this library had always been clean, orderly. Never had Alain found a single tome stacked on the floor or strewn about the furniture haphazardly. Alain wondered if Kazamin had actually read every book in his collection. Judging by the plethora of uncracked spines, he doubted it.

But Alain had no room to judge. After all, his own library was also filled with unread books whose only purpose seemed to be collecting dust.

Kazamin groaned as he lowered himself into the leather armchair directly across from Alain. He and Kazamin had last met only a month ago, yet the dean seemed to have aged several years during that time. He appeared smaller, thinner than Alain remembered. But he couldn't let the old man's frailty deter him from his plan.

"Well, Aventus, I believe congratulations are in order. Finding a way into the Innominate Temple was no easy feat."

"Thank you, sir, though it was far from a solitary effort."

"Humble as ever," he said, smiling warmly. "So, what brings you here today? Safiya said you wanted to talk about something important, unrelated to your recent accomplishments."

"Er, right..."

Alain averted his gaze as he picked at a loose stitch in the leather. It was strange how he was more nervous for this than he'd been for his follow-up presentation. But yesterday's meeting with the High Council had been perfunctory, little more than an extension of the informal meeting they'd held outside Aganast's tower. Mavery had opted to stay home. Firstly, because she hadn't mastered Dauphinian overnight. Secondly, to avoid stoking Lythandus's ire again, amusing as that would have been. But Alain had managed without her. He'd glided through the presentation with ease and, fifteen minutes later, the Sensing spell was approved for peer review and his rank was secure once more. Compared to what he was about to do, he'd rather repeat the presentation ten times over. He took a deep breath before looking Kazamin in the eye.

"I wish to resign from the University, effective immediately."

Kazamin's eyes widened. "Resign? Whatever for?"

"You've read my teaching evaluations over these past eight years. Teaching has never been my passion, and it couldn't be more obvious to my students—and my fellow professors. Recent events have made me realize that I ought to forge my own path, outside the University's towers."

Alain should have felt relief for finally telling Kazamin what he ought to have said years ago. Instead, he felt only dread as his supervisor—his mentor, his friend—gave him a look of utter shock.

But then that look turned into a wide, almost patronizing smile. "I understand your hesitancy, Aventus. I, too, went through a similar phase early in my career, when I believed myself the worst professor to ever walk the face of Perrun. But you are talented, passionate, dedicated. Above all else, you are still young. I have faith that you will—"

"There's more to it, sir." He braced himself, hating that it had come to this, but he needed to get *everything* out in the open. "I've violated the Covenants by having romantic relations with my assistant. Therefore, I'm no longer fit to be a professor."

Kazamin sighed. "Well, yes. *Obviously.*"

"Obviously, I should no longer be a professor?"

"Obviously, you have been having an affair with your assistant." He chuckled at what Alain could only assume was a look of bafflement mixed with horror. "My boy, though my mind may not be as sharp as it once was, my *eyes* remain as keen as ever.

"I've known since you first brought that woman into my office. You looked at her the same way I looked at Safiya during the early days of our courtship." He shook his head. "I had only hoped you wouldn't be foolish enough to *confess* to it."

Alain could do nothing but stare at Kazamin, mouth agape. His head reeled, though this really should have come as no surprise. Ever since Mavery entered his life, he could scarcely remember feeling more content. His mother had known it, as had Declan.

"If anyone asks, I'll forget this conversation ever happened," Kazamin said. "Having a faulty memory does have its upsides."

"But..." Alain shook his head. "Perhaps I misunderstood, but are you saying you *won't* report me to the High Council for this?"

"What you and your assistant do in private is of no consequence to me. So long as it *remains* private, I see no reason to report you. Far be it from me to let a minor slip-up get in the way of your career."

Alain continued to gawk. He'd just confessed to something that ought to serve as grounds for being fired—if not stripped of his rank—and Kazamin had called it "a minor slip-up." Even Declan, the student body's most beloved professor, had received a more severe punishment.

Alain glanced at the portrait hanging above the hearth. Seated next to Kazamin was a graceful Nilandoren woman, Safiya Fel'Shara, his wife and long-time assistant. Of course, Alain should have known Kazamin would be understanding. But Kazamin had been Dean for nearly fifty years, and he'd been married to Safiya decades before the covenant banning such a union went into effect. Never would Alain have equated their circumstances.

"As for your resignation, I cannot accept it."

Alain looked to Kazamin again. "But I followed the Covenants. I gave you plenty of notice—"

"And the Covenants state that a dean reserves the right to deny any resignation that would place undue hardship upon his department. Thanks to the latest budget cuts, the Gardemancy Department is in the midst of a hiring freeze. Had you not been on sabbatical for the past year, you would have known that." Kazamin's words carried with them an abnormal bitterness.

"Speaking of which," he continued, "I will not be allowing any sabbaticals for the upcoming term. Should you decide to take another unauthorized leave of absence, I *will* report you to the High Council. But we both know you would not do anything so unwise. Marya knows the Gardemancy Department cannot afford any more upheavals…"

" 'Upheavals,' sir?"

Kazamin muttered something in Maroban as he shook his head. "Nothing to concern yourself with. Put it from your mind for now."

He struggled to hoist himself from his armchair. Alain rose to his feet, offered Kazamin a hand that was shooed away. Kazamin managed to get out of the chair on his own. He grabbed his cane, hobbled across the library, and opened the door for Alain.

"Take my advice and enjoy your summer holiday. Read for pleasure, travel, do something that isn't related to scholarship. Given what you've just achieved with the Innominate Temple, no one will begrudge you for taking a few months off. Do that, and I fully believe you'll have a change of heart come autumn."

Alain opened his mouth, yet he was unable to find the words to argue with Kazamin further. He simply nodded.

All the way home, he dreaded how he would break this news to Mavery. Since returning to Leyport two days ago, she'd dived head-first into the role of his assistant and had spent most of her time formulating ideas for what to do with Aganast's tower. In fact, Alain suspected her bargaining for the tower had been for her own benefit as much as it had been for his.

When he entered the apartment, he found her amid a pile of biographies. She turned to the door with *The Definitive Biography of Seringoth I* in hand—a tome that could double as a blunt weapon. Seeing her spring green eyes meet his, being on the receiving end of that slightly crooked yet stunning smile... Both were enough to make him fall in love with her all over again.

"As you can probably tell, I've been thinking of the library," she said.

He blinked, pulling himself from his musings. "Er, what library?"

"Yours. More specifically, my idea of moving your books to Aganast's tower. Gods know you've long outgrown this space."

He laughed. "I won't argue with that."

"And then I got to thinking..." She put the book aside and pulled herself to her feet. "Why not do more than simply house your books there? Why not allow anyone to come visit and read your books as they please?"

Alain scratched his chin. "I've never heard of a wizard opening up their private library to just anyone."

"Then why not be the first?" She stepped forward, took his hands in hers. "If there's one thing I remember from my six weeks of Introduction to Arcanist Studies, it's that a wizard's private library isn't like the universities' libraries. Your own book collection isn't beholden to any arcanists. We can ensure Aganast's books, along with anything else we discover, will never again become lost to time—or people like Arcanist Tristan, for that matter."

"Not to mention, we'd be giving back something to the people of Archstone, now that we've deprived them of their main tourist attraction," Alain said. "But I doubt the High Council will be pleased once they catch wind of what we're planning."

Mavery shrugged. "Probably not, but we should still try."

"I'm not disagreeing with you. In fact, I quite like this idea." As he began to raise their joined hands, he remembered his conversation with Kazamin. He winced. "There's but one problem: I'll still be at the University for the foreseeable future. Kazamin wouldn't accept my resignation."

"Did you tell him about us?"

"Not only was he understanding, we have his blessing to carry on in private."

She gaped at him. "You're joking."

He shook his head. "I should have suspected he'd say that, considering he's married to his own assistant—"

"He's married to his *what*!? Why didn't you mention that before?"

Alain shrugged. "He's a dean, I'm only a professor. There are different standards for—"

"Godsdamned hypocrites," Mavery muttered, "the lot of them..."

He led her to the sofa, where he relayed everything else Kazamin had told him. As always, Mavery clung to every word, adding an incredulous scoff or interjection—sometimes with a sprinkling of expletives—in just the right places. He concluded with a frustrated groan as he rubbed his temples.

"What are we going to do?" she asked.

"I don't know. Even if the High Council doesn't give us Aganast's tower, I can't see how I'll manage teaching *and* research *and*—"

"Not that. I mean, what are we going to do about *us*? I know Kazamin said we can court in secret, but I can't say that's what I want."

"That's not what I want, either."

She frowned. "Then maybe I should—"

"You're *not* resigning," Alain said at once, though he silently chided himself for not doing the most sensible thing. On top of everything else, how could he possibly handle a secret courtship with his assistant?

Unless...she wasn't his *assistant*.

"Going back to the library idea," he said, "you were wrong about one thing."

"And what's what?"

"Should we open a library, I will be beholden to *one* arcanist."

Mavery raised a brow; he answered it with a coy smile.

"I'll need an arcanist to manage all these books and ensure they don't get pilfered. Ideally, I'll need someone who can think like a thief. Someone who is intimately familiar with my collection." He leaned in closer, his gaze lowered to her lips. "Someone whose company I find *most* desirable."

She smiled back. "Those are some *very* specific qualifications. Do you have anyone in mind?"

"As a matter of fact, I do." He raised her hand to his mouth, brushed his lips across her knuckles. "Mavery Culwich, would you do me the honor of being my arcanist?"

She leaned forward and kissed him forcefully, as though it had been weeks, not mere hours, since their last. This had become a common occurrence over these past days.

I don't need your magic... I only need you.

A small part of him still believed he didn't deserve this woman.

Perhaps someday that small part of him would realize its beliefs were false.

He pulled back slightly. "Just to be clear, was that a 'yes'?"

Mavery rolled her eyes. "Oh, come here."

The next moments were a blur. He distinctly remembered her straddling his lap, removing her blouse, placing her mouth to his neck.

And then they were back to falling into bed, and into each other. As he buried himself in her, he reveled in her blissful sighs and flushed cheeks. Her fingers gripped his shoulders while her legs wrapped around his lower back. Her gasps urged him to take her faster, deeper. They alternated between pushing and pulling, exploring each other's bodies as they'd done many times over these past days. Yet, each time had always led to new discoveries. Each time had been just as thrilling, just as perfect, as the one before it. As she quavered beneath him, around him, all he could think of was how he wanted nothing more than to have a lifetime's worth of perfect moments like this.

But as they lay face to face, basking in the afterglow, the thoughts that had lain dormant began to reawaken. His mind soon became a swarm of ideas, questions, anxieties. They created such a din of noise, he could hear everything and nothing all at once.

Mavery's fingers brushed his cheek, then his temple, as she pushed a lock of hair from his face. He closed his eyes with a sigh, thankful for her touch. *This,* he could focus on without any effort at all. Her touch grounded him enough to remember that, while there would be no shortage of work in the months ahead, there would be time to worry about that later.

For once in his life, he had all the time in the world.

ACKNOWLEDGMENTS

First and foremost, thanks to my beta readers: Brittany, Matt, Meggan, Isabeau, Babs, and Sarah. Your feedback helped me shape this story into something that was far better than I could have ever imagined, and your enthusiasm kept me motivated during the many ups and downs of the writing process. Some of you amazing people even read multiple drafts!

Thanks to my mom for instilling in me a love of reading from an early age—and for keeping some of my terrible first books.

Thanks to the teachers I've had over the years, from elementary school to graduate school. That includes the late Mrs. B, who always said I would publish a book one day.

And because those teachers would be horrified if I failed to cite my sources, special thanks to the research team at Aberystwyth University for their work behind the Anglo-Norman Dictionary. This was an invaluable resource for bringing the Dauphinian language to life. Vostre merci!

Finally, thanks to my husband for being all-in on this journey, from the first draft to the last. This book wouldn't have been possible without your love and support, and it's no coincidence that I started writing more "kissing books" after we tied the knot. A single paragraph will never be enough to express how lucky I am to have you in my life.

Compendium of Knowledge

The Schools of Magic

Magic comes from the Ether, a fundamental force that most people on Perrun believe was created by a goddess. Magic is an inherited trait, and abilities tend to manifest in early childhood. Every mage has one innate School of Magic. It is possible to learn spells from any of the other Schools of Magic, but those spells will be weaker than those from one's innate School.

Arcane hypersensitivity, or Sensing, is the ability to see, smell, and taste many types of magic. Mages with this ability, known as Sensers, are exceptionally rare. The Senses associated with each School are included below.

Aumbremancy · (**ahm**-bruh-man-see)
 Domain: Shadows
 Practitioners: Aumbremancers, shadow mages/wielders
 Associated Senses: Ash scent/taste
Elemancy · (**el**-uh-man-see)
 Domain: Classical elements
 Practitioners: Elemental mages/wielders
 Associated Senses: None, and the effects of these spells can be easily observed even by non-mages

Faisancy · (**fay**-zawn-see)
  Domain: Inorganic materials
  Practitioners: Menders
  Associated Senses: Saltwater scent/taste, dark red auras
Gardemancy · (**gar**-duh-man-see)
  Domain: Protective barriers ("wards")
  Practitioners: Gardemancers, wardbreakers, wardsmiths
  Associated Senses: Metallic scent/taste. The color of auras depend on the specific type of ward (detonation: red, fireproofing: pink, obfuscation: green, protective: blue, resonating: gold, soundproofing: violet).
Mysticism · (**miss**-tuh-siz-um)
  Domain: Mind-reading and divination
  Practitioners: Mystics
  Associated Senses: Floral scent
Necromancy · (**neck**-roe-man-see)
  Domain: Death
  Practitioners: Necromancers
  Associated Senses: None
Soudremancy · (**soo**-druh-man-see)
  Domain: Healing
  Practitioners: Soudremancers, healers
  Associated Senses: Herbal scent/taste, aquamarine auras
Transmutation · (trans-mew-**tay**-shun)
  Domain: Transformation of space and substances
  Practitioners: Transmuters, alchemists
  Associated Senses: None

Magical Education in Tanarim

Early Education: Magic is generally not taught to children under the age of seventeen. Only a select few schools offer classes on the basics of magic.

University: Tanarim is home to fifteen wizarding universities. Applicants must pass an entrance exam that tests their innate aptitude for magic, as well as their reading, writing, and logic skills. Tuition is not free, and few universities offer full scholarships, so students tend to come from affluent families. Most mages begin university at age seventeen and graduate after four years. Prospective wizards must complete six years. Students ultimately choose one School as their concentration. They may learn spells from most Schools, with the exceptions being Mysticism (exclusively taught at the College of Mystics), and Soudremancy (exclusively taught at sanctified temples).

Becoming a Wizard: A mage must present an original work of scholarship to the High Council of Wizards. The High Council will then decide whether the mage has earned their wizard rank, along with an honorific ("wizard name"). Earning this rank takes, on average, ten years after graduation. In the meantime, prospective wizards will typically serve as wizard's assistants. To retain their rank, wizards must make regular contributions to scholarship, which may include teaching at a wizarding university, writing textbooks, or creating new spells and potions.

The High Council of Wizards: The governing body for all magical education across Tanarim, the High Council consists of eight Elder Wizards, each representing one of the Schools of Magic, and an Archmage who serves as the head of the Council. To become an Elder Wizard, one must hold the rank of wizard for at least fifty years, and serve as the Chancellor of a wizarding university for at least five years.

Religions of Perrun

The Tanarimic Pantheon

Most of the continent of Tanarim worships the Dyad, but there are smaller sects devoted exclusively to other deities. **Yvernal** is the major Pantheonic holiday. Coinciding with the winter solstice, it is a week-long celebration devoted to feasting, gift-giving, and honoring all the Pantheonic deities, which include:

Tanar and Selesta, The Dyad
> Symbol: Pair of crescent moons
> The proto-gods. Tanar created the physical world; his twin, Selesta, created the nonphysical world, including the Ether. Perrun's two moons are named after the Dyad, and the continent of Tanarim is named after Tanar.

Marya, Wardeness of the Beyond
> Symbol: Shepherd's hook
> Marya oversees entry to the Beyond, the Pantheon's version of heaven. Her followers have great reverence for the dead.

Ferne, Sentinel of Enferné
> Symbol: Fire
> Ferne oversees Enferné, the Pantheon's underworld, and is believed to have created the first demons. While he is not inherently evil, worship of Ferne is frowned upon in most parts of Tanarim.

Messun, God of the Harvest
> Symbol: Scythe
> Followers tend to be farmers, who engage in wassailing and other rituals during the harvest season.

Chroniclus, Deity of Records
> Symbol: Hourglass
> Followers devote their lives to being historians and record-keepers. Like their deity, they eschew gender as a social construct, and they believe themselves "observers, not participants" of the world.

Lavestra, Goddess of Afflictions
Symbol: Pair of clasped, bleeding hands
This goddess is associated with the healing arts (Soudremancy), and many infirmaries are managed by the Church of Lavestra.
Illara, Goddess of Fertility
Symbol: Snake
The sister of Lavestra, she is typically invoked by expectant parents during pregnancy and childbirth.

The Five-Eyed Mother

Most Nilandorens worship the Five-Eyed Mother, and their goddess influences many aspects of Nilandoren culture. Nilandorens reach the age of majority at twenty-five, when they have lived "five years for each of the Mother's five eyes." Many tribes are governed by a council of five women.

Calendar

A year on Perrun has exactly 280 days. The nations of Tanarim (Dauphine, Osperland, Maroba, Fenutia, and Zakarza) follow the same calendar. Every month has 28 days, and every week has seven days.

Days of the Week: Onisday, Attisday, Trisday, Middisday, Dredisday, Siddisday, Finisday
Months of the Year: Nivose, Germinal, Pluviose, Verdure, Flureal, Praereal, Fervidor, Messidor, Broumaire, Gelaire

About the Author

N.J. Prynne is the pen name for an office worker who's been writing stories for as long as she can remember. When she's not writing or reading, she's either gaming or baking. She lives in Virginia with her husband, their house panther, and their ever-growing collection of musical instruments.

Subscribe to her blog at www.njprynne.com, or follow her on Instagram @njprynne.